**Look out for the link at the back ~~of the~~
book for a brand new s
free**

Contents

Destructive Interference

Prologue

For **every** decision we make, the alternative choice is lived out in a parallel reality. When the decisions are small, the realities quickly merge again, but more weighty decisions lead to a totally new reality existing at an entirely different frequency.

Sometimes, these frequencies fleetingly merge with unpredictable consequences.

And when life in one reality is at a **high**, whilst life in another is at a **low**, the effects can be devastating.

This is **destructive interference...**

Chapter One

The tear welling in Matthew's eye embraced equal joy and sadness. A turning point perhaps. This moment had grown to have such importance.

It's funny. A particular desire can be so pivotal; so monumental it becomes all consuming; the only focus. And since Abigail's diagnosis occurred at the same time they'd moved here to their dream home in Bristol's cosmopolitan Clifton, having her in her bed completely recovered on Christmas Eve was his.

Blurring the view of his daughter sleeping peacefully in her bed a few feet away, he shook his head in wonder at the good fortune they had enjoyed this year, but the tear clung on.

He smiled at the mixed emotions: the relief it was over allowed him the purging sense of grief at what might have been; at what so easily nearly was.

Acknowledging a squeeze of his forearm, he glanced at his wife. Meeting her delicate gaze constricted his throat as he saw with certainty the same fight in her.

Crying would help, was vital even, to release the despair they had both felt for two long horrific years. But weeping now when it was all over seemed so ungrateful. So instead; incredulous to both of them, they began to laugh.

As the chuckles shook their bodies, they held tight to one another. Praying for the strength not to give in to the darker side of their emotion, they clutched at fronds of cloth hanging from their clothes, loose in the warmth of the house despite the frost outside.

The smile playing on her pretty face as she slept belayed none of the suffering she'd borne; none of the fight. Just a normal eight-year-old girl excited for what Father Christmas might bring her tonight.

She had asked the dreaded question of his authenticity a number of times, and they'd always said: if she's old enough to ask, she's old enough to be told the truth. But they needed the magic this year more than ever. This year with her fit and well and looking her normal self once again, they needed it.

So, it was with grateful grins they watched as she had placed on a tray a glass of milk, a mince pie, and carrots for Rudolph and his reindeer comrades, and popped off to bed extra-early to make sure he'd come.

They had waited until midnight before creeping up the stairs one at a time. Debbie had stood guard while Matthew deftly swung open the hatch and removed the ladder to retrieve the colourful gifts from their hiding place in the loft. They'd peered at their wonderful little girl for twenty minutes to be absolutely sure she was asleep, and they had been rewarded by a successful mission.

The huge pile of presents spilled from the jolly sack, with its pictures of snowmen and reindeer. Tumbling over the floor of her bedroom, there were more than expected. They had definitely overdone it.

They'd spoiled her in hospital last Christmas and the one before of course, but this year, the excitement of their first proper Christmas in ages had proved too much—and that was without counting the gifts to one another under the tree (including a special surprise Matthew could hardly believe he'd managed to keep secret.)

"Come on… We don't want to wake her," Debbie whispered to her husband between sniggers as it became clear their laughing was getting out of hand. Tiptoeing along the landing to their bedroom, they carefully allowed the door to click shut before exploding into raucous guffaws that were every bit as healing as the tears had promised to be.

"It's so wonderful, Matt! She's gonna be thrilled!"

Grabbing both her hands, Matthew swung his gleeful wife in a dance which due to its proximity led quickly to the bed where they fell breathless into each other's arms. Too tired and emotional for anything more, they had at some point during the night taken the sensible measure of getting under the covers. That's where an exuberant Abigail found them snuggled a little after six and still dark.

"He's been, he's been," she shrilled. "I've got so many presents! How did he know I love 'My Little Pony'?"

Shuffling their bums across the bed, they made space for the light of their lives to nestle in beside them.

"I don't know, Abi, sweetheart. He just knows. It's magic!"

With Abi clutching her favourite new toys, the Morrissey family ventured downstairs to their traditional smoked salmon and scrambled eggs breakfast, washed down with an alarmingly early Bucks Fizz.

The knock at the door, absent for the last two years while Abigail went through the worst of her treatment for Leukaemia, was the final signal that normality had returned. It was all Matthew could do to stifle a laugh as he fairly skipped along the long hallway.

Taking a deep breath, their approval assured for a change, Matthew hauled open the heavy door.

"About time! We're freezing out here!" Matthew's dad sneered, but Matthew refused to let it dampen his mood. He'd long learned his father's bolshie belligerence masked deeper emotion.

"Sorry," Matthew smiled as he stared at them huddled in the porch, grins frozen to their faces in the chilly winter air. Wearing fixed smiles of tentative relief stood Matthew's mum, dad and sister, fronted by Abi's cousin Charlotte, and flanked by a bag of gifts.

The magnitude of the moment showed in silent tight hugs as they each crossed the threshold. With Matthew too choked to speak, it was left to Debbie to greet them.

"Alan, Mary, welcome," she said, hugging her parents-in-law before turning to her sister-in-law. "Mandy. How are you?"

Like her brother, she seemed to struggle emitting words, "Where's my wonderful niece?" she rasped. Debbie looked around, surprised Abigail wasn't near.

"Abi! Nan, Grandad, Aunty Mandy and Charlotte are here!"

The hurricane as Abi rushed to see them preceded the sight of her at the top of the stairs.

"Abigail! Darling. Did he come?"

"Yes, Nanna. Come up and see. I got so much stuff!"

The traditional turkey dinner wafted its delicious smells as the family convened in the vast triple aspect ballroom which served as the family's lounge. The tree, large enough for a small town, was decorated impeccably in nothing but red and gold. The pile of presents beneath, not only huge but immaculate with colour-co-ordinated bows and ribbons.

A glass-topped coffee table that would serve most families as a dining table stood between three enormous sofas which faced the roaring open fire. As they all sat comfortably, the routine that had never got off the ground finally prepared to become a well-established family tradition.

The bulky sack of less than beautifully wrapped presents which had arrived with their guests was poorly hidden beside the couch and had Abigail's full attention. She waited with patient interest as the grownups shared out their gifts with teary exchanges as a session for a family portrait at an award winning local photographers was countered with a ceramic plate depicting them all as stick characters that Abigail had made and had fired at a 'Creative Café.'

Charlotte was thrilled with the Barbie dolls Abi had chosen for her, and Abi added more pony merchandise to her collection.

After more shaking of presents, and lots of "What on earth could this possibly be?" there was one final present left.

"This is from me to both of you," Matthew ventured, nodding at his wife and daughter. "But I think I'd like Abi to open it, if that's okay with you?" Debbie at once acquiesced with a smile, and Abigail took the large envelope from under the tree.

"Careful, Abs. You don't want to tear it."

Watching her rip at it with wince-inducing abandonment, Matthew was relieved when its contents were removed unharmed. He wasn't sure Abi would understand what it was, but as she jumped around the room, screaming in joy, he knew further explanation wasn't needed.

"We're going to Disneyland! We're going to Disneyland!"

"Really?" Debbie glanced across at the confirmatory nod from her husband.

"Well. I thought we deserved it. It's for all of us. You too," he gestured to the others. "That way, me and Debs can have the occasional cosy evening meal in the most romantic city in the world while the rest of you do some fun things." Heaven knew, they needed it.

"Yay! Nanna and Grandad coming too!" Charlotte and Abi's jubilant faces beamed with joy. "We can't wait."

Chapter Two

They'd finished their Christmas dinner, including seconds, overfilled on fig pudding and trifle and were contemplating playing a board game in an effort to keep from snoozing and missing any of this wonderful day when there was another knock at the door.

"I'll go," Matthew declared, struggling to haul his Christmas stodged bulk from the winged chair where he'd settled with another brandy (he'd lost count of how many—well it seemed a shame for the pudding to get some and not him!) Sitting on top of this morning's Bucks Fizz and the wine with Christmas dinner, it was an intoxicating concoction.

Shuffling down the long wide hallway, the black and red tiles chequering the floor made Matthew feel like a giddy draught piece advancing for victory. Heaving open the heavy door shutting his perfect world away from the cold outside, he squinted at the figure in his porch.

Hunched over his well weathered cane stood elderly neighbour, Tom.

"Everything okay?" Matthew's tipsy mind managed to inquire with genuine concern.

"Sorry to intrude, only… I've bought a little something for Abigail, if that's okay?"

Nodding vigorously, Matthew promptly ushered him inside, at the same time uttering incoherent assurances that there really was no need and he shouldn't have been so generous.

"I know, but what with everything your lovely family has been through. I'm just so pleased you've come through the other side."

"Thanksh, Tom," he slurred, giving his arm a gentle pat.

Abi and Charlotte were about to give an impromptu 'show' with some brand new puppets Charlotte had brought with her when Matthew arrived with their new guest, so Tom was even more gratefully received by the adults than his welcome presence might otherwise warrant.

"Sit down, sit down, Tom," Matthew's dad implored. "Can I get you anything?"

Whilst the brandy gave its warming glow to the new guest, Abi gingerly took the present the old man held out for her. Tearing at the pretty paper, her eyes shone.

"Oh, wow! It's a Furby! I've always wanted one of these. Thank you so much, Mr King!" And with that, she planted a big kiss on his cheek, red with thread-veins feathering warmth to his rugged old face. Wrenching it from its packaging, she struggled to hide her disappointment as 'Furby' failed to perform.

"Oh, sorry, Abigail. I think his batteries might be flat," he said, and turning to the adults, he added, "I have had it in my house for quite a while. I've been desperate to give it to her since she came home."

Abigail flushed with embarrassed guilt. She hadn't wanted to make this lovely man feel bad.

"It's okay, Mr King. I can still cuddle him, and we can get some new batteries tomorrow," Abi kindly reassured.

But Tom King didn't want her to wait and was already putting his brandy down and shuffling forward in his seat.

"What are you doing, Tom?"

"She deserves her present to work," his voice cracked. "I'll go and buy batteries now. There must be somewhere open."

"No, no. Don't be silly. It's freezing out there," Mandy looked horrified, glancing across at her brother to do something. Matthew stuttered some ill-thought excuses why he should stay where he was, but Tom was almost standing now, and with moist eyes he declared once more. "No. She's waited long enough, little angel. I'll go now."

Debbie leaped to stop him. Patting his hand, she said, "Matthew will go and get some batteries, won't you, Matt?" And despite the not-so-gentle inebriation, Matthew said yes.

Struggling with the buttons on his duffle jacket, he called back in response to Debbie's hollered instructions to get milk and cat food, "Okay, see you soon,"

He didn't know just how wrong he was.

Chapter Three

Turning up his collar, Matthew clutched his coat around him and tightened his scarf (a gift from Abi). Slipping on ice already forming on the gentle incline of the drive, he steadied himself against Mandy's car.

The pause gave him the opportunity to admire the view. When they had moved into their impressive sandstone mansion-esque house four years ago, Matthew swore he would never tire of the panorama. For two awful years it hadn't succeeded in piercing the gloom the family had lived under. But today, it was like seeing it for the first time as the warm glow of a perfect Christmas combined with the brandy in his veins, parting his lips into a huge grin.

Clifton Suspension Bridge, all lit up, looked like Bristol's own giant Christmas decoration. The Avon Gorge, far below, glistened in the moonlight. Glancing up at the house, their own efforts puffed him with pride. Whilst adorned with plenty of sparkle, and gaining Abi's child stamp of approval, it was also effortlessly classy—the type of thing you might expect to see on the covers of the finest homes magazines.

Most places would be closed today, Matthew realised, but one of the advantages of Bristol's multi-cultural society was there'd always be a shop owner not observing the great Christian celebration happy to keep their shop open for the very eventuality Matthew found himself—they probably even had the foresight to order in extra.

A pang of guilt that the particular shop he headed to he'd never been to before pricked his conscience. They were about to help him out in his time of need and he rewarded them by avoiding them at all other times! He should do more to support local business. Maybe it should be a resolution for the New Year.

Many of the houses he passed on his way down the hill dwarfed his own, but that only made him appreciate the affluent area they were privileged to inhabit. He could never ask for more than he had right now, because right now, his life was beyond perfect.

As he gained on the convenience store, the contrast of self-congratulation to what he saw grew his guilt. The shop was mere metres away now, but it wasn't his non-patronage that troubled him. Slouched in the large porch formed by the corner of the shop cut to form its doorway, sat a dishevelled, pitiful presence.

How does this happen? Is there not somewhere they can go at this time of year? Matthew frowned. Gratitude for his own good fortune squeezed shame from deep within, tugging at a knot formed so long ago he had no notion of its origin.

Slowing his steps, he stared at the figure. A male, he was sure, although features weren't visible. Something in the stance as he sat, and the way his green Parka pulled taut over a bony but masculine bulk—something in the utter defeat.

He must be so cold. How can anyone survive in this bitter weather? Pausing at the man's filthy shoes, Matthew stared down, unseen by eyes in a face covered by the hood of the Parka, the fur trim sticking to itself in filthy tufts framing the despair of the strained line mouth. No movement came from the slouched figure. Matthew had to peer to ascertain if he was even breathing.

"Are you okay?" he asked. It seemed ridiculous. How could he be? "Is there anything you need? Anything I can get for you? Food?" Still no movement. "Are you hungry? You must be starving. Here. Let me help you."

Matthew's tipsiness left him a little in the cold evening air, but his clumsy attempt to offer the hand of friendship almost lost his balance when the stranger yanked his own hand away with such ferocity it left Matthew's heart beating wildly.

"Sorry. I didn't mean to..." He wasn't sure what he did mean, so he just repeated sorry again. At least he knew the man was alive. Struggling to know what to do, he had a sudden thought and plucked his wallet from the depths of his duffle coat. There were a few coins and a couple of notes. Dithering a moment, he came to a decision that made him smile.

Picking the crisp £50 note carefully from its place in the designated compartment from within its calf-leather confines, Matthew leaned forward, being careful not to appear threatening, and dropped the folded note into the man's lap.

He made no move to take it.

Suspecting pride may be preventing his gift's acceptance, Matthew decided that leaving him in peace was the best plan. Stepping past him into the doorway, he turned back briefly before disappearing into the shop. "Merry Christmas to you," he said.

Finding batteries proved perplexing after the encounter. Shaking his head, he decided he'd have to ask. Remembering cat food and milk, he added chocolate snowmen and a bottle of brandy—not the finest, but he'd hate to run out—and drummed his lips with his index figure wondering if there was anything he was forgetting. Giving up and vowing to return if needed, he struggled to the checkout with the tins, four-pint bottle of milk and off itinerary impulse buys clutched in reddening fingers.

Plonking his hoard, with some relief, at the checkout, he could see batteries behind the counter. Scrutinising the selection, he realised he had no idea what type he needed. Settling on a good assortment of AAA, AA and C batteries, he hoped they took card payment here because he wasn't convinced the coins and fiver left in his wallet would be enough. His inquiring nod whilst holding up his debit card prompted, "Yes, of course sir," from the friendly shopkeeper.

"Tell me, the man in your porch, has he been there long?"

"What man, sir? I haven't seen any man?"

Narrowing his eyes, Matthew answered. "There was a homeless guy. He must have been bloody frozen. I gave him some money, but I wondered if you'd noticed him before; if he was a regular in your porch?"

"Sorry, sir," and he looked like he meant it, "I don't know who you mean. I haven't noticed, but I can't see from here. Do you have your own bag?"

With nothing more to say, Matthew shook his head and loaded a couple of carriers from the stack by the checkout. Gripping his load with relative ease, dispersed as it now was into the two bags, he arrived back at the doorway.

Pressing colour from parallel lips as they squeezed together in contemplation, he paused in the porch. There was no sign of the homeless man. Eyes straining up and down the street, he was surprised not to see him. "I was right. It must have been pride," he muttered to himself. "He'll be keeping out of sight until I've gone before spending the money. I hope it makes a difference."

Conscience appeased, he strolled with fresh contentment towards the grand houses at the top of the hill, and home.

Chapter Four.

By the time he reached the park, set between the large neat lawns in a square between the houses, things were already different but Matthew didn't notice; the changes too subtle unless you knew what to look for. He would be unable to deny them for long.

As he steadied himself beside a long sweeping sandstone terrace, a squall of panic shook him. Scanning the horizon, he scrutinised each strut of the bridge for the homeless man until, as his eyes settled on the last one with no sighting of a stricken figure, the worry trickled out of him leaving relief in its place. Clifton Suspension Bridge wasn't about to claim another suicide.

Sighing, he let out a whistle. A simple walk to get batteries had given him a new perspective. What might be the very best of times for some underlined the very worst for others—god knows he knew how that felt. With another pang of guilt at his good fortune, he vowed to raise a glass to his new acquaintance when he got back inside.

Looking away from the deep gorge for the first time, his forehead creased. Backing up a few steps, he bit his lip. Something wasn't right. Staring at the street, his frown deepened. No, he hadn't walked past his house. Shaking his head, he couldn't imagine what he could have done wrong. He must have taken an incorrect turn. But that was impossible; there were no turns—just a stroll up and down the hill.

No nearby street signs were around to confirm he was on Clifton Down Road, but he recognised Tom King's large house that he rattled around in since losing his wife. And so the house immediately opposite which looked so unfamiliar *must* be his. Why was he confused?

Well his sister's car wasn't there for a start, nor his mum and dad's. And the Christmas lights weren't on. It was hard to tell in the dark, but they appeared to be missing entirely.

What on earth could have happened? Had they had a row? And what sort of row could possibly have developed in the space of time he'd taken to buy batteries? Surely not one where the guests had left and Debbie had become so disheartened with Christmas she'd rushed out and perilously removed the lights!

It was like returning to a car park certain he'd left his car in zone 'B' only to find it was in an identical looking zone 'D.' Except, there was no zone 'D' either. With no option, he stepped gingerly onto the drive—*his* drive. Shaking his head, he hoped all would become clear when he got inside.

When turning the handle didn't gain the result of opening the door, he shrugged. How much brandy must he have had? When his key wouldn't fit the lock he became certain once more that he had the wrong house. But as he reached the end of the drive, the familiar view of the bridge and the fast flow of the River Avon as it snaked into Bristol was unmistakable. Turning again towards the house, his scowl threatened to scar.

"Can I help you?" the gruff tone of a portly, balding gentleman standing in the doorway demanded.

"Er. I don't know. I think I'm lost." The cold and the shock had sobered Matthew up, but he still expected he must be missing something. "I can't find my house."

Slit eyes barely concealing his irritation, the man sighed before deciding in the spirit of good will to try to help.

"Where do you live?"

"Well… to be honest," Matthew answered, "I was certain it was here… In this house."

The man sighed again, this time adding a roll of the eyes for good measure. "Well obviously you don't. I've lived here for nearly ten years. What's your address?"

"Number twelve, Clifton Down Road."

"Bristol? It can't be. *This* is number twelve."

Matthew stumbled back, head spinning. "It can't be. Number twelve is my house… I'm Matthew Morrissey. I live here with my wife and daughter. My family are visiting for Christmas!"

"Well, you're wrong, yeah? I'm not going to stand here and debate it with you, but you need to get off my property. I *was* enjoying some peace and quiet."

"But…"

"No! No more. You're clearly drunk, or mad, or drugged up to the eyeballs, and if you don't leave now, I'm going to call the police."

Recognising the futility in arguing, Matthew turned slowly and walked down the driveway; *his* driveway? Part of him wanted to rush back, burst in and reclaim his home. But the odd unfamiliarity of it, and the man's confidence stopped him

Across the street, Tom's car was outside his house as usual. And there were lights on so he was likely to be in. Why wasn't he waiting at his house with Debbie and Abi and the rest? Striding over the tarmac, Matthew paused half-way to stare back at the house he was sure was his.

If he'd gone to the wrong house instead of his own, how could Tom's car be there? And it *was* Tom's car, he knew. It wasn't the only Bentley in the area, but it was the only one circa 1965 with the number plate TMK 1NG for Thomas Michael King.

His heart raced as he stepped onto his elderly neighbour's drive. Grasping the knocker firmly, a flurry of butterflies rippled in his chest. How could he explain his muddle? Tom would think him a fool. Before allowing the heavy knocker to fall and connect with the door, Matthew stared across the street once again.

Eyes following the three possible trajectories to the three houses that could conceivably be described as 'opposite,' he had to concede that whilst they did look similar to one another, none of them looked like the Christmas festooned house he had left an hour ago.

His mind could take no more. With a decisive thrust, he allowed the heavy hoop in the lion's mouth to hammer the door sending a reverberating crash through the large hallway beyond. Once the echo faded, the initial silence sunk Matthew's heart into his stomach as he impatiently tapped his leg with fidgeting fingers, but soon faint sounds of life reached his thankful ears.

Another light went on somewhere in the house. Slowly, octogenarian footsteps edged towards him; clip, clip, clonk, as Tom King stumbled along the hallway aided by his antique walking cane. He could see him now through the opacity of the door's glass panels.

Stood inches away, separated only by the wood and glass, words wobbled on Matthew's lips as he waited for numerous bolts to slide and keys to turn. At last, he was face to face with his old friend.

"Tom. Thank goodness. I don't know what's going on," he gushed. Slowing his mouth with a deep breath, he struggled to ask questions that made sense. "I'm surprised you came home, Tom. Didn't you want to see Abi's Furby in action?"

Tom stared at him blankly, squinting eyes unwilling to appear rude until he'd worked out who he was talking to.

Face flushing red at Tom's failure at a forthcoming explanation, Matthew began to rush his words again. "So, what happened after I left? Did they row? I can't work it out." Tom continued to stare blankly at him. "What on earth happened when you left mine?"

A grimace grew on Tom's weathered face. He didn't want to appear impolite, but he was nobody's fool and wasn't about to be conned by one of those unscrupulous distraction burglars.

Putting on his haughtiest voice, he replied. "I'm sorry, but I think you have the wrong house, young man."

Bemusement turned to surreal amusement as for the first time it occurred to Matthew that this was all an elaborate prank. Of course! It was obvious. Even Mandy and Debbie's keenness for him to leave and get the batteries was odd, wasn't it? They had got rid of him to perform this ingenious joke.

"Okay, Tom," he said with a wink. "You've got me." Standing back, he began a slow hand-clap. Talking loudly to the street, he called out. "All right, that's enough, now. Come on out. Great Christmas prank."

But even as he uttered the words he knew they fell far short of the truth. They weren't pranking sort of people. In the thirty-six years he'd known his parents, and the eleven years he'd known Debbie, pranks had never featured. Choosing the first Christmas he had been happy in years to fool him so cruelly was unthinkable.

Panic coursed through him, raising his voice as he spoke. "Tom. Tom, what's happening?"

"Do I know you?"

"Know me? Of course you do, Tom," he spluttered, and another thought struck. It was Tom who was confused. He must be suffering from some degenerative mental condition. It was no wonder at his age. Pushing aside the sincere knowledge that Tom King had always been sharp as a pin the entire time he'd known him, he allowed the familiar stab of conscience to pierce his veil.

Talking slowly, he tried to keep patronising tones from his voice as he explained. "You do know me, Tom. And Debbie, my wife. Do you remember her? And Abi, my little girl?" Blank face. "She's been ill... really ill," he said, tears pricking. What was going on? "You bought her a present... a Furby. That's where I've been," his voice cracked. "Getting these." He wafted the batteries feebly towards his elderly neighbour.

He could see that Tom didn't want to upset him but couldn't tell him what he desperately wanted to hear.

"Look. I'm terribly sorry, but I don't know you. You seem very upset. Would you like me to telephone someone for you? Where do you live?"

"Where do I live? For fuck sake, Tom. I live *there!*" He pointed fiercely across the street, guilt gripping his chest. It wasn't Tom's fault. "There's my house. You were in it an hour ago drinking my brandy. You brought a present over for Abi because she's finally recovered from leukaemia after two years of hell. Tom! It's me, Matthew. Matthew Morrissey!"

Tom's steely blue eyes creased with concern. The unstable man on his doorstep was beginning to unnerve him. He didn't know what he was capable of. "I'm sorry. I can't help you," he said firmly and began to close the door.

"No! Tom, wait. Please wait, you have to help me!"

"Sorry," Tom said again, and this time he shoved the door with a decisive slam.

Matthew rapped rapidly again, but he could already hear the bolts sliding back into place.

"Tom, open up. Sorry I shouted, I'm just scared. I don't know what's happening. Tom..."

Slumping down defeated, a moment of hope raised his chin as he heard Tom's voice again; but only for a second.

"Go away. Please leave my property or I'll call the police."

Fearing he really would, Matthew forced his bewildered body up again and stood blinking in the street light. Staggering forward, his addled mind searched for a logical explanation.

Tom was wrong, obviously. Matthew hadn't noticed him becoming mentally inhibited, but his preoccupation for the last two or three years explained that. He hadn't had time to notice nor worry about his neighbour, he thought, assuaging his shame at the lapse. A few years is a long time when you're in your eighties.

But his own confusion? What was causing that? How much had he had to drink? It didn't seem like much, but he knew drunks weren't the best people at remembering quantities of alcohol. So, he was sloshed. He had to be.

The man at his house, well it can't have been his house. That was obvious. Matthew knew it was he who must somehow be disoriented and had forgotten, or misheard the address the man said. Carefully, he scrutinised each house again. One of them was his. There was no doubt. In one movement of his head he would see his Christmas decorations and wonder how on earth he'd missed it.

He was always hopeless at finding things, and whenever Debbie intervened after he'd declared something (usually his car keys/ and or wallet) they were frequently somewhere he'd already looked. Losing his house was taking that to bizarre new levels, but what else made any sense?

Bright lights soon did fill his vision, but not the ones he was searching for. The blue flashing strobe lamps of a night patrol car pulled alongside him. Ignoring them, he decided now was a good time to leave the area and began walking at pace back down the hill.

Returning to the shop might not be a bad place to begin to understand anyway. He could restart his route home and be really careful not to make the same mistake that had led to this dreadful disorientation.

But he wasn't to get the opportunity.

Chapter Five

The whir of the electric window of the squad car made his heart beat even faster than the thousand beats per minute already exhibited. "Excuse me sir. May we have a word with you, please?"

Matthew ignored them and kept on walking. They'd leave him alone. He hadn't done anything wrong, had he?

"Sir? I have to insist you stop. STOP NOW! Or I'll have to arrest you."

Matthew couldn't imagine on what grounds, but decided he had no choice but to obey. Maybe this was a good thing. Maybe they could help him.

Stepping from the driver's side, a pretty police lady pulled on her hat before pulling out a notebook. "Now then, sir. Perhaps you wouldn't mind telling me what you're doing out this evening? Don't you have somewhere else you'd rather be?"

Matthew shifted uncomfortably. "Well. It's all a bit embarrassing, to be honest."

"Why don't you start by giving me your name?"

"Of course. It's Matthew. I'm Matthew Morrissey, of twelve Clifton Down Road. Somewhere round here!" Matthew passed off with a self-deprecating laugh.

"Mmm hmmm. But it isn't, is it, sir?" she said, scribbling on her pad. A second, male officer had joined her from the car and stood a short distance away.

"I can't seem to find it, that's true. But I left only an hour ago to get batteries for my daughter's Furby... It was a present from a kind old neighbour… Tom King," Matthew rambled in the piercing silence offered by the two police officers.

Pulling her epaulette radio towards her mouth, she spoke words Matthew couldn't follow, but they included his name and address. The crackling response seemed to suggest something was wrong.

"Who are you, really, sir?"

"Really? I'm Matthew Morrissey, as I said before."

"The thing is, sir. We've had complaints… of a gentleman matching your description causing trouble. Insisting he's someone he's not. Shouting and exhibiting threatening behaviour to an elderly resident."

Matthew not appearing a likely hoodlum, she extended some courtesy. "I understand you're lost. If you can convince me where you live, we'll escort you there, make sure you're safe and that'll be that. But we can't leave you out here, can we? We don't know you. We don't know what you might do."

"Do? I won't do anything. I just want to get back to my wife, my little girl and my family. I just want to go home."

"Okay, sir. But home isn't twelve Clifton Down Road, is it? Do you want to tell me where you really live?"

Matthew's perplexed demeanour left an unanswered silence. "Have you taken anything, sir? It's best to say if you have."

Matthew shook his head. "No. I've had a bit of brandy… well, probably quite a lot, but I didn't realise I was that drunk. Sorry."

Stepping forward, the male police officer seemed to have a purpose.

"My colleague here is going to perform a search for drugs upon your person. Before he does, is there anything you want to admit to having." Matthew shook his head again. What on earth was happening?

"Because, we will find it. It'll be better for you; save us both a lot of time if you admit it now?"

"No. Nothing," Matthew stated.

The male stepped even closer. "Put out your arms, please, sir," he ordered. "Now, before I search you, there's nothing in your pockets that's going to hurt me, or you, is there, sir?"

"Nothing," Matthew said again, then added, realising anything was possible on this bizarre night, "I don't think so."

The policeman paused and asked sternly. "Well? Is there or isn't there?"

"No." Matthew sighed and the officer patted him down. The humiliation, Matthew cringed. I'm being treated like a criminal outside (or very near to at least) my own house.

The officer turned to his colleague. "Clean," he said.

"Now then, sir. I'm going to give you one last chance to tell us who you are and where you live."

"I've already told you." Matthew was getting annoyed now.

"Still sticking to your story, are you?"

"I have nothing else to tell you. It's not a story. But if you can help me find it... I seem to have taken a wrong turn somewhere... I'll be out of your hair."

The police lady sighed. "Believe me, sir. There's nothing I'd like more. I don't want to fill in paperwork just because you can't find your house. But if you stick to this story, I'll have no option but to arrest you."

"What for! I haven't done anything wrong." Matthew raised his voice. He was a law-abiding citizen used to people taking notice when he spoke, he understood they had a job to do, but this was getting ridiculous. "Please, just help me find my house!"

Both officers stepped forward. The lady took his arm in a firm grip. "I am arresting you on suspicion of being Drunk and Disorderly, and on suspicion of being a Vagrant. You do not have to say anything, but it may harm your defence..." but Matthew had tuned out. He had no choice, and if he really was so messed up he couldn't find his own house, he'd be better off going with them. He could sort it all out from the station when he was clear about what was happening to him.

"I'm bringing in Matthew Morrissey here for Drunk and Disorderly Conduct and Vagrancy," Matthew heard the woman say as he stood up straight, determined to show his respectability.

"I am neither drunk, nor vagrant and my family will be frantic with worry," he asserted. "If you must insist on keeping me here, then I have to let them know."

The custody sergeant smiled. "Of course, sir. All in good time. Let's just get you booked in first, shall we?" It wasn't a question and Matthew wasn't about to make a scene; only whatever was necessary to go home as quickly as possible.

After another body search (at least not in front of neighbours who might have been looking out at the commotion) he obediently followed the custody sergeant to his cell. As the keys rattled and the metal door clanged open to reveal the grey cube he was expected to spend his Christmas night, Matthew sighed.

"When can I speak to my wife?"

"I can let her know you're here, if you like?"

Matthew stiffened. Was he not even to be allowed to speak to Debbie? Would he even get home tonight?

"It's Christmas. Let me speak to my wife. I'm sure we can straighten this out and I can get home to my little girl."

The sergeant paused. Pursing his lips, he decided Matthew was no threat and led him back to the desk.

"This was supposed to be the perfect Christmas. My little girl, Abi, she's been terribly ill, and this is her first one at home for a couple of years."

The sergeant raised his eyebrows in concerned interest.

"Leukaemia," Matthew confirmed. "But she's well now," and he couldn't help the grin that turned his mouth in a cramp-inducing crescent. He'd be home soon and this confusing incident would become part of the story of Abi's first Christmas at Clifton Down Road. The first of many.

He went silent as he finished dialling and it began to ring. The sergeant looked away to offer some privacy.

"Hi, who's that?" Matthew inquired when he didn't recognise the voice that answered. "Oh. Sorry. I must have mis-dialled," he said in response. Depressing the button on the phone cradle to reset it, he stared at the keys. Rehearsing his number in his head, he was certain he had it right. There was no ambiguity. It rolled off the tongue in his mind with an ease that confirmed his confidence.

Pressing each number precisely, he dialled again. When he heard the same strange voice, the colour drained from his face. His knees buckled forcing him to support his weight on the counter. "Sorry again. Are you sure that's not the Morrissey household? This is Matthew Morrissey here."

"Where did you get my number, you weirdo? First you show up at my door. Then you throw your weight about threatening my neighbour, who's in his eighties for Christ's sake. What are you playing at? I don't know who you are, but if you don't stop harassing me and my neighbours, I'll take you to court. You'll pay for this... Imbecile!"

When the phone clicking had Matthew beaten. The receiver remained glued to his hand for over a minute before he edged it ever-closer to its cradle where replacing it would provide an insufferable stop to his sense of hope

"You okay?" the sergeant asked unnecessarily.

There were no words. Nothing could squeeze through the lump in his throat.

"Did you not get through?" Matthew shook his head. "Is there anyone else you'd like to try?"

Matthew considered. There was his mum and dad, and Mandy of course, but they were surely still at his house; and he wasn't sure he could remember their phone numbers anyway—who could nowadays? So he shook his head. "I don't know what to do. I don't understand what's happening."

The sergeant nodded slowly. "Well. You're a bit the worse for wear at the moment." Matthew was sure he wasn't, but what else was anyone to think? "Sleep it off here. We'll look after you. Do you want some toast?" he offered kindly. "Cup of tea?"

Matthew didn't want anything but didn't want to be ungrateful. Maybe a cup of tea might help to sober him up. "Coffee, please," he asked on a whim of sense. "Make it strong."

The sergeant locked the door and left with an appreciative chuckle. "Right you are."

Chapter Six

When the shutter went back on the eyehole in the door, it was still dark. It didn't matter. Matthew hadn't once succumbed to sleep. He wouldn't rest until he was back home with his lovely family.

His concerns for himself had waned in favour of a tsunami of grief at what his poor family must be thinking. He'd gone out for batteries, and for some peculiar reason he hadn't come home. What would they be going through? They must have phoned the police and the hospitals. It's a wonder they hadn't burst into his cell to tell him Debbie was here to collect him. The fact their phone calls hadn't reached the computer screen of the Desk Sergeant to coordinate his safe return was something he would not take lying down.

He didn't know how he had ended up making so little sense, but anyone should be able to put two and two together and reunite them. Especially at Christmas. It just shouldn't take this long. But maybe Christmas provided the answer: less staff being less diligent, or more likely being completely overwhelmed with emergency calls that the fact he was safe had shaken him down the list of priorities. Fair enough, he thought as the door swung open.

"Matthew. Sleep okay?" It was the same sergeant. He works hard, Matthew thought to himself and so offered him his best smile.

"Not at all, but, hey. It's morning now. I'm sure we can sort this mess out."

The sergeant smiled, but the warmth from last night was missing, or was he imagining it. "Follow me."

It wasn't really following. Matthew walked beside him and another policeman marched behind him. Arriving at a door a short way along the corridor, the sergeant knocked before opening the door.

A woman rose from behind a desk and waddled over. "Matthew?" she greeted with thick lips and a voice like she was in the middle of swallowing a cake. Peering through glasses that made her look as though she was underwater, she nodded nervously, "Come and sit down, please."

As she led him to an orange plastic moulded seat with metal stackable legs, the sergeant spoke. "You know how to fetch us if you need us," he said holding her gaze until he was sure. The lady nodded with a smile which said she knew what she was doing.

As the uniformed officers made a slow retreat from the room, Matthew studied the woman in front of him. He could hardly do anything else, built as she was to fill all but the furthest extremities of his peripheral vision. It was almost as though she had been extruded from a blob of humanoid dough to fill the space—injection moulded human in the form of the end of an interview room and cloaked in an explosion of crashing colours.

Matthew stared, then quickly turned away. He didn't like to judge people by their appearance. The scruffy so-and-so's who frequented his boat yard with cash to buy his most expensive offerings constantly amazed him and they always got on famously. Matthew got on with everyone. But Debbie would struggle to maintain her composure in the face of the fashion faux pas exhibited in number on this lady's full-to-bursting figure.

Her floral dress was made from the type of pattern long since removed from all but the most out of date homes, and then it would have been used as carpeting or curtains. Dominant orange clashed robustly with a peach crochet cardigan that refused to pull over a bust struggling to remain in proportion despite the scope of canvas.

33

It fell short of covering her waist and aided in framing peculiar bulges where her unfeasible chest wedged against a mound protruding beyond the dress's waistband squeezing her stomach. Noticing his gaze, she attempted to pull it further around her, cheeks turning a furious pink that, as well as displaying her discomfort, managed to clash with the cardigan and the dress.

Matthew looked away, his own cheeks flushing. He had no intention of making her feel awkward.

"Do sit down, Matthew, please," she burbled through her cake lips. As her hand waved, he noticed her wedding ring imbedded into her finger. Was it unusually thin, or did scale make it appear that way?

Pulling out the chair, its flimsiness made him worry for its compatriot opposite with its hefty load.

"So, Matthew. What have you been up to?"

Matthew squinted. "I'm sorry. Aren't you going to introduce yourself? If you're questioning me, shouldn't I have a solicitor present?" Matthew assumed he would have to answer for last night's conduct in some way before they released him, but this was very unprofessional.

"Matthew! It's me! Celia. Celia Kay."

Matthew's squint deepened "I'm sorry. I haven't a clue who you are, and I'm not going to answer any questions until I have legal representation!"

"There's no need. I'm not here to question you, Matthew. You're not in any trouble." Matthew's eyes moistened. "I'm not the police. I've come to take you back."

His face relaxed. Pupils which had been steel pinpricks, dilated. Tears of joy brimmed at his bottom lids and he batted them away. "Thank you, Celia," he said, wincing at his uncertainty at her name. It was Celia, wasn't it? Or was it Karen or Kay?

As she stepped back out from behind the desk, he noticed her feet encased in grubby plimsolls that couldn't have been white for a long time. The stitches, straining to contain her fleshy feet, looked stretched to bursting. She must be really limited in her choice of footwear, Matthew considered. Her toes will be frozen.

Expecting cheery farewells from the custody desk now he was finally going home, he was disappointed when everyone acted indifferently. An officer opened the locks with various sets of keys and Matthew and his new favourite stranger stepped outside.

"Goodbye," Matthew volunteered cheerily. He didn't want to add 'Thanks for looking after me,' because he was pissed off that he'd been forced to spend Christmas night away from his family. But it was all over now, and Matthew wasn't one to hold a grudge.

Dawn was breaking outside, and the pair walked out to an eerie calm that no other day would provide—everyone sleeping off the excitement and inebriation of the day before.

"Do my wife and daughter know where I've been all night?" Matthew asked as they stepped towards a car that just had to be Celia's. It was the only one in the vicinity that fit, looking as chaotic as she did.

Even from a distance he couldn't miss the mess. Through the windscreen, the dashboard shelf was littered with food wrappers. The glass itself was covered in dozens of little white rectangles that Matthew recognised as the adhesive parts of dozens of discarded 'pay-and-display' tickets.

Celia paused to unlock the car (he'd assumed correctly.) As the door creaked open, Matthew gagged. The pungent aroma of food, both sweet and savoury, and in many levels of fermentation, reached up his nostrils, shot straight to his brain and gave him an instant headache.

Getting back to Debbie and Abi was about the only reason he'd ever get in this car. Leaning in front of him, Celia dusted crumbs and debris from the seat. "There you go," she offered with a smile showing carpeted teeth that can't have been cleaned since her shoes were white and oddly were the only things that matched her ensemble.

35

"Thanks," Matthew said, covering his mouth. As Celia jostled and slid back and forth forever adjusting her seat, finally adopting a position virtually hugging the steering wheel, her face as close to the windshield as her ample flesh allowed, Matthew was aware she hadn't answered him. It didn't matter; he'd be home in a few minutes.

Bumping away, the car seemed to be begging for a lower gear. Could she even see through the bottle lenses and between all the little sticky oblongs?

Her driving competency indicated probably not, as ignoring a red light, Celia swerved around a cross-roads, thankfully clear so early on this Bank Holiday, but the motion sent cartons of all description sliding along the parcel shelf stirring up their pungent odour.

The danger and the smell and disbelieving glances at his driver peering through the screen with a look of severity, distracted Matthew so that when Celia pulled to a stop outside a building that wasn't his house. Narrowing his eyes, Matthew stared out at his surroundings.

"Where are we? Are you stopping here before taking me home?" Matthew rubbed the nape of his neck. Eyes wide, he noticed his rapid breaths. Closing them for a second, he took a calming breath. He had to remain in control of his senses.

"Why are you ignoring me, Celia?" he growled. Clenching a fist, he didn't know what to do with the ferocity building in him. Slamming his palm on the dashboard, he yelled, "For fuck sake! What is going on?"

Celia shrank into her door and clicked the lock. "Now now, Matthew. Don't do anything silly."

With a scowl, he yanked at the door handle. It took only a moment to decipher the lock. Throwing the door open, he didn't say anything to Celia as she trembled, straining to be as far from him as she could get.

Whack! He hit the floor. Head spinning, he gasped. Instinctively covering his head with his forearms, he flinched, desperate to see his attacker but fearful he'd be more vulnerable.

There were two of them, he could see that at least. Not one accustomed to fighting, he'd have to play it cool and wait for a chance to strike. Curling his right arm—his strongest—away from his head, he coiled it ready to pounce.

"Come on, Matthew," one of the men said with a sneer, leaning in close. Matthew judged a hit from this angle would be ineffective. "That's not very Christmassy, now is it?"

The man's face was no more than a blur as a sudden pain seared his thigh. He could just detect the second man bent down to him too, but they were becoming hazy. Desperately pushing at the floor with all his strength, he had to get away. He couldn't leave himself at the mercy of whoever these freaks were.

Clawing the ground, he made no progress.

"He's nearly out for the count," he heard a voice say, and then his brain contorted as it deciphered the straining grubby plimsolls on Celia's puffy foot. With his lids listlessly closing she stepped back allowing her entirety to fill his view.

Pained eyes stared down at him through her thick lenses. Short nails on sausage fingers were getting a good chewing. Removing them in a self-conscious shake of her hand, he was sure she mouthed "Sorry," before everything went black.

Chapter Seven

Matthew's head hurt. His eyes struggled to open and between the slits of light entering his senses it was impossible to decipher where he was. Attempting to rub away the grogginess, Matthew grimaced to find his arms tethered to his sides.

Yanking at them, he refrained from calling out so as not to draw his captors' attention. Forcing his lids open, the bright light above stung them shut again. Head swimming, he jolted as far to the side as he could and retched.

"It can make you feel a bit sick, I'm afraid."

He thought he recognised the voice but couldn't open his eyes to be sure. Coughing until it hurt, he needed his arms to hold his weight, but his abs were forced to take the strain and he collapsed back exhausted.

"Don't struggle, Matthew. If you behave, I can have your restraints taken off. They're only for your own safety." She paused. "What do you think? Will you be good?"

Matthew had nothing to lose by promising to behave. They were clearly aware he had woken. Restrained, he was defenceless. He nodded.

Hope that the woman was the only one present stalled when she disappeared and returned with both the men who had attacked him. If he didn't have their measure before, he had no chance feeling like this. He would find out what they wanted and come up with a better plan than fighting them.

Moving towards him, one of them leaned in and grabbed his wrist. Mechanical ratcheting echoed round the room and was the first clue to his surroundings. When a hand helped him up, recovering from the pounding in his head, he saw the clean, boxy room. It was no surprise but he still didn't understand.

"Feeling better?" the woman asked. He recognised the rubber-lipped, fashion-less bulk of Celia.

Matthew scowled. When he decided to speak, his lips were dry and his tongue slow to move. "Where am I? Where have you brought me?" he demanded with as much force as he could rasp.

Celia looked at the two thugs in turn, her micro squint belying her uncertainty. "Come on now, Matthew. If you're ready, we can take you to your room?" she asked, eyebrows raised above the tortoiseshell of her severe glasses.

"Ready for what?"

With one man either side, and Celia leading the way, they led Matthew down a long empty corridor. His back felt cold. Where was his coat? And his boots, he wasn't wearing his boots. He staggered and was caught under the armpits to stop from falling.

As he was virtually dragged along, posters dotting the walls depicting jolly cartoon images entered his view as he struggled to focus. One caught his eye displaying a list in red with a large cross underneath, and a similar list on the opposite side of the page, written in green with a large tick at the bottom—do's and don'ts. Matthew's bleary brain couldn't comprehend any of them.

Rubbing his eyes to regain focus, his hands were slapped down.

"We're not going to have to restrain you again, are we, Matthew?" He let his arms drop and made no attempt to read anything else.

Reaching the end of the long passage, they came to a pair of robust looking doors. Celia keyed in a code to the keypad being careful to cover her hand so Matthew wouldn't see. There was little chance he'd remember even one of the digits as his mind fought to give its power into just keeping him upright.

There followed another corridor, shorter with more doors leading off. Two or three doors down, Celia paused again. Extracting a key from an impressive bunch, she slotted one into the lock. Reddening, she realised she'd selected the wrong one. Scrutinising the rest of the bunch, she tried three more before either through luck or reason, the door opened.

"Here you are, Matthew. Your old room. You're lucky it's still here. You've been gone quite a while."

What are you talking about? He wanted to scream. But instead, he shuffled forwards towards a bed. Collapsing onto it, the restricting grip of the two gorillas made it a more graceful landing.

"I'll be in to see you in a bit," Celia assured. "Get some rest, yeah?" she advised before waddling out, the three of them pausing to re-lock the door. The large window next to it allowed a view of them right the way down the corridor—and they, a view of him.

With a sudden rush of consciousness, Matthew shot his eyes open wide. Unaware of even falling asleep, he wasn't sure if he'd slept for a minute or a month. Glancing at the brightly lit ceiling, he was pleased to acknowledge he felt more alert. Pushing himself up, he swung his legs round onto the floor and sat up. With a resolute sigh he offered an ironic smile to Celia—his captor.

Unsurprised to see that again she wasn't alone, at least the lady with her was marginally less menacing than her male associates, only insomuch as overpowering her would be easier. Her hair scraped back, taut faced countenance was made more severe by her threatening stance clutching a clip-board and pen.

"I'd like to take a few details from you. Get you properly settled if that's alright?" She sounded surprisingly pleasant and meek.

"I don't want to be settled. I want to go home!" he stood up.

"Sit down, Matthew. Please."

"Look. I don't know what the fuck is going on, but I want to go home to my wife and my daughter, NOW!" Out of breath from his outburst, wiping spittle from his mouth, he continued, "I don't know who you are, but Celia, here—if that's her real name—promised to take me home. How the police let me into her custody is a mystery. And then I was jumped by your two goons and when I wake up, I'm tied to the fucking bed!"

At first he thought it was amusement passing in glances between the two ladies, but then he saw the bewilderment and recognised the fear.

"Matthew!" the clip-board woman shouted. Celia ducked behind her. They were afraid of him. "Please sit down and we can talk about this."

Talking about it was what he wanted too; frightening them would gain nothing. Perching on the edge of the bed, ready to run if he needed, he sighed, "Okay."

"How are you feeling… in yourself?" Matthew's glare was of complete bafflement, but it seemed to come across as aggression because the clip-board woman was struggling with her next words. "Any thoughts to harm yourself… or anyone else?"

His eyes widened. He had to get away from these crazy people. When his feet hit the floor, he noticed he wasn't wearing shoes… or trousers. Gulping down a pang of panic as he saw his limbs cloaked in an unexpected fabric, he flopped back onto the bed.

Holding out his arms he gasped. Finally, he understood where he was. '*For hospital use only*,' was written hundreds of times in faded orange and green stripes all over him. Covering his arms and chest and partway down his legs. But not his back. The chill he felt on his skin told him what he knew already, recognising his attire—his back was bare.

The words were as insane as the situation. 'For hospital use only!' Thanks for the warning. I was going to wear it to Marks and Spencer's, Matthew shook his head in incredulity.

It was almost possible to hear the cogs start in Matthew's mind. He was in hospital. Specifically, hospital for the mentally ill. He'd believe it all to be a case of mistaken identity if they weren't so sure of his name. There couldn't be someone else who looked like him, also called Matthew.

It made the issue of getting out of here different. These people were *trying* to help him apparently. He was convinced if he explained, he would be understood and be home very soon. "I'll do what you want," he agreed. "But you must let me speak to Debbie and Abi—my wife and daughter, to let them know I'm safe. They will be frantic."

The clip-board woman smiled. "I'm sure we'll have let them know already."

"Well, could you check?" Matthew insisted.

"Of course." Drumming the side of her board with her pen, the noise chased her smile to the opposite side of her face making her expression lop-sided. Pausing, pen in mid-drum, she straightened her mouth again, "I think it's probably best if you speak directly to Doctor McEvoy, if that's alright?" she said. "You don't want to be answering the same questions from me twice, do you? It'll save time."

Matthew was all in favour of saving time. The quicker he could clear up this misunderstanding, the better. "Of course. Whatever you think," he added to be sure to sound nice and cooperative.

"I'll arrange it. It might not be today though."

"Wait! What? I have to get home today! Debbie and Abi will be frantic!"

With a cough, she added, "Sorry, yes, of course. Debbie and Abi. I'll see what I can do."

"Make sure of it. Please," he said.

She left the room and marched down the corridor, presumably to get things moving.

"There. That wasn't too bad, now was it?" Celia's rubber lips caught on the words. They still flapped even though she was now silent. Matthew shrugged. "I'll leave you to it for a while then, shall I?" Matthew shrugged again.

He wasn't sure if he was welcome to leave the room, or if the two men might come and restrain him again, so he lay back and stared at the ceiling. What was happening to him? And why?

He understood why the police had arrested him. He had been drunk and couldn't tell them where he lived. What else could they have done? But Celia? He knew now she must be a social worker, or a psychiatric nurse or something like that, but why? He'd see the doctor soon and demand answers.

It was a relief that it was a hospital, he supposed. The brutal kidnapping he thought he was suffering would have been an unknown quantity. Now he just had to satisfy the doctor of his sanity, which should be straight forward.

He shot his head round at a shuffling noise in the corner of the room. He hadn't heard him come in, but there stood a slight built, lank haired man. Stood, Matthew decided, might be an overstatement. Stooped, or cowed might be better. The man looked terrified.

"Hello," Matthew offered. The man's dark eyes widened. Edging around the room towards the door, he clutched at the wall for support, and when he reached the opening, he shot through with a wail of emotion like an injured child running to Mummy.

Matthew jumped from the bed and strolled to the door to see what had happened to him. A glance down the corridor saw him batting at the double doors at the end. Sensing Matthew's presence, the man darted round to face him.

Backing up, trapped by the locked doors, a whimper echoed from the hard wall. Matthew took a step towards him which felled him to the floor. Clutching at his knees he forced himself into the corner where the doorframe met the wall and pushed with his legs.

"It's okay," Matthew tried to reassure. "I won't hurt you."

The crying grew louder and the man began banging the back of his head against the wall muttering, "No, no, no… No, no!"

Brow creased and eyes wide, Matthew struggled to contain his disbelief at his effect on the trembling figure. With no idea how to make it better, he walked slowly back into the room he was waiting in. The room Celia had referred to as 'his.'

Closing the door, he took a deep breath and walked over to the bed. It was the only place to sit. There was no chair, or table or anything else. Just the bed.

Matthew perched on the edge. Fingers found their way to his temples and he began to massage in a circular motion. Pausing to squeeze the bridge of his nose, he screwed his eyes and let out a sigh.

There was nothing to do but wait and so he swung his legs around and lay back. Having counted the polystyrene ceiling tiles, and then passing an inordinate time constructing faces from their dimpled patterns, the rage at the injustice ruptured like the first seismic tremor of an angry volcano.

His jaw clenched, his arms went rigid and he balled his fists, clawing at the bed sheets until his nails threatened to rip through.

Repressing a scream in his throat, he let it warble, mouth clamped closed and lips turned in to insulate the room, and anyone listening, from the cry. Tensing every muscle, he released his rage in one expulsive breath.

"Keep calm," he coached himself. "It will all be over soon."

What time was it? Matthew didn't know. And where was his watch? Why hadn't he brought his sodding mobile phone with him? All this could have been avoided if he had. They would have laughed, but they'd have come to guide him home. And now, stuck here, he could have phoned them; let them know he's okay.

But no. He didn't even know where it was. He'd switched it off on Christmas Eve and declared "I don't want to be disturbed. This is family time." And now it was anything but.

Swinging his legs round and standing up in one swift motion, Matthew stomped from the room with a fresh determination. This was ridiculous.

He didn't get far before the same doors that trapped the trembling man prevented his progress. There was a buzzer to one side of the door which he pressed. His natural politeness gave way to frustration when no-one answered his call and so he pressed it a few more times, pressing harder each time to no effect.

At a distance, a face behind a desk creased and peeped out from a doorway. Tilting her head, she seemed to be inviting him to tell her what he wanted; from a distance and through a tiny Georgian wired window. Matthew shrugged at her preposterous request. He'd had enough.

He could see her sigh. Planting her feet on the floor from where she had been sitting, she pushed herself up with both palms flat on her thighs as if moving were a great effort. Taking her sweet time down the corridor, she paused when clip-board woman exited a side room and the pair proceeded to chat.

Matthew could feel his fists balling again and consciously unclenched them. He never liked upsetting anyone, but their control over his situation fuelled his rage.

He'd been excused many the minor traffic violation with his polite subservience, whereas Brian, his boat-building business partner was almost carried off to the cells on occasion when his apoplectic rage roared at the very existence of the police in his life. "Why weren't they out catching *real* criminals?"

So Matthew knew the drill and understood he wouldn't get out of here any faster by losing his temper. The pair of women stopped abruptly, ending their chat and quickening their pace towards him. Without the barked instruction to "Stand back," clip-board unlocked and opened the door.

Anticipating he was chasing up his doctor chat, she began with excuses which Matthew strained not to react to. "He's ever so busy at the moment, I'm afraid. I'll get onto him again now. I know you're keen to see him…"

Matthew coughed. "If you could, yes. But I wanted to speak to my wife, please. Now," he added with an authoritative air.

The nerves showed themselves again in the jittery response. Her mardy colleague stood silently beside her, chunky arms folded tight across her chest in its tatty maroon gilet. "Er... I don't think that's going to be possible just yet."

"Why not?" Matthew seethed.

She shuffled from foot to foot. "Just not right now, yeah? Maybe after you've seen Doctor McEvoy..."

"Well, have you at least told her I'm here?"

She added knuckle cracking to her fidgeting. A shared look between the two women left Matthew none the wiser to what they were trying wordlessly to communicate, but something was up.

"We let them know... Yes."

Why the strangeness? Why hadn't they told him? As if reading his mind, gilet butted in with, "Yeah, sorry we didn't come and tell you, but we've been busy."

With an elevated last syllable, she conveyed that expecting them to run around telling patients every phone call they make in the course of their busy day was beyond unreasonable. Matthew ignored her rudeness.

"Are you sure?"

She raised her eyebrows and snorted. "Yes. I'm sure." Matthew glimpsed her rolling her eyes as he turned his attention to the friendlier lady nodding enthusiastically.

"What did she say...? Debbie, was she angry?" Wondering if he'd given the wrong impression: that she was upset with him when he'd meant with this bunch of fools, he didn't bother to correct the possible inaccuracy.

"She thanked us for letting her know."

"Is she coming to collect me, because she'll need directions? She's not very good at knowing where places are." The shuffling and knuckle cracking restarted in earnest, and rude woman folded her arms extra-tight.

"Let's see what Doctor McEvoy says, yeah?" and before Matthew could object the door swung swiftly closed and locked automatically. He wrestled his arm back to his side and refrained from banging the glass as the two women sped down the corridor away from view, not looking back even once.

Matthew trudged back to the little room but couldn't face sitting or lying on the bed again. The only window in the room was too high to offer a view. Tempted to shove the bed over to use as a step up, but he'd already noticed it was bolted to the floor.

Matthew pondered for a moment his surroundings. Had anyone ever ended their life in this room? He shuddered, but a quick inspection indicated that to be unlikely. The room had been designed for safety, Matthew understood that. The bed had to remain static to avoid access to the window. Not that escape would be possible. Only a child could squeeze through the gap, but broken glass could be used as a weapon for harming the nurses or oneself.

With the bedframe immovable, it was impossible it could be utilised to tie something to provide the opportunity for suicide. He could see no other way. There was conspicuously nothing else in the room: no hooks to hang a jacket, nor chair to kick away.

The ceiling he'd studied for hours, counting the tiles and entertaining himself making pictures, was unusually high. No-one could possibly reach up and remove a tile and rummage around in the area reserved for pipes and wires to come to any harm.

Relieved at the limited gruesomeness the room presented, he suddenly shuddered looking at the bed. How many troubled souls had slept there? Not for a few hours, like him, but for days, months, or perhaps even years.

The austere safety precautions would be difficult to live with. They'd push the sanest of individuals over the edge of reason. Once hope is lost; hope of taking control in any way, what's left. Nothing. The human psyche has evolved to cope by shutting down, by becoming depressed. Not caring could be the only way to survive.

A gentle knock at the door roused him from his reverie. "At last!" he exclaimed, calling "Come in," just as he would have in his plush office on Bristol Quayside.

He fell back in dismay as the visitor's intention was not what he'd expected: not to take him to see Doctor McEvoy and release him from this madness, but to keep him even longer with the hideous offering of a tray of food.

Even that was safe. He was certainly in no danger of sustaining burns from the cold slop that the nervous girl in a burgundy uniform accented with jarring green piping informed him was Cawl. Matthew had been to Wales plenty of times, and he'd never seen Cawl like this.

To wash it down, there was tepid tea in a harmless cardboard cup; no sharp plastic to stab with, or polystyrene to choke himself on. The tray itself was also cardboard and threatened to dissolve in the gloopy mess if left for too long.

"No thank you. I shan't be staying long enough to warrant eating this." And by long enough he meant, 'I'm not about to succumb to malnutrition, and even then I'd consider eating the bedclothes first.'

"Nurse says you have to keep your strength up. You'll feel sick if you don't line your stomach before taking your medication."

Unwilling to waste his energy arguing a point with someone with no authority, he smiled and allowed her to place the tray on the bed. How dreadful, he thought. They may as well put it in a bowl on the floor.

Hours passed. Further forays into the corridor failed to bring anyone to his aid, and now daylight was disappearing fast. Standing with his thumb permanently on the buzzer, Matthew was shocked no-one came. But through the doors, he could hear the reason: screams and shouts from patients brought alive by the diminishing daylight.

Walking up and down the short corridor beyond the double secure doors offered no reprise. There were two other doors; three if you included the toilet. One of the rooms must be the man he'd terrified by saying 'Hello.'

Knocking gently at the first door, even though it was pitch black inside. He didn't want to frighten the man again, but he needed to understand his surroundings because waiting for the bloody doctor was losing its attraction. He had to seek alternative ways out other than via protocol.

He wouldn't stay here a minute longer than he had to.

No answer came from his knock, which could mean a dark empty room, or might mean a frightened man hiding. And if he was hiding, he may be about to pounce from behind the door or beneath the bed.

He tried the door. It wasn't locked. Pushing it open with his foot, he paused before taking a primed step into the room. Arms up in a Kung Fu-cum-boxing stance, he had no idea what he'd do if he got jumped, but being ready for it couldn't hurt.

Standing stock still, he quietened his breath. If anyone else was breathing in the tiny room, he'd hear them. Happy he was alone, he switched on the light.

It was identical to the room opposite. The same bolted down bed, the same high inaccessible window vent.

Exiting, he decided to check out the toilet before disturbing 'timid man', especially as he was even more convinced now that his room would be another carbon copy of his.

The toilet had no liftable seat, but instead a moulded soft plastic multi-purpose base that would suit all functions. All purposes, that is, apart from harming anyone. Nothing to break off here. And no window. He supposed the only room where staff couldn't see into from the corridor needed to be extra-safe.

The windows from the rooms were likely the same super-strong glass he'd witnessed gorillas at Bristol Zoo Garden's throwing themselves at. No patient was getting through that, and apart from to cause self-injury, what would be the point?

There was nowhere to go; nowhere to hide, nothing different in any way.

If they wouldn't play ball, there was no way of escaping this corridor. He prayed Doctor McEvoy wouldn't be conducting his assessment in this high security area. There had to be a fire escape somewhere in the building. If necessary, he would find one and go.

With one room left to check, expecting it to be no different, was it even worth the effort, he wondered. But he was thorough and wouldn't rest if he didn't get a peek inside. It might offer something.

It was like Russian roulette; dramatic perhaps, but with one room empty and his room accounted for, this last one would probably be occupied. With his heart pounding in his head, he grasped the handle. Turning it enough to open it if it wasn't locked, he pushed slowly. It opened.

"Hello. Don't worry. I won't hurt you." This time when he paused to listen for breath, he could hear it. In, out, in, out—short nervous little pants. "It's okay. Honestly. I don't want to hurt you. I just wanted to see in your room."

An unmistakeable whimper emanated to his ears. Matthew batted the wall for the light switch and the room burst into light. Sitting a few feet away on the bed, the man from earlier sat facing the wall.

"Hello," Matthew ventured again, the illumination making the scene feel new. It seemed rude not to try to speak to the man. If his presence was really so disturbing to him perhaps he shouldn't, but if he could just help him realise he had nothing to fear.

He took a step towards him. The whimpering grew louder.

"It's okay. Look at me. It's all right!"

Shooting his hands up to his ears, the man screwed his eyes shut, "La la la la laaa! I can't hear you. You're not here! La la la la laaaa!"

Matthew shook his head. He was never getting through to him. About to turn away, something caught his eye. Drip.

Blood oozed from the man's arm, dripping into a large pool on the bed.

"Shit! Are you okay?" How did he find anything sharp enough to do this? "I'll get help," Matthew said, but before he turned to go, the question of how was unquestionably answered.

The man shot his head round and screamed, "Leave me alone!" and when he did, Matthew saw blood; a lot of blood: dribbling from the corners of his mouth, a gruesome burgundy coated his teeth.

"Oh my god!" Matthew shot from the room.

"What are you doing?" It was one of the men who'd restrained him before. He took in the scene and screeched at Matthew. "What have you done? You evil bastard!"

As he rushed to the timid man's aid, the other man hurried through the double doors. Responding to a mouthed instruction from the first man, he flew for Matthew and rugby tackled him to the floor. Effortlessly, he held him in an immobilising grip that seemed to tighten the more he struggled.

Joined by more men, they hauled him up by his arms and legs, splayed him on the bed and proceeded to strap him down. As Matthew wriggled against the indignity, they screamed at him. "Shut the fuck up, Matthew. Evil fucker."

Matthew wanted to scream out, but words refused to come. His lips didn't open and soon his eyes wouldn't either.

Chapter Eight

Matthew screamed out whenever his mind rallied enough to make the effort. He'd been drugged, he was sure, but that's as far as he got with his deliberations before oblivion clawed at his thoughts, dragging them to the point of nonsense.

Resurfacing, they'd gargle and fire enough fear in Matthew's mind to call out, but no-one would come, and no-one would help.

"Debbie," he yelled. "Mum! Dad! Help me."

For hours, the same cycle, but each time he breached the surface of his consciousness it was with a little more vigour. Eventually he succeeded keeping his eyes open for a minute or more at a time.

Jolting his head from side to side brought spurts of relative alertness and he came up with a plan: to bide his time, be very obedient and get to see the doctor. He couldn't risk giving them any reason to think he needed further assessment.

He knew they could have no interest in keeping him here against his will if he could explain, but they also seemed to work on a presumption of insanity. Without waiting to hear his explanation, they had assumed his guilt in hurting the nervous man when it was obvious, wasn't it, what had happened?

No-one considered Matthew might have been trying to help, which while it wasn't his primary incentive had been what he was doing when they stopped him.

Granted, they caught him fleeing, but that was only because his presence made the man worse. With a sigh, he knew he was examining it too much. Whilst he possibly understood why they might have jumped to the wrong conclusion, that's exactly what it was. Once he could explain to Doctor McEvoy, it would all be over and they'd apologise, or not, and he'd be on his way.

The perfect Christmas had been ruined, but it was the first of many, he reminded himself. They were no longer on borrowed time. And at least they knew where he was now. He didn't have to fret about what they might be going through and hoped they could enjoy what was left of the Christmas break without him.

It was an experience. He'd come through the other side stronger, he was certain.

Quietly accepting another meal—breakfast—and grateful he'd been unstrapped to eat it, Matthew sat on the bed, swinging his legs whilst munching on an unfortunately bland bowl of porridge and some cold toast. Demonstrating what he hoped was a warm smile, he asked the nurse who pottered nearby in a poor effort of appearing unconcerned (she was there to watch him, and he knew it) "Will I see Doctor McEvoy today?"

Pausing in her examination of the doorframe she turned to him with a smile. "This morning. He's keen to see you."

And I'm bloody keen to see him, Matthew thought but merely turned up his grin and gesticulated his thanks with a triangle of toast.

She waited for him to finish his food. "You'll not want to see him in your gown, I don't suppose?" Matthew couldn't give a shit. Whatever was quicker, but he supposed a barely concealing hospital robe might be distracting. "I'll fetch you something."

Matthew dreaded to think what. Goodness knows the state of anything banished to lost property in this place. "Can I just have my own clothes, please?"

She shook her head. "Not safe. Maybe soon, yeah?"

Why did they all do that? Presume to ask him if something suited him by adding 'yeah?' to all their sentences. It particularly annoyed him as he doubted his approval was actually being sought. They'd do whatever they wanted regardless.

When she brought what amounted to a grey track suit, he recognised it as being similar to the others attire. If this was some kind of uniform, he could think of a more uplifting colour for the depressed and mentally unwell than grey. With no option but to put them on, it had an eeriness that rattled him; like he'd be wearing this longer than he could bear. At least they looked clean.

"I'll leave you for a minute to get changed," she said. Stepping from the room, she turned a key somewhere next to the window and the glass became tinted. Matthew was pleased and surprised that he was allowed to be alone. Pulling the bland items on took less than a minute, including towelling slippers.

Trying to imagine he was at an expensive spa on his way for a treatment, he forced the smile back onto his lips and popped his head round the door. "I'm ready."

"So," Dr McEvoy smiled. "How arr ye?" The Christmas tree on his desk tried desperately to raise its needle clad hand. 'Drink. Please! I'm so thirsty!' But its temporary nature meant that despite the Tesco label denoting it as a 'miniature *live* tree' it seemed sure to relinquish the title before the celebrated twelve days.

Matthew stared at the feeble thing. It was the only nod to Christmas he'd seen since his arrival. The torn posters on the walls demonstrating perhaps why they hadn't bothered. Picking up strewn decorations throughout the day would get tiresome pretty quickly, Matthew imagined. And now, his perfect Christmas was reduced to this. He wondered if someone who could ignore such a blatant cry for help from a plant flashing its tiny LED's for attention was the best person to have caring for the needs of this ward.

Doctor McEvoy grinned lop-sidedly across the desk. His mop of dark brown hair in a neat Lego fringe above piercing emerald eyes. He was so quintessentially Irish, he would have suited a Leprechaun suit instead of the crumpled indication to his position of respectability that hung loosely from his shoulders like he'd recently lost a great deal of weight.

Reassured by the calming sing-song lilt of the doctor's voice, Matthew answered the question. "I've been better, Doctor."

There was the smile again. This was going well. He'd be home soon. Doctor McEvoy scribbled on a pad. "Uh huh. I'm sure you have. Do you want to tell me what you've been up to?"

Matthew didn't know what he meant and said so.

"You know. In the big outside world?"

Ah, he understood now. It was just his way of asking who he was and what he did for a living. "Well, I was enjoying a wonderful Christmas with my family. We've bought a lovely house after I managed to pull off a brilliant deal supplying amphibious craft to the military. It's my own design. Brian, my partner—business partner," he over-clarified, "he didn't think I could do it. It took a long time, to be fair, but it happened and we turned a tidy profit… A very tidy profit."

The doctor's friendliness was such a relief. Chatting normally like this was so comforting. "But we'd never enjoyed a Christmas there because my beautiful daughter has been so unwell…" Even though he knew she was well now, just mentioning how close they'd come to losing her choked him up and he struggled to carry on. "So this was our first proper Christmas, and I've ended up in here!" he rolled his eyes as if being arrested for drunk and disorderly conduct on Christmas day and being taken to the asylum was just one of those things, but the tear rolling down his cheek was a drop in the ocean of his depths of despair.

"Uh huh." He scribbled more on his pad, the pen scratching so fluidly it was hard to consider it forming words, and Matthew imagined him doodling silly pictures. "Tell me about your family."

Matthew was keen to cooperate. The questions, whilst unnecessary, seemed very normal. "Well, there's my wife…"

"Wife?"

"Yes. My wife," Matthew said slowly. Why was that hard to believe? Had he misconstrued the word 'partner' despite him being extra-clear?

"You haven't mentioned her before. Where do you see her?"

Not mentioned her? Matthew's grief gave way to annoyance. Was this guy for real? How much were the NHS paying this joker? Was he fulfilling another Irish stereotype: being pissed?

"Where do I see her? In our home… I don't know what you mean." It was a supreme effort to control the anger brewing; catching him by surprise forced him to gulp it down. He couldn't risk an outburst.

Nodding vigorously, Doctor McEvoy squeezed his features tight in a weird facial contortion. "No, no, don't worry. You're doing fine. And your daughter? Where is she?"

"Where do you fucking think she is!" he didn't say. Instead, speaking extra-slowly—this guy seemed to have trouble with plain English—he told him how she was at home, hopefully enjoying her presents in his unexpected absence. Struggling with the words, every time he thought about where he should be, it filled him with an intoxicating cocktail of emotion.

"Okay. And where is this… home?"

Matthew shook his head in bewilderment. Coughing to regain his composure, he made sure to look Doctor McEvoy straight in the eye, but it was hard. He wanted to hide somewhere and regroup. This weird tint to proceedings was unnerving him.

"Do you mean, what is my address? It's twelve Clifton Down Road. Bristol. We're planning to name it but haven't felt like it yet," Images of Abi lying stricken in her hospital bed flooded his mind. It was over. This would soon be over.

"Mmm, hmm. And what about your sister, you haven't mentioned her?"

If I haven't mentioned her, how do you know about her, Matthew puzzled? "Er, she's fine, thanks."

"Fine? Really? Your sister is fine?"

"Look! What is going on? Is there a script you want me to follow? I just want to get out of here and back to my family. I want to cooperate, but you are beginning to piss me off." Matthew was puce now. Keeping the anger at bay had funnelled it to an acrid geyser of rage he could barely control.

With an irritating calm, he smiled at Matthew. "What do you think is going on? Mmmm? You see, it really doesn't matter what *I* think, only what you think. Does that make sense?" he nodded along with his own logic as if every word were a gem of wisdom.

I bet, Matthew inwardly scorned. I'll just go now then, shall I? "I think my moderately drunken behaviour has been blown out of all possible proportion, and you guys here want to come across like you have done your job before you send me on my way. Well done. You've been very thorough. Now I'd like to leave. Please."

The scribbling took on a furious pace. His eyes sparkled. He was in his element. "And where would you go?"

"Where do you think I'd go? I just gave you my address. Why do you care anyway? What difference does it make to you if I walk out of the door and take a world cruise? What? Tell me!"

"Okay, Matthew. I can see you're getting agitated. I'm pretty sure what course of action to take, but there are a couple more questions I need to ask. Please don't take offence. I ask everybody the same." He cleared his throat and looked Matthew straight in the eye. "Do you have any notion to harm yourself… or anyone else?"

Well not until a few minutes ago. Now I'd quite like to smash your stupid smug face into the desk! "No," he answered "I don't"

Slapping his book shut with an air of finality, he said, "Good! That's good. You're doing great. It doesn't matter what you've been up to. You don't have to tell us. You're here now. Safe."

This didn't sound like he was going home. "So I can go now. Can someone bring me my own clothes, please?"

Doctor McEvoy sighed and looked down at his shoes. "I don't think you should go anywhere just yet. It would be irresponsible of me to just let you go. We don't want anything to happen to you, do we?"

Blood drained from Matthew's head to his boots, filling them with dead weight, like the iron in his blood had magnetised him to the floor. It was all that prevented him falling. So they weren't planning to let him go. His pale, weary head could summon no suggestion why on earth they wanted him to stay, and he sat open-mouthed and defeated.

What could possibly have led them to the conclusion he wasn't operating with a full load? "You can't keep me here." His ethereal voice echoing from the silence of Doctor McEvoy's office hit an unfamiliar note that didn't even sound like him. "On what grounds?" he rasped. "I'm not mad. I'm perfectly sane. Please just let me get home to my wife and daughter!"

Doctor McEvoy sighed again. He'd suffer hypoventilation if he carried on. "Mad isn't a term we like to use here, Matthew. But you do need some help. That's all. There's nothing wrong with that, so there's not. If you help us, we can help you. You'll soon be right as rain, so you will." And with that he leaped from his chair and offered a hand to shake.

When Matthew took it, he used it to help him from the chair and steer him towards the door. Opening it onto the corridor, still holding Matthew's hand, he paused. "But I am happy for you to have the run of the place. Catch up with the others in the rec room. Enjoy meals with them. It's all part of the process."

Gripping onto the doctor's hand. Matthew wasn't happy to leave it like that, of course. "If I'm not going home, you have to at least let me to speak to my wife on the telephone, *please*," he was careful to include. Holding his gaze until the doctor shrank away from it, his breath wouldn't come and his heart pounded in his ears as he awaited his response.

After consulting the floor, Doctor McEvoy stared hard into Matthew's eyes before answering. "We'll see what we can do, okay?"

Matthew knew when he was being fobbed off, and his mind rallied in the waning opportunity. "Well, I just need a phone, that's all. We can go to the office now, can't we?" he added, forcing the corners of his mouth up into what he hoped resembled a smile. "I'm sure it would make me feel so much better."

Doctor McEvoy crinkled his mouth and tilted his head before smiling assuredly. "You'd be surprised, Matthew. One of the advantages of being in here is that you don't have to worry about things in the outside world."

"But I'm not. I'm not worried at all. I just want to speak with my wife who I haven't seen since Christmas Day! Surely that's not too much to ask?"

He was reluctant to assign a motive for fear the doctor would turn it against him. He couldn't say he was worried, because the doctor would reply that they had spoken to Debbie already and she was fine. And he couldn't say it was for his own benefit because Doctor McEvoy was the self-proclaimed expert in what was good for him. So he just held the smile, forcing him to react.

"Matthew. You need to leave my office now. I have other patients to see." There was no doubt he was being threatened.

Matthew released the grip. He knew what would happen if he didn't: they'd use force and he'd be tied to a bed in the security wing again. He didn't understand why they wanted to keep him, but he was more certain than ever his wellbeing was not at the top of the list.

Chapter Nine

Standing alone in the corridor his breathing became faster and faster. A group of three nurses walking towards him smiled. The kindness in their eyes pierced his grief, and he turned to hide his face.

The toilet sign further down the passageway became his goal. Stumbling over his feet, using the wall for support, he had to get there. Heaving open the creaking door he was confronted with two unisex doors. Relieved neither were occupied, Matthew rushed into the nearest one and crumpled, the seat of the toilet groaning and creaking as it supported him from collapsing to the urine streaked floor.

His mouth gaped, cries of anguish too raw to make a sound, escaped into the ether, adding to the scent of despair. His throat ached with the effort of releasing even a fragment of the pain he felt. Clasping his face in his hands, he rocked back and fore, breathless until the need for oxygen outweighed the expelling grief and he gasped for breath.

Creaking air into his screaming lungs cranked his mouth open further and fuelled the next silent wails. The toilet rattled as he trembled. Snot joined tears as liquid streamed from Matthew's face.

Eventually came a kind of resolute calm. Less peace, more determination.

He didn't have to make sense of it. He just had to get away. Splashing water over his face from the wash-hand basin, Matthew couldn't see if his swollen features had improved enough to leave the room without provoking 'concern' from anyone passing him because there was no mirror.

Shrugging it off, he opened the door and peeped out, relieved the corridor appeared momentarily silent. Not far away he could see the office from where the nurse who answered his frantic door buzzing yesterday had sat. From where Matthew stood now, it appeared empty.

Matthew took a deep breath and steadied himself. Strolling with a confidence he didn't feel, he walked straight to the office. The door was ajar. On the desk, another of the little supermarket trees stood, skewed, half-propped on a notebook so that it had lost some of its soil. It looked even worse than its compatriot. Perhaps they were 'pining' for one another, Matthew failed to smile at the pun.

Next to it, mere feet away from where he stood was a telephone. Matthew had no new numbers to try, but he'd been drunk last time he'd dialled. He knew his phone number. He'd had it for several years.

Putting out of his mind the misdialling of two days ago, Matthew stepped towards the phone. Picking it up, there was no dialling tone. What did they do in his office, dial 9 for an outside line? Looking into the middle distance as he made sure he recalled his number correctly, he jumped as the receiver was snatched from his hand and slammed back into its cradle.

"What are you doing?" a gruff deep voice demanded. The rage grew in Matthew and he struggled to keep it corked. Turning, he wore his warmest fake smile.

"I'm phoning my wife. She must want an update now I've seen the doctor."

"Oh, don't worry. We'll do that," the male nurse grinned. "You get yourself off to the rec room, yeah?"

Matthew's fists clenched. "I'd like to phone her first." He plucked the phone up and began dialling. Blocking as best he could the advance of the nurse behind him, he heard ringing when, at once, the line went dead.

He turned to see the nurse with the phone wire in his hand. "Faulty, see. We've been asked by the telephone engineer not to use the phones while they sort it out. But don't worry. We'll definitely tell your wife how you're doing."

Matthew smiled. His best bet was to be a lot more careful and come back. "Oh, sorry. I didn't realise," he said.

"That's okay."

No sooner had Matthew stepped from the room than keys were thrust from pocket to lock, barring any further attempts. "Rec room's that way," he said pointing with a sneer.

"Of course. Thanks," Matthew said, and began a slow amble in that direction. The two patients he'd met so far had been very distracting. He didn't want to find himself strapped on the bed again, accused of assaulting another one he hadn't even been within three foot of.

The nurse didn't wait to confirm his safe arrival. Now the office was locked, he had other important duties to attend. Seeing him disappear, Matthew turned away from the recreation room towards the office and a number of doors. Doors led somewhere, which meant an opportunity to escape this ridiculous place.

Having composed himself, he was able to affect the look of any other patient, casually sauntering up and down familiarising himself with his surroundings; reading posters, glancing here there and everywhere, which of course he was. But not to settle in. Matthew was scrutinising the best and fastest way to get out of here.

With muscles tensed and his chest taut, he wanted to run screaming through the nearest exit. But they were trained for that. What they weren't prepared for was perfectly sane individuals taking stock and intelligently making their move.

He soon reached the office again, adjacent to which appeared to be the main entrance. He recognised the space outside where Celia had parked her hideous little car on Boxing Day. If he could make it there, he could get away for sure. There had been no guard at a gate or anything like that. Matthew hadn't even known what type of building it was when he arrived. No. This was going to be easy. It wasn't prison. Just a hospital with overworked, underpaid staff.

Doing his best to look as though he was waiting for a member of staff for a not-very-important reason. If the same nurse returned, they would think he was asking to use the phone again. He was happy to annoy him if it meant finding a way out. Leaning against the wall giving occasional glances at his fingernails, he looked with disinterest up and down the corridor, and peripherally at the entrance/exit.

There were two security measures in place. A scanner that could be deactivated by electronic keys which hung on lanyards around the neck of staff, and a combination lock like the one that led to his room. A little observation would afford him the code. They might change it often, maybe even daily, or they might not; he'd soon learn.

That would take time—days even, and Matthew hadn't given up hope of finding a way out sooner than that. Oh for a fire exit. There were none in the high security end of the ward, he already knew that. But there had to be laws in place to ensure the patients and staff didn't all burn to death, didn't there? And with mentally unstable people in a kitchen, that seemed all too likely.

Maybe they weren't labelled clearly. Staff knew and could direct patients to the right door when necessary, but if he saw one, he was sure he'd know. He understood it would probably not exit onto the street, or everyone would escape, but outside had to offer more of an opportunity to escape than inside.

As he strolled, casually tapping his legs with hands hung from thumbs at his pockets, he was surprised how far he was able to wander uninterrupted. Turning a corner, he blinked at stark lights too bright for the white space. He could barely see the end. Walking along, he felt he was disappearing and the relief made him giddy. Straightening his spine, he took a final glance around him before launching into the brightness.

Faced with a set of double doors similar to the ones he was already familiar, he pressed his face against the window, cowling his eyes from the intensity above. Through the glass he could see into the passageway beyond. Step-ladders leaned against walls on both sides. Dust-sheets and pots of paint were strewn around as work had stopped abruptly, quite likely downing tools for a pre-Christmas drink two nights ago.

They might be back tomorrow and their noisy presence could give him cover to escape. But what about when they weren't there? Heart thumping, a plan formed rapidly in his mind. He was going to get out of here now.

Strolling with purpose, he paused every few yards to take a calming breath. Halting at the office, he was pleased that his act earlier added credibility to his current plan.

Noticing him hovering, a nurse approached. "Can I help?"

"Thank you. Yes. I'm feeling a little bit overwhelmed and wondered if I might be allowed back to my room?"

The nurse rolled her eyes and turned down her mouth. "Yeah. Of course." Glaring at Matthew, she flapped a dismissive hand, "Go on then."

"I need someone to let me back in. It's locked." Her face softened as the penny dropped. "Sorry, yeah. Matthew isn't it?" he nodded. "Follow me."

Arriving at the double doors, she reached out and keyed in the code, careful to cover her hand and Matthew cursed her. He'd seen the first two numbers, but there were four more he had to decipher.

With the door open, Matthew didn't go through straight away. "Go on," she said tersely He took a step forwards and began shaking.

"I can't."

Tut-tutting, she sneered, "Make up your mind!"

Matthew took another step and the trembling got worse. "If you don't wanna go in, don't go in. I don't care. It's you who wanted to!"

Turning to her, eyes wide with pleading, Matthew begged, "Come in with me."

Rolling her eyes, she accompanied him to his room as he mooched painfully slowly, resisting the urge to speed up when he heard the click of the door re-locking, he reached his room, and sighed with relief. "Thank you."

A false smile flashing on her face for a Nano-second, the nurse walked briskly away. Pausing at the door, she keyed in the code, this time, without Matthew at close range, she didn't cover it with such care.

Squinting eyes committed what he witnessed of the code to memory. He assigned the numbers to ages of family members and famous dates and they were locked in. Rushing to the door before the nurse got too far, he banged on the glass and pressed the buzzer until his thumbs glowed red.

Her shoulders slumped. Turning lazily, she mouthed 'What?' Banging louder, Matthew drew her in. She'd have to come to tell him off at the least.

This time, completely distracted and more than convinced that Matthew's mind posed no threat, she forgot to cover the code at all, and now he was certain. "What is it?" she snarled.

Matthew squealed and darted past her. "I can't be alone. I can't!"

Her head shook slowly as she directed him to the rec room. There was no code for that. Patients were free to come and go. Inside, groups of other patients sat playing cards and board games. Most ignored him. But Matthew's eyes shot to the table closest to the window, as a chair scraped back against the floor, setting his teeth on edge and a judder down his spine.

"It's you!" Striding across the room in three giant steps, the mountain of stretched and stained grey fabric stood as an impenetrable barrier before him. He wasn't sure how to answer the question and wanted to be on his way as soon as the nurse was out of sight. An altercation with a patient could give him reason to bolt. "You're alive!" he spat the words like an accusation.

"Shouldn't I be?" Matthew braved asking. The sweat stained hulk stared up and down, looking for the catch.

Prodding him hard with a finger of incredible circumference and firmness, he looked pleased at Matthew's yowl of pain.

"You're alive," he repeated with a smile. "Nice one."

Moving back to his table, shuffling now, not striding, the brute slumped on the plastic chair showing greater confidence in its integrity than sense would consent to.

Left standing, ignored by everyone else, it was easy for Matthew to make his departure. Not expecting to arouse suspicion, he still sauntered into the toilets rather than walking directly to the other security doors.

This was it. His heart raced readying him for action. Popping his pale face around the door, the corridor was empty. Stepping out in the direction of his escape route, a sudden noise made him freeze to the spot.

A door slammed open and banged against the wall. A woman screamed at him to "Fuck off!!" which he did, gladly, glancing back only to see her tackled to the floor as she ripped pictures and posters from the wall.

"Karen! Behave!"

Matthew was gone. Karen was a godsend. Scurrying to the end of the corridor, he panicked that he wouldn't remember the code; and then that it might be a different one and he'd be back to waiting.

Reaching out to the keypad, he rehearsed the number over and over in his head. Pressing each one slowly and firmly his heart throbbed in his fingers and his head. "Come on!" he hissed under his breath.

With a final glance back down the corridor, Karen, whoever she was, had done a sterling job of causing a distraction. CLICK, BUZZ, it opened! Matthew bolted inside. Ducking, he hid in the dark. Breathing hard, he had to stifle a satisfied laugh.

Blowing through the circle of his lips, he straightened when he was sure no-one was coming and crept away from the wall. Risking a longer look, he could see the bright passage was completely empty. Smiling at the sense of freedom, he scanned his surroundings. There were the ladders and the paint he'd already seen. Paint rollers, brushes and scrapers were in buckets where they had been hurriedly rinsed; unfortunately, there were no sledgehammers or power tools to smash his way out!

What should he do? Inspecting the ceiling, he imagined himself crawling along heating ducts like so many American films. But no, when he popped a polystyrene tile, the space it revealed was mere inches. A mouse would struggle to escape through there.

His attempts to come up with a plan had put him in his element; a distraction from the peculiar turn Christmas had taken. Being inventive was him. It's what he did, but he'd have to hurry. His absence would soon be noticed.

Chapter Ten

"Thanks again for the Furby, Mr King. I love him." Abi squeezed the furry little creature hard. It would be brilliant when her daddy returned with the batteries and he came to life!

"Can we do our show now?" a miffed Charlotte whined. She didn't enjoy being interrupted so her cousin could get even more attention *and* another present.

The adults shared amused glances. "Charlotte, I think Abi wants to wait for her daddy to come back, don't you, Abigail?"

"Yes, Mummy. Let's wait for Daddy. He won't want to miss it." Grinning at Charlotte, presuming her agreement, she skipped off holding silent Furby's hand. Charlotte didn't agree. They'd wait, and then she'd be busy with her new Furby! They would never do their show, would they, Charlotte glowered? Slinking away, she kicked an errant Barbie shoe under the dresser and smiled before skipping off to play again with her cousin.

"This is a smashing place for Christmas, isn't it? You must be so happy," Tom declared, eyeing every corner. "I love your tree. I wasn't going to bother at all with mine. You know? Since Betty died…"

No-one knew what to say. Tom stared at his brandy. Swirling it around, he drained it and held up the empty glass to the light.

"More, Tom?" Mandy offered, her brother's expensive brandy having not left her hand. Nodding he smiled up at her from the leather chair he'd sunk into.

Mandy sloshed a generous measure into Tom's glass. "Let's play charades!" and she immediately took her place in front of her audience and gesticulated wildly.

"Film…"

"Four words…

"First word, 'The.'"

They collapsed in hysterics when after twenty turns, Tom took the stage and after establishing his idea was a one word book and film, his teeth fell out when he re-enacted 'Jaws.'

"Oh, Tom! I'm sorry. It's not even funny! Here, let me help." But it was funny, and Tom laughed the loudest.

When the gnashers were retrieved, they had become encrusted in pine needles the tree had shed after its week in its unnatural new home.

Tom leapt forward and slapped his thighs. Tears streaming down his face, he could barely speak from laughing. "Well, I said the tree looked nice, didn't I?"

When the hilarity died down and Tom's freshly rinsed teeth were back in their correct place, they were putting the world to rights.

"So, business good?" Tom asked, and then nodding to the house in general, added, "It must be."

"Yeah. Great, thanks. It's the boat yard's tenth anniversary. We've always done well, but it was all Matthew. He managed to get this contract with the Ministry of Defence. Worth millions!" Tom nodded along, eyebrows raised, rapt. "It took a lot to persuade Brian, that's his business partner—senior partner—didn't want to get involved 'cause the MOD take forever to pay.'

"They did: two years, but they did pay and we bought this house. And now with my little Abi-angel all better, we can actually enjoy it."

Tom nodded with a sad smile. He knew how the loss of the light of your life made normal joyous occasions meaningless.

"I'm so pleased for you all. It's nice to see such hard work rewarded."

"Thank you, Tom!"

"We're really proud of you all," Mandy joined in. "Aren't we, Mum and Dad? ...DAD!" Alan jolted awake, falling off the prop his elbow had provided against the arm of the sofa. "We're proud of Matthew, aren't we, Dad?"

"What? Yeah. Of course. Why?"

Rolling her eyes, she snorted, "This house! The business! We're really proud."

"Oh, yeah! We love this house. Brought up from nothing. Grew up in a council house."

"There's nothing wrong with that, Alan. Your business is great, too. People rely on you." Alan shot his wife a glare. "And we're proud of both our children."

The sickly smile she offered Mandy was gratefully grasped. "Thanks, Mum."

"And both our granddaughters."

Mandy squinted, "Awww. You are lovely," she cooed, blowing her a kiss.

"Yeah. We're proud of you both, and I'm not unhappy. I'm not saying that, but this place. Well I'd never have thought."

"And he puts it down to you, Alan," Debbie smiled. "Letting him help you in the garage and the remote control boats. It all started there, he always says." Debbie knew he lapped this sort of thing up. Other issues of childhood, the entire Morrissey family seemed blissfully unaware. Debbie saw. Her own mum being so transparent perhaps made her more critical.

Alan's grin creased his face and he sighed a contented sigh.

"More brandy anyone?" Mandy piped up again, and realising it was the final dribble, "or cognac, or something else?"

"Won't Matthew mind you raiding his drinks cabinet?" Alan admonished.

"It's Christmas. Be quiet, Grandad!"

"He won't mind, Alan. Don't worry," Debbie diffused.

"Where is my brother, anyway? Where has he gone to buy these bloody batteries? Taiwan?"

The rest considered. They didn't know what time he'd left, or what time it was now, but they had performed a lot of charades.

"He must be having trouble finding somewhere open. Good job you didn't go, Tom."

"Yeah," he nodded. "I can't walk so far anymore."

"Shall we see what films are on?" Mandy asked, remote control already in hand, the giant screen twinkling into life.

When the final credits rolled, the Morrissey family, and Tom King, sat in silence. Matthew still hadn't come home.

"I'm gonna have a drive round, see where he's got to. If he's walked that far, he must be knackered."

"Alan, you can't," snapped Mary. "You've had too much to drink."

"Well, what then?"

Everyone sat in various positions of anxious thought: Mary drummed an extended and manicured index finger against her glossy red (Christmassy) lips, Alan patted the arms of his chair, Debbie chewed an errant fingernail to the quick, and Mandy stood at the window, commenting whenever she feared she hadn't spoken in a while that he really should have been back by now.

"I should have gone," ventured Tom. "It's my fault." All eyes shot to him, but no-one could be bothered to point out again how that would have been ridiculous.

"Nobody should have gone," Mary snapped. "There's obviously nowhere open. Abi was happy to wait until tomorrow. It's stupid."

Pushing up from her chair, she took her place staring out of the window next to Mandy.

"Nothing's happened to him, has it?" Debbie removed her finger from her mouth long enough to ask.

"He'll have just got carried away and tried every shop. He's nothing if not thorough, is my Matthew."

"Our Matthew," Mary corrected her husband.

Oh, I thought it was my Matthew and your Mandy, Alan inwardly seethed.

"Try his mobile," Mandy suggested brightly.

"Okay. He never has it with him, but it's worth a try." Pulling the phone away from her ear with a grimace, "Straight to voicemail," Debbie sighed.

"I think I'd like to go home now," Tom said, hauling himself with visible effort from the chair. Grasping at his stick, he struggled to straighten up. "Sorry for all the trouble," he choked, shuffling to the door.

Debbie wanted to reassure him it was okay, but she couldn't. It *was* his fault, and if anything had happened to her husband (and she was sure nothing had, wasn't she?), then yes, he probably was to blame.

A tumultuous explosion of little feet invaded the lounge, "When are we doing our show? Why is Mr King leaving? Where's Daddy? Isn't he back yet? He's been ages. I want to play with Furby!"

"Can we do the show without Uncle Matthew if he's not coming back?" Charlotte asked, tugging at Mandy's blouse.

"I should think so," Mandy began.

"No! I don't want to see it until Matthew gets home!" Debbie screeched. Moderating her tone, she added, "Sorry girls."

"Okay, Mummy," Abi said through a tight hug before disappearing again to the land of play.

"It'll be fine, Deb," Mandy gave her sister-in-law a reassuring pat on the arm.

"I haven't drunk too much. I'm going out to look for him."

Anxious glances were shared, but they trusted Debbie. They hadn't a clue how much she'd had. It was easy to assume they had kept pace with one another, but Debbie had been busy in the kitchen, and they hadn't seen her drinking.

"I'll come!" Mandy cried, bustling from the window to fetch her coat from where she couldn't remember putting it.

Desperate for some peace; time away from her in-laws; time to wonder where Matthew might actually be, Debbie sighed. "It's okay, Mandy. I'll be all right on my own. I could do with the peace and quiet."

"No. I'm coming. I won't hear another word."

Turning to disguise her rolling eyes, Debbie mouthed, 'Great,' and headed to the front door without waiting, grabbing her keys from the hooks that dangled from a little blue boat by the front door.

Hopping into the convertible Saab that Matthew referred to as 'a classic,' Debbie put the key into the centre console by the long hand brake and longer gear stick and started the engine.

"Wait up, sis!" Mandy shrieked. Seeing her silhouetted in the doorway with its border of fairy lights and glorious wreath looked so hopeful, she had to wait as Mandy tumbled over herself in her hurry. Grabbing open the door, she hopped in still sliding on an Ugg boot. "I thought you'd forgotten me!"

Debbie shot her a smile, "Of course not." If she was worried, Mandy was probably worried too. Leaning across, she patted her knee. "Thanks for coming along to keep me company."

"Which way? Where's the nearest shop?" Mandy peered up and down the street

The closest shop was the little corner one quite close. As they approached and it was open, Debbie's heart stopped. "If he came here, he'd have been home within an hour! And why wouldn't he come here?"

Bumping the Saab onto the kerb, Debbie fumbled to release her seatbelt. Mandy's ashen face either meant she was travel sick and was about to revisit the brandy, champagne, cognac and goodness-knows-what-else, or she had caught Debbie's worry.

Marching into the shop, Mandy followed chaotically behind.

"Hello," Debbie hollered to gain attention.

"Good evening, beautiful ladies," the man behind the till greeted. "What brings you to my little store on Christmas night?"

Debbie walked up to the counter. "I was wondering if my husband has been in? He came to buy some batteries, I'm not sure what time, but it was hours ago now."

The man looked thoughtful. "I have sold batteries today. What does your husband look like?"

Whilst Debbie fished her phone from her coat pocket to get a photo, Mandy interrogated. "Have you been open all day?" The man nodded. "And has it been you here all day? I mean, could someone else have served my brother?"

"I have been here all day. I live here. When I see somebody on the camera, I come out to serve. Ah yes. I remember him," he said, peering across the counter to Debbie's phone. "It was ages ago, though. Why are you looking for him? Has he not come home? To such beautiful ladies, I cannot understand."

"No he hasn't," Debbie sighed. "and I'm getting very worried."

The man puckered his lips, his brows pinching together. "What is it? You look like you're thinking."

Leaning on meaty, hair-covered forearms he spoke in a stage whisper. "I didn't see him, but there was another man. A homeless man, your husband said. In my porchway there. Your husband gave him some money, so he said."

"Oh my god!" Debbie's hand shot to her mouth. "That's it. He's been attacked! The silly sod got his fat wallet out and someone's spotted it, haven't they? Oh, no! No, no, no!"

Scraping hair from her red face, Debbie bolted to the door. Staring up the brightly lit street, then down, she screamed at the top of her lungs, "Matthew! MATTHEW!"

"We don't know that is what's happened," Mandy reassured, but even she went quiet at the venomous stare from her sister-in-law.

"Why didn't you call the police? Heh?" Shaking her head in disgust, Debbie turned away from the shrugging man and snorted her contempt.

Back outside again, she resumed her screaming of her husband's name.

"What are you doing?" Mandy dashed after her.

"If he was at that shop giving money to homeless men, and then if he was mugged he'll be close by, won't he? He'll have headed home and been followed. Come on!"

Mandy had to agree. The cold air and the seriousness of what was happening had sobered her up. Scampering after her taller companion, her own cries might have seemed half-hearted, but they were heart-felt. With every cry of her brother's name and every non-reply, a wave of fear crashed over her, rocking her on her toes.

"Matthew? Matthew!" they called in unison.

With silence the only response, Debbie turned to her sister-in-law "We're going to have to report this to the police,"

Chapter Eleven

"Good evening, ladies," a burly, shorn headed young police officer hailed, stepping from the squad car. The blue lights blazing atop combined eerily with the flashing red, white and green Christmas lights shining from store windows and hanging over the little street on the Edge of Bristol. Debbie and Mandy stood shivering in the shop doorway having exhausted their search walking almost all the way back to the house with no sign of Matthew. "Do you want to tell us what's been happening?"

The officer and his robust colleague took a brief account from them both, and the man behind the counter. Their expressions left Debbie and Mandy in no doubt they shared their concerns and they'd done the right thing in calling them.

"Can I ask you a few questions about home?" he asked, removing a small notepad from a concealed pocket on his vest. "I just want to build a bit of a picture, you know? Don't take it the wrong way, but was Matthew happy at home?"

Debbie and Mandy both nodded earnestly. "Never better. We've had a difficult couple of years with our little girl being unwell, but she's all better now. We were happier than ever."

"Any money worries? I know this can be an expensive time of year."

"Again, never better. Matthew was paid for a big contract. We have a lovely house, and quite honestly, we're set for life with the money Matthew's made."

Mandy joined in. "They've got the nicest house. Overlooking the bridge up there on Clifton Down," she said dreamily.

Mention of Bristol's best known land mark produced a sharpness in the policeman's eye he didn't need to explain, but without cause: it didn't sound like suicide was going to be a likely explanation in this case.

"Did he often give money to homeless men?"

Debbie clenched her mouth, sending her lips askew. "No. To be honest. I don't wish to sound harsh, but those ones in the city centre, it's like they're proper con men. They all have a story and I think they're raking it in."

The policeman made no comment, but scribbled away in his notes. "But he is generous. We give a lot to charities via regular Direct Debits. You know, the usual: Cancer Research, British Heart Foundation, NSPCC, RSPCA; all those. So if Matthew did give money, the man must have looked genuine."

The policeman smiled. "There are a lot of 'genuine' homeless, Mrs Morrissey. Would he have been carrying much money in his wallet?"

Debbie reddened and nodded. "I don't know, but he often has £50 notes from customers paying deposits for their boats."

The policeman barked some instructions into his epaulette walkie-talkie, then scribbled furiously on his little pad. "I think we've got enough to go on for now. The best thing you can do now is get off home. He might well be there already."

Debbie was sure he wasn't. "Do you believe this homeless man saw his money and… hurt him?"

"We will definitely look into that. But there are other possibilities. We'll call into any establishments in the locality and ask around. Try not to worry. Nine times out of ten, there's a perfectly reasonable explanation."

Debbie and Mandy headed back to the car, not imagining there would be any reasonable explanation at all. Matthew wasn't the type to go off on a jolly to pubs or clubs on any night, least of all Christmas night!

No, the police could check all the pubs if they wanted. Maybe someone there might know the man who attacked him, but she was beyond certain they wouldn't find her husband in any of them. She had to push that certainty aside. Right now, it was the only hope she had.

The Saab crunched on the gravel drive as the pair sped in. When the momentum stopped, Debbie sat in silence as she switched off the engine, and Mandy uncharacteristically joined her. Still silent, she took her cue when Debbie shoved open the large Saab's door and swung her legs onto the stones underfoot.

Staying a few paces behind, she wasn't looking to take centre stage in the telling of her brother's disappearance. Detecting the moistness in Debbie's eyes, she clutched her hand and gave it a gentle squeeze to say, 'It'll be alright,' but neither of them felt confident that it would.

Centre stage was thrust upon Mandy despite her reluctance when Debbie stood in unbreachable silence before the others, mouth opening and closing but making no sound.

"What? What is it? What's happened?" Alan barked as his wife stood beside him, gaping mouth covered by her splayed open fingers, eyes open almost as wide.

"Well, we haven't found him… but we know he went to the shop, and we know he gave money to some homeless guy. The police…"

"Police? Why. What's happened to my boy?"

"The police are saying not to worry. Nine times out of ten there's a reasonable explanation."

"For what? They're saying he's missing?"

"They reckon he might be in a pub or something."

Mary snorted. "Not my Matthew. That's not him at all. On Christmas Night? With his family waiting! I hope you told them there was no chance he'd be in a pub!"

Debbie spoke her first words since stumbling through the front door in a daze. "I don't believe they do think that, Mary. They suspect he's been mugged, and the fact he's nowhere to be found anywhere near the shop he was last seen, he's either really badly hurt, or…" Debbie didn't want to consider what.

"So, to be honest, I hope he is acting out of character and getting pissed in a pub or something!"

"I suppose he could have seen Brian. It's a long shot, but he'd feel obliged to go for a drink with his boss."

"Brian isn't his boss," Debbie objected.

"Sorry, 'senior partner,'" Mary corrected. "What are you doing?"

"Phoning Brian… Hi, Sue, yes… Merry Christmas to you too. The thing is. Has Brian gone to the pub?" Her face slackened into an almost smile. "He has? Do you know if he met up with Matthew? … No Matthew doesn't normally do that sort of thing… Yes, it is Christmas… His mobile's on the table. What pub does he normally…? Oh. Okay. Thanks, Sue." Debbie stabbed at her phone savagely. "Looks like the police might be right, Mandy. Brian's out—without his sodding phone, just like Matthew. I'll kill him!"

Not completely reassured, it made sense, and when Debbie phoned a few pubs and put out a call for the pair and no-one had seen either of them, one of Brian's little secret dens seemed to be a plausible explanation. Matthew would turn up really, really apologetic sometime soon, and everything would be okay.

"When is Daddy coming home?" Abi asked tearfully, no mention of her and Charlotte's show.

"Come here, sweetheart," Debbie invited, arms spread wide and welcoming. Abi and Charlotte rushed to the arms of their mothers and clung on tight to their waists.

"I think Uncle Matthew has gone to the pub with his boss. You two ought to settle down in bed, and if he comes home soon, I'm sure we can send him up to tuck you in, Abi." Looking to her sister-in-law for approval, Debbie nodded along.

"That's right Abi. You don't want to get too tired and moody, do you?" Abi shook her head.

"Can I have another mince pie before I go up?"

"I'll bring a couple up to you, with a glass of milk?"

Both girls nodded enthusiastically. Charlotte wasn't too keen on mince pies, but the idea of a midnight snack in this big house excited her. It felt like St Trinian's. "Can we have some biscuits too," she pushed her luck.

Debbie smiled. "We'll see."

As soon as the girls disappeared back upstairs, she allowed the clouds of despair to colour her face once more.

Shuffling silently to the kitchen, Debbie prepared a midnight feast fit for Christmas night. The cupboards were well-stocked, and unsure what Charlotte liked, she placed a generous and varied selection onto a tray, along with milk in cups with straws.

Once done, the distraction was over. Steadying herself on the marble worktop, she snorted at her own pathetic sensitivity and batted a tear from her eye. "Lots of husbands go down the pub on Christmas Day, and he wasn't exactly sober enough to make the best decisions, was he?" she asked herself, shaking her head in acknowledgement that it was supposed to be the first sign of madness. Her desire to argue her logic, the second.

Forcing a smile for the girls, Debbie collected up the tray and steadied her grip as the milk trembled in its glasses. Walking through the back of the kitchen, straight into the hallway rather than meet the gazes of the others as she walked through the dining room and living room, she padded up the gentle curve of the exquisite staircase rising from the chequered floor below.

She was relieved to hear giggling from Abi's room as she approached. Knocking gently, balancing the tray carefully on one hand, she stepped in and plonked the gleefully received offerings onto Abi's dressing table.

Noticing a twinkle in the pair's eyes, Debbie grinned. "What are you two up two? Are you going to settle down?"

Charlotte giggled and agreed a little too readily. When Abi asked before she reached the door, "Can we watch a movie?" Charlotte looked disappointed that permission had been sought, as though the naughtiness of sneakily staying up when they were expected to be asleep was half the fun.

Her face dropped further when Debbie declared, "Yes. Why not? It is Christmas." Contrary child, Debbie thought as she quietly closed the door behind her, the absence of giggling making her roll her eyes as she walked away.

Trotting back downstairs, a glance at her wristwatch brought hope and anxiety in equal measure. Hope that the lateness made Matthew's return evermore imminent, and fear that it would serve to underline what she suspected from the start: that something terrible had happened to her husband.

"Phone the police again! Phone the hospital. There's no way he would stay out so late. The pubs probably aren't even open now." Mary snapped her orders. Her unfortunate tone riling Debbie, despite her agreeing with every word.

She phoned Brian's home number again. When it rang and rang, she was tempted to hang up, but then a breathless Sue answered, giggling.

"Hi, Sue. Is Brian still out?" she already knew the answer. The hilarity evident down the phone had the air of intimacy to it. Brian and Sue had never had children, though not for want of trying. They spent the years since giving up on the idea taking advantage of their never-interrupted bedroom.

"Mmm Hmm," she giggled. "Matthew?"

Debbie moved the phone away from her ear to give it an incredulous stare. "No, Sue. He hasn't come home and I'm really worried."

"Stop it…" she overheard Sue snigger to her drunken husband. "Sorry, Deb. Brian didn't see him. He'll turn up. We'll let you know if we hear anything… Stop it, Brian!" She dropped the phone and there was an agonising minute before she realised, leaving Debbie unable to make any other call and forced to listen to the amorous antics.

Grateful for the click and resulting silence, Debbie dialled the phone number on the card the police officer had given her earlier.

"There's no sign of him in any of the pubs," he said, having just returned from his beat to fill his nightly report. "And no-one heard anything from the homeless man either. Colleagues are all still looking out for him, but at the moment, I'm sorry, I don't have any more information."

Debbie couldn't speak. She just managed to expel an "Uh-huh," through the lump in her throat to let him know she was still there.

"Let us know if he comes home. If he doesn't, we might have to consider him as a missing person... Officially."

Debbie just rasped, "Thank you," before pausing her thumb over the red 'end-call' button on her screen. Turning, the faces of her in-laws were no comfort. They were all certain Matthew was in trouble.

Chapter Twelve

"What's the time?" Mary's first words as she disentangled from Alan's embrace, snuggled for comfort in his thick arms.

"Four o'clock in the morning," he barked without a pause.

Pushing herself up, she rubbed her eyes spreading a generous amount of mascara around her face. No-one cared. Silhouetted in the bay window, Debbie stared through the glass, arms folded, expressionless, like a ghost from Bristol's past awaiting in vain for her beloved to return from sea.

No words were needed. It was clear as day Matthew had not returned. Searching out her other child, she spotted her, draped over the arm of a chair, spittle dribbling down her chin, a snore trapped in her nose as air sucked in and out.

Wriggling free from her husband's grasp, she left his motionless figure to join Debbie to stare from the window. As she placed a caring hand on her shoulder, Debbie wrenched away.

Arm hanging in the air, Mary allowed her lips to open only a crack to disguise the escaping sigh. Standing next to her daughter-in-law was too uncomfortable to bear, and she shuffled away with a vague murmur of putting the kettle on.

"I'm going back out to look for him. He has to be somewhere," Debbie spoke in a daze.

"I'll come," Alan creaked forward in his chair. Arms resting on his knees and hands hanging between his legs, he looked as shattered as he felt.

With no more words, the pair made their way to the car, either deliberately or distractedly ignoring Mary's shouts of did they want tea.

The Saab had gained a coating of frost in the few hours it had been still and they had to wait in icy silence as the heaters fought Mother Nature for control of the vision and safety. With a side-plate sized hole, Debbie wouldn't wait any longer. Throwing the stick into reverse, with a quick backwards glance that offered little visual information, she floored the accelerator.

Gravel sprayed as the wheels spun. The tarmac gave no grip, hidden beneath a sheet of sub-zero slipperiness. Regaining control seemed unlikely as the car spun onto the main road running through Clifton Down, but just as the adrenaline flowed and Alan thought his fingernails would pierce his hands gripping the handle above his left shoulder, the car came to a serene standstill.

As though that was the way she always left the house, Debbie drove on, lurching forward, rubbing pointlessly at the screen as she rolled on down the hill. "He's out here somewhere, Alan. We have to find him. We can't leave him out in this freezing weather overnight."

Driving down every side road, and side-side road leading off them, Debbie drove with the windows rolled down and the heaters on full, calling "Matthew! Matthew! Where are you? Where the *fuck* are you?!"

Stopping in a particularly quiet road, Debbie reached up and pushed the button to lower the roof. About to object, Alan's mouth stayed open but silent. If his son was enduring this cold lying in the gutter somewhere, then he could manage to search for him in the open air Saab without moaning.

Zig-zagging up this street and the next, there didn't seem a single one they hadn't driven up at least once. Where else could he be? Pulling into a space occupied by ice-cream salesmen in the summer months, Debbie clawed at her face, peeping through frozen fingers at the view below.

Exhausting the roads left few choices for Matthew's whereabouts. The river glistening red, gold and green in reflexion of the jolly lights adorning the street in such stark contrast to the mood in the car, suddenly had a dark demeanour.

"He won't be in there, Deb. Why would he be?"

"Well, he's bloody somewhere." Throwing open the door, Debbie tiptoed, slipping in the ice, her arms flailed before she steadied herself at the water's edge and scanned the riverbank. Could he be in there? Something catching his eye and he slipped in? It seemed all too possible. Turning away, she couldn't bear to look.

Huffing at the concentration of not slipping in the ice, Alan joined Debbie's scrutinising the surface of the water. "Do you think he's fallen in there?" Alan gasped.

Debbie nodded once. "What else could have happened to him?"

"The man in the shop said about the homeless man…"

"The homeless man who was so angered at the gentleman giving him money and a few kind words, he what? Mugged him? Murdered him? It doesn't make sense."

"But the police said it might have been more people… a gang. Seeing him with all that money… People are murdered for a fiver!" Realising he was arguing against his son having drowned in the river by suggesting he might have been murdered stopped him in his tracks. It all seemed so unreal; like it was happening on TV and he was trying to work out the clues.

"No. You're right. What gang would be out on Christmas Day? There'd be scant pickings. No-one's about. And Matthew would have gladly given the money. He wouldn't have risked," he was going to say his life, but settled on a more palatable, "anything."

Debbie nodded. "No. He wouldn't. But what he might do, is try to get a closer look at some wildlife on the river; especially if he thought it was in trouble.

As the sun slowly warmed the hearts of the night-time searchers, they both knew any clues to Matthew having slipped into the icy water could soon be clear in the growing light.

Faced with that ever-likely reality, it was time for some reassurances.

"He might have been carried down river and be sheltering somewhere to keep warm. He's a really strong swimmer." Debbie knew that strong swimmers died in mis-judged forays into open water all the time, never mind being steaming drunk in sub-zero conditions. But it was hope, and hope was all they had right now.

Birds in the surrounding trees broke into a frenzied cacophony that made their hope seem well-placed. With the fanfare cheering them to their grim task, they edged, hand-in-hand for safety, along the towpath. Every lap of water they were convinced was a hand, or Matthew's head bobbing above the waves. Their straining eyes could have been persuaded the Loch Ness Monster had made an appearance if that's what they sought.

When they reached one of the many bridges traversing the River Avon, they had excited themselves to an almost certitude that Matthew would be found, clinging and grateful, to one of the supports holding the bridge's walkway high above the water. When he wasn't immediately visible, they hurried over the bridge, stopping in the middle to peer beneath them at the centre struts.

Not bothering to speak of his failure to appear, they decided with a glance to carry on over the bridge to examine that side of the river. Treading over the flowing water to the opposite side seemed a significant change. Maybe their luck would change too.

Gaining a comfortable pace was difficult. Too fast, and they wouldn't feel sure they hadn't missed him. He might be clinging on for dear life to an outstretched tree root, or perhaps lying unconscious on a beach formed at a bend in the river. Too slow, and they might never reach him before the river carried him further from their reach.

The tendency was always to hurry though. If they couldn't see him where they were, then he had to be somewhere else: *they* had to be somewhere else.

The swift flow of the river carried a little piece of hope with it at every turn; optimism speeding away with the flotsam and jetsam collected along the river's seventy-five mile course.

The sun having risen high in the sky, Debbie stopped abruptly. Shoulders sagging, she allowed herself one final scan of her surroundings before declaring, "This is hopeless!"

"Phone the police again. Maybe they've heard something."

"They'd have phoned home. Mary or Mandy would have called us."

"Is there signal all along the river then?"

Debbie moved her head from side to side as she jostled with the notion of allowing hope back into her head. "I don't know. There might not be." Checking her phone, her heart raced. One bar! It was possible the police or her other in-laws had been trying to phone. She dialled home first.

"Any news?" Mary's breathless voice answered.

"No. I hoped you'd have some."

"What now?"

Debbie murmured through her angst about registering him as a missing person, but her voice failed her and she clicked to end the call.

"Are you going to call the police station now? They might have heard something.

Debbie slowly nodded. Trembling fingers tapped away to bring up her last dialled numbers. The one she recognised as the police officer's popped up where she expected, displayed next to the time *23.11,* on the *25.12.17,* Heart pounding in her ears, she was desperate to hear that Matthew had been found and was safe.

"Hold on," was the response to her inquiry. "I think that particular officer is off duty today. I'll see if I can get his notes up… Ah yes. It's still been less than twenty-four hours, hasn't it?"

Debbie grunted her confirmation into her phone.

"I know it's not what you want to hear, but we wouldn't be that concerned at the moment. It's hard for you left behind, but literally thousands of people go missing every week. The good news is that most of them turn up after a short time, and haven't gone very far."

"If you're suggesting he's gone missing on purpose, that's ridiculous. We're the happiest we've ever been, for Christ's sake!"

"It says here on your file that your daughter has made a recent recovery from leukaemia? I'm pleased for you, but perhaps the time before... when her recovery was er, in question. Well, maybe it took more out of your husband than you realise?"

Debbie was silent. What could she say?

"We're optimistic he'll turn up again soon. Certainly our investigations thus far haven't found any ominous signs. No-one heard a struggle, there was no sign of him having gone near the river, as far as we can tell, and there's no sign of anyone matching his description at the hospital. I think it's a case of no news is good news. I know it's hard, but waiting is the best thing you can do."

Debbie's voice was no more than a whispered rasp through the lump in her throat. "What do I tell our daughter?" she squeezed through the gap.

"Be optimistic. Keep calm, and please be reassured that nine times out of ten, things work out just fine. Okay?"

Debbie coughed in her attempt at regaining her voice. "The policeman last night mentioned making an official report; registering him as missing?"

There was a confused silence for a moment. "No. There's no need. We are already taking the matter seriously, let me assure you. He could have been talking about the charity, 'Missing People.' They may be a comfort if he doesn't turn up really soon. Or the Missing Person's Bureau. They have a useful fact sheet..."

She couldn't blame them. It was their job to remain detached and impartial.

Turning to her father-in-law, she forced air into her lungs and tried to sound optimistic. "They say not to worry. He's bound to turn up. She reckoned maybe Matthew was more stressed with Abi's illness than we realised."

Alan nodded, willing to grasp onto anything. "Maybe her getting better has let out some long restrained emotions? And the deal at work with the MOD; making the perfect Christmas... It got too much for him."

Strolling back to the car, they offered occasional optimistic titbits to one another.

"He did this after his GCSE's. Fine all the way through, then when he finally got his results and they were brilliant, he locked himself in his room for a week!" Alan shook his head with a smile. "I'd forgotten about that. Thinking about it, going missing isn't so out of character after all."

Debbie did her best to smile. "My mum. She was an SRN. A more capable woman you couldn't hope to find. But one day, she cracked. My dad had died a couple of years before and she'd kept it all in. 'Coped wonderfully,' everyone said. Ended up spending a week in the local nuthouse. She was on anti-depressants after that." Alan's downturned mouth showed he was giving the story due consideration. "She's fine now. You'd never think it possible."

"You never would," Alan agreed.

By the time they reached the Saab, they were as happy as they could be that Matthew was just taking a much needed break and would return requiring their compassion and support, and perhaps a little medical intervention.

Chapter Thirteen

"Where's Daddy?" a yawning Abi greeted as they stripped off coats and slumped at the kitchen table.

"Coffee," Mary hovered with a fresh pot, and poured at her husband and daughter-in-law's nods.

"We think he's taking some time away. Having a bit of a break."

Abi's pout was a relief and preferable than the anticipated tears. "At Christmas?" she said, eyes wobbling to say 'That's crazy.'

"I know. But I think Daddy was a bit more stressed than we realised."

"About me?" Abi's high voice seemed perfectly upbeat.

As Debbie floundered for an answer, her brain was too fatigued to come up with an explanation that didn't sound like she blamed her beautiful little girl.

"Not just that, honey," Alan interrupted. "He's been under a lot of pressure at work and everything."

"When's he coming back?" It was the most reasonable question in the world.

"Soon, love." Alan did a convincing job of detaching from his distress to comfort his granddaughter. "I'm sure he'll be home really soon." The sound of the words echoing from the oak cabinets were oddly reassuring. Alan sipped at the scalding coffee. Thumbing the handle fondly, he allowed himself a small smile. He'd been right. His son would be home soon. Why wouldn't he?

"Why don't you get some rest?" Mandy had sat on the sofa next to Debbie, staring at her in between sips of tea. Hugging the tepid cup to her chest with both hands, her leg swung irritatingly back and fore, hooked over its grounded partner resting on tip-toe to extend her short leg to the floor.

Her short glossy brunette mane glistened in the lights of the Christmas tree like a glorious accessory, her full lips wet with the tea combined with saucer eyes to affect the epitome of sympathetic grace.

Debbie stared into space, ignoring the question because it was bloody obvious. She couldn't get any rest, wound like a coiled spring, ready to unleash kinetic force in any direction that opened itself to the possibility of finding her husband. How Mandy looked so immaculate; could even bother to brush her hair, or find pleasure in a cup of tea when her brother was missing was unfathomable.

Stiffening at the hand patting her forearm, combining distastefully with a squinting of those big eyes into almond smiles, a microgram of tension evaporated as Mandy slid off her seat to the announcement she would 'Leave her in peace.'

Debbie sighed. She was being unfair. If Mandy looked immaculate and was relaxed about Matthew's disappearance, it meant she was sure he was fine. Moping would get her nowhere. Maybe she should take a leaf out of her book and copy some of that optimism. God knows, she could do with it.

She couldn't shake the feeling something terrible had happened. If Matthew had needed space, it was a big enough house to keep to yourself in. *"He stayed in his room for a week…"* Alan's words echoed round her head. Of course!

"Has anyone actually checked in the house?" she cried out. "We have three spare bedrooms!" There was no answer so she hopped from the couch and hurtled to the kitchen. Repeating her request met with stony stares and reluctant nodding. Mandy and Mary had looked everywhere—even under the beds and in the attic—both remembering clearly how oddly Matthew had responded to the good news of his sterling exam results.

Perhaps witnessing that was what was keeping them on an even keel now.

"Even keel!" Debbie said out loud. "The boat yard! His work. We haven't even checked there, have we?" She leaped up with a yell. Her eyes bright, met the stares of her in-laws. This time it was vigorous shaking heads that greeted her question, and it was obvious they all thought they knew exactly where to find Matthew.

"Phone him… on the office number," Alan instructed, looking at the reconditioned seventies phone hanging on the wall. "Tell him he can stay there if he wants but we've all been worried sick."

Debbie glowered. Why the criticism even now? She shook her head. "No. I've never known him like this. If he's unstable in some way, we don't want to guilt trip him. He might run away."

Capering down the long hallway, she fairly skipped to the car and was sat behind the wheel before anyone else had a chance to be included in the plans.

She saw Mandy, and then Alan and Mary as they squeezed together through the front door, hurried down the steps and planted their feet onto the gravel, disquiet lining their faces, but she pretended she didn't.

Wheel-spinning, her eagerness to be away her only thought. As her house faded in her rear-view mirror, a rage at the ridiculous and unnecessary heartache Matthew had put her through filled her and released in a flurry of punches on the steering wheel.

"You bastard! You fucking, selfish, self-absorbed, selfish," she repeated, "BASTARD!" and she pummelled the steering wheel again. Salty tears wet her cheeks, dribbling into her mouth and down her chin. A bead of her raw emotion fell onto her sleeve. She watched as the droplet grew and pooled before plummeting onto her lap.

It was good letting it out. When she saw him now, she could just hold him and love him, not berate him.

The river grew wide here, butting onto Spike Island. Brunel's S.S. Great Britain dominated the quayside, Matthew's luxury launch business within sight of it was close now. Pulling the Saab into the car park which served the tourist attraction of the world's first iron hulled ship, some swanky new apartments, and a range of new bars and restaurants to sustain them, was the first thing that slowed her racing heart.

It was crowded. Boxing Day was not the 'stay at home with your family' day for everyone. Loads of youngster's, possibly students (although wouldn't they have gone home to families around the country?) spilled onto the pavements from bars and cafes, the hubbub of conversation a constant buzz, Matthew might have found the crowd a comfort, but more likely it would have repelled him.

Despondency was brief as the next image which filled Debbie's mind was Matthew having arrived at his office last night, now trapped because of the constant noise outside.

Striding across the tarmac, the plush office of Marsden-Morrissey Marine rose abruptly in front of her, numerous impressive yachts moored alongside. It didn't look the sort of place you'd expect the military to use for manufacturing specialist equipment, but Matthew's dogged determination had paid off. Of course, there were no examples of the amphibious craft on display. They weren't exactly top-secret, but they observed a degree of confidentiality.

Pausing at the front door, she prayed it would be open, to fuel her certainty she'd find Matthew inside. When it was resolutely secure, she tried to maintain positivity and fished her key from its place on the Saab's key ring.

Her hand rested on the light switch. Leaving the room unlit, she breathed quietly and peered into the dusky light. The stillness of the air sucked the buoyancy from her mood and she knew no-one had passed this way for days. The idea that Matthew may have, but had been deathly still since his arrival, wasn't something she was willing to entertain.

Stepping past the huge framed posters of boats, along with accompanying models and pamphlets, Debbie padded up the plush carpeted stairs to Matthew's office. Keying in the entry code—Abi's date of birth—she stepped inside, switched on the light and closed the door.

Silent and untouched, the large space felt paused, confirming her original verdict that no-one had been in since the office closed for Christmas a week ago. Stepping to her husband's desk, she sat in his plush leather captain's chair.

The view over the huge expanse of oak, flanked either side by floor to ceiling Georgian windows glazed with rippled antique glass offering timeless vistas of open water to one side, and Brunel's masterpiece to the other, would cheer the dourest mood. Pictures of the three of them adorned the walls, along with photos of Matthew and Brian shaking hands with some well-known faces: some celebrity customers, others, big business magnates and investors, including HRH The Prince of Wales.

If Matthew had been feeling distressed and had found his way to the office, then she could think of no reason why it wouldn't cheer him up—unless there was some reason she didn't know about.

Throwing open the top drawer, Debbie began a thorough search to uncover a possible motive for Matthew's disappearance. Not really sure what she might be hunting for, she had vague notions of unknown money worries attempting to enter her thoughts. Shaking them off, she knew that couldn't be the case, but she still glanced at the bank statements she came across in the drawer.

If anything, it might provoke concerns of how to spend it all. Not that Matthew had hidden anything, they didn't really talk about the specifics of the business, but there was even more in there than she imagined when he had declared the payment from the MOD had left them 'comfortable.'

Scanning the sheet further, there were no anomalies. No odd, unexplained amounts to a letting company for a mistress's flat, no regular amount to a possible blackmailer's account, no off-shore accounts, nothing like you see in the movies. Nothing. No clue.

Debbie's lips pressed so tightly together they squashed the colour right from them, leaving a pale line mirrored by her straight brow stressing pin-prick pupils as her quick mind tried to fathom the situation.

If he had come down here, and the bars were even half as busy as they are today; and perhaps he'd popped into one for a drink, and maybe someone saw his fat wallet... That opened up a whole load more possibilities, didn't it?

Her pale lips now represented the only hint of colour on her face. If she were not already sat, she'd have fallen as her legs turned to jelly.

Quickly concocting the worst story, her mind tortured her with ceaseless sickening scenarios—Matthew mugged and shoved into the dock, his body sluiced along the vast Avon River joining the huge tides of the Severn estuary and washing out to sea. She could see the newscast now... Man's body washes up on beach; dog walker discovers, and then she imagined infinite beaches around the world where the Atlantic swell might deposit her love's husk.

It wouldn't even have to be a mugging. He was drunk when he left. If he'd had more in one of the bars, he might have fallen in the bloody river all by himself with no need of assistance from a villainous third party.

She would hurry down to the bars, ask around; check the bins for his wallet. It was gruesome and she hoped it led nowhere; that she'd got it all wrong, but in the front of her mind she could not escape that logic had decreed the quayside as Matthew's most likely destination, and logic now provided infinite ways why he might never have returned.

She would phone the police, of course she would, but she didn't want to be told not to make inquiries. She understood that questioning anyone involved might tip them off, but she didn't expect that she would be doing that. Just finding out if anyone had seen her husband. And she didn't want to be ordered not to do that, because it would drive her insane.

Closing the drawer, Debbie swung the chair round and planted her feet firmly on the dense pile of the carpet. "Here goes," she said, standing up and nodding to the dozen or more photos of Matthew on the wall.

Striding into the first bar, she was greeted by three hipster beards at three different heights. The tallest one smiled down at her. Detecting her upset, he rushed a stool under her and insisted she sit down.

"Can I get you anything? A beer? A glass of water?"

The kindness opened the floodgates. As she sobbed, water and beer were brought to her, and her face reddened in the concerned stares from fellow patrons.

In-between sobs, she managed to tell them why she was there.

"Missing since yesterday? I can't believe it," Middle-beard shook his head.

"Matthew Morrissey? Yeah we know him," short-beard volunteered. "He comes in some lunch times. Always tries whatever craft beer is on the specials board and leaves a tip. Showed us round the boats one time… beautiful. I'll buy one one day," he said looking around him to express, 'when this place is paying enough.'

No-one had seen Matthew. They hadn't been open yesterday, nor had any of the other bars or cafes as far as they knew.

Debbie walked into all the establishments on the wharf to be thorough, but after the bearded men's discouragement, she wasn't surprised when no further information came forth.

There were a few litter bins dotted about, but it was impossible to check their contents because they were designed to remain closed with a small resealing aperture to receive litter. It was a good design to prevent interference from gulls and escaping odours, but bad for seeing inside.

It would have been a needle in a haystack anyway, and with no-one seeing him there, she hadn't been hopeful of finding anything even before she had examined the impregnable bins.

So much hope a couple of hours ago, evaporated now like steam from a puddle of piss. What was left to do? Wait? She couldn't just do that.

Walking back to the car, she dialled the police as she went. By the time she opened the door and slumped into the driver's seat, she was talking.

Listening to Debbie's sobs, they talked her through a course of action that included nothing more than she had already done, and agreed to escalate the investigation. With those words, Debbie could take no more. When terms like 'missing due to misadventure,' echoed from the earpiece, she was no longer listening. On autopilot, she said polite goodbyes.

A few seconds of silence passed before she broke down. There was no doubting it. Matthew was gone, and right now, she was beginning to believe she would never see him again.

Chapter Fourteen.

He couldn't tell, but he hoped Karen still occupied the nurses' attention. Once restrained, there would be retribution, maybe taken to a secure section, Matthew wasn't sure, but felt confident he had a little bit of time.

A whole new wing was under construction. Large panes of glass on each of the rooms suggested they were to be further high security rooms, like his. Sighing, a fire-escape seemed improbable but he had to know.

Dusk was setting in, drawing light from the corridor like liquid to a sponge. Matthew had to hurry to see, but the cloak of imminent darkness would be good cover if he could find a way out.

And there it was!

The last room at the end of the corridor glowed lighter than the rest. And the reason was, it had a door! He imagined it being some sort of therapy room, taking advantage of open air on a summer's day. It was a new door. Nothing special; no key code or camera or anything. Whatever security was planned, it hadn't been installed yet. Just a one-key multi lock stood between Matthew and outside! That and a massive pane of thick glass.

Eyes scouring the corridor with pin-prick pupils, his heart raced as panic set in. Why did he think this was a good idea? Big panes of glass like this were always safety glass—it was law. He knew it would be a waste of time hitting it with anything; the paint cans, scraper, even the stepladders would be useless, but he knew a way.

From his own use of tempered glass he'd learned that until fitted into position, they were fragile. An accidental knock along the edge of the sealed unit would see it shatter into a million pieces. He recalled the corners being the most susceptible.

But he still needed something the right weight and solidity to attempt it. Anxiously glancing back down the corridor, he knew his luck and his solitude couldn't last forever.

The sharpest point was the handle end of the scrapers. But it would be impossible to use any of them on their own. Weighing a stepladder in his hands, his mind whirred, trying to engineer something quickly to produce the most force.

With two stepladders he might balance a lever. They were long, so he could place the pivot point more than twice as close to the glass as the area he would apply weight. He was almost smiling. This was definitely going to work.

He was about to tape the scraper to the pane to use as a point when he found something even better: a tatty, paint covered screwdriver that must have been used to prize open pots of paint. The sharp point would multiply the power even more.

Testing it all in slow motion, it worked perfectly. Climbing a third ladder to the top. He wasn't sure of the height so he couldn't calculate accurately his force, but his weight, multiplied by whatever speed he achieved in the time it took to fall from this height, he was sure would be enough.

Perched high up the ladder, he was certain his plan was good. He had only to land anywhere on the rungs below to affect a massive potency. With a deep breath, Matthew jumped, easily landing on the furthest end, striking the screwdriver in the perfect point to instantly shatter the glass.

Before the momentum of the fall had even been fully spent, Matthew knew he had made a terrible mistake. There was another aspect of breaking toughened safety glass that had escaped his recollection until now, but as the ear-shattering noise echoed like a bomb had gone off, he knew he'd have company soon. And the glass, now crazed, still remained a barrier.

Piling the ladders against the entrance wouldn't stop them, but he hoped it might buy some time. As the first foot came round the corner at the end of the corridor, Matthew knew he had to act fast. Diving through the window, tiny crystals cascaded in a shower around him as he tumbled to the floor. Leaping up, he brushed broken safety glass from him and smiled. He was in the room. Now for the door.

Grabbing the screwdriver that had helped so much already, he had a different job for it this time. Squeezing the blade into the corner, he wriggled free the glazing bar that held in the glass. Pulling two off with one deft movement, the neoprene gaskets fell off like long black snakes swaying in their new freedom.

He could hear the door open and the ladders rattling. They were doing their job but wouldn't forever. Peeling away the opposing corner, he freed the remaining bars and immediately attacked the glass, prying it from its place.

Breaking the seal, it fell backwards just as his makeshift barricade gave way and flooded the small corridor with Gestapo nurses.

"What the fuck is going on here?! Christ!"

They reached the room as the glass toppled and exploded on the floor. Matthew shot through the opening he'd created and he was outside, but without a clue where to head, he was trapped; hemmed in by walls on all sides.

Flinching his shoulder away from the grab made by one of the nurses, his instinct was to lash out. His lunging swing was more effective than he'd expected as the screwdriver he'd forgotten sliced straight into his attacker's hand.

Squealing in agony, the hand let go and Matthew was free to run around like a headless chicken. There was nowhere to go; no way out.

Running back over to the nurse he'd injured, by the time the colleague arrived it was to a terrible scene.

"Now, now, Matthew. Don't do anything stupid."

But it was too late, he already had.

The point of his screwdriver pressing into the man's throat was his only ticket out. He couldn't give up now. The trouble he'd be in would be so severe, it was now or never.

"Let me out of this crazy fucking hell-hole, and I won't press this point through his fucking neck, yeah?" he said mocking their habitual false affirmative and pressing hard on the nurse's throat.

He did it to be taken seriously; and to steady his trembling hand: the hand of a meek, generous man. This was not him at all, but these arseholes were keeping him from his family and they had to believe he would kill for them.

"Come on, now. We can talk, can't we? You can tell me what's bothering you." Edging closer, the nurse took a step back when Matthew prodded, and snarled. "Okay. Not me, then. Is there someone else you'd be happier talking to?"

Matthew snorted. "Oh, let me think. Is there anyone I'd like to speak to? How about my fucking wife? Why won't you fucking bastards let me speak to my wife? Hey? HEY?"

Thrusting so hard, he wasn't sure himself if he might not pierce this jugular in his grasp, see his tormentor lying on the floor clasping frantically at his life draining away with every desperate pump of his heart—but he knew he never would. He never could.

But this lot didn't.

He had to get somewhere quickly before they crowded him and found a way to overpower him.

"Get me to the nearest exit, and I'll let him live. Do it. *Now!*"

"Okay. Keep calm, okay? You don't want to hurt anyone, do you?" Matthew ignored the question and made his demand once more.

"You'll need to follow me inside. There are no exits out here."

"Liar!"

"Look around… There's nothing. Come on. It's this way."

Matthew had a screwdriver, not a gun. How could he keep the burly bouncer/nurse under his control whilst he walked along the corridor to the exit? They were trained for this. He was chancing his arm in the most stressful circumstances.

But he couldn't give in. This was his only chance.

"Here's what you are going to do. You are going to walk calmly to where the exit is so I can see you. I will walk with my buddy here, and my other buddy," he said nodding towards his weapon, twisting the point of the grimy tool. "And when I'm satisfied you aren't tricking me… When *I'M* satisfied… I'll let him live!" Squeezing his arm further into his captive's neck, he screamed, "Do you understand?"

The other nurse nodded, two more strapping specimens appeared at the doorway and Matthew stiffened. "You two keep back as well! All of you, keep back." They nodded and stepped aside.

It must have been obvious how much Matthew was struggling with his task. He was wiry, and efficient, but not strong; not in a brutish way at least. But obvious it appeared not to be, as with a huge relief, Matthew scuffled past the side-stepping figures of all who stood between him and his escape.

The nurse he'd told to show him the exit, stood at the end of the corridor and pointed round the corner. Apparently the only way in and out of this place was the main entrance, or maybe he should think of it as just 'the entrance,' in light of that.

Shuffling along, his charge offered no resistance. He'd done a good job persuading them he actually was a psycho. When he reached the corner, the nurse moved to the door.

"Open it!"

Tapping in the code—the same code Matthew had used already, the nurse presented his lanyard key and the door slid open to reveal a porch with another set of doors which led to the outside world.

"Open those too." Matthew calmed a little. He could hardly believe how well this was working.

The nurse sighed, reluctant to let this nutcase out, but for the safety of his friend and colleague, he had no choice. No code this time, just the lanyard. The breeze was the most welcome sensation Matthew had felt in days.

Backing from the door, he was outside with the nurse still inside. Shoving him with all his might, and with the adrenaline, that was surprisingly hard, he was free.

His only plan now was to run fast before they could catch him.

But he would never run. Before he had even begun to turn, the piercing, excruciating pain as twelve hundred volts seared his skin, the warning, "Taser! Taser! Taser!" occurring simultaneously, not before as he was sure protocol decreed, felled him in an instant.

They swarmed around him, the injection entered his thigh and relinquished its load in one fluid movement. His thoughts drained from his head like an emptying bath, swirling around and leaving inescapably.

The last thing he heard before everything went black was the hissing contempt in his ear of the nurse he'd attacked. "You'll pay for that, you lanky fucker."

Chapter Fifteen

Gasping for breath, Matthew jolted, clawing at his sides, he had to get away.

His arms wouldn't move. Muscles spasming, he felt restraints on his wrists. Trying to look down at what was holding him still, his head moved stiffly and a sudden nausea giddied him.

Searing light hurt and he slumped, defeated.

It had all gone horribly wrong, hadn't it? He was back in high security and now he'd be under closer scrutiny than ever.

His mind stalled, unable to push past the drugs clinging for a free ride around his blood vessels. Pinching his eyes together, bringing his attention to the front of his head to flood his brain with consciousness, achieved nothing more than exhausting him until he had no choice but to give into sleep, drawing him under until even the brightness couldn't penetrate the fug.

Panicked. Matthew jolted at the not-so-gentle shaking of his arm.

"Meds," was the only explanation offered as Matthew whirred forwards as the electric motor of the adjustable bed raised him to a high sitting position. "Open up," the male nurse, in jeans and a scruffy T-shirt depicting some gruesome looking thrash metal band, said to him as his right hand approached his lips with a little pot of pills.

"Open UP!" he repeated, shouting the second word as he pressed the plastic pot sharply into Matthew's mouth. Leaning in, he spat the words into his ear. "If you don't open your mouth voluntarily, then know this: we are well within our rights to make sure you have your medicine. We think it's important, and you… You have proved beyond doubt you are not to be trusted. Open your f'ing mouth if you know what's good for you."

No sooner had Matthew's lips parted than a small handful of pills in a variety of shapes and colours were forced between them, swiftly followed by a beaker of tepid water.

"Drink," he barked.

With no choice, Matthew swallowed the tablets in his mouth. He wasn't sure if he imagined the swooning giddiness that overcame him immediately, but he couldn't fight it.

The room spun. A nausea, so strong, swirled inside and he could barely recognise up from down. When the blackness returned, Matthew was grateful.

It was silent as Debbie stared from the large bay window in Clifton Down road. Her husband had been missing for days now. She wasn't even sure how many. Moving her head slowly from side to side, she was almost amused at her failure to recall. Almost.

She had always thought that under these sorts of circumstances, she would know to the second. But maybe that was only for the spurned. For the utterly bewildered and numb, time meant nothing.

The in-laws had returned to their respective homes yesterday, or was it the day before? And now it was just her and Abigail. Keeping in a light mood for her daughter had been her intention, but she knew she was failing miserably. Or failing depressed-ly, or distraughtly, hysterically, or on the verge of becoming unhinged-ly.

Where was he? Where? Where? *Where?*

The police had begun to take things more seriously, and had, in their own words, 'extended the search.' They weren't dredging the Avon, but they had looked.

Their efforts had mainly been 'extended' in providing her with leaflets and scruffily written websites and local groups she might try—groups full of people like her with husbands, wives, and children missing.

The pamphlet from the Missing Person's Bureau hurt the most. It was sympathetic but hopeless. 'It's hard for those left behind…' it said, and 'Most people turn up within forty-eight hours close to their home.'

It hurt because the advice for what to do if that timescale was exceeded seemed geared to coping rather than finding. And it *had* been longer than that. She might not be sure to the second, but forty-eight hours? That had passed a long time ago.

The statistics were terrifying. People missing for years, and the website was full of them. Dozens of new entries had been added since she first looked for Matthew, and she was sure the only people monitoring the pages were those with loved ones missing.

Hundreds, no, thousands of faces smiled out at her from the screen. Black, white, Asian, male and female, representing all classes and areas of the country, and none even looked unhappy. Not one showed any indication they were about to disappear from the lives of the people who loved and cared for them.

The photos were surreal. Happy, smiling faces now being frantically missed. The very photos taken to bring back a joyful memory now gnawing a festering sore.

Debbie's blank stare left the window for a moment to answer Abi's request.

"Yes, you may help yourself to another mince pie." Mince pie! Anything to do with Christmas made her angry now. Standing quickly, she stomped over to the tree with the intention of flinging the infernal reminder of Matthew's disappearance as far as she could. To smash it; destroy it. But the few steps in its direction quelled the desire.

What good would it do? A momentary release of her anger would hurt Abi. With a faint but resolute smile she determined Matthew would return. Something had happened, something terrible, but he would overcome, and he would come back to them. Debbie had only to keep their loving home in order until then.

Chapter Sixteen

"Eat."

The orderly had demanded this of him for ten minutes now. He'd interjected other words occasionally—usually expletives letting Matthew know just how much of a pain he was being not eating, but he could muster no appetite.

Being unstrapped from the bed was the only benefit to meal times. His arms ached with the lack of movement. He tried to shift his weight from time to time to avoid bedsores and cramps, but the rawness on his buttocks and hips showed it hadn't been enough.

"Sit up and eat your fucking food or I'll force it down your fucking throat!"

He would, too. They'd come in mob handed a few days ago and he'd opted for spooning a few mouthfuls in rather than be choked with a dry sandwich.

It wasn't that he wanted to misbehave, on the contrary: the sooner he could get in their good books, the sooner the opportunity for escape might re-present itself. But it was impossible. His limbs failed. His mind failed. He wasn't really here at all.

Whatever they were giving him for his 'psychotic' episode left him unable to think; unable almost to blink. And using no energy, even with his mind, meant he had little use of food.

Moving his desert-dry tongue around his mouth, he didn't know if he would speak, or even if he might attempt to eat. Its movement woke the terrible taste: chemicals and iron, like he'd sicked up blood after drinking petrol.

Attempting to push himself up from the mattress, his arms were too weak for the job. The orderly launched at him and shoved him forward. "That's it. You gonna eat now, yeah?"

The 'yeah' grated on him making him want to throw the plate across the room, but he didn't. He kept control and forced a few mouthfuls between his lips. Swallowing was another story. "Drink," he hissed, mouth caked in bread sticking his epiglottis and stopping him breathing. "Drink…" he hissed again.

"Give me a fucking minute, will you?" Shuffling away at a speed suggesting Matthew's choking to death wouldn't bother him, he poured stale water from a jug into a white plastic beaker and thrust it in Matthew's direction with his meaty, tattooed forearm. "Take it then!"

Matthew reached out in-between gasps for air. The cup shook in his feeble grip and as his other hand instinctively shot to aid it, he dropped the plate of food.

"Stupid fucker!" the orderly screamed.

"What's going on?" a calmer voice entered the room.

"Oh, it's Matthew dropping his sandwich, Doctor… Sorry I got a bit frustrated. I should know better."

"Indeed you should. I'll take it from here," her gentle voice had a calm authority. Noticing the large man's attitude towards her was amusing; like a cat telling off a bear. "Go and clear up the rec room or something, will you?"

As the diminutive doctor strode towards the bed, the orderly grinned at Matthew. "I'll leave you to it then, mate, yeah?" Reaching a fat hand out, Matthew wasn't sure if he was expected to shake it, but instead, he received a fond pat of his arm. "See you in a bit." Turning to the doctor, he smiled at her and added, "Give us a shout if you need anything." And with that, he strode from the room and even had the audacity to give a tuneless whistle as he went.

"So, how are we today?" she smiled over her glasses.

Matthew couldn't speak, but at least felt confident he didn't have to persist with his charade of eating. "We're going to restart your therapy. Maybe not today, but you need to do something soon. We want to get you better. Back to your old self."

This was the most positive thing Matthew had heard since being forced through the doors goodness knows how long ago. He nodded.

Draining the last of the stale water, his arid lips formed the words, and a hushed whisper fell from his chapped lips. "Can I speak to my wife? Please?"

The little doctor shuffled from foot to foot for a moment. "We'll see what Doctor McEvoy thinks, shall we? He's in charge of your treatment. What? Sorry?" she answered Matthew's rasped response. "Oh, when will you see him... Give your therapy a chance for a few days, or a week, and you'll be back on ward rounds like everybody else," she smiled.

Back on ward round. Yay! Matthew had no choice but to go along with whatever plans. He'd spotted the diversion and wasn't at all convinced the Irish doctor would give him his phone call no matter how 'therapy' went. He wouldn't hold his breath anyway.

"Do you want to follow me to the rec?" she asked, eyebrows rising above her spectacles.

Matthew nodded. As he shuffled from the bed, his legs collapsed and he clung to the bedframe. Forcing himself up, he took a determined wobbly step towards the door, and followed the doctor along the corridor.

The exertion pumped adrenaline through his body just to give him the strength to walk. His brain cranked into action, fighting the medication for control of his senses. Pausing at the double doors, the doctor offered her lanyard to the sensor before covering her hand with her clipboard as she entered the presumably new code.

Matthew glanced away feigning disinterest. If he was going to get the new door code, he'd have to play it calm.

Shuffling into the rec room, the doctor saw him to a seat before smiling proudly at him and announcing, "I'll get you started with therapy as soon as I can, okay?" and for once, the question appeared genuine. He'd stumbled upon the one person who seemed to care.

Others in the room looked up at his arrival and quickly looked away again. Ignoring him was unanimous and seemingly deliberate. It suited Matthew. He had no desire to talk to anyone; apart from Debbie.

"I'm busy now. I can't talk. No! I told you, I'll call you later!" The person holding the phone stopped mid-stride when he saw Matthew. He moved the device from his ear with gentle care and held it in his hand a few inches from his face.

The bright screen cast shadows on his pock-marked skin, pores so deep and black a gentle abrasion would cause a cascade of blackheads to fall like sooty snow.

The griminess continued in his greasy locks which hung over his face in dark triangles as the hair stuck together through adhesion rather than styling. Lowering the phone, Matthew watched in horror as the man proceeded to rub the screen on a T-shirt so filthy it had no hope of cleaning anything.

Cautiously, Matthew shuffled forward in his seat. "Where did you get that?"

The man gasped and held the phone close to his chest. "It's mine!"

Matthew nodded, "Of course. I just wondered where you got it because I'd like one, too. May I see it?"

The man squinted, deciding whether to trust Matthew or not. Without moving closer, he held it out in Matthew's direction so he could see the screen. The wallpaper depicted a skew-whiff photo of the garden through the doors at the end of the room. It was badly lit, and someone's blurry arm had been caught in the image as they walked past.

"Nice," Matthew whistled. "Can I hold it?" The deliberation clear as it contorted the man's face, blackheads threatened to burst from their cautious purchase on his bulbous nose. Holding the screen to his wholesomely clean ear was something Matthew would usually avoid at all costs. But if he spoke to Debbie, or Brian, or anyone, they couldn't keep him here. It wasn't normal; not right to retain him and deny him access to his family.

Backing away, the man screamed, "NO!" and thrust the mobile out of reach in the depths of his equally disgusting grey jogging bottoms. Matthew sunk back into the chair. He had to get that telephone, but he had to do it without upsetting another patient. He couldn't risk being strapped to the bed again.

Minutes later the man was sat at a table near the window, legs swinging in carefree contentment. Matthew approached, he hoped, in the least threatening manner possible; which given his emaciated pallor should have been easy. But as he shuffled slowly forward, shoulders rounded, eyes down to the floor, he suspected that threatened is exactly what the man felt.

His leg stopped swinging and rested on the floor. Bouncing up and down, his extreme anxiety at Matthew's approach was undeniable.

"Wanna play a game?" Matthew quickly decided that perhaps winning use of the phone could work better than friendly persuasion. Interacting somehow might ease the distress.

The knee stopped jumping. Covering the mobile with his grubby palms, he looked at Matthew before his eyes darted to the window.

"You like looking out there, don't you? How about Eye Spy?"

A flash of excitement lit the man's eyes for a second before he reigned himself and shrugged.

"I'll start if you want?" When no response came, Matthew began searching a suitable object. Instinctively choosing something easy, he was glad he did when after ten minutes guessing, and more than a hundred suggestions (many of which were the same but in a different order), he struggled to get 'Grass,' despite its dominance of the window's vista.

"My go!" he yelled when he guessed right. Bouncing with excitement, his eyes narrowed in thought. "I spy wiv my liddow eye... sumfin 'ginnin wiv...wiv..." He glanced round the room, agitation causing his leg to vibrate again.

"How about if I guess, you'll let me have a go of your phone, just for a minute?"

"wiv... "

"Deal?" The man pouted. "Deal?" Matthew asked again, hand extended to shake.

Grasping Matthew's hand, he shook it and repeated, "Deal." Matthew smiled and resisted the urge to smell his fingers. Suffice it to say they would need washing at the earliest opportunity.

"L!"

"Okay," Matthew said, looking outside. "Lawn?"

"No."

"Lines... between the paving slabs?"

"No."

"Light?"

"No!" he squealed with delight.

It went on. And on. After ten minutes suggesting everything he could think of outside, Matthew turned his attention to the room and alighted on dozens of possibilities, "Lamp? Lamp shade? Light switch? Leather shoes?"

"No, no, no, no, and NO!" His eyes were ablaze with the thrill of his obscure object. "Do you give up?"

Matthew shook his head. "It's not you, is it? Your name's not Lenny or something, is it?"

The man scowled. "No. My names Malcolm. Why would you think it's Lenny? Who told you I was called Lenny?" he eyed the room suspiciously.

"No-one told me." Seeing the leg twitch under the table, Matthew got on with the guessing before Malcolm lost interest and decided not to give him the phone. "Linoleum? Laminate?" He was grasping at straws, scrutinising every corner. There had to be something he was missing. "Lock? Label? Laces?" he said without even seeing them before remembering laces were considered too dangerous to have on the ward.

"Do you give in? Do you? Have I won? Have I? Mmm?"

Matthew couldn't afford for him to win. He needed that phone. If he couldn't see it soon, he'd have to hope their newfound friendship prompted a better response if he asked to borrow it again.

Desperately scouring the room, he took a deep breath. Come on Matthew. You're missing something. When he tells you and it's bloody obvious, you'll kick yourself.

"Leaning?" he said, looking at Malcolm resting on his elbow.

"No! Give up. You know I've won! Go on, give up."

It seemed important to him; and pleasing him had been a major consideration in playing a game, so reluctantly, Matthew said, "Okay. I give up. What is it?"

Malcolm couldn't contain his joyful glee as he pointed at his wrist.

"What, Malcolm. I don't see it."

Malcolm scoffed. Matthew was being thick. He shook his wrist in Matthew's face, and even though the object was right in front of him, and the idea that this cretin had made an alphabetical error stared him in the face, he was still shocked when Malcolm jumped from his seat and skipped around the room, "Lastic band! It was right there on my wrist the whole time, you thick bastard! I beat you good, see? Las-tic baaaand!"

Matthew's annoyance at the foolishness didn't stop him noticing the phone unattended on the table. Scooping it swiftly, he stood and strode away, hoping he'd make it to the door before Malcolm noticed.

"Hey. You stole my phone! The nurse give me that cos I bin good. You can't take it, you lost."

Matthew paused. "Look, Malcolm, I just need it for a few minutes, and then I'll give it back. I promise."

"No! You lost. I won. You couldn't guess lastic band. You never got it!" Malcolm lunged for the phone but missed as Matthew hoisted it out of reach.

"I couldn't guess, Malcolm. No-one could, because there's no such thing as 'lastic band.' It's E-lastic. Elastic!"

"Fuck off. It's lastic band. Everyone knows that!" Malcolm pitched for the phone again. This time, Matthew blocked him with a gentle shove.

"Five minutes, Malcolm. That's all I'm asking. Five bloody minutes."

"Hey leave him alone." There could be no question the man in front of him would have little trouble stopping him, but that didn't hinder the rest of the rec room's residents from standing and joining the beast in solidarity. "Give him his phone back, now, or I'll break your face."

Matthew couldn't. He needed this opportunity, this might be it. His only chance.

In one swift movement, he grabbed a chair, bolted through the door and propped it against the door handles, leaving an angry mob trapped in the room.

The monster-man picked up his own chair and flung it at the door making the glass shudder at the impact. Matthew scurried down the corridor. Any room would do. He just needed enough time to dial. Simply hearing his voice would let Debbie know that whatever they were telling her were lies. He was alive and well and in dire need of rescue.

Avoiding the toilets was preferable—it would be the first place they'd look when they escaped his blockade. But luck was on his side for once. A room beyond the office was empty, he could see through the glass. And when he tried the handle it opened!

Scuttling inside, Matthew rushed to the furthest corner and ducked down behind a chair. Stabbing at the screen with a quivering finger, he dialled his home number. Nothing. Was there no signal in this room?

Risking being seen, Matthew hurried to the barred window and raised the handset aloft to see if that would help.

"What are you doing?" A nurse demanded, marching towards him, her arms already reaching for the phone. "That's Malcolm's. You can have a go when you've behaved well enough, which at the moment seems very unlikely!"

Matthew jumped away from her. "Listen. I'll give it back. I just need to make a call. I have to speak to my wife!" Dialling as he sprang from her reach, Matthew pressed the phone to his ear again. Nothing.

"You won't do it with that!" Matthew stared, waiting for the bombshell. "It hasn't got a SIM card. We just give it out so you can use the camera and play a few games. There's no SIM, and no Wi-Fi! You'll not get far with that." She was laughing now. "Come on Matthew. Give it back."

Staring at the screen, Matthew was dismayed to see she was right. That's why there was no signal. That's why he couldn't hear anything! The little antenna icon at the top of the screen confirmed it 'Insert SIM' the blinking message warned.

Matthew placed the phone on the table and slumped in the chair.

"Come on. Out you get."

With a dejected sigh, Matthew stared at the ceiling. "Just give me a minute. Please."

Chapter Seventeen.

Matthew was relieved that despite the ruckus in his attempts to use Malcolm's phone he had not been forced to stay in his room, and the straps had been removed from his bed. It was like the staff were confident in his staying put now. He'd made a few attempts at freedom, but, like a wild animal in the circus, they had trained him into submission.

But Matthew was waiting; watching. This caged beast was determined to escape at the first opportunity.

"Matthew? Doctor McEvoy is ready to see you now," the friendly little lady doctor advised, peering up at him through her square black glasses. "Come on."

Matthew followed happily. He would have to be careful, but he wanted answers from the good doctor. Taking his choice of seat from the three scattered around informally in the room Doctor McEvoy had selected, he chose the one nearest the desk. He didn't want to give the impression he was anxious about this meeting at all.

Poorly drawn and coloured-in hearts adorned the wall and Matthew shuddered that he might have missed Valentine's Day. He would always surprise Debbie with flowers and a meal in the finest restaurants, and now, he was sure she didn't even know he was alive. How poignant must the day have been, thinking she'd never see him again? But she would. Of that, Matthew was prepared to promise.

"So, what about ye, Matthew, eh?" the leprechaun impression began. "You've not done so great since I last saw ye, have ye not?"

Matthew smiled. He knew a lot more about his stay here since the bewildered state he'd last seen the doctor. And with that knowledge came a new confidence.

"All I wanted to do was speak to my wife. I've been fobbed off every time I ask, and looking at the love inspired walls, it looks like I've been here for weeks. What on earth is going on?"

Doctor McEvoy sighed and sat back in his chair. Crossing a shiny black shoe over his grey suit trousers revealing alarmingly jolly Tweetie-Pie socks, he prodded his chin with steepled fingers. "You still going on about that, are ye?"

"Still going on about it? Talking to my wife? Er, yes," Matthew snorted. "I was picked up by the police on Christmas Day, which was bizarre enough in itself, and then you have kept me here, an isolated prisoner, until the middle of February!" Matthew shook his head and leaned forwards. "I haven't worked out why, but it's not on, and it can't be legal."

"Oh, it's legal. And the quicker you engage with the treatment, the better for all of us!" Doctor McEvoy stopped as he noticed his own rising temper. With a deep breath, he rolled his shoulders and forced a smile onto his face. "Now, Matthew. We just want you to engage with us. Stop trying to escape. Stop frightening the other patients. And just engage. Let us help you. Will you do that, Matthew? Will ye?"

Matthew stared at the doctor, forcing his will into him with a piercing stare, desperate for the power of hypnosis to declare itself under his mastery. "Just let me speak to my wife, and I'll do anything you want!"

Doctor McEvoy sighed again. Leaning forwards, placing both palms flat on the desk, he smiled a crooked smile. "You're not going to let this go, are ye?" he shook his head to himself.

Matthew increased the stare. It seemed to be working! "No. Never," he asserted.

"Okay. Okay," Doctor McEvoy said, drumming the desk with his fingers. Matthew felt like jumping up and dancing, but his request was so simple, his glee was dampened by a growing fury at being denied this for so long.

"I'll have to tell you the truth."

The rage bubbled up. He was going to deny him again, wasn't he? Just when he thought they were about to allow him the minimum of human kindnesses and let him speak to Debbie, this stupid doctor was going to refuse!

"The truth is, Matthew... And I didn't want to have to tell you... I hoped it would just fizzle out like your other ideas. The truth is..."

Matthew waited before deciding whether to leap across the desk and kill the bastard opposite him.

"... We haven't let you phone your wife for your own protection."

Matthew's fist grew tight, the blood squeezing from his white, hard knuckles. "Explain," he demanded.

"We didn't want to get you all upset."

Screwing his balled fist into his thigh, the beginning of pain released some of the pressure and allowed him to speak again. "And why, for the love of all things holy, would talking to my wife upset me? Please, do tell."

"Well, don't shoot the messenger, but the truth is, Matthew," he sighed the deepest sigh. "The truth is you don't have a wife. You've never had a wife. She's just a figment of your psychosis along with all the others."

"Never had a wife! Are you quite mad?" he regretted it immediately. But his plan to stay composed struggled against such nonsense. Lowering his tone to sound calm, he added, "I was with them until the police brought me in on Christmas Day. What are you saying? I've imagined my whole life?"

Matthew's stare remained. What did he expect? Surely not that he'd believe this bullshit? Why were they doing this? He had no clue, but he would have. He was determined.

"You're going through some issues at the moment, for sure. We're pleased you're back..."

"Back? What on earth are you talking about?"

There was the sigh again. "Listen, I don't know what you've been through out there. The police picked you up in Clifton, so I suppose you were heading to the bridge again. Were you going to the bridge, Matthew?"

Matthew stared. "What are you talking about?" he protested again.

"It's okay. We can help you now you're back." He smiled from beneath his jet black fringe. "You're safe here."

Matthew added opening and closing his mouth to the staring routine forcing Doctor McEvoy to fill the silence.

"So, you can see why we didn't want to tell you. Although you do seem pretty calm about it. I presume it's ringing true in that head of yours somewhere, yeah?"

Matthew forced himself from his bewildered haze and smiled. "That must be it. Thank you, Doctor." He knew he wasn't going to get anything from them that made any sense voluntarily. His only hope was to comply, and in so doing, convince them they didn't have to watch him.

He had to get out of here. If someone was this desperate to keep him locked away from his family, then he was sure they must be in danger. And that was all the motivation Matthew needed to escape, whatever the cost.

Chapter Eighteen

'Dear Mummy. Sorry Daddy isn't here to give you this, but I still love you.
Abi xxxxxx'

Tears streamed down Debbie's cheek as she read the Valentine's Day card for the hundredth time. It upset her in so many ways. Obviously it was a painful reminder that her husband wasn't here, and on this day that he always made so special... made *her* feel so special. But more than that, it was how Abi must feel to have written it.

Hovering her hand above the mantelpiece, unsure whether to display the card again where it would taunt her from every angle. Opting for laying it flat, she could tell Abi it fell if she asked.

Why was Abi sorry? Did she worry it was her fault Matthew wasn't here? She knew she was guilty of discussing how the stress of Abi's illness must have affected him more than any of them had realised.

Abi taking his place in writing the card must mean she thought he had a choice; that she had to right what he was doing wrong. Debbie couldn't deny the thought had occurred to her too, and that upset her perhaps the most, she realised, and the guilt stung.

Were they as happy as she thought? Or had the success of Marsden-Morrissey Marine made him want more? Was he living off the proceeds she'd helped to build? Living it up on an exotic island with a newer, younger, mysterious girl on her arm?

She was ninety-nine percent sure that wasn't the case, but it happened, didn't it, to some people?

Pursuing the MOD deal, and then payment for that contract had taken a lot of energy. Caring for, and caring about, Abi had been shattering. What if that had held their marriage together? All that energy with its focus and purpose? What if she wasn't enough—had never been enough? What if she'd just been along for the ride of *his* success?

No. She shook her head and bit her lip. He loved her; adored her. And he adored Abi, there could be no question.

He'd been missing for nearly eight weeks now. The arrival of Valentine's Day had brought that hideous timescale home hard. Shaking her hand when she realised she was chewing a fingernail, usually immaculate, now shabby and torn, her hands hung conspicuously at her sides like a smoker unsure what to do with them the first week into a New-Year resolution.

Squeezing them into her skirt pockets was a comfort, but now she didn't know if she should sit or stand. It didn't matter. Nothing seemed to matter anymore. It was too much. First, years of hell with their daughter, now a living nightmare of utter misery for both of them.

A new emotion rocked her, and she tried at once to quash it: anger. Not at Matthew. She was already almost certain he was away from them by some dire necessity. Her anger directed at Abi. Her hand shot from pocket to open mouth as she gasped at the notion. Why would Abi act like her daddy was away from them on purpose? If she didn't know how much she was loved after all she'd put them through…

Nausea at her own crassness clawed at her face, drawing her mouth into a downward horse-shoe. "He loves you, silly girl," she sobbed to the empty room. And then she wasn't sure if she was angry with Abi for underlining the possibility he may have chosen to leave them, or with herself for entertaining it for even a second.

Quickly absolving Abi of any blame, she condemned herself entirely. It's what Matthew would want; to take any pain from

Abi. She couldn't be made to feel something she didn't already suspect, so it was all her fault anyway, there was no uncertainty.

Slumping onto the sofa more from necessity than through choice, Debbie closed her eyes. Oh to fall asleep and wake from this nightmare. But sleep was as elusive as ever, her eyeballs bounced around under their lids trying to escape their sightless incarceration. Pinging open, they continued their scrutiny of the minutiae of the décor—patterns in the Laura-Ashley wallpaper taking on a life of their own as faces and beasts constructed themselves in Debbie's mind. If only they could construct something useful.

Her eyelids suddenly concurred with her desire to close and remain shut in response to a knock at the front door. Knowing she had to answer it, and persuading her eyes open again with the promise it may be news of Matthew, she hauled her legs round and stood shakily.

Taking a breath to steady herself, she strode officiously to the door and heaved it open.

"Hi, Debs. How you doing?" Mandy stood in the porch with an artificially bright smile plastered on her boyish face. "I know. Terrible, right?" She didn't wait for an answer, nor an invitation, before bustling past her sister-in-law into the lounge. "It's awfully dingy in here, Debs. Do you want a hand having a clean-up?"

It wasn't dirty, or even untidy—the cleaner came three times a week and there wasn't a thing out of place. But their beautiful home had soaked up Debbie and Abi's misery and spewed it back through its every pore, poisoning the atmosphere like an emotional smog.

Mandy's initial impression of chaos caused her to shake her head as she examined the spotless room with wide eyes. "Maybe a bit of a dust then?" but wiping any surface showed that didn't need doing either.

Debbie shrugged and resumed her position as part of the furniture. Mandy sat beside her and patted her leg to break the silence. She was distraught at her brother's absence, of course, but it must be harder for Debbie.

Mandy wouldn't see her brother from one month to the next anyway. For Debbie, noticing little clues every minute of every day must break her heart. And the rejection, if he was happy and healthy and keeping away by choice, was a rebuff of Debbie, not her.

She supposed that was the reason why she looked pristine, and her sister-in-law looked like she hadn't washed in weeks.

"Do you want a cuppa?"

Debbie shrugged again. She couldn't care less, but she prayed Mandy might leave her in peace and disappear to the kitchen for a while, so she asked for a sandwich as well.

Giving very particular instruction, she made it sound complicated—this amount of butter, that thickness of bread, this mayonnaise not that mayonnaise, triangles not squares— in the hope that Mandy would be conscientious and take her time. She needed to ease into to the idea of company to cope.

"So, what's the plan now?" Mandy sat cradling a hot cup in her manicured fingers. Debbie dragged her gaze from contemplating the steam rising from her tea and stared at her sister-in-law. "Do you have any plans?"

She was trying to help, and she deserved her attention, so, grudgingly, Debbie sat up, cleared her throat and dug deep. "I've done everything I can think of. I badger the police and missing person's bureau every day. I've put his photo all over social media…"

"I saw. A lot of comments. He's very popular, my brother."

"Lots of comments, none of them useful."

"I've seen your posters. Anything from them?"

Debbie tried not to glare.

"I suppose you'd look a bit happier if there had been news." Noticing Debbie flush red, she probed, "What is it? What have you heard?"

Debbie shook her head. "Nothing. But, sometimes I've been pleased that no-one knows where he is…"

Mandy's eyes clouded as she awaited what she could possibly mean.

"… rather than hear he's left me for some floozy!" and she broke down into silent sobs, pounding her thighs with enraged fists. "Abi thinks so! Look at that card. Go on, read it!"

Mandy slid the Valentine's Cards from the mantelpiece. She wouldn't rather her brother stay missing than having left Debbie. She didn't care about Debbie that much. She was just her brother's wife. She supposed she loved her, well you have to love family, don't you? But if it came to choosing loyalties between her and Matthew, there was no contest. Whatever he'd done, and however selfish and misguided he'd been. He was her brother.

"She's just trying to make you feel better. And she doesn't understand. To her, anger at her daddy leaving you is marginally more palatable than the alternative, and for you too by the sounds of it." Wondering where she was going with her point, Mandy tried to dig herself from the depths. "But I'm sure there's another explanation."

"Thanks, Mandy. Thanks for trying to make me feel better, but you're right. I probably would cope better with him leaving me than something terrible having happened to him. Wanting to leave me, I can understand. I'm not all that. I'm just… Debbie."

Mandy rushed to hug her; a rare occurrence. She knew at once she'd been too harsh. Replaying her own opinion in her head sounded so unfair. "He loves you, Debbie." Kneading her shoulders, she added, "I'm his sister. We're close. I'd have got a hint if he wasn't happy. Mum would've too. He said he was the happiest he'd ever been…"

"But maybe not with me."

"Yes, with you! He adores you."

A smile flickered onto Debbie's face for a mere second, before sinking into the quagmire of reality. "So something terrible has happened to him, then. That's the only explanation, isn't it?"

Mandy's mouth opened and closed. They'd come full circle and she had nothing else to add. "He'll turn up," she said unconvincingly. "You'll see."

Debbie sighed and shut her eyes. She supposed they would see, one day. And when they did, she couldn't imagine anything but the very worst. And she envisaged it in so many upsetting ways.

Matthews's stricken face loomed at her from every angle. Pain, torture, streaming from his eyes as someone valuing money more than human life, and the devastation taking it leaves behind, cast him away like the flotsam of life. The rage boiling up for whomever could do that consumed her, but was quickly offset with exasperation at his carelessness in showing his thick wallet to anyone in the vicinity.

But then she imagined him throwing away his own life with no-one else to blame. What was it the police called it? "Death by misadventure?" something like that. He was a gung ho type who may well have got too close to the river and fallen in. She didn't know what sort of drunken state he'd been in, but he'd been drinking since breakfast... their special Christmas Day breakfast.

Halting her thoughts, trying to release some of the grief in concealed weeping didn't help. Closing her eyes, she willed sleep to take her, to offer respite in the world of dreams. But she knew, if unconsciousness did claim her thoughts, it wouldn't take her somewhere nice. Instead she'd be forced to relive the torment she endured every waking moment, adding new terrors to suffer as soon as she reopened her eyes.

"Another cuppa?" Mandy's bright voice echoed in her ear after an attention grabbing pat on the arm. Debbie didn't remember drinking the first one, but she nodded and closed her eyes once more.

Chapter Nineteen

Matthew sat in the rec room. He had a cup of tea he'd allowed another patient to bring him and, under their scrutiny, he was even debating taking a sip.

"So, why are you in here, Natasha?" he broached. "Is it okay to ask?"

The girl nodded. "It's fine." She appeared completely normal, but when she pushed up her sleeves, her arms heating with the conversation, the raw scars of a hundred attacks on herself were striking. She held them up on display. "I get pretty down... Hear voices that tell me *this'll* help... and it does in a weird sort of way. But I bloody wish I didn't have to do it."

Matthew nodded, cupping his mug and finding the tea surprisingly tasty. "How long have you been in here?"

Resting her own cup on the arm of the chair—its precariousness causing Matthew to grimace in nervous anticipation—Natasha hooked her feet up, crossing her legs. Collecting her cup up again and hugging it to her concave chest, she gladly lay herself open. "On and off... about two years." Sipping her tea as punctuation, she smiled, her face emitting a welcome warmth.

"On and off? You go home, then? How often?"

"Most of the time, I'm home. But when things get on top of me," she pointed to her right arm with a bony left index finger, "I act up."

"What sort of things get on top of you?"

Natasha shrugged and lowered her cup. Looking away, her eyes stared out of the window, when their gaze finally returned, Matthew cringed at their wetness. He'd been unfair, but

Natasha was the realist person he'd met. Talking to her was a relief, and he hoped she might be able to provide useful information about this place.

But she didn't deserve this interrogation. He should do less talking and more listening. "Sorry. It's just that you seem nice and I'm interested."

The smile returned and she attempted to answer. "Just stuff... you know?"

Matthew took that to mean it could be anything, and it didn't matter. Everyone's troubles were different. It was of no consequence if he considered what had been Natasha's tipping point would also be his.

"Does being in here help?"

Natasha resumed sipping her tea. Pausing before nodding, she decided to add, "Defo, man." With a chuckle, she gurgled in-between sips, "I think it's because I fucking hate it in here! My brain reboots just to get me out!" Slopping a small amount of tea from her mug as she shook with mirth, she stopped and grinned. "Great. This is my best top as well!" Her laughing grew louder as she mopped at the stain on her standard issue grey T-shirt with a tissue. "How about you?"

Matthew told her everything, ending with his failed escape attempt and grabbing at Malcolm's phone.

"Whew!" she whistled. "You're going through a rough time, aren't you?" A final swig of tea made her gurn in revulsion. "Blah! It's cold." Arcing forwards, she eased the mug down, clutched in her long fingers at the end of her gangly arms and set it on the floor in front of her. "But I don't know why you've had so much bother. I can walk out of here anytime I want."

Matthew gasped. Why?

"I think it must be cos you've been a bit aggressive by the sounds of it. But if you want me to get you something from the shops, just say the word."

Matthew gasped. Natasha was a godsend! "A phone? Could you pick me up a phone?"

She snorted. "Nah, man. I ain't got them sort of readies. I mean sweets or a cake, or a paper."

Matthew couldn't hide his disappointment. "Thanks. I guess a newspaper might be good."

"Any one in particular?"

Matthew shrugged.

"I'll get the cheapest then, if that's okay?"

"When will you go?"

"I have to ask, then they arrange it. Do you want me to ask if you can come too?"

Eyes wide, Matthew nodded. He didn't imagine they'd say yes, but what if they did? What if him not asking personally made a difference? "Yes, please." He hopped off his seat to give his new best friend a hug. Regretting it mid-step; she might hate physical contact; he was relieved when she clutched him to her tightly.

The closeness pierced the boil of emotion he had repressed for weeks and it cascaded from him in a torrent of tears and body-shaking sobs.

"Ah, it'll be okay. You'll see," she said, stroking his hair.

"Thank you," Matthew managed through his thick throat.

Days passed with Matthew not seeing Natasha. He hoped he'd not put her under too much pressure. He was musing the point whilst watching the most incredibly unskilled game of pool he'd ever witnessed when she came skipping up to him.

"They're not keen. I don't know why, but you have seriously blotted your copy book, Matthew! I'll try again another time, but I didn't want to push it. I didn't want to arouse suspicion."

"Thanks. What did you say?"

She pursed her thin lips; everything about her was thin. "I asked if I could go to the shops. They said 'Fine.' And then I said I'd made a new friend and wondered if they could come too. They were fine until they realised it was you! Then they warned me to keep away. Said you weren't to be trusted."

"*I'm* not to be trusted? Cheek!"

Keeping his voice low as a nurse walked into the rec room, he smiled his warmest smile. "Are you looking for me?" he greeted, none of the hatred he felt at his imprisonment showed in his voice. He knew the game now, and he was going to win.

The nurse nodded whilst ticking his name on her clipboard. "Doctor will see you now."

It was his weekly ward round, Matthew thought. He'd lost track of time, his mind numbed by stress and the medication they insisted him taking every morning and evening. A small nugget of his brain stayed focussed; honed on his plan to get out of here. But it was surrounded by the cotton-wool of his intoxicated grey matter and was struggling to be heard. But Matthew was unwavering in his determination to listen.

Striding into the side room with unnatural poise, Matthew sat neatly on the nearest chair to Doctor McEvoy, nervous of his ability to remain calm and unthreatening. It was vital for his escape.

"You look... well, so ye do," he nodded in Matthew's direction. "How are ye feeling?"

Matthew's brows knitted, demonstrating his careful consideration of the question. "Much better, thank you."

The doctor nodded. "Any visions?" Matthew shook his head. "Of your sister? Or your wife? Or your daughter, or anyone else?"

Matthew smiled as he could answer quite truthfully. "No, I haven't seen them at all."

"And what about wanting to phone them? You still thinking that's a good idea?" Matthew shook his head again and allowed a little chuckle to fall from his lips. Once more, he could answer honestly.

"No. I realise that was a mistake now. Foolish of me."

The doctor nodded, but Matthew thought his honest replies were not hitting their mark. They sounded too diverting. So, he decided to lay it on thicker. "I think the medicine's doing the trick. I'm a lot calmer. I wondered if there might be some talking therapy I could do? To understand why I have these hallucinations in the first place, rather than just keep on medicating? I do feel a bit groggy."

Other patients had reported the doctors lapping that up. They loved their therapies. Although, in reality, they tended to be baby-simple advice dished out in the most patronising tones, they were generally considered preferable to medication side-effects.

It was with surprise then, and some dismay, that Matthew greeted the doctor's response.

"We'll keep things the same for now. Perhaps we can look at adding more therapies when we're sure you're stable, yeah?"

Matthew hid his white knuckles beneath his thighs as he prized a smile onto his lips. "Sure. Whatever you think."

"I'll see you in a week or so, then, okay?"

Matthew maintained his smile as he left the room. What could he do to ingratiate himself? Nothing. He wasn't like the others. All the therapy and the medication had only one purpose: to keep him here. But why?

The idea that kept coming back was the only explanation that made any sense to Matthew. The work he'd done designing and building a military craft was a lot more important and secret than he'd understood.

Brian had warned him not to get involved. And now, at the whim of some secret bloody agency, these people were keeping him locked away: away from his family, away from his life; and away from his work.

They would be in full production soon; the amphibious tanks. The contract had been agreed, the design paid for, the raw materials procured. They were notorious locally, maybe even nationally. So what did Matthew know that was worth keeping him away? What was worth this ridiculous charade?

Matthew was going to escape, and he was going to find out. He just didn't know how.

They would never let him walk out with Natasha. He wasn't operating under the same rules. And despite only being a hospital ward, the prison capabilities of these walls were undeniable.

The line for medicine was beginning to form. Matthew joined, grateful for the chlorpromazine to take the edge off his anxiety. Maybe tomorrow he'd wake with a plan.

Chapter Twenty

"I can help you out of here!" The small man crouched in front of him, peering at him through bulging eyes, and Matthew half expected him to shriek 'My precious!'

It was hard not to raise his hopes, but anything he suggested was likely to be insane. And he didn't disappoint.

"I can organise a crack team. They'll smash through the windows." He leapt up, animated now, thumping an angled, bony fist into his waiting palm. "Smash!" he pointed a window, and then another, "Smash, smash, smash!"

Perching on the arm of the chair, he breathed heavily. "You just say the word," he winked, "and I'll get it done." And with that, he slid off the chair and sauntered away muttering military plans to himself.

"You've met Wayne, then?" Empathetic eyes met his through thick lenses from across the room. Sliding the tortoiseshell glasses back up his nose, they promptly returned to the thick red ridge further down. He thrust himself up, giant palms with thick long fingers pushing against long muscular legs.

Striding across the room, he paused halfway to blink hard three or four times, then hunched his hefty shoulders and rolled his head on his solid neck.

Slotting his mountain body next to Matthew on the couch, he pressed one of his huge hands on Matthew's thigh and leaned in. "You wanting to escape again, then?"

Matthew didn't consider his last attempt to have been an escape, but he nodded anyway.

"I'll help."

Matthew's forehead puckered. "Go on?" he invited.

"When you get out, you'll have to do me a favour." Matthew nodded readily. "Bring me back a cheeseburger! I bloody hate the food in here."

"If you can get me out, why don't you get out yourself?"

The man looked down at his boat-like shoes. "Nah. I'm good, thanks."

After the upset he'd caused to other patients, Matthew didn't pry. "What's your plan?"

It was simple. He would go outside in the enclosed garden, making sure to leave the door ajar for Matthew. He insisted he could lift and even throw the metal benches, and he'd do so in such a way they could provide a ladder up the wall for Matthew to scale.

The nurses would be distracted by the raucous rage he'd enact and Matthew could disappear from the ensuing chaos.

"Won't you get in trouble?"

"Don't matter. We were close, you and me. Before you left last time."

"Last time? What do you mean?"

The man shrugged. "You don't remember. Doesn't matter, I remember; you helped me. You're a clever one, you. And now I'm gonna help you."

Matthew's mind whirred. What did he mean, 'last time?' Was he in on it? Could it be a trap? He seemed so genuine.

Suddenly it clicked. He was confusing him with someone else. Easily done when you're on this medication and you're not quite with it in the first place. Matthew would trust him. His heart fluttered. This could be it. At last.

Anticipating time to plan; to prepare, Matthew didn't react when the man stood up. It wasn't until he heard the grunts and strains from outside that he realised it was time for action.

Nurses rushed past him, and the other patients in the room crowded at the window to watch the show.

"Now then, Adrian. What do you think you're doing?"

The bench snapped away from its rotten floor bolts, something Adrian must have noticed and kept stored away in his weary head. Tossing the bench aside, narrowly missing the approaching male nurse, he immediately turned his attention to the table.

As the nurses encircled him, ready to pounce with their chemical cosh, loaded and sharp, it was the perfect opportunity. The spontaneity was ingenious. With no plotting, no conspiratorial nods to raise suspicion, he'd never risked unwanted attention. And the cover of darkness was invaluable.

Watching the pack tighten the circle, they were almost ready to make their move and seemed oblivious to the risk of escape the bench offered propped up against the wall.

Heart pounding, Matthew could scarcely believe that after weeks; months, he could see the end.

Seeing the look in the lead nurses eyes, a slight tightening of the eye socket, and if he'd been closer, he'd have seen a sharpening of the pupils, Matthew made his move.

It happened in slow-motion. They pounced, the injection speared Adrian's thick thigh, and they tumbled onto him in an ungainly scrum which took all the attention of the small crowd.

Dashing across the garden, Matthew hopped onto the bench and made the sprint to the top with ease. He had little idea where he headed, but a quick glance back to the kerfuffle below gave him hope he had time. Scanning his surroundings, it was dark beneath him, and he wasn't sure if it led to a way out.

But next to where he stood atop the wall he noticed a low roof. If he could reach that, he could run along to the front car park and at least see where he was leaping to the ground before committing himself.

With a deep breath, Matthew gave one more glance to the ward garden to gauge his time. Adrian grinned up at him from the small gap his face protruded through in the crook of a nurse's arm before the injection took its full effect. Their eyes met, and it was the last thing Matthew saw before taking a leap of faith onto the adjoining roof.

Chapter Twenty-one

It was a soft landing. The awful slippers they provided on the ward offered little grip, but they were quiet. Ducking down, he padded along the flat felt to the other end. There were no security measures in place, just the small car park edged with shrubbery, and beyond that what looked like a construction site where they must be extending the hospital.

Matthew ran to the corner, considered jumping onto a car roof, but instead eased himself down the drainpipe expecting a car alarm to be set off by such an impact.

Before he decided where he would go, his immediate concern was to make sure he took the most unexpected route. Following the hedge, Matthew's eye caught an area of greenery. Imagining open fields and farmland, he tore through the hedge to find himself in a patch of allotments.

Whilst the sheds at the end of each strip of muddy ground could provide shelter until he came up with a workable plan, they were likely to be the first place someone looking for him would suspect.

Glancing over his shoulder, he wondered if his absence had been noticed yet. It couldn't be long before they'd be chasing him, and if they caught him, who knew if he'd ever get another chance?

But God was smiling on him. Beyond the allotments, Matthew was sure he glimpsed the reflection of moonlight on water. The river! Hopeful he'd find something to float away on, he rushed towards it.

The path from the allotments led through rows of houses. No-one was out on this chilly spring evening. If someone had seen him, his grey tracksuit wasn't that unlike what you might witness any jogger wearing anyway. The slippers might take some explaining, but it was dark, and who examined passer-by's feet?

Passing a sign declaring his location to be Lakewood Road, Matthew was soon facing the water he'd seen, and as if by holy decree, there was a boat. In fact, there were two. A large one on a trailer, and a small tender hanging from the stern.

Nimbly untying the tender, Matthew dragged the small fibre-glass structure to the water's edge. He could see a sign which declared 'Private swimming lake—members only' and decided to take the stream a few metres away that drained the lake; not because he was keen to adhere to the rules, but because he doubted he'd get far on the lake.

The minimum draught of the light craft proved the perfect vessel to drift down stream, but it was soon obvious the stream went barely further than the lake! It forked, extending his range only a few hundred metres. It was still the right choice, though, because now he enjoyed the benefit of cover from a small woods at the water's edge.

Hauling the little orange dinghy up the bank, Matthew sprinted for the woods and collapsed, exhausted, to the ground. Keeping to the edge, he hid in the first line of trees. From there, he figured he'd be able to see a search party before they saw him.

No-one came. Distant sirens, always part of Bristol's soundtrack, didn't turn in his direction. Breathing a huge sigh, relief bubbled from deep within and exploded from his mouth in an ill-controlled chortle.

Staring out from his hidey-hole in case he'd been heard, he sighed. He couldn't risk resting more. He had to push himself on. His head-start now was such that he had to be in with a fighting chance.

He desperately wanted to run all the way home, throw the door open and hug Debbie and Abi and never let them go. But that would be the first place they'd check, wouldn't it? No, he'd have to hide out for a while, stakeout the house and make sure it was safe before risking showing himself. "It's been weeks. A few more won't hurt, and I can't risk getting caught," Matthew soothed.

He had to focus on his immediate requirements: food, and changing from his conspicuous clothes and shoes. Then he could think about where he might hide overnight. His instincts were what must be the usual choices for those without a fixed abode—shop bins.

He couldn't turn up to a homeless shelter, he'd be found too easily, but Tesco? There'd be discarded food, and he knew there was a charity clothes bin too.

It seemed wrong to steal from a charity, but he doubted anyone's need for clothes could be greater than his own. He walked through estates rather than main roads to give more opportunity to hide if he was pursued. And he felt less suspicious in his inappropriate attire if his poor choice of clothes could be explained by his proximity to houses. He'd worn worse when he was at home, strolling round Bristol's streets in dressing gown and slippers to send a teething Abigail to sleep. The memory brought a stab of pain. "Soon, my angel. I'll be home soon."

As he walked from path to pavement and through alleyways between the houses, he was heartened to see no sign of any pursuers. If they were onto him, they were being uncharacteristically subtle.

Tesco's enormous red and blue sign glowed visibly a short distance away now. Cautious of late night shoppers and CCTV cameras, Matthew paused. He had no choice. Did they even check those things, anyway? They must have better things to do with their time than watch recycling bins on the extreme off-chance someone tampered with them; even though that's exactly what he was about to do.

He wouldn't stay here. If he was spotted, by the time his presence was investigated, he'd be long gone. A surreptitious glance at the lens gave no clue whether he was being watched so he decided he'd be quick.

Flipping the door open at the top of the bin, Matthew fed in a stick he found nearby snapped from the perimeter hedge. He couldn't see inside but the stick connected with something fairly high up. Twisting the stick, he hoped it would tangle in the plastic of a bag of charity cast-offs and enable him to haul it out. As soon as it dug in, it loosened again and the sound of tearing polythene followed by garments tumbling softly into the depths of the bin mocked him with muffled contempt.

"Damn!" he exclaimed, prodding desperately inside the bin again. The clothes he'd freed from their bag now prevented the stick from snagging another.

Pausing, Matthew took a breath to calm his nerves before carefully sliding in the stick again. Closing his eyes, slowly he began to feel what the end of his prod might be latching onto… something hard, and more plastic, firmer this time. This was smaller; a carrier bag perhaps.

Heart pounding in his head he tapped around the package and located the handles. It wasn't going anywhere so he could take his time slotting the end through their holes. He could feel the tug, and like a skilled angler, he edged his catch to the top of the bin.

He could see it now, and from that first glimpse it looked like he'd lucked out… shoes! Close enough for him to reach in with his hand, he grabbed the bag out. Dealer boots with elasticated sides. Not his size, slightly too big, but not bad condition. Not bad at all. Faintly scuffed leather, worn down but crack-free soles. Excellent.

Poking and pulling garments from the bin, most presented in remarkably fine condition but were for women, apart from a couple of tiny girl's cardigans. Encouraged by his success with the boots, he carried on. Latching onto something heavy at the back of the bin, he was soon gratefully sporting a barely worn duffle coat! Three of the toggle buttons were missing, but it was just the job.

Hanging below his hospital T-shirt, it disguised his look enough that combined with the boots, he felt comfortable he wouldn't attract attention—and he was warm.

Popping his slippers into the large pockets of the duffle coat, he added a few of the lighter, more unisex garments and ran from the CCTV camera so that if anyone was watching, they'd witness his exit and his direction up the hill away from the superstore car park.

Doubling back out of range of the cameras, he walked in the opposite direction towards the vague area of his home and work. He knew he couldn't go there yet; not until he was sure he wouldn't endanger himself or his family, but it felt great. To even be this close felt fantastic. He paused in a copse of shrubbery and laughed.

Chapter Twenty-two

There came no obvious sound of pursuit. He must have been far enough away when they noticed him missing there had been no sign of him. But Matthew knew they'd be around. Watching. Waiting.

He knew they'd expect him to turn up at his house sooner or later. Seeing Debbie was a temptation he couldn't deny. So whether going sooner, or later held any advantage, he hadn't decided. Either way, he'd need to keep his distance.

Taking back-roads through residential streets, his heart raced as he gained ground. It was miles, but he could walk it in a couple of hours. Tightness squeezed his chest. Was he making a huge mistake?

Right now, he was closer to the hospital than to home, and that didn't seem like the best way to remain undiscovered either. He could head into the countryside and take cover in woodland. The border with Somerset wasn't far. He could be in a different county somewhere soon, did that make a difference? How much effort would they put into finding him? No-one had ever suggested he was a criminal.

Juddering in his sleeve was the first indication he was cold, and he stared at his trembling arm in surprise. Obviously his newly attained coat wasn't as warm as he'd expected. Chewing dead skin from the edge of his index fingernail, he had to decide what to do. He could walk on and hope he'd make it home where the warmth and safety of his life would envelop him, or he could take shelter where he found it like the homeless must in this weather.

The urge to push on for home was strong, but memories of the last time he'd headed there tugged at the fabric of his wellbeing. The mesh of his resolve hadn't allowed doubts to surface when he was on the ward, it had been vital to focus on one thing—escaping. Now he was free, his brain couldn't help but attempt to reprocess what had happened the last time he'd headed home.

He hadn't found it. That was what he had to comprehend; he was so paralytic, he couldn't even remember where he lived, even though he didn't remember having drunk much.

But a part of him feared he *had* found his home; or rather his house. And he'd been greeted by a stranger. His mind cramped at a solution, anything he could think of was completely outlandish, but he had to let his thoughts run, because whatever had happened was not ordinary and he wouldn't find the solution believing it was.

Everything that had happened since then, everything anyone had said, attempted to undermine him; chip away at his sanity. It hadn't worked, he was as sane as ever. So if a strange man stood at his front door denying any knowledge of him, he must be part of the collusion.

Like a magic show. Sometimes it was easier to just believe in magic than to try to work out what was going on. But not for Matthew. And what was going on was usually far simpler than anyone ever guessed!

So why? That was the question now. Why would someone pretend Matthew's life was not as he said? Someone with a lot of influence wanted him to believe he was insane, or wanted the world to believe it so he had no credibility. And who could possibly have that sort of clout and care what he thought? It had to be the Ministry of Defence or one of the agencies under its umbrella, as he'd already supposed. It was the only theory that made any sense.

Knowing his foe helped him plan, but he also suspected by reputation that such agencies stopped at nothing to reach their goal. If only he'd listened to Brian. The money on offer only mattered because it offered security for him and his little family. And now, all that security had amounted to nothing.

But even that didn't gel in his head. Rubbing his temples with frozen fingers, he tried to massage out the answer. The project wasn't even secret. He had signed no official secrets orders. He hadn't even been warned not to talk about it. The local press, even TV, had hailed their success with bringing jobs to the area and the prestige the scheme offered Bristol. So, if they'd changed their mind, could they not have asked him nicely first?

Pain!

A shooting in his legs made him cry out. His arm wasn't just quivering now, but shaking. Violently.

Glancing around, if anyone saw him, they'd wonder what was wrong. Ducking into a covered alley, he squealed at the agony. Cramps swelled and flowed, felling him to his knees. Head pounding, he held his face in his hands as his body convulsed in spasmodic eruptions.

The medicine, topped up compulsorily every twelve hours, had been due when Adrian had implemented his escape plan. Now it had been free from his system for a dangerous amount of time and he was paying the price.

Hugging his legs, he rocked back and forth. It would pass, but he had no idea how long it would take. His only experience with coming off hard drugs was watching *Trainspotting,* and that did not fill him with optimism. He hoped the brief time he'd been fed this poison might save him from hallucinating dead babies crawling on the ceiling.

The shuddering and aching took all the processing power of his brain. He thought he should find better shelter, for warmth and for cover from the authorities looking for him, but he couldn't move: a sitting duck for anyone who wanted to abuse him.

Chattering teeth bit down on his tongue, the taste of iron disconcerting. Crying out, he prized a timorous hand from the warmth of his pocket to stifle his own screams. Kicking, his boot-clad feet echoed in the confines of the passage where he squatted, ringing in his ears and twisting the knife in his head.

"Stop! Make it stop! Someone. Please!"

Growling, snarling at the audacity of this feeling, so alien. This wasn't him. He'd never wanted any of this, it had been forced upon him. Literally, mouth held open, pills poured in, force.

Shifting position, sitting, lying one way then another, his legs kicking beside him, thumping on the wall, bludgeoning his head. Crawling along, desperate to hide away, he reached his arm out but his weak hand couldn't support him. Crashing to the floor, his face hit the tarmac hard.

Aware, somewhere in his addled mind, that he detected a trickle of something warm on his face, with equal fear of what might happen to him in his stricken state, and relief that unconsciousness might give him respite from the pain, he slipped away.

Chapter Twenty-three

"You okay, buddy?"

Matthew jolted, coaxing his exhausted muscles to shuffle him away from the owner of the voice. 'Don't be a nurse. Please, don't be a nurse.' Squeezing his eyes open a slit, Matthew peered at the person leering over his afflicted body.

"What you doing here, mate? Did you sleep here? Have you got somewhere to go?"

Matthew leaned against the cold stone of the wall and nodded. Holding up a hand in front of his face, the shaking had definitely reduced. Scraping a dry tongue on the roof of his mouth, Matthew tried to speak. And failed.

"I probably shouldn't do this, but you've landed on my doorstep for a reason. Would you like to come in for a warm and a cuppa?"

Tears welled in Matthew's eyes. That could be fantastic. He'd take the charity, he wasn't proud, and he needed every advantage for the next phase of his endeavour. He wanted to cry out, "Yes! Thank you so much. Yes!" but his mouth wouldn't open enough to form the words.

Matthew's Good Samaritan was a young man. When he'd hauled Matthew up from sitting on the floor, he stood much shorter. Shuffling along the passage, Matthew followed him to his house a few metres away.

"Take a seat," the man invited as they stood in the kitchen at the front of the small house. "Tea? Coffee?" and then in deference to what he might be dealing with, the man thoughtfully inquired, "Something stronger?"

144

Matthew blew his cheeks out in revulsion, but realised withdrawal from 'Something stronger' was exactly what was wrong with him.

"Water," he managed to squeeze from his dry mouth. "And coffee. Please."

The man stepped to the sink and proceeded to fill a pint glass with cold water which he passed to Matthew before filling the kettle for the coffee. He allowed Matthew to sit in silence while he poured boiling water into a cafetiere, loading up a tray with cream and sugar and an intriguing looking 'Darth Vadar' biscuit barrel.

As he popped Darth's head off he invited Matthew to 'join him on the dark side.' "Biscuit? There's rich tea and digestives. There might even be a couple of custard creams."

Matthew smiled and took as many as he dared without looking greedy.

"So, friend. How did you end up shivering in my alley this cold morning?"

The water had lubricated Matthew's mouth a little, but he was shaking too much to talk, so he offered an apologetic shrug instead. The man didn't seem surprised. Plunging the hot water, he poured two cups. "Help yourself to cream and sugar," he invited.

With the sugary nourishment of five digestives and three custard creams combined with the caffeine of the dark coffee, finally his cold turkey was warming.

"Thanks so much for your hospitality. I'll have to repay you when I get back home."

Two raised palms conveyed there was no need. "I'm Ben, by the way…"

"Matthew," Matthew answered in response to Ben's arched eyebrows, declining to add his surname in a sudden flurry of fear. "Thanks for the coffee and biscuits. It helped a lot, but I'll be out of your way now," Matthew garbled, keen suddenly to be away from someone who could identify who and where he was.

"It's okay. Why don't you stay and get warm? Don't worry. I won't call the police or anything. Let me clean that nasty-looking cut on your head. It must be sore?"

Matthew's hand gingerly touched the throbbing in his head and he flinched. Gratefully watching as Ben used some of the water in the kettle to soak a cloth, his shoulders relaxed and he managed a half-smile.

Returning to the table with hastily concocted first-aid supplies, Ben noticed, and while he dabbed at the grit filled cut on his patient's head, he asked, "You in some kind of trouble, Matthew?"

The swell of emotion couldn't be dammed. There was no need to answer. As tears cascaded down Matthew's cheeks, over his chin and into his lap, it was the first he'd realised he wasn't in the slightest bit confident he was as close to reuniting with Debbie and Abi as he'd pretended to himself.

The reality of his memory merged with his incredulous weeks up until last night, leaving questions that only time could answer.

"It's okay. You don't have to tell me, but I might be able to help."

Why was this man, Ben, so keen to be involved? Did Matthew look so non-threatening that he trusted him implicitly? He'd always considered himself charming and charismatic, but the other patients had typically displayed fear in his presence. Just a bunch of neurotics, he supposed. Or did Ben have other motives?

Hoping he was being paranoid, it still seemed unlikely he'd be able to help.

"There. That's not too bad. It's better than it looked. I'll just pop a plaster on it." Peeling a fabric strip from its roll, he deftly secured it to Matthew's head and declared him done. "Do you have somewhere to go? Family? Friends?"

Matthew stifled a chuckle. "Yes, thank you. I do. That's where I'm going now," he said, rueing his inclusion of the information. "I just had a funny turn this morning. That's all."

Ben gave a solemn nod. "Okay. If you're sure. Make sure you get yourself checked out though?" he implored. "You don't look well."

Matthew smiled and pushed his chair back to stand. "I know, but don't worry. I'll soon be fine." He prayed his display of optimism was doing more than just persuading Ben. Stepping to the door, Ben offered no resistance and Matthew was convinced he really was just doing his Christian duty.

He paused at the end of the path to offer a polite wave of thanks. Despite his faith in Ben, as soon as he was out of sight, Matthew doubled back and walked in the opposite direction. With all that had gone on, he couldn't trust anyone.

The closer he got to home, the worse he felt. Another twelve hours had passed in the alley without medication. It didn't compare to last night's agony, but it still affected him.

Squeezing his head in his palms, desperate to coerce his headache away, he moved his hands to his eyes and pressed the heels into his sockets. Open mouthed, he squinted at the horizon. Below him was the bridge. He'd definitely come the pretty way, but he was nearly home. Another hour could see him at his door. Should he go there so soon? How would he feel when he got there? And who would he see?

"Worry about that when you get there. You need to arrive safe and unseen first," he directed himself.

Hopeful the unusual route he'd taken, and his change of clothes, had left him undetected so far, the closer he got the more at risk he felt. He didn't even have the 'home advantage.' The couple of years at the house had been preoccupied with work and Abi's health. There had been no time for neighbourhood strolls, so he didn't know the surrounding streets any better than anyone else.

Summiting the hill and striding towards a bluff high above the Avon Gorge allotted as a 'viewpoint,' offering spectacular views of Brunel's masterpiece suspension bridge, Matthew put his charm into action. Several cars were parked in the small car park that gave access to a variety of leisure activities—

walking, climbing and abseiling, and the gentler pursuit of breathing in the surroundings.

In the far corner, an elderly couple had set up a picnic beside a bench. A tartan flask stood next to a wicker hamper, but neither were attending the food. They were taking turns looking through an enormous pair of binoculars; the strap around the man's neck pulling him to one side whenever the lady took her go.

Heart pounding, Matthew closed his eyes to induce calm. Plastering on his best reassuring smile, he ambled curiously towards them.

A few feet away, the man turned to meet his gaze, straining against the strap. Muttering something to his wife, she turned and Matthew cranked his smile up a gear.

"See anything interesting?" Matthew cringed at the corniness. 'No we're staring at nothing,' would not be the sarcastic response. Instead, they beamed; thrilled at the chance to share their enthusiasm for the view.

"Only the whole of Brizzle!" the man declared triumphantly, straightening his hat that had been knocked by the to-ing and fro-ing of the binoculars.

"We were looking at our house!" the lady chuckled. "Drive five miles up here and spend an hour staring at our own home! I know… we're proper crackpots."

Matthew joined the laughter. "Not at all. I couldn't have a look at my own house, could I? I've always wondered if I could see it from up here." He hadn't finished his sentence before the dual lenses were being thrust in his direction. "Oh, really? Are you sure?"

There followed a lengthy tutorial into their every nuance, but Matthew didn't mind. Eventually he was left to enjoy the fruits of the couple's obsession.

Buildings, undetectable with the naked eye, loomed at him through the cylinders making no sense to his mind as it reeled in surprise. Using the bridge as a datum, he swept the horizon a number of times before from nowhere his house jumped out at him.

Training the lenses back, he struggled to find what he'd just seen, but then he was certain and a little shocked at how clearly he could see into his back garden. If his theory was correct and his nightmare was at the hands of government agencies, they could have observed him effortlessly and undetected for as long as they wanted. Gulping down the bile that rose in reaction to his realisation, he felt a fool, but how could he have known?

"You finding what you want?" the binocular's owners inquired.

"Oh yes, thank you. It's taken me a while, but I've found it now. Could I look for a few more minutes?"

The couple shifted uncomfortably, glances of disdain pierced the air between them. Matthew didn't wait for their approval. He had to know what his chances were before he could risk getting near his home. This old couple would just have to wait.

The front of the house; the driveway and the cars, weren't visible from here, but he could see along the street. Occasional cars dotted the road; none that looked suspicious, but what would suspicious look like anyway?

There was a familiar figure: old Tom King hunched in scrutiny of the front tyre of his vintage Bentley. By the time Matthew had walked the distance down the hill to Clifton Down Road, he'd probably be back inside, but he'd have to be careful not to be seen. Matthew had decided: he was going to risk it. He was going home.

Chapter Twenty-four

The room was different again. It seemed every time Debbie walked into the lounge it had been altered. Cursing under her breath, she forced on a smile as Mandy strolled in from the kitchen with a laden tray.

"Ah. You're awake! There's coffee here. Or would you prefer tea?"

Without answering, Debbie slumped onto the nearest sofa, checking behind her first in case it bloody moved again. For some reason she couldn't fathom, it wore a soft throw blanket over the top.

Seeing the direction of her gaze, Mandy explained, "Makes it look more homely. Don't you think?"

Debbie shrugged and leaned towards the coffee pot. As she poured unaltered strong black coffee into a small espresso cup, Mandy continued.

"We thought rearranging things might be good for you and Abi. A new focus, you know?"

A new focus from the fact that her husband, and Mandy's brother had been missing for months and hope of his safe recovery was dwindling with every passing minute? Yeah. Moving the couches and displaying tasteless blankets was sure to help. Debbie grimaced at the bitter coffee, doubtless another change in their routine.

She knew they meant well. And they were worried about her, but it was frustrating never knowing how a room would look if she left it for more than five minutes. Maybe it was helping.

Surprising her mind stirred up the quagmire and allowed it to function a touch more.

"Abi seems to be loving having Charlotte here. They've become inseparable!" Mandy carried on, and it was true.

Abi demonstrated anger more than upset at her father's absence. She'd heard snippets from police officers and missing person's experts in the large lounge—possible explanations, and how her daddy was a grown man who may well have decided to leave them.

She'd witnessed the theories that it might have been the stress of her illness that drove him to the edge; or work, or unknown debts. None of it sounded like her daddy at all. She felt she didn't know him. And if he had abandoned them for any reason at all, she didn't think she wanted to.

She understood why her mum was so distant. She still clung onto hope there was another explanation. Grownups could be so unrealistic sometimes. Abi had seen death and looked it in the eye and won. It gave her, at even her young age, an intolerance for bullshit. Life changes. Get over it and move on. That's what she'd done, and that's what her mother had to do. But now she too had virtually deserted her, because she might as well not be here.

Grandpa, and Nanna, and Auntie Mandy and her cousin, Charlotte wouldn't abandon her; they'd made that very clear every day. She was pleased they were here again. They were upset her daddy hadn't come home on Christmas Day. She knew that. But they were realistic; like her. And they weren't going to waste their lives, nor hers, waiting for him to come home. She felt their disappointment in their son and she shared their disgust.

Moving rooms around had helped her cope. It didn't look like the same house her daddy had left many months ago, and she was grateful.

They might have to move house. She'd heard the talk. Her daddy's shares in the boat company couldn't sustain them forever in his absence. The grownups talked of plans to save the business, but none of them had the skills. Selling their bit of it to her daddy's partner had been a talk she'd overheard.

She didn't care. This house, lovely and big as it was, had never been her home. The local hospital felt more familiar. When she'd languished in there, it wasn't this house she'd longed for, but the small terraced house in the quiet street the other side of the city where her friends were. Friends she hadn't seen for years and likely never would again.

If they left this house, Abi couldn't care less. In fact she almost welcomed the idea, but she wouldn't hope for it. She didn't care enough. So long as she had today, she'd live it, whatever it held. And when tomorrow came—and it was *when*, not *if*, as it had been for so long, she'd live that too. Everything else could do what it wanted.

"So we were thinking about a trip to the zoo. It would be great to get out. Or maybe Cheddar Gorge. We haven't been there for years and I know the girls love it…" Mary and Alan had joined them on the opposite sofa and were trying to plan a day out. Debbie's constant shrugs made it difficult, but also underlined the need. "So what do you think? Zoo or caves?"

She held her hands either side of her, scales weighing up the pros and cons. When Debbie shrugged again, she added with a grin, "Let's ask the girls."

Running in, the two of them jostled with the choice for only a few seconds before declaring the zoo the winner. It was a short drive and the red pandas, oh they were so cute!

"…so if you get yourself showered, we'll get going, okay?" Alan ordered, struggling not to show his exasperation with his daughter-in-law. The best way to beat depression was to get out and bloody do something. He knew that. Debbie wasn't helping herself wallowing like this. And it certainly wasn't the best way to bring his son back.

If he ever did come back, he'd need to see normality. Not least, to show these sorts of shenanigans had no place in adult life. He understood Debbie's reluctance to face facts, but it was his GCSE's all over again. He'd try to be patient with her. He had agreed to do that.

Chapter Twenty-five

Edging along the road, Matthew felt highly conspicuous. His only hope was that his surveillance had been correct and the way was clear. But why? He had to be missing something.

Still a good distance away, he could see his driveway and was surprised not to see cars. Were Debbie and Abi out somewhere? Or was he to be greeted by the stranger of Christmas Night?

Walking with a casual gait, Matthew paused and looked at an imaginary wristwatch. Ducking between two of his neighbours houses, he was able to approach his rear garden from Rodney Road which ran parallel. It was too easy. Taking note of the *This is a Neighbourhood Watch Area* signpost, he scaled the fence and plopped onto the lawn; his lawn, of his own house. A giddy euphoria rang in his ears. Could it all be over?

His heart pounded so fiercely in his head, he feared it might explode. Edging towards the window. Mere feet away from seeing inside, he felt sick. What would he see?

Picturing it exactly the same, even expecting to see the Christmas tree with all the family sat around in festive jollity awaiting his return with the batteries for Abi's Furby, as the spring sun beat down on his back, he knew that was fantasy.

Leaning into the window, eyes shielded from the daylight by his hands cowling against the glass, he let out a gasp. Not only was it not the same, it didn't look like his house at all. Dashing to another window confirmed it. Nothing looked the same.

He had to get inside. Debbie and Abi could be in there being held hostage! Or they might have been forced out. Wherever they were he would get to them and make this all right.

One of the bathroom windows was ajar. The vent was too small to get in, but if he could reach his hand round, he might reach the larger vent below. He was sure he'd squeeze through that.

Clambering onto the shed roof, Matthew hauled himself towards the open window by clinging to the grey downpipe. The soil and vent pipes that had bothered Matthew with their ugliness were suddenly very welcome as he climbed the tree of cold plastic.

He was high up now. One slip could see him badly injured, or worse, but he had to take the risk. Cursing his poor diet, he reached trembling fingers towards the sill of the bathroom. Trusting he had a strong grip, he allowed his weight slowly to transfer to his furthest fingers. When they held, he pushed forward.

There was a distinct lack of grab holes, but he was so close now he could almost reach. Exhaling hard, he flung his weight right, stretched and swung then grasped hold of the edge of the window. Holding firm, his wiry arm reached inside. It was a stretch, but he could almost touch the handle.

Pressing his feet on extended toes his fingers brushed against it. Straining further, he couldn't quite move it to the open position. Pulling his stretched right foot further up the pipe, he took a risk and lunged for it.

With a gasp, he almost missed the handle as his oversized boot slipped and lost its hold on the pipe crashing him into the wall. Stifling a cry of horror, reddening fingertips hauled with all his might. Making it onto the sill, he rested, breathless, on his knees and nodded his gratitude to the concrete slabs thirty feet below that were so nearly his last view.

Offering a silent prayer, he pushed the handle and opened the window. Easing carefully from his knees to extended toes, he squeezed inside. A sigh of nervous relief and exhaustion fell fast from his lips and he closed his mouth to stop the sound. He might not be alone.

Covering his face with a towel he didn't recognise to muffle the sound, Matthew allowed himself some good deep breaths. With his heart rate slowed, he took his first step toward the door. He would search the house from top to bottom. If Debbie and Abi were being held anywhere, he'd know before he reached the front door.

Pausing on the landing, the house had the silence he'd expected from the empty driveway. Still, he'd be cautious.

Everything was different. How and why they had redecorated he could only guess. And he guessed the government agencies responsible for his nightmare were thorough. If he described the home he remembered in a court of law, it wouldn't match the house he stood in now. Clever.

When he creaked open the door to Abi's bedroom; last glimpsed on Christmas morning as he delighted in her opening her presents, it was a shock. Despite his certainty it would be different, seeing its purpose reallocated as some sort of craft/knitting/crochet room struck him as heartless. They'd have done their research. They'd know what the family had been through. But they didn't care about them, only about whatever their crazy plan was.

Sweat dribbled into his eyes as he wiped hair from his face, swallowing for the hundredth time, he forced himself on. His slippery palms struggled to grip the handle of the next doors in this surreal twilight zone which used to be his life. With a deep breath he detached himself from his hideous reality and diligently examined the other rooms.

His purpose was still to recover Debbie and Abi, but in his heart he wasn't expecting to find them. They couldn't have been allowed to stay and cause a security risk, but he had to check. He couldn't formulate a new plan until he'd exhausted this one.

Fears confirmed, he walked in a daze to every room and each one had been changed. Every single one. Matthew shook his head in horror, and admiration for the trouble they'd taken. A niggling in the back of his mind—the leprechaun voice of Doctor McEvoy—sliced into his conviction. *You haven't got a wife. You've never had a wife. She's just part of your psychosis...* For a Nano-second he gave it credence before shaking it out of his head. They were in on it too.

They were good, though. He had to admit that. They were really good.

Padding down the stairs, Matthew was no longer surprised by the transformed décor of the lounge, nor the new cabinets in the kitchen. There had been no sign of his wife or daughter. The stabbing in his mind fell to his chest and twisted. This nightmare was not over by a long chalk.

Stepping towards the front door, he knew where he was headed next. The boat yard couldn't be adjusted so easily. Brian would have to tell him what was going on. He owed him that.

Keys!

The unmistakable sound of the front door being unlocked preceded a moment of arm flapping panic before Matthew was confronted by a lady, probably in her mid-sixties, immaculately dressed in a pastel two piece. She put him in mind of Her Majesty, The Queen at any point in her illustrious reign.

The bag of shopping she'd clasped in the crook of her arm as she'd thrust the key into the lock fell to the floor; sticky mess of jams and butter quickly patterned the parquet tiles before she had the presence to scream.

Thoughts of overpowering her and forcing her to tell him what the fuck was going on quickly dissipated at the arrival of her husband: the man he'd last seen on Christmas Night. Who else would he have expected?

156

It took a beat, but the man recognised him too. "You. Again!" Striding in front of his terrified wife, who was readily recovering in the confident company of her husband, he plucked a sturdy looking umbrella from the stand. It looked pathetic in his bear-grip and he looked tempted to discard it.

Pulling his phone from his trouser pocket, he instructed his wife. "Keep back, Ange. This guy's a nutter." Pointing the umbrella at his intruder, he blasted. "Stay where you are, you! I'm calling the police."

"Who are you?" Matthew demanded. He may as well find out what he could before escaping the police. "What are you doing in my house?"

The accusation stunned the man into open-mouthed silence for a moment before he re-iterated his original point to his wife, "This guy's completely mad!"

"So everyone keeps telling me. But we all know the truth. You two better than me, because all *I* know is since Christmas Night, you have been imposters in my house!"

Stepping back in fear of Matthew's rage their greying pallor told him he'd hit the mark. "Do you know what I've lost? Do you?" Matthew slammed the side table. "Of course you do. But did they tell you my little girl had just recovered from leukaemia? That this was our first Christmas; *proper* Christmas here…" He gesticulated the space of the house. "How much are you told before you take a job like this?"

He'd run out of anger. Seeing the fear in their eyes calmed him and he decided upon a gentler approach. "You look like decent people. You can't have known, I bet. But you can tell me. I'm not the risk they seem to have decided I am, I promise." As he calmed, they calmed.

The sound of the police car pulled into the drive. That was quick! "Please! Is there anything you can tell me?" he knew they'd divulge nothing. You didn't go to this much trouble and put a couple of amateurs front of house.

Matthew bolted for the back door, turning the key, he flung it open and made it to the fence before the police could have

157

arrived at the front door. Keeping an eye out for another officer patrolling the rear, his eyes widened with surprise and gratitude there was no-one.

Vaulting the fence, Matthew ran down the maze of streets. Puffs of exertion combined with a sigh of relief as he felt safer with the distance. Without a dog, they'd have no idea where he was headed.

He'd watch first, they'd certainly expect his arrival at Marsden-Morrissey Marine before long, but he'd make sure to find the perfect time. Brian Marsden was going to give him answers.

Chapter Twenty-six

Fury burned his cheeks. The audacity. *Marsden-Morrissey Marine* no longer displayed its livery on Brunel Quay alongside the magnificent SS Great Britain. No. In its place was flaunted a simpler logo for Marsden Marine. *Marsden*, with no mention of him.

Bizarrely, it appeared Brian must have been forced to give back a lot of the money paid to the Ministry of Defence, because the premises were half the size; the other side being given over to a railway museum!

It had happened so fast. It was like he'd never been here.

Blending in with the tourists, a cap and sunglasses he'd liberated from outside a touristy shop on the way, helped disguise his features. Even expecting him, anyone would be hard pushed to recognise the dishevelled man he'd become.

Laughing at a joke he hadn't shared with a family standing nearby, he regretted the move when their incredulous stares burned into him making him more conspicuous than if he'd stayed quiet. But no-one else looked. No-one else seemed to care about his presence at all. And given his ease at getting in and out of his house, he could take a confidence that this would be easy too.

But it was a confidence which upset him, too. Because if they weren't following him, they had to be pretty secure that what they'd put in place was enough to put paid to any threat he offered.

He'd take one step at a time. Debbie and Abi were somewhere, and some*one* knew where. If Brian didn't, he had to know who they were dealing with, and why.

Blending in with different groups, Matthew patrolled the quayside like a prowling cat. He'd never seen the office door remain shut for so long. But it was no surprise business wasn't booming. Watching it shrink so dramatically would hardly inspire the purchaser of luxury boats with confidence. They wanted prestige, and Marsden Marine lacked what Marsden-Morrissey had enjoyed in abundance.

Unsure of the time, the quality of remaining daylight suggested late afternoon to early evening. He'd be coming out soon. Matthew could wait by Brian's car, but a survey of the area showed no sign of his partner's Jaguar. Had he waited here for no reason? Was the office closed?

No. There he was. He looked different; unkempt. He wasn't just wearing his usual designer suit un-pressed. It looked like an entirely different, cheaper one altogether. Matthew took satisfaction that what he'd been forced to do to him and his family had aged him so. Satisfying because he deserved it, but more that his obvious guilt made him more likely to spill what he knew.

The reason for the Jaguar's absence was obvious now, but watching his exuberant friend amble towards a ten year old Mazda still shocked him. Closing the gap between them with three giant strides, Matthew was clutching Brian's arm in an iron grip in half a second.

"What! Get off!"

Matthew held his arm firm. "Don't make a fuss! I don't want to hurt you, but after what I've been through, I'm not beyond it."

Brian peered at him. The spark of recognition ignited in his eyes. "Oh my god. Matthew! It's Matthew, isn't it?"

Matthew glowered. What did he think had happened to him?

"I'd heard you'd fallen on hard times. That you weren't... well. Are you okay? Do you need anything?"

Matthew couldn't believe it. "Let's just go back inside. Back into *your* office, shall we?"

"I'm meeting someone." His face reddened. "It's a date, actually."

A date? Sue had left him then. But did he seriously expect him to be pleased? "She can wait. We need to talk."

"But…"

"Now!" There was no denying the threat in Matthew's demeanour. Brian nodded and the two of them headed inside.

It was shocking. Nothing of the old firm remained, and it was no wonder this shit-hole wasn't pulling in the business. Brian knew boats, but he sure as hell didn't understand their customers. "I like what you've done with the place," Matthew snarled as they entered the foyer.

"Thanks," Brian grimaced.

Matthew followed him up the familiar stairs to what had been their joint office. As the door creaked open, the disorganised chaos of the one desk was of unfeasible proportions.

"How have you got in such a state in a few short months?"

Brian didn't answer but offered a quizzical gaze. Slumping behind a pile of papers, he perched on the edge of what had perhaps once been a quality office chair but now looked like it might be time to relinquish it to the local recycling centre. Indicating the shabby chair opposite with a wave, Brian waited for Matthew to take his seat before he spoke.

"So, Matthew Morrissey, what can I do you for?"

Matthew coughed, waiting for Brian to just come out and say. Did he really have to prompt him? When the silence grew uncomfortable, Brian was forced to speak again. "Come on. You accost me in my car park," he said with a smile ready to excuse his tone if Matthew took umbrage, "you criticise my décor and my office. I'm missing a date for this. I told you that. So I assumed it was something important, but…" Brian pushed up on the arms of his chair ready to stand, taking Matthew's stunned silence for impassiveness.

"SIT down!" Matthew ordered. "It is important. You fucking know how important. And you will give me answers or god help me, Brian, I'll fucking beat them out of you!"

Ashen faced, Brian sat in silence.

"You can probably guess what those questions are, Brian, can't you? Why you'd expect me to believe this bullshit," Matthew indicated the room where they sat, "I can't fathom. So let me make it crystal clear."

Confident of Brian's full attention, Matthew cleared his throat. "You were right. I presume that's what all this is about. We should never have taken the MOD consignment."

Brian didn't move, his face regaining none of its colour. "Since I last saw you, I've lost everything," then he corrected, "for now. But don't you worry. I'm getting it back. Debbie and Abi must be frantic, but I'll find them. And this place? I'll deal with that later. Priorities, Brian. Priorities."

Brian remained stock still.

"Am I speaking a foreign language?"

Reluctant to answer, when he did, fear turned to spite in his weasily eyes and Matthew could just see him happily making a deal with whomever asked. He wouldn't have given him a second thought before selling him down the river. He could see that now.

"I think you must be, Matthew, because I don't have a clue what you're talking about. I'm sorry things have been hard for you. Divorce can be tough. I know. But what issue you have with me and my boat yard I don't get."

"Don't you, Brian? Well. Call me touchy, but I am a little bit pissed that my whole life has been turned upside down. Everyone wants to convince me I'm crazy, and you... You must be stupidly sure they've been successful if you think I haven't noticed the business we built together now bares only your name, you stupid shit. *That* is what's wrong."

Brian snorted. "Built together? *My* boat yard? How do you work that one out?"

"Don't be a prick," Matthew lunged forwards. "You're *really* pissing me off. We grew this business. You and me!" Matthew thumped his chest. "Until I insisted we produce boats for the Ministry; mainly for the millions of pounds it was worth—which you were very happy to spend, if I recall—and the prestige; for our company, and for this fine city," Matthew gave a general gesture through the window. "But it's all turned to shit. Just as you warned it would. I should have listened. But now you have to help me. I don't care about the money, but tell me what they've done with Debbie and Abi."

"I don't know what you're talking about! If you're saying you should have listened to me, listen to me now."

Matthew paused from grinding his fist into his leg.

"This business? We didn't build it together. And as for a million pound contract. Does it look like I've got that sort of money? Cos I can tell you now, things are hard. Bloody hard. Other boat yards are taking my business every day. I'm struggling. My wife, Sue, left me. 'I couldn't keep her in the manner in which she'd like to become accustomed.' And now you've turned up making crazy accusations." He sighed. "I'm sorry things are tough for you. I'd heard a little on the grapevine. I'm sorry about your wife and kid, but I understood you'd never married. That you were in and out of the nut... hospital."

"Wife and kid? Debbie and Abi, you mean! You've been on holiday with us, for Christ's sake!"

"No! No, I haven't. I haven't seen you since school."

Matthew flew at him, the punch knocking him and his flimsy chair to the floor. Looming over him, Matthew shouted, "Brian! I'm not falling for this. Bravo! You've made the place look shit, I'll give you that. Who would believe that months ago we'd just been paid three million pounds? 'Tell him he's crazy.' That's what they told you, is it? They must really have their claws into you, but I couldn't give a shit. Do you hear me? I don't care what you've got to lose."

Matthew kicked viciously at Brian's torso. Wincing, Brian rolled away but Matthew stooped down, grabbed his thinning hair, and dragged his head round to face him.

"Brian. I've been nice. I haven't ripped your head off. But if you don't tell me where Abi and Debbie are, I'm gonna take my frustration out on your face. Do you understand?"

A whimper fell from Brian's mouth.

"What's it to be, old pal? Hmm?"

"I can't…"

Smack! Matthew hit him hard. Hurting his hand, he thought he'd best find something else to use if this was going to take more strikes. He'd never hit anyone before. The sound as it reverberated around the room, and the undoubted pain it caused, sickened him. But he'd have to man up. Brian had to believe he was capable of hurting him. They'd got him scared. Matthew had to make him *more* scared, so he threw his all into this performance. Brian had to believe he was in more danger from Matthew than from them. Then he'd talk. He'd have to.

Shoving his compassion aside, he had to force the truth. This wasn't a mugging, or indulgence in bullying; this was life and death for the most important people in his life. Grabbing around for the first hard thing he could find on the desk, when he saw it was just a stapler he discarded it in favour of a bronze statue of Brunel sporting his regular top hat and cigar.

"This is going to hurt, Brian, so I'll ask you again. Where are Debbie and Abi?"

Brian stared up at him, terror pouring from him in salty tears. "Matthew. I don't know. You're unwell. You need help."

Crash!

Isambard Kingdom Brunel sliced into Brian's neck and shoulder, and he grimaced in agony. "Matthew. No! I'd tell you if I knew anything."

"That's right, Brian. You will tell me, because I know you know. It's not possible that you don't know. Where have they taken them? Have a guess. You can have a guess, can't you, Brian?"

"Relocated. Somewhere in London."

"More. I need more, Brian."

Brian wailed. "I don't know. I only said that because you said 'guess!'"

Matthew brought the statuette down hard on Brian's arm. "Don't, Brian. Just tell me, or I'm gonna fucking kill you!"

The police would probably do better if they didn't announce their arrival with flashing blue lights. "Shit, Brian. Did you call the police?"

"No! Honest. You've been with me the whole time."

Still holding Brunel, Matthew waved it, rage pulsing through his arm until he threw it down at Brian's legs. His partner's whimpering echoed whilst Matthew busily made his escape through the back door and onto the tow path. Within seconds, he was back mingling in crowds outside bars and cafes before disappearing into the swanky new apartment blocks of Spike Island.

"I'll be back, Brian," he hissed under his breath. "And you will tell me. I promise you."

Chapter twenty-seven

It was a half an hour walk along the river and over the bridge to Matthew's next port of call. The impressive Harbourside Apartments all enjoyed wonderful views, but the penthouse boasted the best.

Matthew was cautious as he walked. His unusual attire might attract attention, but the charity duffel coat had been quality in its day making him not so different from the early evening dog-walkers and boat-tinkerers who were a friendly lot, and of course, he shared an affinity. In less pressing times, he'd be tempted to hop on board; perhaps offer some expertise and even secure a lead for a new customer.

But tonight, his sister's home was his only focus. What could he expect there? It seemed doubtful, with all that had gone on, that she'd be happy at home. They'd never been incredibly close. More resentful of one another, really. But there was love. And there was loyalty. She wouldn't rest while her brother was missing for half a year!

He'd paid the deposit; or rather Marsden-Morrissey Marine had paid it when a penthouse apartment overlooking their own impressive office seemed a good idea for accommodating clientele from further afield. But Mandy's firm of interior decorators (which he'd helped to fund but she'd taken from success to success) had worked its magic and she was now the live-in caretaker.

Would she have continued paying the rent in his absence? Or, more likely, would it have been acquired by his unseen foe in its battle to wipe memory of him from the face of the city?

Pessimism seeped into him like a leaking cesspit of gloom. There was no way Mandy would be in her flat, was there? They'd have moved them all. But why? It still made no sense. He'd go anyway, despite it being the most obvious place for him to go. He'd had no trouble so far. Whoever had arranged all this displayed little concern about him finding out. Maybe it was even part of their plan: to actually drive him insane.

But he'd never give up. And for now, he'd push his certainty that he was to be disappointed again aside and pump himself up in anticipation she might be there, and she might have answers.

It was impossible to tell from ten storeys down, but that didn't stop Matthew from craning his neck to try. There was a keycode at the door, and he typed in the usual number. With a rarely displayed smile, Matthew pushed the door open as the lock clicked and buzzed his entry.

Standing in the foyer, he took a minute to compose himself. The last time he'd stood here it had been with a supreme confidence; like he ruled the world. Now he could barely bring himself to take the first step.

He opted for the stairs, rather than the lift, to keep aware of the risk of ambush. It struck him as unlikely, but not unfeasible. It was no time to let down his guard. Popping his slippers from his pocket, he sat on the third step and swapped his boots for them to aid his quiet ascent.

Every few steps, he stopped and listened, straining against the silence he became more and more comfortable that he was safe. Striding now, chest out, there were just two more flights to go.

Safety was only one of his concerns. What would he find when he knocked on his sister's door? Aware of his rapid breaths, he stumbled the last few steps. Wiping damp palms on his trousers, the door loomed at him. Behind it could be the answer. The first successful step towards his life reshaping. Or, he tried to push aside burgeoning despair, yet more turmoil.

The landing looked empty. No police or psychiatric nurses waited to imprison him and he took the final step towards the door. Dabbing his palms again, he ran them through his hair and smelled his breath in a cupped hand. He couldn't smell it, but assumed it was rank. It didn't matter. His sister would hold him tight. She'd welcome him and help him piece it all together and he'd be back with Debbie and Abi.

If she was there.

Rapping white knuckles on the sturdy wooden door, he thrust his hand to his pocket and attempted to affect a mature pose suited to seeing his sister for the first time in months.

He shuffled from one foot to the other trying a nonchalant lean on the wall, but shrank away from it when it didn't feel right. Unfolding his arms which had clasped themselves together for comfort, he didn't want the fear he felt to show.

Excruciating seconds passed and he knocked again, harder. Allowing a minute this time, when there still came no response, he banged louder. Flapping the letterbox, he bent forward and called out, "Mandy! Mandy, it's me, Matthew. Answer the door!"

Ear pressed to the open oblong, Matthew listened to the silence assaulting his ear. Then a noise did come; not from inside the apartment, but from a few stairs away; a concerned neighbour investigating the ruckus.

"Can I help you?"

Matthew stood up to his full height. Refraining from offering his hand, realising it might be unpleasant after his night in the alleyway, he smiled. "Ah. Good evening. I'm trying to locate my sister, but she doesn't appear to be in."

The neighbour nodded. "There's no-one there. It's up to let, I think."

Matthew believed it, but surely that wasn't possible. The lease they'd secured was for two years. "I own the lease," he objected, causing the neighbours facial expression to change little.

Shifting his posture, he squinted barely detectibly before addressing Matthew again, his discomfort at engaging with this odd old acquaintance clear. "I don't know about that, but the previous lady has gone travelling."

What? She must be searching the globe for him. It made sense. Unless… of course. That was the story, but the truth would be she'd been relocated with Debbie and Abi. It's what he'd anticipated with every step walking here.

"You don't know where she's gone, do you?"

The neighbour shook his head. A sly smile crept onto his lips. "Sister you say?"

Matthew nodded.

"Which one of you was adopted, then?"

Brow furrowed, Matthew stiffened. Why had he assumed this stranger to be what he appeared? Nothing was as it appeared. "What do you mean?" he asked, knuckles hardening, buried in his pocket.

Despite his hidden hands, the man picked up on Matthew's change in attitude; almost as though he'd expected it. He pushed himself up from the wall, ready for what wasn't clear yet. "Well, you can't expect me to believe that Thu Ling is your sister, mate. Who are you, and how the fuck did you get in here?"

Matthew lunged, thrusting his hands from his pockets to the man's collar in a stiff manoeuvre which despite its lack of poise still had the man rammed against the wall.

Matthew forced his wiry forearm into the man's throat, muffling his cry, "Sarah! Call the police!"

It seemed unlikely Sarah had heard, or even that she existed. His eyes were wide. Pin-prick pupils struggling to keep his relentless stare belied his bluff. If she was real and was now on the phone, Matthew reckoned he had a good few minutes before anyone would arrive. Enough time to force this arsehole into giving up what he knew.

Thrusting his arm further into the man's throat, he released only when the choking looked like it might prove more damaging than useful.

"Who are you? Who do you work for? And what have they done with my family?" Releasing just enough for the man to answer, when he failed to do so, his flickering eyes bulged at a ferocious punch to his abdomen.

As he convulsed, choking and rasping for breath, Matthew leaned in and pressing his dry lips into the man's ear he growled. "Who are you, who do you work for, and what have they done with my family?"

The man forced himself up in his first show of strength. Catching Matthew off guard, he gained ground until Matthew's sheer force of desperate will thrust him backwards again.

Clawing at the bannister as he stumbled over his feet in the tumult, the man pitched headlong down the short flight of stairs coming to a confused crash at the bottom. Matthew leapt the few steps and loomed over him, adding a sturdy body kick for good measure. "I won't ask you nicely again!"

Cowing in the onslaught, the man spat his retort, blood mixing with saliva staining the floor as he spoke. "I don't know what you're on about. I don't know your fucking family, you weirdo!"

About to exact further torture on the lying bastard, Matthew stopped in his tracks at the "Stop. Police!" echoing from the foyer below. Snarling at the man, and cursing how the unexpectedly real Sarah had managed to get the police here so quickly, Matthew knew he couldn't let them take him. His family were in danger, and he wasn't prepared to lose them.

Plying the heavy fire extinguisher from the wall, Matthew jumped the first few steps, ran along the landing and leaped the next flight in a single bound. The momentum when he collided with the policeman on the next stairwell was sufficient to knock him flying.

As he lay winded, Matthew could see him bark warnings into his epaulette radio, but not fast enough. When Matthew

170

encountered the officer's colleague at the doorway, he hurled the fire extinguisher crashing it into the policeman's shoulder, felling him to his knees.

As Matthew side-stepped him, he slumped to his face with a groan. Matthew had made it fifty metres along the towpath before looking back he saw the first officer in fast pursuit. Matthew increased his pace. He'd never been one for running, but now he found his long legs were perfect for the job. A glance back confirmed it; he was gaining ground on his pursuer.

More blue lights on the road beside him were the first indication there were more of them. As two burly men rushed at him from the side, Matthew could see two more a hundred metres away, hurtling towards him.

Despite having gained ground on the first policeman, there was no chance he could make it back. There was only one escape route open to him, and in this cold, it might kill him. Matthew saw no choice.

Running at full speed, he launched himself high into the air at the perfect trajectory to fly far from the path. The icy water parted at his feet, the hospital jogging bottoms protecting him from the worst of the shock. His slippers, jumping ship, drifted away in an eddy towards the bank.

By miraculous chance, the huge duffle coat ballooned in the down force of Matthew's descent and now buoyed him along the fast flow of the river, watching from a comfortable distance as one of the policemen dived in after him.

Thrashing arms achieved little in their pursuit. Apart from needing to leave the water at an unexpected point, and requiring fresh, dry clothes, Matthew was home free. Free to do whatever he could think of to get at the truth. But ideas were dangerously depleted.

He wasn't dead yet, and while he still had breath, he wouldn't rest.

Chapter Twenty-eight

As the duffle jacket soaked up more of the rapidly flowing Avon, its buoyancy diminished. Edging himself to the bank, his choice of where to exit the freezing water was limited to his ability to withstand the cold.

The coat and layers of other clothes had prepared him for the shock, but it couldn't repel the cold forever. Without something dry to wear, Hypothermia was a certainty.

If he managed to find some coins, he might be able to dry his clothes at a launderette. A long shot, perhaps, but he took heart that he'd found change left in machines one time when they'd used the launderette whilst they waited for a delivery of a new washing machine years ago.

He recognised where he was, having chartered the river hundreds of times, and he remembered a launderette not too far away. Maybe lady luck would grace him with her presence. God knows, he needed it.

Exiting unnoticed from the river at a convenient slipway was easy enough, but walking to the launderette with a puddle pooling beneath him would surely get some looks; memorable looks that could be passed onto the local constabulary.

What choice did he have? He hoped that the night time inhabitants of the Powders Laundromat were not busy-body informers. When the smell of recreational herb greeted his approach, it seemed a safe bet.

A scruffy man sat on the front step, his fat blunt the obvious source of the odour. Ignoring Matthew until drops of water splashed down, his mellowness quickly gave way to a tirade of abuse.

As Matthew side-stepped him, he hunched in the doorway and went back to puffing on his joint. The room was empty but for baskets and bags of washing dotted around that people were trusting would be there when they returned.

Several machines were running, washers and driers. From the dial, Matthew could see the drier furthest away had the most time to run. His clothes were too wet to add to the load tumbling round, but if he removed them one at a time and rung them out, maybe it would work.

Or maybe he should have a look in some of the bags? Double checking that pot-head was his only company, he smiled thinking of him as an early warning of a disturbance.

The first bag eluded giving away the jackpot, but by bag three, Matthew had pieced together a fair wardrobe. Not his usual attire, and all the better for it.

Prizing out the sodden shoes he'd stuffed into his pocket in his attempt at a quiet approach to Mandy's front door, he thought it a pity they weren't laundry items too. Blatantly opening a drier, he popped them in with whoever's clothes were occupying the machine and closed the door. The damp garments provided useful cushioning for the boots as they clumped around and around.

While they dried, Matthew removed his joggers, his modesty maintained by the long coat. Replacing them with jeans he'd found folded and warm, he cringed as they wrinkled the baggy boxers he'd already found in another bag. Someone else's pants—nice.

Taking off the coat, he checked the pockets, confirming the rest of the items he'd acquired at the charity clothes bank had been lost to the Avon's current, he added it to the drier. He couldn't afford to leave that behind. Removing the last of his hospital attire, he stuffed them into the bin filling the corner of the room and put on a new shirt and jumper.

He looked clean, and smelled okay considering his river bath, the floral fabric clothes softener helped. A woman walked in tapping away at her phone and Matthew remembered his desperation to use Malcolm's SIM-less one.

She looked up at him but didn't give him a second glance, still tapping on her phone screen as she walked to a machine; thankfully not one containing Matthew's coat and shoes. Her disinterest indicated he wasn't sporting her husband or boyfriend's shirt and jeans.

As she emptied one machine into another, Matthew removed his coat and shoes and put them on. She stared at him forcing the leather back into shape. Her next text would surely mention the odd man in the laundrette. But it didn't matter. Matthew was ready.

Plucking the pile of other people's clean washing he'd gathered, he placed them carefully into the empty bag an unfortunate someone had planned to take their washing home in. Oh well. His need was greater.

Mouthing a combined thank you and sorry to the powers that be, Matthew stepped back onto the street, confident he looked very different to the description that would be circulating. That was, of course, until someone reported the theft of clothes.

The disastrous campaign to retrieve his life had to pause. He had to lie low or risk arrest. His priority now had to be food and warmth. For that, he'd learn from the masters. Striding with confidence to one of the city's less desirable areas where he knew from experience homeless beggars frequented, he would keep warm with his vagrant comrades for a couple of nights; eating what they ate and sheltering where they sheltered. God, how had it come to this?

Stopping dead in his tracks, the distraction of putting into place what he had thought until today would be a joyful reunion had kept him from connecting with his emotion. Facing the graffiti tarnished walls (albeit some of them priceless works of art) allowed it to flood him, brimming and cascading in a torrent of despair.

He couldn't take another step. A tremble turned to a violent shake. Cold and hungry, Matthew's need for shelter was outweighed by the overwhelming trauma that all hope was lost. Nearly. Hiding his face with the collar and hood of the duffle coat, tears refused to come. Instead they prickled at the back of his eyes, focusing needle-sharp rage at the street.

No! Now wasn't the time for despair. Now was the time to re-energise and come back stronger. They wouldn't be expecting that. But they didn't know Matthew Morrissey.

Chapter Twenty-nine

The girls were loving the zoo. Debbie could take heart in that. She was pleased, no, more relieved, that Abi was taking Matthew's absence so well, but she resented her too.

He was in trouble. She knew it. The rest of the family's willingness to believe he'd just upped and left—on Christmas Day of all days—left her feeling distant. She didn't want to come to terms with having lost him because she didn't believe she had.

"Come on, Mummy! Come and see the red pandas. They're so cuuute!"

Debbie sighed and shuffled from her bench. Pushing up on her thighs, she struggled to find the motivation to stand. But she did. And she cooed over the red pandas and the baby gorillas and the penguins. When it was time to leave, she picked up gifts and souvenirs from the shop, just as she'd done the last time they'd come here as a complete family. And every second hurt.

"Matthew, where are you?" she sighed under her breath. "Where on earth are you?"

The lounge had been moved around again. She'd thought they were trying to expunge Matthew from their lives and that made her angry. But moving things around again seemed pointless. It was her house, not theirs (apart from Abi, of course.)

What were they even doing here? Their return, having left after Christmas, had been gradual. Cooking for her one night, Charlotte sleeping over another, and now she wasn't sure if they ever went home at all. They always seemed to be around whenever she engaged enough with her surroundings to notice.

Abi might take comfort from their company but they were no comfort to her. They were a constant drain on her optimism.

In fact, they'd stopped her doing things that could find him. With all their busy-bodying and re-arranging furniture, and days out. She didn't know what she could have done; she'd exhausted her brain. But if she'd been left alone, maybe she could have thought of something else.

If they'd left her in peace, perhaps she'd have fallen into a deeper depression. Okay, she conceded; almost definitely, and where that would have left Abi? She couldn't bear to think about it. But it didn't mean she had to like it. She'd ask them to leave. Or at least find out when they were planning on doing so.

Slumping down on the sofa, she ignored the gratitude that had fossilised into resentment that Abi was content, happy even, and closed her eyes. Sleep was her only refuge, and even that betrayed her, giving into restlessness throughout the night. Exhausted, she forced her eyes shut.

When she heard the banging, she wasn't sure if it was a dream. Pricking her ears, she was sure. Someone was at the front door. "Great! Why has no-one answered it? I'm exhausted!" she called out to whoever might be listening. But no-one came, and the banging persisted.

"Fine! I'll go." Flouncing as much as her exhaustion would allow her, she reached the door. Instinctively pulling the chain over, as she pulled it open ready to give whoever was disturbing her short shrift, she let out a gasp.

Waiting on her doorstep stood the police lady she'd seen a few times before. She'd taken notes and sympathised in a supremely professional manner. Swaying in shock, Debbie watched detached as the warm smile rested uneasily on the police woman's face. Unsure if she was to be allowed into the Morrissey home, she blurted out her key information at the door.

"We've found him!"

Chapter Thirty

Knees buckling, her hurry to remove the door chain and allow the glorious angel in her police lady uniform into her home to confirm what she thought she heard, only made her fumble. At her third attempt, rattling the links to no effect, she paused, took a deep breath and smiled.

Pushing the door completely closed, the chain slid from its keep in the effortless manner it was designed, and Debbie pulled the door open wide. "Come in," she invited with a wave of her hand. "Please."

Understanding the shock, the WPC took a timid step into the vast hallway, her eyes following the long line of the straight Victorian corridor with its multitude of doors as they had every time she'd stood here. One day, if she won the lottery, she nodded to herself.

Debbie ushered her into the lounge, cursing in her mind the insensitivity of the room's rearrangement. They could venture putting it back to normal, tout suite. Breathlessly, and barely able to speak through the huge grin bisecting her face, Debbie asked, just to confirm, "So, you've found him? Really?"

The police lady nodded. "Yes." Eyes moving around the room, even her less familiar eyes recognised the changes. She awaited Debbie's confirmatory nod before taking a seat. "He's in a bad way."

Debbie's mouth retained the contour of a smile, but her eyes clouded. Slowly, like memory-foam returning to shape, her lips centred and reformed into the line that had graced her dour countenance for months. "Oh?" she forced through the gap.

"He was spotted at the top of the gorge. Passers-by thought he was probably…" she paused, not wanting to appear too insensitive, "heading for the bridge."

The not-so-subtle intimation at a possible suicide attempt was lost on Debbie. All she could think was how incredible he'd been so close all along! She could have looked from her window and seen him! "Why had he not come home then?" she demanded with a puzzled scowl.

The police lady sighed. "He's… not quite himself, I'm afraid."

"What do you mean?"

Leaning towards Debbie in what she hoped was a comforting way, she refrained from taking her hand, her face reddening at the abandoned notion. "He is a bit confused. Doesn't seem sure who he is or where he's supposed to be."

"You're sure it's him, though, right?" Panic widened Debbie's eyes, the whites glowing manically. Their gaze softened at the firm nodding from the seat next to her.

"Yes. He knows his name. And he does look like the photos. Albeit, a rough-sleeping, heavily bearded version."

Debbie gasped and rushed a hand to her trembling lips. "He's been sleeping on the streets?"

"It seems that way, yes," the policewoman confirmed. "We don't know what happened. Whether he's been victim of a crime is of less importance than his immediate well-being. We can get to the bottom of what happened to him when he's ready to talk."

She edged forwards on her seat ready to stand. "We'd like you to come into the station to see him."

"Of course!" Debbie leapt up in her eagerness.

"I'll drive you there if you like? You seem a little overwhelmed to drive safely." Debbie nodded. "He probably won't come straight home." Interrupting the 'Why?' poised on Debbie's lips, she explained, "We just want the doctor's to give him the once over. He seems fine, physically, but with him having been gone for so long, we'd like to check." Her eyebrows raised awaiting approval.

"Yes. Of course. That's fine. Whatever you think." Debbie's power of reason had deserted her weeks ago. She'd agree to anything the police lady suggested.

Following her to the police car, a little hatchback, she hopped in beside her. Reaching round for the seatbelt clasp, her fingers shook and she had to concentrate to grab it and slot it into place.

Stuffing her hands under her legs to keep them still, she gazed out of the window as the car made lamentably slow progress to the station. The views were pleasant, fields and occasional glimpses of the river far below, but they meant nothing to Debbie.

Grimacing, she removed a shard of fingernail from her mouth. She hadn't known she was chewing them. She didn't even remember moving her hand from beneath her leg, but she must have. Forcing it back, she concentrated on the scenery.

Gradually the outlook changed as the little police car edged into a more urban layout, and suddenly a large cube of concrete and glass loomed in the near distance. That must be it, Debbie pursed her lips. That has to be where they're keeping Matthew.

Her heart thumped against her ribs as if it too couldn't wait for the first glimpse in months of her beloved husband. The car pulled into a designated space and lurched to a halt, the handbrake click-clicking into place.

"Ready?" the woman smiled at her.

Nodding, Debbie yanked at the door handle and leapt from the car, instantly springing back with a winded thud as the seatbelt hauled her into her seat.

With an apologetic smile, her trembling fingers fumbled with the button until the policewoman leaned in and unclicked it for her.

Stepping with ease from the car now, she followed on tentative tiptoes to the front door of the large new-looking building. The door whooshed open and they were inside, the atmosphere cramming professionalism and crushing oppression into the same space: unrest's swirling around one another in fragile unease.

They stopped at the custody desk and the police woman spoke to a man in uniform behind the desk. Debbie wanted to listen; they might even be talking to her, but her mind was already with Matthew, clutching him to her breast and squeezing; never to let him go ever, ever again.

With no further instruction, Debbie was led through security doors to a cell door a few along from the main entrance. Glancing through a peephole, the officer from the desk pushed down hard on the handle and the door swung into the cell.

A man sat on the bench at the end of the room, knees to his chest, matted fur on the hood of a green Parka obscuring his face. Debbie's plan to rush over and take him in her arms stalled. Who was that?

"Matthew?" the officer called out. The man didn't move. "Matthew, your wife is here." Motionless, a snort of heavy breath moving straggly tufts from the hood was the only movement the man made.

Debbie took a step forward, fear gripping her: fear there had been a terrible mistake, and the police hadn't found her husband at all; and also, fear of this man. He had an air that withered her. "M M Matthew?" she ventured. "It's me."

Almost imperceptibly, the face hidden by grubby green fabric tilted up. A second, or an hour later, his features were clear to see.

With a gasp, Debbie flinched before rushing over to her husband. "Matthew. Oh, Matthew. What on earth has happened to you?"

Throwing her arms around him, she clutched at the filthy fabric, the smell of dirt and urine stinging her nose. Matthew remained still. He made no move to reciprocate the affection, just sat still like a mannequin.

It must have been awful for him, Debbie understood. Obviously he was distressed. What had she expected? She had to admit, the part of her thinking she'd walk in to see the same person who'd left her on Christmas Day sitting smiling at her, was foolish. And she didn't even want that anyway. No. If he'd chosen to stay away from his family, there had to be a reason. And this? This looked like a reason to her.

She'd do whatever it took; be whoever it took to help him back onto his feet. Her in-laws had been right. He'd clearly had a nervous breakdown. She'd assumed he'd coped with Abi and her leukaemia, but assuming was never good.

They'd rarely talked about it. They had sat in doctor's appointments, after specialist's appointments, again and again with a good old British stiff-upper-lip. There didn't seem anything more to say whenever they'd gone home from the hospital. They both knew if Abi miraculously recovered, life would resume better than ever. And if she didn't, then it never would. They knew that. They hadn't needed to talk about it: to live it before it had happened.

And in the end it didn't happen. So they'd done the right thing. But, now it seemed they hadn't, because two years of unfelt grief had obviously crushed Matthew as soon as he'd deemed it safe enough to feel it, and it had overwhelmed him. It wasn't so difficult to comprehend.

And she would. She'd be the most understanding wife anyone had ever known, and they'd put it all behind them.

"Come on, my lovely. Let's get you home." She held out her hands, palms down in invitation to haul him up from the hard little bench. Matthew stayed still. "Don't you want to come home?" the thought wounded Debbie. Why had she assumed he would? He'd kept away for months, why presume he'd be ready to come back just because the police found him?

His head jolted up and he stared straight into her eyes, the vacant look behind the dry shine of the pinhead pupils sent a shiver through her. But not as much as what he said.

His dry lips parted. Fetid breath oozed from between brown furred teeth. It was the first time she'd heard her husband's voice this year. She'd longed for him to phone her, just to tell her he was okay, or at least that he was alive. But when he spoke now, it wasn't the comfort she'd craved. His words, now, wounded like a hunter's spear, ricocheting round the cell.

Taking a deep breath, he sighed slowly, as though not wanting to waste his expelled air on the words. "Who *are* you?"

Chapter Thirty-one.

Life force bleached from Debbie's face. "What do you mean?"

Matthew slumped back. The effort of the question too much for him.

"What do you mean, '*who am I?*'" Debbie demanded again, immediately regretting her tone.

Jolting at a touch on her arm, the kindly face of the young police lady squeezed a smile in her direction. "He's not really himself, as I said. He may have had a blow to the head which has caused his amnesia. But that's definitely him, isn't it?"

Debbie nodded. It was definitely Matthew. A very different Matthew.

"You can see why we're keen to have him checked out. The doctor's on his way. I expect they'll want to give him the once over in hospital though."

Debbie's throat was too tight to speak. Turning her head, she concealed pools welling in her grey eyes. She didn't know why she felt the need to hide.

"You can go with him, if you like."

Of course. She wasn't going to let him out of her sight any time soon. Pivoting on the spot, her instinct to sit next to her husband was under attack from an unexpected unease at his gruff manner. Opting for standing near him, his obvious discomfort in her presence told her she'd made the right choice, and ripped at her heart.

Noise from the corridor preceded the entry of a bustling scruffy man on the morbid side of obesity, dirty hair hanging in stringy tufts on an untrimmed hairy face. Struggling to hold a pile of papers affecting their escape from a worn briefcase he gripped in both hands, as though the handle had abused his trust in the past, he lurched to a halt in front of Matthew where his high-pitched voice announced him as the duty doctor, Doctor Kay.

Matthew treated him to the same indifference he'd greeted Debbie.

"And you are…?" the doctor's freaky falsetto carried around the cell. When Matthew failed to answer, Debbie interjected.

"Matthew. Matthew Morrissey." The doctor peered at her as though only just noticing her. The long black caterpillars balanced above each eye arched their backs. "I'm Debbie Morrissey. Matthew's wife."

The caterpillars relaxed. 'What's wrong with him?' so nearly spewed from Debbie's lips, but she doubted this unhealthy looking specimen had answers yet.

"Matthew," he yipped, and in different circumstances his high screech would have been comical. "Matthew, I'd like to test a couple of things… reflexes, neural responses; things like that. Give me your hand," he ordered, holding out his own meaty sausages.

Matthew remained statue still. The doctor reached out further and took his hand. Matthew shot his arm back, bashing it into the wall behind the bench. "Get off me!" he roared.

Stumbling back in surprise, the doctor's heel entangled with the cascading papers falling from his briefcase. He slipped, glanced at what was troubling his feet and lost balance. With a hefty thud, he crashed to the floor.

"Now then! There's no need for that!" he squealed, shaken and winded.

The police lady and the custody sergeant lunged forward to protect the doctor but Matthew had already resumed his position of silent stillness. The bubble rippling in Debbie's throat erupted as a wail into the unforgiving acoustics of the featureless cell, attracting sympathetic glances from the two police officers.

Heaving his mighty mass from the cold floor, the doctor dusted himself off, brushing at his knitted tank top with sweaty palms. "We need to get him into hospital. There are lots of reasons he could be displaying these type of symptoms. I take it this isn't Mr Morrissey's usual mode of behaviour?" he directed at Debbie.

Thank goodness, she thought. He was offering an explanation; a reason her husband was behaving so irrationally. She had worried he'd end up in trouble, arrested, or sectioned or something. "What might be the matter?" she managed through a new optimism.

The doctor squinted, blowing raspberries through rubbery blue lips. "Well, like I say. Any number of things. Given he's been sleeping rough, he could be suffering from low sodium levels, or perhaps he's sustained a knock to the head? He's not diabetic is he?"

Debbie shrugged and shook her head.

"He may be malnourished; low blood-sugar, low salts, both those can cause confusion and violent outbursts. Or..." He rubbed at his matted beard. "He might be experiencing withdrawals from... substances, or possibly suffering from a mental health issue. We'll know once we've run a few tests at the hospital."

Debbie sighed, heartened that a smile had grown quite naturally on her lips. She'd have him back soon. They'd give him sugars and salts and medicines and whatever else he needed and he'd be back to his old self. And at least now she knew he was safe. She wasn't counting the days of her despair anymore.

A giggle burst forth, surprising her. She'd be able to tell Abi, and Mandy and Alan and Mary! They'd be thrilled and relieved. Despite Matthew's odd behaviour, there was no question; today was a good day.

Chapter Thirty-two

It was with undeniable reluctance that Matthew followed the doctor to his awaiting vehicle. His mind churned through the options which boiled down to two: go to the hospital, or stay in the custody of the police. Keeping his face hidden under his hood, he slumped into the back seat of the car emblazoned with *Doctor* livery on the doors and bonnet.

Debbie slid in beside him and fought the side of her that wanted to reach out and hold his hand. He wasn't well. There'd be plenty of time for that when they'd topped up his minerals. Poor Matthew. What had he been through?

Resting her chin on her chest, she allowed herself another little smile as the driver sped them through the city centre to the hospital. Tall buildings hemmed them in giving an odd sense of security in their confining opulence.

Arriving at the hospital, the car pulled into its allocated space and the scruffy doctor bustled from his seat presuming their compliance in following. Debbie noticed Matthew's eyes darting to the exit. Her heart jumped to her throat. No! Don't go! But he didn't. He stepped in behind the doctor and the three of them walked through the swishing doors.

Keeping up with the wheezing doctor took no effort. By the time they reached a side room along a corridor he was sweating through his shirt. Wafting dark pits in the air as he rolled up his sleeves, he heaved out a chair and invited his patient to sit on the couch while he caught his breath. Debbie was left to stand wherever, so long as she wasn't in the way.

Approaching Matthew, the doctor reintroduced himself as Doctor Kay and stood back as he made his intentions clear.

"Mr Morrissey. May I call you Matthew?" he squeaked. Assuming his agreement, he continued. "Matthew, I need to carry out a series of tests. But I can't put up with the sort of behaviour you demonstrated at the police station." He removed his thick spectacles to make absolutely sure their eyes connected. "If I am unable to rely on your behaviour, then I will call the police. Am I making myself understood?" Matthew didn't move. "Will you behave?" Matthew still didn't move, but Debbie was sure she detected a grunt. That appeared sufficient for Doctor Kay to proceed.

Cautiously, he reached for Matthew's hand again. The effort was intense, but Matthew forced himself to allow Doctor Kay to take it. Holding it loosely, he examined it before replacing it; almost as though he had no need of it but wanted to test he could.

"Follow my finger," he instructed. Matthew's eyes followed the doctor's Bratwurst as he moved it up and down and left to right. "Good," he said before pulling what looked like a pen from his pocket. The pen was a bright torch which he shone into Matthew's eyes. "Good. Now, can you touch my finger? And your nose? Again?"

The hatred pouring from Matthew went unnoticed by the physician. Debbie saw. Why? He was only trying to help him. Trying to find out what's wrong so he can help.

Holding out both his hands, he requested Matthew's and the effort was still evident. Debbie supposed she'd be reluctant to hold the doctor's hands too. She didn't know where they'd been, but under hot soapy water seemed unlikely given the rest of his appearance.

Unhidden now, she saw his hands. There was no mistaking the absent wedding band, and she gulped down flames of rage that plumed from the fiery pit of scorn she never knew existed within her. She could only imagine what had led to its removal, but Matthew's grungy look in no way suggested another woman. She sighed, fuming, but she had to let it go. For now.

Matthew looked away, detaching himself from the unwelcome sensation of touch, Matthew pushed and pulled his arms as instructed. His strength didn't look lacking to Debbie's eyes, and the satisfactory outcome was confirmed by another affirmation of, "Good," from Doctor Kay.

It was the doctor's turn to display discomfort as he asked Matthew to remove his shoes and socks, but despite his having been on the streets for months, the effluvium proved less offensive than expected. Doctor Kay used the handle of his rubber mallet to scratch the soles of Matthew's feet, his toes curling in response gained satisfied nods.

"I'll arrange for a nurse to take some bloods. Once we've got the results back, we'll know more about why he doesn't appear to remember everything we'd like." He smiled at Debbie, the high pitch of his voice still reverberating the room. "I'd like him to stay in…"

"NO!" Matthew yelled. "I'm fine."

"Matthew! Don't start being difficult again. I won't have it, you hear?" the doctor yipped

Matthew sat back to appease the doctor, but the notion to run still flashed in his eyes.

"We need to do some tests. You may have had a bump to the head."

"I haven't," Matthew spat.

"Or you might be diabetic, or there might be underlying problems."

"I'm fine. I haven't had a knock to the head. I'm not diabetic. I'm fine!"

The doctor sighed and flashed an anxious pout in Debbie's direction. It was the first time he'd included her since they'd arrived.

"Can't I just take him home? I'm sure that would be best," Debbie's eyes pleaded.

"I'm sorry. I can't advise that, Mrs Morrissey."

189

"But we've missed him so. I think getting back home might be the best thing for him."

Doctor Kay patted his top lip covered by matted moustache. "I'm really worried about him, Mrs Morrissey. Why don't I run a few tests and we'll go from there?"

Debbie turned to her husband. "That would be okay, wouldn't it Matt? Get the bloods taken. Make sure you're okay before I take you home?"

"I'm fine!" he seethed. "…But okay. Run your tests." He sunk back on the examination table and awaited his fate.

The doctor disappeared to find a nurse to bring him what he needed for taking samples of blood. The grim silence between the pair left in the room gnawed at Debbie's heart as she fought not to cry.

When the doctor returned with the nurse and a stainless steel trolley laden with sharps boxes and kidney bowls and other packages, the room filled quickly.

"I'm afraid I'm going to have to ask you to wait outside the room; perhaps go to the dayroom at the end of the corridor. I'll come and get you when we're done."

Debbie glanced back at her husband as she left the room. He couldn't care less that she'd gone.

Muddled emotions swirled inside her leaving her nauseous. It was great to have Matthew back. But now she was rushed headlong into desperate worry for his health. She was expecting too much. Just as she was preparing to give in to the risk that she might never see him again, here he was. And he was in one piece. Whatever was wrong with his mood could be put right, she was sure of it.

As they'd talked about for months, the stress of Abi's illness whilst growing the business into the million pound success story it had become had pushed him over the edge. It wasn't a weakness. He wasn't a weak person. It just showed he'd taken his strength for granted for too long. They all had.

She would never take him for granted again. Although she hadn't realised she ever had, she could see it now. Whilst she'd had the chance to spend time with Abi, he'd been forced away with work. And she'd had the opportunity for grief, and later for joy too when she'd made her miraculous recovery.

The assumption they were feeling the same thing had been a mistake. Not talking had been a mistake. And this was the result. Something about Christmas Day, maybe even how perfect it had been, had flicked a switch in Matthew's brain and given it permission to feel all that he had missed. No wonder it overwhelmed him.

Shutting himself off was what he did. It wasn't something Debbie had witnessed in eleven years together, but he had form. Her in-laws had known, and whilst she'd resented every word, they had been right. It wasn't a bad thing. He'd recovered before and he'd do it again.

The doctors would know what to do. There'd be a plan. And she could make super-sure they did everything possible to help. This time next year it would all be behind them. Her own mother had a nervous breakdown when her father died ten years ago. And no-one could call her weak. Her dominance in the male-dominated area of law and its implementation in industry had been legendary—still was. Her embarrassment at not coping had surprised everyone.

It was a distant memory now, but maybe she was troubled still. A pang of guilt wounded Debbie realising she didn't know. They didn't talk either. A new blame was taking shape, and Debbie was becoming sure it was hers. "Stop it. You have to stay strong; for Matthew."

In the spirit of doing the right thing, she was pained by more self-reproach that she'd been with Matthew for ages and hadn't even let her family know. Part of her wanted to keep it to herself. Their almost-contempt in their certainty Matthew had not coped and it was 'GCSE's all over again riled her. Now they'd been proved correct, she didn't want to hear the inevitable 'I told you so's'. But it was wrong not to have told them as soon as she'd known. They showed it in a different way but they were upset too.

The payphone in the corner beckoned. She could phone them right now and tell them all about it, keeping some of the details to herself for now. At least until the prognosis was clearer. Fumbling in her pockets for coins, she pulled four or five pound coins and fifty pence pieces from the depths of her jeans pocket; more than enough to phone home.

Mary picked up after three rings, but Debbie was unable to speak.

"Debbie! Where are you? We've been worried sick!"

There was no covering her emotion as planned. She could barely get the words out. "Sorry," she began. "It's Matthew…" Realising her dour tone would provoke severe anxiety, Debbie did her best to hurry. "The police came to get me…" she rasped. I'm making this worse, she tried to rush on. "He's fine. A bit confused, but physically well…"

"Oh my god! Mandy! Alan! They've found Matthew!" And it was difficult not to grin in the face of their exuberant celebrations. The phone rattled as from the other end of the line they jumped around, screaming in delight.

"When's he coming home? When can we see him?"

The positivity rubbed off on Debbie, freeing her constricted throat enough to talk more lucidly. "Like I say, physically he seems okay, but they just want to check he's not malnourished, or had a bump to the head or something. They'll probably keep him in tonight, just to run whatever tests they need."

Pouncing like a hunter to a wounded prey, Mary barked, "Bump on the head? Why? What's he saying?"

Playing it down, Debbie explained, "Well, that's just it. He's not really saying a lot. And he's really edgy." She didn't say he couldn't remember her. It made her too sad, and who knows, he might piece it all back together really quickly. She might return to a much warmer welcome.

The door swung open, and a nurse popped her head in. "We've finished with Matthew for now," she didn't pause in interrupting the phone call. "Sorry it took a while! Not very forthcoming veins." She wandered off again before Debbie could finish up. She would have liked to ask a few questions.

"I'll have to go now, Mary. The nurse has just come in. I'll phone again when I know more."

"Wait! When can we come and visit him…" Debbie heard as she was replacing the receiver. Ignoring her, she let the phone go click.

Hurrying after the nurse, she was shocked she was already out of sight when she stepped from the day room. Breathless, she craned to see in both directions. Giving up, there was no way to guess her route so she headed back down the ward to the little room where she'd left Matthew. Eyes narrowing, her racing heart dismayed her. Why was she being so negative?

When she pushed open the door, she hung her head before lifting her eyes to gaze upon her husband. With heart-stopping shock, she flinched at his absence. "Oh, Matthew! Where are you?"

Through the pane of glass in the door, the calm scene at the nurses station; files open with frowning faces poring over them, told her they were unaware of Matthew's absence. With a sigh and a smile, she thought, unless he's just gone to the toilet, or been taken for a scan or something. Shaking her head, she approached the nurses' station.

Behind the desk, the car park was visible through a small square of window in the staffroom. Gazing out, waiting for one of the busy nurses to have time to attend her, she was about to speak as one looked up when what she saw through the glass turned her to jelly.

"Can I help you?"

Debbie didn't answer. She didn't have time.

"Sorry… Excuse me… Sorry," Debbie scurried down the corridor. Where was the exit? Why was it so confusing? On instinct, she followed a gaggle of what appeared to be visitors on their way out. Her hunch proved correct. As she stood at the front of the hospital, there was no longer any sign of Matthew. "Shit!"

Hands in double salute shielded her eyes from the sun. Scrutinising the street in both directions, there was no sight of him. Coming so close only to lose him again was too cruel. Stepping into the road, she had to find him. She'd seen him a minute before, he can't have gone far.

But of course he could have. Even though he'd been seen ambling slowly, that would have been so not arouse suspicion. Out of sight of the door, he could have hurried away in any direction. How on earth was she going to find him now?

The sob working its way from deep within wounded as it stretched Debbie's insides, rising through her body to her throat. As it heaved upwards, Debbie's face creased to squeeze it out.

Even as her desolation creaked into the air, her eyes focussed like hawks. With a sudden gasp, she sucked back her wail as luck leaned on her side. Squinting in the afternoon light, she stopped herself rushing to him when she saw Matthew not far away at all. She knew he might run if he saw her, but why? He was confused and distressed, she knew, but what could she do to help him? He needed to go back to hospital and get the medicine to make him right again.

Using passing cars as cover, Debbie ducked down lower than their rooflines. Matthew hadn't seen her. Keeping a distance, but with him in sight, she allowed him to walk further away. She wanted to see where he was heading, and she didn't know what she'd even say to him when she caught him.

He crossed this road and that, into shops and out. If anyone from the hospital came out to find him, they would stand no chance. The crowds of people rushing into Cabot Circus, shopping, or grabbing a bite to eat on their lunch break, stared at Matthew, his grubbiness marking him out as one of the homeless who hung around begging for money. Debbie wondered if he was going to approach the people crossing the street as had happened to her countless times.

She'd felt guilty and donated the pound for a cup of coffee on many occasions, but their brazen confidence; threatening almost, had made her avoid their attention. Now she watched to see if her husband was one of them.

Keeping his head down, his face was obscured by the tatty hood of his coat; where had he even found such an item? Debbie observed as he glanced in shops along the way. Was he remembering the numerous occasion's they'd shopped in the expensive boutiques? Picking up a designer handbag at Michael Kors, browsing round Jack Wills and Ted Baker's stores before lunching on the top floor of Harvey Nicks with its award winning food and views over the city?

If he was, then what he did next was even more bizarre. Pausing at a gourmet hot-dog and burger bar at the end of the line of expensive street food that was all the rage, he didn't join the line and order. He plunged his hand into the bin at the end and grabbed two or three polystyrene containers.

Scurrying away, he plonked himself into a doorway of an office building and proceeded to scoop leftover sausage ends and cold fries into his mouth. As he scoffed the revolting leftovers, passers-by threw money near him, muttering about the poor man as they walked by.

But he wasn't a poor man. He was likely the richest man in the street! Why was he doing this? What had happened to him?

Chapter Thirty-three

Debbie crossed the road towards the doorway, keeping Matthew firmly in her sight. When she reached him, he didn't look up until she spoke.

"Why are you doing this? Eating out of bins! For pity's sake, Matthew."

"Go away." His eyes diverted back to the cover of the raggedy hood. "Leave me alone."

"Matthew," she said softly. "I don't know what's happened to you… what you've been through, but it's over now." She sighed at her simplification. "It can be."

Detecting no movement in response, Debbie had no choice but to continue her persuasion. "You're not well, Matthew. The doctors at the hospital…" she didn't get to finish the sentence when Matthew threw the boxes of food debris into the air in frustration. As they fluttered back to earth without a bump, Debbie wondered if he was amused or extremely disgruntled at their lack of drama.

"No!" he spat, aware the soft food trays may not have made the point sufficiently. "I'm not going back there!"

Debbie dropped to her haunches and instinctively placed her hand on Matthew's arm. "Okay. Come back home with me. You'll feel better there."

"I don't want to."

Debbie scowled. "You'd rather stay on the streets and eat your dinner from bins than come home to your family?"

"Family! I haven't got a family!"

This was harder than she thought. "Matthew. My love. You do. You have a family who love you very much."

"Why are you doing this? Who sent you? How do you know my name?"

Debbie sighed. "I know everything about you, Matthew. I'm your wife." Matthew snorted. "Born 31st July 1981 in Wexford Road, Bristol to Alan and Mary Morrissey… Sister, Mandy, born…" she had to think to remember, "born 8th January 1988…"

"Stop it! Stop it! Don't you talk about them. You hear me? Don't!"

Debbie had never seen this side to Matthew, but his reaction at mention of his blood family suggested these problems went deeper than she realised. "Would you like to see them? They're all staying with me… us. In our lovely home. They can't wait to see you. And Abi…"

"My mum and dad and sister are staying at our house. That's what you're saying?"

Debbie nodded. Matthew looked down at his hands, holding them out as though seeing them in a new light. Something she'd said had got through to him, she was sure. Holding out a hand, she stood, the blood rushing back into her legs giving her pins and needles. "Come on," she invited.

To her immense delight and surprise, Matthew took her hand and allowed himself to be helped up. Striding hand in hand towards the nearby taxi rank, Debbie stopped at the first one and pushed Matthew inside. Leaping in herself, she closed the door before addressing the driver.

"Twelve, Clifton Down Road, please."

The taxi-driver's eyebrows raised as he nodded, "Posh," he declared, pulling out into the line of traffic, then creasing his face as the whiff of his blatantly un-posh passenger reached his nostrils. Winding down the window, he drove off with a scowl etched on his face.

Matthew stared out of the window. The tall buildings drawing his eyes skywards. Bustling river-side bars and cafes

197

took Debbie's eye, remembering all the times they'd walked hand-in hand beside the water, enjoying some pre-show drinks or a bite of something delicious to eat.

It was a strange thing to hark back to because it had been the early days of Marsden-Morrissey's success. And before Abi's terrible diagnosis. It's like she wanted to erase those two years and plonk the family into the scene that would have unfolded if the leukaemia had never happened.

Turning her head further towards the window, she hid a tear as it tracked down her cheek. They'd come through the other side until Matthew's tangent from wellness took all her focus again. It had been hard. Desperately hard. Her throat thick with the pain of it all, a flood of salty orbs followed the route scouted by the first, she tasted their bitterness as they skirted her quivering lips.

At some point during the journey home, their hands had separated and Matthew sat, insular, as far from her as the confines of the back seat allowed. Debbie tried not to care. She was bringing Matthew home. Everything was going to be alright. She had to believe it, her very being depended on it.

The scenery opened to green fields, the river snaking its seventy-five mile length through the nineteen miles from source to sea as the crow flies, cutting its steep, rocky gorge that had delighted them as the view from the magnificent home.

Would Matthew find joy in it again, seeing it now, the bridge that he'd stared at for hours in wonder in his love affair with the great Isambard Kingdom Brunel, his hero and his inspiration? A glance across revealed needle-sharp eyes staring at the iron structure, but there was no joy there. It was unclear what he was feeling looking at Brunel's masterpiece, but it certainly was not joy.

Debbie's heart sank. Who was this stranger? Would he ever return to the Matthew she knew and adored? It had been hours. Not months, the little voice of reason raised its hand in Debbie's head. Give him a chance!

With a smile, Debbie accepted she had to reign her expectations. Whatever he'd been through would take more than a drive through the city to overcome. She was in for the long haul, determined to help him become well again.

"Here we are!" she declared triumphantly as the taxi drew to a stop outside the wide driveway of twelve, Clifton Down Road. Its tower of stone bay windows looming above them, displaying a quiet confidence in the stunning scenery they knew they commanded.

No recognition glinted in Matthew's eyes. No smile played on his lips at the grandeur they gazed upon.

"Sorry. I'll just need to pop inside and get my purse... I left in kind of a hurry," Debbie apologised. The taxi-driver was happy to wait, and she would give him the anticipated generous tip.

"Come on, Matthew." If he resisted her again now, she wasn't sure if she could cope. With breath held sharply in her throat, she waited as he alighted his seat and stepped onto the wide tarmac expanse of the street. She would pay the driver any amount to give chase if he eluded her again.

Thankfully it wasn't necessary. He didn't look built for a successful pursuit. Matching Matthew's sloth-like pace toward the front door, she didn't understand his reluctance. Memories flooding back; too hard to cope with, she expected. Maybe bringing him straight home had been a mistake. But what choice did she have?

The front door flew open to reveal a beaming Mandy with a hug loaded and ready to deploy. Her arms sagged slowly as she realised a show of affection wasn't what was needed here. "Oh my god," she hissed under her breath in reaction to her brother's dishevelled appearance.

Debbie feared Abi's first sight of her daddy in such a shocking state, the worry entering her head with a stab of guilt that it hadn't surfaced before. "Where's..."

"Out with Mum and Dad and Charlotte. You probably passed them in the playground?"

Debbie hadn't noticed but was thankful for the chance to clean Matthew up before he re-met her. "Take my purse and pay the taxi. I'll get Matthew cleaned up."

Matthew stiffened as he crossed the threshold. Was it the changes they'd made? Debbie cursed her in-laws' insensitivity. "Come with me. I'll run a nice hot bath for you." Was that pleasure glinting beneath the surface on those indecipherable dead pool eyes? She smiled. She'd only ever wanted to make her husband happy. It's what she lived for.

With the water steaming, Matthew stripped and Debbie failed to stifle her gasp. Without acknowledging her, he shuffled his filthy, bony build to the edge of the bubbling pool of water. Raising his right foot, he offered it to the boiling broth and dipped it in.

This time the smile was unmistakable. Stepping in with both feet, he grasped the handles and eased himself into the steaming heat. Watching as he closed his eyes, Debbie could see his tension merging with the steam from the bath. Swirling in the air it condensed harmlessly, high up, far from him in the vastness of the Victorian splendour.

His eyes remained firmly shut, and she took it to mean he wanted to be alone. Drumming her fingers against the doorframe, she decided it was safe. He looked content—not about to run off again. Grabbing the grubby garments from the floor, she left him in peace. Pausing outside the door, the silence was only broken by her own creaking footsteps as she tried to pad silently away.

Creeping down the stairs one careful step at a time, she finally breathed out when she reached the bottom, knowing she couldn't hear anything no matter how hard she tried. Mandy handed her back her purse, which felt cumbersome with the armful of laundry, and she stopped to place it in the sideboard drawer by the front door on her way through to the utility room.

Drifting absently back through to the lounge, a cross-armed Mandy waited until they were both sat before she could contain the barrage of questions ramming her lips no more, and allowed them to burst forth. "Where have you been? How did you find him? What on earth has happened?"

The first two questions were easy to answer, the third brought Debbie to tears.

Mandy leaped up and thrust her arms around her. "What is it? What's wrong?"

Sucking in streaming tears, Debbie forced the words out. "He doesn't want to be here! He ran away from the hospital and I had to chase after him… had to persuade him to come home with me in the taxi!"

Mandy was silent as she thought of something to say.

"He doesn't seem to remember me." Debbie paused and clawed her face with her fingers. "He didn't even remember me, Mandy…" she placed her hands carefully in her lap and continued. "He remembers you, though. It was mentioning you that got him to come home."

Mandy flushed. "I'm sure it'll be a short-term thing. And it explains why he hasn't been home. If he couldn't remember… What did the doctors say?"

"They didn't get much of a chance to say anything. He worried it might be down to his emaciated state. You know, missing salts or sugars." Glancing down at the floor before meeting Mandy's gaze again, she went on, "he mentioned mental illness."

"Well, obviously. You don't leave your family on Christmas Day if you're fully compos mentis, now do you?"

Debbie smiled at Mandy's light-hearted take on it.

"No, I suppose not."

"It'll be like we said all along. Stress got to him, and he had a breakdown. Happens all the time, particularly to those in Matthew's position; people relying on him; multi-million pound deals. And Abi."

"I know that's what you said but…"

"Look," Mandy sat forward in her seat. "He's home. That's the important thing. We knew he'd be suffering from stress related issues, didn't we? It'll be fine. You'll see."

And for the first time, Mandy's trivialisation of what had distressed her so for months was a welcome relief.

They both turned to a sudden sound of Matthew huddled in a towel, dripping in the doorway. "Where are my clothes?" he demanded. He seemed annoyed, but he couldn't mean the disgusting stiggy outfit he'd come home in.

With a timid voice, Debbie informed him, "I've put them in the laundry room, but I expected you'd want to throw them away." Regretting the suggestion when she saw the shocked look on his face, Debbie added, "You can put some of your nice clothes on now, can't you?" Knowing he probably didn't remember where their bedroom was, she raised herself to her feet and walked towards him. "Come on," she said, extending her hand in invitation. He didn't take it and was clearly reluctant to go with her.

As his eyes screwed in his scrutiny of his situation, Debbie waited. With little choice but to wear a towel forever or go with her, he chose the lesser of two evils and followed her upstairs.

When they reached the door to their bedroom, Matthew was still a couple of steps behind. Debbie pushed it open and stepped inside.

Matthews's eyes gazed upon the decorative masterpieces as though he'd never seen them before and he whistled a "Wow," under his breath. Striding to the walk-in wardrobe, Debbie slid open the doors and waited for her husband to join her.

Approval shone from his eyes at the tailored outfits hanging colour co-ordinated and pristine along every side of the small room. Checking with his host before touching anything, when he was assured it was okay, he fingered a few of the jackets delicately.

"Choose whatever you want. They're yours. I'll see you back downstairs in a while." She was surprised at her desire to leave him alone with his clothes. She justified it with ideas that he might remember more if he relaxed, but she suppressed a fear that she just wasn't enjoying being with him.

Watching him treat their home as a stranger sliced into her every minute she witnessed. She hoped her justifications were right; that he would come downstairs more himself, memories of his old life creeping through the cracks in the façade he'd constructed. But even if he didn't, she needed a break.

"Okay?" Mandy inquired, surprised to see her returning alone.

Nodding, she stumbled in and perched on the edge of the sofa. "Pour me a stiff drink, please." As Mandy attempted to ascertain a preference, Debbie waved a dismissive hand. "Surprise me!"

Mandy joined her on the sofa with two large French Brandies. Debbie took hers in trembling fingers and took a soothing sip. Smiling over the glass, she inhaled a deep breath, readying herself.

Footsteps echoed down the stairs and into the hallway and Debbie's heart clenched in anticipation. He wore a smirk on his lips and Ralph Lauren polo with a blazer and chinos on his body. With a scarf tied at the collar he looked very nautical as well as disguising his gauntness; not quite his usual style but it worked.

"That's better, Matty," Mandy nodded approvingly. "Much better."

Matthew said nothing, but still wearing the odd smile, he took a seat on the wing chair in the corner. It was always his 'reading chair' but had rarely been used for reading; more a 'drinking brandy and falling asleep chair.'

Fingering the studs fixing the leather to the chair arms, he seemed oddly self-satisfied.

"Brandy," Mandy offered with a shake of the bottle. Matthew nodded slowly, enjoying being pampered. He deserved it after what he'd been through.

He'd just taken a sip when noise echoed through the house from the back garden and Abi, Charlotte and Matthew's parents could be seen entering the back door. Debbie stiffened. She hadn't come to terms with her husband's oddness;

particularly his failure to remember her and she didn't feel like explaining it to Abi and her in-laws.

At the same time, she was thrilled. They would be so excited to see him, and at least now he was clean and presentable, although his beard was a little long. He'd always been meticulously clean-shaven but a beard couldn't disguise him.

In her mind's eye she pictured Abi running in and throwing her arms around him. "Daddy, Daddy!" she'd cry bringing the memories flooding back to Matthew. What father could resist the affection of his little girl?

"Oh, hi, Debbie!" Alan said, surprised to see her. Abi and Charlotte could be heard chattering in the hall. "How long have you been back?"

"Not long," she said, eyes twinkling in anticipation.

Following her gaze his eyes fell on Matthew and stunned him into silence. "Matthew," he declared matter-of-fact; cold. He crossed the room and sat next to Debbie, failing to manifest the emotional reunion with his prodigal son Debbie had anticipated. But he didn't kill the fatted calf. Instead, he folded his arms and stared silently into space.

His displeasure fully on display, Debbie's chest tightened; her lips moved but no words came. Why was he being like this?

Abi skipped in, play-acting with Charlotte as the bossier of two Disney princesses. As her eyes looked resolutely in any direction but Matthew's, Debbie observed in disbelief. Did she not see him? Had she deliberately ignored him?

Finding her voice with her authority over her daughter, she exclaimed with dramatic glee, "Abi! Look! Look who's home." Muteness returned as she watched her blatantly ignore Matthew and carry on her game with her cousin.

"Abigail Morrissey! Don't you dare ignore your poor daddy like that!" She was furious. This wasn't the action of a little girl. She was clearly under the sour influence of judgemental grandparents. No wonder Matthew had held onto his emotions until he could bear them no more. He'd been taught that showing your pain was weak. It made perfect sense.

Well Alan could behave like a heartless git, but she wouldn't have it from her daughter. "You go and give your daddy the hug he must be desperate for, young lady. I can't believe you'd be so horrible!"

Abi paused and looked for confirmation from Grandpa who looked away in the face of Debbie's ferocity. With no choice, Abi shuffled over to her dad and half-heartedly leaned in for a hug. Debbie was disgusted. What was wrong with them?

And he was no better! Matthew didn't lean forward and scoop his little girl into his arms, squashing away all the doubts she had that he might not love her anymore.

He'd left her on Christmas Day. Her first one in years she could properly enjoy. He robbed her of that. So the least he owed her was his undying, unconditional love. What was he playing at?

Sitting in silence as things refused to bend in the direction Debbie desired.

"More brandy?" Mandy offered to silence. "I'll go and put the kettle on," she excused herself. Debbie felt like joining her, but worried what might be said in her absence. She couldn't risk Matthew wanting to leave again.

"So, where have you been, Son?" Alan asked, arms folded, steely stare at the floor as he spoke.

"Since when, Dad?" Matthew spat in reply.

"Since Christmas Day. What do you bloody think?"

"Oohh, let me think." Matthew was angry. Drumming his index finger against pointing lips in an am-dram performance of rumination. "Which Christmas do you mean?" Standing up with a ferocious stomp, "Don't act like you fucking care all of a sudden!"

Storming from the room, he gasped as he barged into the incoming figure of his mother as she bustled in removing her coat from her time away at the playground with her grandchildren.

"Matthew! You're back!"

"Oh my god," he hissed, and it was the last thing he said. Colour drained from his face and he crashed to the floor.

At that precise moment, the bizarre blue lighting of an emergency vehicle illuminated the half-light of the dusky hallway preceding a loud banging.

As Debbie stooped over the unconscious figure of her husband, Mandy rushed from the kitchen to open the front door. Stood with staid deportment were two burly policemen. "Good evening, madam. We are here to speak with Matthew Morrissey. Is he here?"

Chapter Thirty-four.

When the policemen entered the hallway, they were not alone. The scruffy Doctor Kay joined them, sweating so much, Mandy wondered if she should insist he stand on some newspaper to protect the parquet floor.

Despite his attendance with the police, they were all grateful to see a doctor given Matthew's sudden collapse. Helping him back to the wing-back chair, Debbie passed him a glass of water and Mandy added another sugar to his tea.

"What happened, Matthew?" Doctor Kay shrilled, and in reply to Matthew's shrug, he added, "You fainted. I really think we need to get you back into hospital."

"No! I'm fine."

Everyone remained silent, unsure how to proceed for the best.

"Clearly not, Matthew. Fainting could be a sign of an underlying problem."

"I'm fine. It was just the shock, that's all."

"It was when he saw Mary, my mother-in-law; his mother," Debbie over-explained. "He looked stunned. The next thing we knew, he collapsed."

Doctor Kay screwed his eyes in contemplation. "Why was that, Matthew?" He shrugged again. "Listen, Matthew. It is my professional opinion that you need to be in hospital."

"I've told you, I'm fine."

"I'm concerned about you, that's all."

"Thank you. But there's no need."

The doctor shifted his hefty weight from one foot to the other, his face reddening as he glanced round the room at the faces scrutinising his every move. Forcing himself up straight, he smiled at Matthew. "I can insist." Extending his arms, he waved his hands from the wrist, trivialising his threat. "I don't want to, you understand? But if I think it's in your best interests, I can section you under the mental health act. You do know that, Matthew, don't you?"

The high pitch made his words even more patronising.

Edging forward in his seat, strength restored, Matthew stared challengingly into the doctor's eyes, whose wet pools couldn't maintain their gaze. "On what grounds?"

Doctor Kay manifested a handkerchief from nowhere and held it to his mouth while he cleared his throat. "You're confused, Matthew. You couldn't even remember your own wife, could you? And then you left hospital against my advice. If I think you are a danger to yourself, or others, that's grounds for me to bring you in."

Matthew nodded along as though he had something up his sleeve. "I was confused. But I no longer am. So there are no grounds anymore. I'm sorry I left without telling you. That was wrong and you were clearly worried about me." Matthew lit his face with a simpering smile.

"But regarding my health. I just needed some TLC. I've had a hot bath, something delicious is cooking and I really don't want to miss out on dinner with my family. Not when I've only just found them again!"

"Your family whom you don't remember?"

Matthew let out a little laugh. "Of course I remember. I was upset, that's all. I was determined not to do what you wanted me to; not to say what you wanted me to say. It seems so silly now."

"So, aren't you going to introduce me to your family, Matthew?"

"Sorry. Yes, of course." Matthew gestured to each in turn. "This is my wife, Debbie. My father and mother; Alan and… Mary," he said after a pause.

"And…" Doctor Kay demanded, seeing several faces he's not known.

"And, my daughter."

"And?" he pressed. "What's her name?"

Matthew's lips wobbled, wondering if blurting out just anything might fool the doctor. In the end, he slumped with a defeated shrug. "Not everything has come back to me yet. You've taken my blood. I'll happily come to see you and discuss the results, but please don't take me away from here tonight. I need your help. I know that. But not tonight, okay?"

Doctor Kay's eyes were so tight, it was impossible to see if they were even open.

The policemen relaxed. Their previous tense stance calmed to an 'at-ease' slouch. Matthew was talking sense.

"You're the medical professional. But if he's not in any immediate danger, is sectioning him really the best way forward?" one of them queried the doctor.

"We can't expect these good people to cope if he becomes confused again," the Mickey Mouse modulation of Doctor Kay filled the room as he panicked, his authority questioned.

"We'll cope," Debbie shot at the doctor. "We don't want him to leave. Anything you need to do can be done as an outpatient, surely?"

"We don't know if he's damaged his head…"

"I haven't. Honestly. I've experienced a breakdown, obviously. But my head's fine. Check with a scan or something if you like. I'll do anything you want. I just don't want to do it tonight, and I don't want to stay in hospital. I want to stay here."

Debbie could feel the huge wad of fear dissolving. He'd said it. He *wanted* to be here. She wasn't going to lose him. The escaping misery ran down her face in stinging streams merging bizarrely with a smile which refused to wane.

209

Doctor Kay sighed. The police looked more than happy to leave the situation in the obviously capable hands of this successful, affluent family.

"Well," he finally said. "I suppose…"

And it was settled. Matthew would stay home until such time as concerns for his health; either from the blood tests currently taking place, or from observations by Debbie, or the others deemed otherwise. Appointments for relevant scans would be sent out in the post.

Doctor Kay shuffled his bulk back through the door. He didn't seem happy about it. The police were last to leave, their posture and their words full of apology. "Do telephone us at the station if you become worried about Matthew. Any time, night or day."

Debbie's smile warmed. "Yes, of course. Thank you."

Car doors were heard to slam and the vehicles drove away down the street, without blue lights.

Debbie walked back to the lounge. Everyone was sat on the couches studying Matthew like a scientific subject. He drummed his irritation at the scrutiny on the brass studs on the arm of the chair again. After an unbearable minute of silence, he launched himself to his feet and glared at them. What was wrong now?

"Where am I to sleep?"

Debbie's legs lost balance as a nausea swept over her. "In bed with me, of course. Why? Where do you want to sleep?"

Matthew's mouth fell askew. "I need my own space, thank you. The house looks plenty big enough."

"Yes. Of course. While you find your feet," Debbie forced through her abruptly arid throat. She walked briskly from the room. She hoped the others would think she was making up a fresh bed. She might, but the real reason was she had to leave the room.

Her body shook with the distress erupting from her. The hot and cold of Matthew toying with her threatened to break her.

How could anyone cope with this? Why was he being so horrible to her?

When she reached their bedroom, she ran over to their four-poster and threw herself on the soft covers. Burying her face in the four duck-down pillows, and confident she wouldn't be heard, she let out the wail of despair that had begged for release since she'd first walked in to see the stranger in the police cell.

It did her good. Thoroughly spent, she breathed in the feathery softness for a minute before pushing herself up to sitting. Smoothing her jeans with rigid palms from thighs to knees, she let out a deep sigh. It was just going to take time, that's all. He wanted to stay. That was an improvement to chasing him around Cabot Circus.

Remaking the bed, she left the room and went to the linen cupboard on the enormous galleried landing. Selecting sheets and covers for the spare bed, she made it up not for Matthew, but for herself. Sleeping in their bed would surely be beneficial for him and his struggling memory. And time away for her without the constant reminder that the other side of the bed was filled with her strange husband might prove a comfort too.

When she was done, she strode to the top of the stairs and stalled at the sight of Matthew taking his first step. "Hi," he said with a smile that may or may not have contained a fleck of warmth. "I'm exhausted. I'd like to turn in, if it's okay with you?"

Debbie had imagined her husband's return hundreds of times. In all her musings they'd laughed and chatted through the night; all the times she'd pictured him alive, anyway. "That's fine. Let me show you where to go."

When Debbie opened their bedroom door, Matthew objected. "This is your room. I wanted my own space." His face was the picture of dejection: pouting lips and a deep scowl. Thrusting his hands into his pockets, he turned to leave.

"But all your things are in here. I thought seeing them might jog your memory."

Matthew paused, patting his belt loop with an anchoring thumb. Wordlessly, he squeezed past Debbie into the bedroom. He strode to the walk-in wardrobe before addressing Debbie again.

"Thank you," he said with an air of finality. "I'll be fine now."

Debbie was torn. "Would you like me to stay? We could have a cuddle."

Matthew's eyes blinked this way and that, without looking up, he replied, "Maybe soon, okay? Sorry."

Debbie allowed the tears to trickle down her cheek. She wanted him to see how he'd hurt her. But she respected his wishes, turned, and walked away. Pausing at the top of the stairs, she took a firm grip of the bannister before descending; she couldn't trust her wobbly legs to carry her safely by themselves.

Silent stares greeted her as she swayed into the lounge.

"Brandy?" Mandy offered for the hundredth time, like a PR girl at an alcohol exhibition. But this time, Debbie nodded with such ferocity Mandy filled her glass and left the bottle within reach.

Sipping at the fiery smoothness, her eyes pleaded with her in-laws to reassure her; to say something to make it all right.

Shifting uncomfortably in their seats, Mary was the first to speak. "It's like his GCSE's all over again." Raising her eyes to the ceiling, she tut-tutted and shook her head, adding a curve to her lips in her pretence that this was perfectly normal in the world of Matthew Morrissey. "He'll come round. Best just to ignore him."

The rage festered in Debbie. She didn't have the energy to fight, but their unfeeling coldness was unbelievable. "I don't know how you're managing to stay so calm," she managed tactfully, hiding the snideness in her remark.

Mary took it as a compliment. "Well. It will do no good getting hysterical. It was too much sentiment that sent him running in the first place. No. he needs to see how normal everything is. He'll come round, you see if he doesn't."

Seeing her mother's distress, Abi scurried over and slunk in for a hug. Basking in the closeness and controlling the sharp stab of emotion it dislodged, she stroked Abi's hair until she was able to speak.

Drawing her face close to her own, she looked deeply into the sparkling blue of her eyes. There was love in there. And pain. She knew exactly why she'd not welcomed her daddy home with welcome arms. She needed to forgive him first.

"Abi, my love, are you not pleased Daddy's home?"

Abi pulled away and shrugged.

"Are you angry with Daddy, sweetheart?"

She shrugged again. A pout combined with a vicious tangling of her brows to suck the colour from her bright eyes leaving them grey and angry like her own. The storm brewing in Abi would not dissipate with comforting words from her mother, Debbie realised. There needed to be a storm.

Abi was so brave. She'd proved that. Debbie would have to leave her to find her own way through this. "Just so long as you know you can talk to me... about anything." The storm crackled and fizzed within her but she nodded.

"Charlotte! Shall we play something before bed?" she called out. Meeting Debbie's eye for approval, it was given readily, grateful that such approval was even being sought. Abi skipped off upstairs like she didn't have a care.

Chapter Thirty-five

He hadn't seen her. Stood inside the walk-in wardrobe, he failed to detect the handle turn and the door swing open. Abi stepped in, the tempest in her eyes about ready to strike.

Padding across the floor, her dainty feet made no sound.

"What are you doing?" she demanded loudly.

Her desired response of watching him clutch at his chest and declare she'd made him jump out of his skin failed to happen. Instead, he turned calmly and simply stared without answering, making her wonder if her entrance had been quite so undetected after all.

When he'd treated her to enough of his unblinking glare, he returned his attention to the hanging clothes. The open leather holdall was already full, but Matthew forced a few more shirts in before squeezing the heavy metal zipper closed.

"Are you leaving?"

Matthew ignored her again.

"Don't go!" she said, and threw her arms around his legs. Matthew stared down at her. His hand hovered above her silky blonde hair before he returned it to his side without touching her.

Pulling abruptly away, Abi squealed, "You're not my daddy!" Running from the room, her socked feet skidded on the polished floor at the edge not covered by the long woven runner that stretched the length of the landing. She tripped and fell headlong into the wall, her head bouncing off the plaster with a thud.

Matthew cursed and threw the leather bag down. Rushing to the girl as she lay on the floor, he didn't know what to do to help her.

With a sudden flash of movement, Abi twisted thrusting clenched fists into the floor, propelling her almost back onto her feet. But not quite.

It happened in slow motion. Her slip-sliding along the edge of the landing. The stairs looming like a cobra ready to strike. Matthew lunged forward, grabbing at her foot as she pitched headlong between the bannister posts. He watched as she disappeared from his view before glancing down at the white sock in his hand.

Scarcely able to move, he forced one foot in front of the other. He had to see what had become of her.

Reaching the top step, Abi was clinging to the newel post, her instinctive grabbing as she fell saved her. Matthew reached down and took her hand. Hauling her slight figure the few steps she'd fallen he seized her up and brushed her off.

"Get away from me," she said in a hushed whisper. Matthew stood up straight. She was fine, thank goodness. "You're not my daddy," she wailed as a balloon of tears blurred her blue eyes. As she scurried away to another door, the other child blinked out at him.

Matthew turned away and answered under his breath. "I never said I was…"

"Everything okay?" Mandy hollered from the hallway. Matthew returned to the top of the stairs and glowered down at her.

"Perfectly fine. Thank you." And with that, he strode to his room and closed the door with a competent click.

"What happened?" Debbie asked with a slur.

"Nothing much. Matthew wandering around upstairs. He's back in your room now."

Debbie nodded and swilled the dribble of amber liquid around the bottom of the glass trying to decide whether to add to it. She drained it. As she watched herself struggle to right it on the table beside her, a spark in her brain just reached her consciousness and told her she'd had enough.

"I'm gonna go up now, too. See you in the morning." Kissing the tips of her fingers, she blew them to the room as her way of saying goodnight.

Swaying at the foot of the stairs, she held the rail for support. "What a day," she shushed, and plonked a heavy foot on the first step. Heaving herself to the top, she began to turn to her room. "Naughty, naughty," she admonished herself before walking to the spare room she'd selected with its view over their back garden.

Stripping to her underwear, she realised she'd forgotten to include a nightie when she'd brought through the sheets. Growling at herself, she hopped into bed and hauled the duvet over her. It was perfectly warm so she removed her bra and knickers.

Making a 'sheet-angel' under the covers, the cool of the satin on her skin soothed the day away. "What a day!" she said again. The next time she blinked her eyes tried to open but slammed shut, closing herself away from her burdens.

Dawn had broken and it was a bright day. So bright, Debbie feared she may have slept through to afternoon. Scouring the floor for her discarded clothes, she sniffed at yesterday's knickers and considered going commando.

With a rueful shake of her head, she tugged them over her legs and tried to forget the face she'd pulled. They were soon covered by her jeans. It would do until she'd had something to eat. She'd shower then, and hopefully she'd be permitted back into her own bedroom!

Trotting downstairs, she selected a bowl and browsed the larder for a cereal she'd like. She opted for a fruity granola and had half a grapefruit to start.

Placing the filled bowl, spoon, milk and grapefruit on a tray, she carried it through to the breakfast room. Pushing open the door with her foot, she gasped, surprised to see Matthew dressed and staring through the window at Clifton Suspension Bridge.

"Good morning. Did you sleep okay?" she asked as she took the seat at the end of the table; not beside him. He didn't seem any more receptive to closeness than when she'd last seen him.

He nodded and sipped at a black coffee. This was good. If he'd made himself a drink and found his favourite spot with his favourite view, that was a step in the right direction.

She scooped the grapefruit into her mouth and shuddered at its bitterness. She wasn't sure she even liked them, but there was something in them her body craved. When she'd finished and she could pour the creamy cold milk onto the sugary cereal, she was thankful.

Chewing a fruity mouthful, Matthew interrupted her and stopped her jaw mid-chew.

"What's this all about?" he said, glancing down in examination of his fingernails; their cracked grubbiness seeming to bother him.

"What do you mean? What's *what* all about?"

Matthew sighed and turned to face her. "It's all very convincing. I did wonder how you knew so much about me, birthdays, where I was born. But now I understand; my father must have told you. I feel foolish because that's why I agreed to come back with you."

Debbie still hadn't chewed and the mouthful of oats was absorbing every drop of moisture in her mouth.

"Everyone seems to be playing their part, but I can't for the life of me work out why."

Debbie reddened. She needed to fetch a drink to save herself from the congealing food in her mouth, but her brain had seized in the onslaught of Matthew's bizarreness.

"Who's the girl?" he asked, taking another sip of coffee.

Debbie brought her napkin up to her lips and daintily ejected her dry mouthful into in. Replacing it to her lap, she thought it added perfectly to yesterday's outfit. Fighting back the rage, she coached herself before responding. He's confused. He's in

217

the middle of a breakdown. He's not meaning to be as offensive and ridiculous as he's being!

"Abi? She's your daughter. *Our* daughter."

Matthew was unnervingly calm. "Are you sure about that? She doesn't seem so convinced."

Well who can blame her! I'm not sure who the hell you are either! -she didn't say. "I'm sure," she confirmed with a smile. Just stay calm. That's all you can do. It's what he needs.

"And the red-head?"

Stemming the irritated sigh aching to leap from her lips, Debbie replied. "That's Mandy. Your sister. I thought you remembered her? You told the doctor you remembered her."

"Oh, I do. I remember her very well." He was making no sense. "So the red-head is Mandy, my sister. And the other woman is Mary, my mother. Right?"

Debbie beamed. He was getting it. "Yes, that's right."

"Bullshit!" Matthew screamed and flung his coffee cup at the wall, shards of bone china showered the floor. Throwing back his chair, he stomped to the door and slammed it so hard it rocked the room.

Mandy was yawning and stretching as she entered the kitchen. "Hi Matthew. You okay? What was the noise?"

"Oh, hello, '*sis*'," he spat in disgust. Pushing past her, he thudded up the stairs.

Chapter Thirty-six

"What on earth has got into him?" Mandy breathed into the breakfast room. Stopping in her tracks, the sharp look on her sister-in-law's pale face made her scurry round the table and hold her. "It'll be okay. He's not well, but this isn't the real Matthew. With our support, he'll come through this." Squeezing tighter as Debbie clung to her, she added, "Don't upset yourself. He's home, and he's healthy—physically. It'll just take some time," and maybe some medication, she thought.

Debbie let out the sigh she'd held back for Matthew's benefit. "You're right. I know you're right. But we've been through so much. Abi's illness took us to the edge and we came through. And then this! I'm not sure I can cope, Mandy." Burying her face in her arms, she collapsed onto the table in front of her, furious sobs shaking the table and echoing woefully around the room.

Dewy eyes stinging, Mandy stroked Debbie's head. "Come on, Matthew. Sort your shit out," she breathed silently, vowing to make having a little chat with her brother a priority. They hadn't always got on, but they'd always had that understanding only siblings could have. She wouldn't take his crap. Upsetting her like he had poor Debbie was not a likely outcome.

Her stroking of Debbie's hair became more forceful and Debbie raised her swollen face to wince up at her.

"Sorry, Deb. But he's made me cross. I'm going to have a talk with my darling brother!"

"Don't make it worse! Don't upset him."

Upset him? He really had got her fearing what he might do, but Mandy had seen it all before, and if anyone could get him out of his big sulk, it was her! Of course, she knew there was more to it, but some home truths would be just what he needed to get him to take responsibility; the first vital step.

Then, she'd be as caring a little sister as you could ever hope to find. She'd make sure he went to appointments; make sure he took medication (if they gave him any) and make sure he bloody well got back to normal as quickly as possible. His little family had gone through quite enough.

Stopping with a fixed smile, she offered coffee and returned to the kitchen to get some thought-aiding sustenance in the form of caffeine and sugar.

Clattering around in the big kitchen helped to disperse a little of the anger she felt towards her brother. That was probably helpful. Whilst she was keen to take a firm hand, she didn't want to fulfil Debbie's fears, upset him and make things worse.

Debbie stared through the window for the entire time it took for Mandy to devour two syrup filled waffles and two cups of coffee. Mandy presumed she'd taken comfort in her determination to sort her brother out. There was certainly no point in persuading her things would get better. She'd leave her in peace and actually make it happen.

Marching up the stairs topped up her resolve, but she had to put it on hold as too much coffee demanded its release from her bladder. It was surprisingly quiet upstairs. Abi and Charlotte not making their usual ruckus. Pulling up her knickers and trousers she puckered her lips askew, pondering if she should check on them before speaking to Matthew.

Unwilling to delay the inevitable, she assumed they were sleeping—exhausted after the excitement of Matthew's return (albeit well hidden excitement.) If she woke them, she'd be on breakfast duty, or at the very least, she'd be drawn into their exuberant plans. No. She needed to stay focussed. It wouldn't take long.

Knocking firmly so that he knew she meant business, when no answer came she knocked again. Silence from beyond the sturdy oak door disconcerted her. Electing instantly to risk his annoyance and open it, she was surprised at her relief that it did open, appreciating the significance of a locked or barricaded door.

Matthew mirrored his wife's stance, staring aimlessly through the glass. She was certain he was aware of her, but he ignored her until she stood next to him.

"I don't understand why he's doing this," he sighed.

It was then Mandy noticed the bulging leather holdall at his feet and his hand gripping the handles ready to run at a moment's notice.

Ignoring his comment because it didn't make sense, and his apparently imminent departure being a more urgent priority, she spoke in a calm, slow manner. "You're not thinking of leaving us again, are you, Matthew?"

Tightening his hold on the handles, bloodshot eyes turned and met hers, the pain behind them a shock. Mandy reached a comforting hand to his but stopped half-way as he stiffened in dislike of the prospect.

"I can't stay. Why would I?" he shook his head, the question swirling, unanswerable.

Mandy drew out the chair beside him. Unsure what to say, she joined him in staring through the glass. Fingering the seam of her trousers, pinching the fabric between thumb and forefinger, she eventually broke the silence. "I don't understand, Matthew. I don't know what you've been through or why you're acting like this, and I won't pretend I do."

"You don't know what I've been through? That's doubtful."

He was upset. One of those 'If you don't know what's wrong, I'm not going to tell you' stand-offs. Suspecting getting it wrong would be a bad idea, she kept her platitudes generic but tried to be comforting.

"I know it's been hard. I know we should have realised you weren't coping; spotted it sooner. Not Debbie so much. She had enough to cope with, but Mum and Dad…"

The suddenness of Matthew's bolt from the chair sent a flood of adrenaline through Mandy. Heart racing, her brain stalled at the change of pace and she welded to her chair.

Matthew stood, the bag banging against his legs as he propelled it away with flexed thighs every time it came to rest. The angry pendulum slowed in Mandy's silence.

"Sorry," she said. And she was. She'd wanted to make things better, but she could see now. He was more unwell than she'd ever seen him. This was so much more than his exam breakdown, and she should have realised.

He'd built a future, far greater than anyone else ever had in their family. Maybe it was the GCSE's that had spurred him on. You hear it a lot. He hadn't given in to the pressure his good results had mapped out for him. He followed his dream He didn't go into accountancy or law, despite plenty of pushing from Mum and Dad. He did his own thing.

So with a determination, he embraced the tangent of his dreams, put himself through college and learned everything there was to learn about building boats. He met and fell for the love of his life, and together they'd produced the apple of their eye in Abigail.

When Abi got sick, Matthew hadn't had Debbie's luxury of being with Abi all the time they believed they might lose her because he was building their business (and hers, truth be told. Her interior design company wouldn't exist if it wasn't for his generosity.)

She could see it now: he'd never grieved. He hadn't had time. So expecting him to cope just because it all turned out okay was naïve and lazy of them. How they hadn't seen what that had done to him would be a source of shame to her forever more. But she'd make it better, and she'd never let him down again.

"Sorry," she said again. "I've let you down."

"Let me down?" Matthew sputtered. "Let me down! You are a cruel, manipulative bastard. You must get what this is doing to me. You must have some clue. He must have told you!"

Breathless from the agony crushing him inside, Matthew collapsed back onto the chair, the bag drooping to the floor escaped his grip. He didn't have the energy to go anywhere.

Watching the result of her comforting words upsetting him more, Mandy didn't know what to say, but she was relieved his departure seemed less imminent at least. "I get it, Matthew," she lied. "You're angry. But you're safe now."

His legs twitched, testing their ability to speed Matthew from this torture before flopping, knowing they could not be relied upon. The grief overwhelmed him and he allowed his limbs to melt. "I thought I'd got over all this… well as much as anyone can. He must have gone to a lot of trouble to set all this up. To find you, and that 'Mary' woman."

"Mum, you mean?"

"Oh stop it! For fuck sake, just stop it, will you?"

Mandy's lips moved up and down, her eyes taut crescents of confusion. "I don't understand, Matthew, I honestly don't. But as your sister…"

"Sister? But you're not my sister, are you!"

Mandy's mind whirred. Had Matthew discovered some family secret? Was he adopted or something? Of course! Having gone through all he had, something must have been said on Christmas Day that rocked him to his core. And he was angry with Dad; denying Mum, and her as his sister.

"Matthew, I'm so sorry. I had no idea. What did Dad say to you then?"

Matthew's eyes squinted. "Say to me? He hasn't said anything to me. Which makes this even more preposterously cruel."

"Well, you're going to have to explain. Why am I not your sister, 'cos it's news to me." She hoped her own ignorance of the family secret would bond them. Surely it had to help?

"Don't be ridiculous!" he raged.

"I'm not. I have no idea what you're talking about."

A coldness clouded Matthew's eyes. The pain pushed down into their deep pools. "So, despite what I've been saying: how upset it's made me, you are going to sit there and insist you are my sister? Amanda?"

Knowing it would aggravate him, but with no other option, she stammered, "But I am."

His limp limbs found a sudden ferocious velocity as his hand slammed down on the table in the window in front of them. "No! You're NOT!"

Mandy shuddered in the sheer kinetic explosion of his utter fury. Finding herself matching his angry scream, she yelled back. "What are you talking about? How do you know I'm not your sister?"

Matthew slowed his breathing, leaned forward in his seat so their knees were almost touching and forced the intensity of his hate-filled stare into her eyes. Boring into her, he opened his mouth, ready to destroy her.

In a deep, slow breathy baritone, Matthew unleashed his closing argument. "I know you're not my sister… because my sister is dead!"

Mandy gasped. She hadn't expected that. But what he said next stopped her heart cold.

"And I know my sister is dead…" he paused, eyes falling to the floor, the effort in saying the words creasing him. Puffing out his chest, he forced his gaze to meet hers once more. "… I know she's dead, because *I* killed her!"

Chapter Thirty-seven

Matthew had stood in Wexford road for at least half an hour. Watching. Waiting. Confident as he could be that he had been unseen, his heart pounded as he stepped towards the front door. This was it. This was the last chance to find out what was going on. If he came away with no answers, he had nothing else to try. He'd be finished.

The heady mix of optimism and despair edged him closer and closer to the home of his childhood. Reaching the gate, he pushed it open with an eerie creak but couldn't bring himself to step onto the path.

"If this is the end, there's nothing to gain by delaying it," he muttered, shuffling on. Throwing back his shoulders, he strode to the front door. With his finger poised ready to ring the bell, he paused again a hair's breadth from the button. A final clench of tenacity drove it forward, the shrill reverberation from beyond the door thrust him to the point of no return.

There was no answer, but Matthew felt sure the place wasn't empty. Pressing hard on the button again, an unreasonable anger surfaced and he carried on pushing even though the jarring noise already echoed in the hallway beyond.

Shadows moved behind the stippled glass, and a figure made slow progress toward him. Leaving his finger on the bell, he waited until he was sure he'd get an answer.

The door pulled open. Memories of the weird doorstep encounter with Tom King all those months ago robbed him of relief even though inches from him stood his father. Matthew opened his arms ready to hold him; the only friend, the only familiar person he'd seen for half a year. "Dad," he cried, "You're here! Oh, thank heavens." Tears flooding down his face, he flung himself at Alan and drew him close.

The embrace was cold; one-sided, but Matthew clung on for his life. It would be over now. He had finally returned to reality. It might be bewildering but he'd understand at last. The discomfort of the unreciprocated hug confused him and he pulled away.

A palm on each of his dad's shoulders kept him square as Matthew stared into his cold gaze. "What's happened, Dad? I know it's bad, but I'm here now. Tell me. I can fix it!"

Alan sighed a heavy sigh. "You'd best come in." Turning, he left Matthew to follow him as he opened the door to the lounge. Matthew flinched in surprise at the mess. It was never usually untidy, but the room was littered with dirty cups and food wrappers and an ashtray so full it threatened to dislodge in a heap of ashy scree onto the crowded coffee table where it took pride of place.

Alan hefted a stack of newspapers from the sofa so his son could have somewhere to sit. "Crosswords," he said, nodding to the pile in his arms. "I keep them for the crosswords."

"Oh," Matthew replied. There was nothing else he could say.

Balancing the stack of papers on their new temporary home on the kitchen worktop, Alan paused to fill the kettle. Ambling back to the lounge, the sighs escaped his mouth with every breath. Slumping as softly as he could on a chair at the fold-down dining table, he crossed his ankle over his knee and waited.

Matthew drummed his fingers on his thigh. He had a million questions, but gawping at the chaos, one snaked its way to his lips before any other. "Where's Mum?"

Alan squirmed in his seat but didn't answer. Well, that can wait, Matthew supposed. "I am so pleased to see you, Dad. Aren't you going to tell me what's going on? My life has been blown apart. I've got my theories, but I need to hear it from you."

Alan sighed again. "They said you might come."

"They? Who? What do you mean?"

"Doesn't matter," Alan shrugged it off. "What do you want?"

This was weird. Just when he thought sense had returned to his life, his Dad was being as bizarre as everyone else. "Dad! I want to know what's going on. Where's Debbie and Abi? What's happened to the apartment and where's Mandy? And Mum?"

Alan shook his head. "They said you were being like this again."

"Who, Dad? Tell me."

"The bloody hospital, who'd you sodding think?"

Matthew stiffened. They'd got to him too. Had they convinced his whole family he was mad. Is that why Debbie had gone? Taken Abi to keep away from mad Matthew? "What did they say… exactly?"

Matthew could see the cogs crunch into life as Alan considered his response. "They said you were confused… In denial. And of course, they told me you had escaped again."

"Great. Now how about you tell me what the fuck has been going on since Christmas Day? You're pissing me off. Obviously you and Mum are having issues," he said pointedly glaring round the room. "And I don't doubt my disappearance has had a lot to do with it and you're angry. But I haven't been gone on purpose. And I didn't need to be in hospital. They were keeping me against my will and I had to get out. I had to save my family."

"Bit late for that, boy."

"Why?" Matthew screeched. "You have to tell me. This isn't fair."

Alan perched on his seat regarding his son. "Are you crazy? Are you seriously asking me these questions?" Slapping an open palm to his forehead, he sat back in his chair. "What am I saying? Of course you are. You need to go back. Get help."

"I need you to tell me where the fuck I can find my wife and child."

"What wife and child? Who are you talking about?"

"Dad, you're scaring me. Stop it!"

"No, you stop it! Do you think yours was the only life destroyed by what happened? By what you did? I lost everything too. But I manned up and got on with my life as best I could. Didn't scrounge off the state, and I certainly didn't try and kill myself! Maybe I should have killed you, you stupid little bastard!"

Matthew lunged for him. Grabbing his collar, he hauled him up, the chair falling backwards catapulted horded crap in a shower of debris. "I don't understand, Dad. I don't have any idea what you're saying." Tightening his grip, he moved his face within an inch of his father's. "So I'll make it crystal clear. You are going to tell me exactly what happened when I left on Christmas Day. Now!" he shook him fiercely.

"Left where?"

"My god, Dad! I can't believe this. What happened on Christmas Day, after I left you and Mum and Mandy and Charlotte, and of course Debbie and Abi, to go and get batteries?"

Alan flopped in Matthew's grip. His weight too much to hold, Matthew bent to right the fallen chair and lowered his dad back onto it.

"You're crazy," he wailed.

"Just tell me."

"You're making stuff up. You have to be. You can't actually believe this bollocks."

"Where are they, Dad? Where's Mum? Mandy? Abi? Where, Dad?" Matthew's shaking fist brushed against his dad's lips. "Where? Tell me, or so bloody help me…"

"Dead, you stupid shit. They're dead, aren't they!"

Matthew released his grip and fell back. Catching himself on the edge of the sofa. It took an age for his mouth to form the words ricocheting round his head, but at last he squeezed one word through the lump in his throat, "How?"

"Oh. For Christ's sake, Matthew. I don't have the time or the inclination to go through it all again! I've got on with my life. Coped the best way I knew how. You haven't. I get it. But I won't let you drag me down with you."

Matthew's mind whirled but any other questions he thought to ask were interrupted by a sturdy knock on the door and the bell shrilling into life again. Alan stiffened.

"Who's that?" Matthew demanded.

"Look, son. You need help."

"For fuck sake, Dad. You phoned the police! That's why you took so long answering the door!" Matthew bolted from the room to the back door. He'd seen the unmistakable silhouette of two police helmets and wasn't prepared to stick around to find out what they wanted. Scarpering along the path, he vaulted the fence at the bottom of the garden and sprinted to the next street.

He was sure they'd be in pursuit, but he knew these streets like only someone who'd lived here as a chopper-riding nine-year-old could. Weaving this way and that, he effected his escape easily, but what was the point. Unless his dad had gone completely mad, what was the point in anything?

Chapter Thirty-eight

Mandy stood and backed into the window. "What do you mean? 'You killed her?' I'm not dead! I'm here." She gestured fiercely up and down her body. "Whatever it is you think you've done, you haven't. Do you see?"

She could see the strain in his eyes as he tried to compute the situation. Jabbing on, she knew she'd reach her mark. "I'm here. I'm fine. You haven't killed anyone, Matthew."

"Not *you*! Mandy. My sister. When she was a little girl."

Mandy's legs buckled and she staggered into the table. "Oh my god, Matthew. What have you done? What have you done!"

"I told you," he cried as Mandy fled from the room. Charlotte, Abigail. She should have known that quiet was too quiet. Bursting through Abi's bedroom door, she could see both girls lying completely still in Abi's huge double bed. The covers were pulled up to their noses.

"What did you do, Matthew, what did you do?"

Edging towards the pair in the bed, she reached out a trembling hand to her little girl. "Charlotte, Charlotte, sweetie." Nothing. No movement.

Her arms shook so much, but she couldn't bring herself to touch her daughter and confirm her worst nightmare. She could almost feel the cold, clammy flesh of death kneaded between her fingers. With a resolute shake of her head, she thrust her fingers forward.

Before her hand even reached Charlotte's skin, the two girls leapt from the bed throwing the duvet into the air.

"Mummy!"

"Auntie Mandy!" they cried, bouncing around on top of the covers. "Did we scare you?" they giggled.

As Mandy's heart thudded against her chest, she nodded. "Oh yes. You got me good." And she scooped them into her arms. As they faced behind her, she allowed the tears of relief to fall. Batting them away, she brought the cousins around to face her again. "Come on. We'll go and get some breakfast, shall we?"

"Yay! Can we have pancakes?" they skipped.

Mandy walked slowly behind. "You can have whatever you like."

As the girls trotted down the stairs, Mandy popped her head back into Debbie and Matthew's bedroom. He still sat, staring out of the window. He didn't look up as she waited in the doorway.

"We have to get him help. We can't do it by ourselves."

Debbie nodded. She knew Mandy was right. "Where's that doctor's phone number?"

The necessary calls were made, and a short while after the pancake debris had been cleared there was a knock at the door.

"Should we go and get him, or let them go up to him?"

Debbie shrugged. "We'll let them decide, I guess."

Mandy pulled open the door. "Mrs Morrissey?" a gangling figure held out an ID lanyard. "I'm Steve, one of the psychiatric nurses from Southmead. And this is my colleague, Gemma."

Steve's long limbs gave him the appearance of an insect. His striped woollen jumper, too warm for the time of year, jarred with his shock of ginger hair, which fought with his freckles which in turn managed to offend next to the fabric of his jumper. Even the gold of his wedding ring made an unpleasant addition to the orangey hue.

Gemma, in contrast to Steve's pole body, was robust, round and solid. She almost looked as though she could roll away;

like she might wobble, but not fall down. Her full blonde bob accentuated the circumference of her face. Between them, the pair stood with uncomfortable smiles looking like a modern take on Laurel and Hardy.

"I'm Mrs Morrissey. Please come in. Thank you for coming so soon."

Steve grinned, a nasty yellowing of a tooth set back from the rest added one colour too many. "That's quite alright. We were in your neighbourhood, so…"

"Where's Matthew, then?" Gemma asked, her Bristolian accent the strongest Debbie or Mandy had heard in a long time.

"He's upstairs. Should we get him, or do you want to go up?"

"Is he expectin' us?" Gemma asked, and in response to the ladies' shaking heads, she tapped Steve's arm and said, "We'll go up to him then. Is that okay?"

Debbie continued nodding. "Right at the top of the stairs. It's the first door on the right."

"Hang on, do you want some background first?"

Stepping back from the stairs, Steve took on his listening stance; head cocked and hands clasped in front of him.

"Well, the thing is, he seems to think he's killed someone."

Debbie gasped and clasped Mandy's arm for support. "Who?" she whispered, and Gemma and Steve cocked their heads like dogs at the rustle of a biscuit packet.

"Well, that's the weirdest thing. He says he killed me. When I was a girl."

Steve nodded as though this was all part of a normal day. "Thanks. We'll go up and have a chat with him now." Extending yet more orange with his nicotine stained fingers, he brushed Debbie's arm, "Try not to worry."

Tramping up two steps with each stride, Steve made rapid progress to the top, while Gemma took a one foot meets the other half-step at a time snail's pace. He happily waited at the top sporting what he seemed to presume was a confident professional smile.

Reaching the door, Steve gave a gentle rap before the inevitable louder knock when Matthew didn't answer. Pushing the door open, the pair stepped inside to see Matthew sitting in a chair at a table in the bowed window.

"Hello, Matthew. Do you mind if we have a quick word?"

Matthew turned to face them. His eyes lit up in recognition. "I can't believe they've called you, but I might actually be glad to see you."

"That's great. My name's Steve," said Steve, arm outstretched. "And this is my colleague, Gemma."

"Aright, bod?" she greeted with a smiling nod.

Matthew stared. "I know," he glowered.

"Do you mind if we take a seat? P'raps Gemma could sit on the bed. Would that be okay?"

"Yes. Whatever. Do you think you could explain what's going on, please?"

They took their positions, Steve placing his hands flat on the table like blueprints of their plans. "What it is, Matthew, your family are worried about you. I understand you've been missing for a while. Is that right?"

Matthew remained motionless and Steve continued. "Mandy, your sister, tells us you might have something troubling you. Why do you think she might have said that, Matthew?"

Matthew sat forward. "She's not my sister."

Steve nodded, but Gemma spoke. "Tell us what happened to your sister, Matthew."

"I've told them all before. At the hospital."

"Humour us?"

Matthew sagged back in his seat. He didn't want to talk about it, but then he wanted answers. He really did want those. "My sister is dead."

"And how did she die, Matthew?"

Smoothing fingertip against the fabric of his trousers, Matthew looked up, moist eyes meeting Gemma's. There was a short version and there was a long version. The short one was too abrupt. It placed the blame on Matthew far too quickly. If he was going to tell them what happened, he needed to ease up to it.

"It was Christmas Day. I was seven. My sister, Amanda—Mandy—was two and a half." He stopped. The pain evident in his face as his cheeks hung in dour demonstration. Pleading with his eyes to make it stop.

"Carry on. I know it must be hard, but we need to hear it if we're to help."

Matthew nodded. "We'd opened all our presents. She'd got more than me. Well it seemed like it. There was a shared present that should have been mine, but…"

"What was that then?"

Matthew hung his head and garbled. "A computer. Mandy had loads of doll stuff: a pram, a rocking crib, a cooker… all sorts. I had one action-man, and my share in the computer because it was 'expensive'."

"Okay, Matthew. So what happened? Take your time."

"It was all my fault. Mandy was in her room so I snuck into the box room at the front which was now the new computer room. It was all set up. It took my dad most of the morning and a lot of swearing, and then of course he had to have a go, but he didn't know what he was doing.

"When it was finally free, I loaded up one of two games we had. Took forever with the little tape player. I had to get the volume just right or it wouldn't load. I remember it like it was yesterday; 'The Hunchback of Notre Dame.'" Matthew sighed and blinked his grey eyes.

"I'd barely started playing, when suddenly Mandy was tugging at my arm wanting to have a go. 'In a minute, Mandy,' I said. 'It's not your turn.'" The tears streamed into Matthew's mouth. "I'm sorry," he spluttered. Can I have a minute?"

"Of course." She turned to Steve. "Why don't you get Matthew a glass of water?"

Easing his gangling height from the confines of the bay window, Steve stepped to the door. He paused in the opening, hoping Matthew wouldn't restart without him.

As soon as he was out of earshot, Gemma hopped off the bed and took his seat. Resting her forearms on the table, her smile was warm and encouraged Matthew to talk again.

"I pushed her. I pushed my little sister because I cared more about a fucking game!"

Gemma was sure she knew what happened next, but the details seemed important. "Then what happened. What happened to Mandy then, Matthew?"

The words trembled between Matthew's lips. Once released they could never go back. Blinking his eyes shut, he uttered the next line with them closed. "She fell," he rasped. Shuddering. He couldn't say another word. Burying his face in his hands, he clawed at his skin, guttural cries echoing from the walls as pain of the memories sliced into him like mortal spears.

"Here's your glass of water, Matthew," Steve said as he closed the door. Looking up, he saw Matthew's distraught face. "Oh. Is everything okay?"

Gemma nodded. "It will be."

Matthew brought his knees so his feet sat on the cushion, and he swayed back and forth and side to side.

Steve placed the water in front of him but Matthew didn't touch it. Muttering under his breath at his lost seat, he took Gemma's place on the bed.

"What happened when she fell, Matthew?"

He stopped rocking and turned his gaze to her. Moving his feet back to the floor, he rested his hands on his knees. "I don't know… I'm not certain. She screamed. I looked back…" Matthew screwed the knees of his trousers in his fists and began swaying again, his glazed eyes stared into space.

"When I looked…" A sob creaked in his throat. "… she was gone. Then I heard Mum crying and Dad was yelling. The bannister posts had snapped. She must have fallen into them and broken them," he sobbed, the swaying making the chair legs bump off the ground.

"When I peered over the edge…" he stopped talking.

"Oh my, Matthew. How awful." Reaching across, Gemma placed her hand on his arm. "Poor Matthew."

"Mum took it worst. They both blamed me. And they should. It was my fault. I killed my sister. And my mother too."

Struggling to keep her hand in its comforting position, Gemma had to ask, "Your mother? How? What happened to her?"

Matthew's eyes still stared at nothing. He needed the detachment to continue. "They blamed me. *I* blamed me. We never got over it. School work suffered, but it was better than being at home. They called it an accident, but I knew they didn't believe it. They never hugged me. They barely even spoke to me again." Gemma squeezed his arm for him to continue, but she feared where this tale might finish.

"The next year. Christmas. My dad had put a tree up, but Mum made him take it out. There were no presents. I don't think I would have wanted any. It was hard. So, so hard. And like I say. Mum took it worst. Dad tried to make it a bit Christmassy when Mum went up to bed early. We pulled some old crackers from the year before and watched 'Back to the future' wearing silly hats. But then the screaming started again…"

"She was dead, Mum. Taken loads of pills. Dad called an ambulance, but she'd been dead for ages by the time they got there. And I'd never spoken to him since until yesterday. It must be his revenge. He must think I haven't suffered enough. But it's weird."

"What's weird?" Steve piped up.

"Getting these people to pretend to be my family. The Mandy girl doesn't even look how I imagined my sister turning out. She was much prettier. But the mum? Wow, he's done a fucking good job finding her, I'll give him that. And it's worked. It's brought it all back. And now I feel like this." His eyes flashed. "Like I did before."

"And how's that?" Gemma asked with a caramel soothing voice.

"I don't want to be here."

"What do you mean 'here?' Here in this house?"

Matthew shot a look that indisputably clarified it was more than just this house he wanted to leave.

"Don't do anything silly, Matthew. Leave it with us and we'll find out what's going on, okay?"

Matthew nodded. He knew what was going on, but having his cruel dad forced to admit it to the nurses oddly satisfied him.

Chapter Thirty-nine

The family, minus Matthew, sat in the huge lounge on two of the sofas, leaving another frce for Steve and Gemma to take centre stage. When they'd repeated Matthew's versions of his unforgettable Christmas, there followed a stunned silence.

Debbie, hands clasped tightly, stared at the floor, her in-laws exchanging incredulous glances. Eventually, Alan spoke. "That's some story. Where has he come up with that?" Gnashing his teeth, he fumed, "It makes me feel sick!"

"It's difficult to say, but he is pretty convinced it's true," Gemma replied with a stern nod.

"But how?" Debbie's soft voice rose from the corner.

Steve tilted his head. "I don't know, I'm afraid."

But Gemma was more willing to have a stab at a diagnosis. "I think you guys have got it spot on." With all eyes on her, she basked in the glory. With gregarious gestures, she explained. "The last couple of years have taken a lot out of him. His brain identified issues from his childhood and that's where it took him."

"Issues? There are no issues in Matthew's bloody childhood."

"No offense, but it's obvious Mandy's your favourite," Debbie carried on despite the gasps from the other three. "You seemed to change a bit when he had success with the boat yard, but what did you do? Demand he set Mandy up in business!"

"He was happy to do it."

"He was. Of course he was," Debbie agreed with her father-in-law. "But I'm sure it bothered him that it was your first consideration. It bothered me."

Mandy uncrossed her legs and crossed them the other way. "Sorry," she said, but her face couldn't disguise her true feelings. "But I'd have done the same for him…"

"Listen," Gemma commanded. "All families have their problems. When I mentioned issues in Matthew's childhood, it wasn't to apportion blame. Do try to understand his perspective though. He needs your support. He hasn't invented all this on purpose."

Steve took up the mantle now, his uncertainty of moments before giving way to a new authority. "Do you have anything to convince Matthew he's remembering wrong? Photos, childhood teddies or toys. You know, sentimental things."

Debbie left the room without speaking and returned with an armful of leather-bound albums. She passed them out, one each, leaving the remaining couple on the seat beside her.

"Where did you get all these?" Mary mumbled.

Debbie glanced up from the photos she was staring at. "Matthew's childhood ones? There weren't that many, admittedly, but they're all from your loft. Don't you remember? I got them out when we got married. For the wedding. That one of him holding two ice-cream cones was in the foyer of the hotel at the reception." Mary nodded. "Next to one of me in a sandpit with my face covered in sand!"

"It's all round your mouth! Did you eat it?" Alan scorned with a smile

A chuckle rippled around the room. Its relief welcome. "You said I could keep them because they were no use to anyone in the loft. So I did. There's only about a dozen of Matthew and hundreds of Mandy. Half the ones of Matthew have got Mandy in them!"

Mary quietened. The instant of laughter now tempered by the harsh critique of her parenting.

"We're really proud of him!" Exclaimed Alan. "He's done really well."

"Until he had a breakdown with all the stress. I can see it written all over your faces! 'When's Matthew going to pull his finger out and get back to normal? Get back to earning?'"

"That's unfair, Debbie," Mandy tried to be the voice of reason.

"Is it?!" Debbie yelled, slouching back into her corner. She'd said enough for now.

Rising up from their seats in unison, Gemma and Steve stood. "We'll take a couple of these up to Matthew, okay?" No-one answered, so they backed quietly from the room, sharing a look when they were sure they were out of sight.

Striding with new verve back to their patient, they were relieved though not surprised to find him exactly as they had left him.

"What was the yelling? Have I done something wrong?" Matthew asked, staring still.

Gemma was shaking her head as she sat opposite him, Steve clenching his teeth, silently cursing her for taking the lead role and the lead seat. "No, my lovely. You haven't done anything wrong." Seeing the relief in his eyes, she leaned towards him and placed a closed photograph album within reach. "I think you might like to look at that, Matthew."

He held his hands over it and drew them back close again. Performing the same movement half-a-dozen times, when he did allow himself to take it, he plucked it from the table and opened it in one brisk motion.

Steve and Gemma stared, scrutinising his expression as the meaning of the photos seeped into Matthew's mind.

Turning the pages, then turning them back, his brow furrowed in confusion. "I... I don't understand. How have they done this? How did they make these?"

Gemma smiled. "They are photos from your childhood, Matthew. There you are with Mandy. That is you and your sister, isn't it?"

Matthew nodded. "It looks like it, but this…" he pointed at a particular image of the pair of them in front of a grand Christmas tree. "This never happened!"

"How old would you say you look in that photo, Matthew?"

Matthew peered. "I don't know. But Mandy's there, so I can't be older than seven."

"And what about Mandy? How old does she look?"

A tear had formed in the corner of his eye as he stared at the picture. "She can't be older than two and a half, can she!" he yelled.

"Don't be angry, Matthew. I'm on your side. I'm trying to help," Gemma cooed. "Look again. How old does she *look*?"

Matthew forced himself to peer again at the picture of him and his little sister in blissful anticipation of Christmas. "I suppose she looks about six."

Gemma stifled the smile crinkling her lips. "Turn the page, Matthew. What do you see?"

"Me."

"What are you doing?"

"Riding a chopper bike, but I never had a chopper. I never had any bike. Dad put me into care after Mum… No-one ever took me into their home again, and who can blame them? All those kids in care because their parents are abusive, or they've been orphaned. Why would anyone take a selfish bastard who killed his sister for a go on the computer when there's kids like them? No-one. And I never had a bike. This must have been done with editing software."

Ignoring his objections, Gemma pressed on. "In the background, there's someone else. Also on a bike, a smaller bike, can you see?"

Matthew squinted. "Mandy! She looks like her, but it can't be!"

"I know this is a lot to take in. But I think you need to at least entertain the idea that what you're remembering might be faulty. Do you know, we never really remember anything?"

241

Steve interrupted, keen for some of the glory. "We only remember the last time we thought about it! That's why the details are so vague: what you wore, who was there. They're all really easy to manipulate."

Gemma smiled at the poor confused face gawping at her. "Just think, Matthew. If you at least look into it, you might find out we're right after all. And the reality waiting for you here is much nicer than the one you've constructed in your head."

Chapter Forty

He ran until he was absolutely certain he'd lost them. That's if they even bothered to chase him. Resting his back against the wall, he shook his head in disbelief and determination. So his dad was in on it too! The bastard. "I knew they were jealous of my success, but this?" he questioned himself. He never would have believed it, but here he was living it.

What had they been offered? It had to be down to the bloody amphi-tank and the MOD. He'd got involved in something he didn't understand, so they got rid of him.

Where was his mum and sister? His mind whirled. If it was money, his dad didn't appear to be reaping the rewards of compliance. Had he refused to be a part of it? Is that why he was on his own in an untidy, dirty house?

Did that mean his mum and Mandy had taken some sort of pay-off for their cooperation? Those two had always been bloody cliquey. He'd never managed to penetrate their close bond; taking themselves off doing jigsaws and playing games he was excluded from as a kid. And then going away for spa days together on *his* money when Mandy grew up!

Did it really bother them so much that their good fortune was *his* fortune? It was beginning to become undeniable. But Debbie and Abi would never have submitted to demands of silence. They can't know. With help of his conniving mum and dad and sister, it wouldn't have been too difficult to convince them that Matthew was never coming home.

But he would find them. He was smart, and he was determined. Someone knew where they were, and Matthew would too. It was the only thing that mattered.

Chapter Forty-one

As the bell peeled around the house, Debbie brushed down her skirt. It felt odd. Why was she doing this? Who was she trying to impress? The doorbell chimed a second time and this time she lugged open the heavy lump from its aperature. "Hi," she invited Gemma, pleased she was alone.

Gemma rolled through the door and waited to see which room she'd be directed. Following her hostess to the lounge, it was her turn to be relieved at its emptiness.

"I'll fetch Matthew," she said.

Nodding, Gemma fought not to ask if the argumentative rest of the family would be joining them, and instead half mouthed, half whispered, "How's he doing?"

Debbie smiled. It wasn't huge. Not a grin, but it was genuine. In the eyes, not just the mouth. Gemma was pleased. "Better. Thank you," she replied.

She disappeared. Moments later, Matthew, alone, tiptoed into the room as though unwilling to disturb the calm.

"Hello, Matthew," Gemma greeted, standing. She almost gasped as Matthew accepted the invitation to shake her hand. "Everything okay?"

He nodded.

"What are your thoughts on what we talked about?"

Matthew hunched on the sofa. Tapping his thumbs together, his hands clasped, he looked a nervous wreck. "I want to believe you. It would be wonderful. Disturbing. Worrying. But wonderful." He choked back the tears already welling. "But I can't. I have a lifetime of memories. Awful, terrible memories.

And then there's the photos, and I don't recognise any of them. It's like a different person."

Gemma nodded. It was complicated, but she had to try to put this poor family back together. "You say that, but are you prepared to admit now that it isn't a different person? That it's you but you don't remember?"

"I've been poring over the photos every minute since you left. I haven't slept. It looks like me. It even looks like the sort of things I would like to do. The family here seem lovely."

"You have spoken to them, then?"

"Yes. But I meant the family in the photos. Every picture is so full of love. The Matthew Morrissey in these pictures has it all."

Gemma edged closer to him. "The Matthew in the pictures is you. You do know that, don't you?"

"I don't know it. It doesn't feel true. But I can't argue with the evidence."

Gemma nodded and sat back, trying to appear relaxed. "Do you know the little girl in the pictures? Not Mandy. Abi?"

Matthew stared at the floor. "I don't recognise her at all apart from the family resemblance. She's a beautiful kid."

"Yes. There's another album I've kept from you. I'd like you to see it now. It might explain things."

Matthew took the book of photos from her. It was tied with a black ribbon. If he opened it and still nothing made sense, what then? He had no choice. He had to know.

Peeling back the first page, he jolted at the image. He could barely recognise the girl, she looked so ill. So pale. He didn't know her but for the photos, but it broke his heart. Seeing anyone so close to death would move anyone. "What happened?" he asked flatly.

"Don't worry, she's fine now. You recognise Abi? Your little girl?"

Matthew clutched at his chest, wringing the material of his shirt in his hand.

"Have you heard of Retrograde Amnesia?"

Matthew shook his head.

"It's a type of amnesia where you don't remember anything before a particular point of time—often an accident, maybe brain damage, or psychological trauma." Matthew turned all his body towards her, desperate to make sense of what she was saying.

"Your little girl was very ill, Matthew. It was certain she was going to die from leukaemia, but then miraculously, she pulled through."

"Then why don't I remember?" Matthew mumbled.

"You never got to express your grief. That's what your family believe, and I agree. So you shut yourself off, remembering nothing of your life before."

"Before what? Because I don't remember any of it. Not the version here anyway."

"Something triggered it on Christmas Day. My guess is that this accident, that happened with Mandy when you were seven, lodged in your brain far more significantly for you than it did for your mum, dad and Mandy.

They remember the computer. They even remember you and her screaming at one another for a turn, but nothing more. Mandy wasn't injured, let alone killed!"

Matthew collapsed into the chair in huge sobs. "How? How do I remember it differently?" he rasped.

"Confused I guess. You blotted out everything that had happened to Abi and projected the result you hadn't had the chance to grieve for onto what was a very clear image for you—a Christmas row with your little sister. You probably felt guilty for your behaviour—I don't think you have anything to feel guilty about, by the way." She smiled. "They got confused in your mind. You invented the rest. Your brain filled in the gaps."

Matthew shook his head slowly in disbelief.

"There are no records of you going into care Matthew. No records of Mandy having died. Everyone here is who they say they are, I promise you."

It was too much to take in. But it had to be true. A whole lifetime of false memories. He was going insane.

"I'm going to call in to see you every day. Help you integrate all this."

"Will I get my memory back one day?"

"It's possible. Sometimes it's temporary. You might get all or some of it back."

But of course, he never would, because it wasn't his memory to get back.

Chapter Forty-two

Matthew was never seen without one of the photo albums in his grasp. Everyone was giving him time and space but there were no cross words as he gazed into the world beyond the pages.

Gestures of affection no longer elicited his flinching agitation. Matthew was slowly coming home. It was a long way up a steep hill but they were on the journey at last.

Sitting beside him on the sofa, two steaming teas on the table in front of them, Debbie smiled the warmest of smiles at her husband. Risking a squeeze of his thigh, she leaned in. "How are you doing?"

"It's weird, looking at all these pictures and not remembering anything I'm seeing. But I like it. It must have been a good life."

"Oh, it was… Still is. You will get through this. And I'm going to be here for you every step of the way."

Turning and meeting her gaze full on, he spoke two words that touched her and filled her with optimism more than anything she'd heared since his return. "I know," he said, falling back into the allure of his unknown past living in the pages of photographs on his lap.

Debbie sat back with her tea and allowed him his time away in his mind.

Debbie drove as Matthew insisted he'd never learned. Sitting outside Marsden-Morrissey Marine in the vintage Saab Matthew had insisted on keeping, he sat and stared.

"Don't you want to go in?"

He nodded but added, "Not yet though. I just want to watch a little longer."

People bustled in and out, with smiles on their faces when they went in enlarging to huge grins by the time they came out again. Beautiful cars filled the car park while their owners decided on just what they wanted from a luxury sailing yacht, and whether to buy pre-owned or have a bespoke one made to fit their every whim.

Just seeing the boats resting on the water filled Matthew with an excitement he'd never known. They held such possibilities. Resting on the surface ready to cleave a path to a new land, a new adventure. Bobbing in his seat, Matthew laughed. "I want to go in, now!"

Debbie took his arm as they strolled over to the main entrance. Glancing back at the car, with its roof off, she tried to guide her husband to the doors, but he was already pulling her towards one of the smaller boats.

"It's incredible. So full of promises."

Debbie squeezed his arm and choked back a mass of pure joy as he reciprocated. "Yes," she agreed.

"Would I be able to get one, one day? You said we have plenty of money," Matthew met her eye with childhood zeal. "What's so funny," his eyes crinkled as Debbie couldn't control her mirth.

"One day? You already own this boat, Matthew. You own every boat here... well Marsden-Morrissey Marine owns all the boats and you own half of that!"

His eyes could scarcely open wide enough to take it all in. Staggering, he allowed himself to be guided to the double doors that swished open when they were close enough. A vaguely familiar figure walked towards them. Who was that? Someone he'd known from school a long long time ago. It couldn't be.

"Hello stranger!" Brian greeted with a slap on the back. Grabbing Matthew's hand, he pumped it vigorously, stroking his arm at the same time. "Great to see you, really great!"

Still with his hand on Matthew's arm, he guided him gently towards the stairs. "Come on up, I've got a bottle of your favourite up here."

Matthew and Debbie trotted dutifully upstairs after him. As the door to the office swung open, Matthew whistled. "Nice," he said, nodding enthusiastically.

"I don't know how much you remember, but here's your desk. You always had the best view and I've kept it for you. I was tempted once or twice to swap in your absence," he joked with all his teeth on display. "Here," he thrust an exotic looking leather box towards his friend and business partner. "I got you this for Christmas, but I never bloody saw you, did I!"

Matthew held the box which surprised him with its weight. A gold clasp held it shut and when Matthew popped it open, the most exquisite, intricate bottle he had ever seen sat in velvet luxury, its golden liquid content basking in the afternoon sun as it blazed through the venetian blinds.

Matthew's bright eyes looked impressed, but Brian filled in the gaps of his memory. "Blended from over twelve hundred different eaux-de-vie," he declared with an impressive turn of French. "Some of which are over a hundred years old!" Pointing to the neck of the bottle, he blustered, "24carrat bloody gold, that is. Remy Martin, Louis XIII. Two and a half grand a pop. Enjoy!" he said with a waft of his hand.

It looked exclusive, the neck of the bottle seemed to be pure gold. *Actual* pure gold as Brian had said. The glass of the bottle itself was not simply smooth, but finished in hand blown droplets all around the edge, the shape almost a circle with a hole in its centre bridged only by the delicate embossment of the Remy Martin livery.

"May I have a taste?"

Brian's head bowed, "I insist!" he cried. "I've been waiting half a year to see your face when you do!"

While Matthew glanced around for something to drink it out of, Brian leaned over him and pulled open the bottom drawer of his desk. "Ta-dah!" he exclaimed, revealing some cognac glasses almost as impressive as the bottle.

Carefully releasing the intricate fleur-de-lis stopper from the bottle's golden neck, Matthew did the honour of pouring the honey liquid into three glasses.

"Not for me, Matthew. I've got to drive, don't forget."

The bottle hovered above Debbie's glass for a second before Matthew settled it on his desk and replaced the top.

"To your return to your family, and your rapid return to work!" Brian hailed.

The first sip fired in Matthew's brain as it burned his tongue, the fiery smoothness warming him like nectar. "Shit! That is good stuff."

Brian beamed. "It should be. Two and half grand, that cost!" he repeated. But Matthew didn't mind. It was money like he'd never dreamed of, splashed on him just so he could have a drink in a fancy bottle!

"Listen," Brian murmured. "No pressure, but how would you like to spend the afternoon here? You can stay in the background, just get a feel for the place again. What do you say?"

"Yes. I say, yes. Please."

"There's no need for please. You own half the bloody place."

Debbie was stunned, and thrilled. It was like seeing the old Matthew; the old spark in his eye. The spark that without it, Marsden-Morrissey Marine would be a struggling, middle-of-the-road boat builder. It was her husband's unfailing genius that had made it what it was today.

"Can you bring him home after work, please, Brian?" Brian squinted, cocking his head. "He can't drive."

"Say no more," he said, raising his glass in the air.

"Or, if you end up drinking any more of that, I'll come and get you both!"

"I wasn't planning on it, but it is one hell of a special occasion," he declared, longing looks directed at the exquisite bottle.

When Debbie had left, Brian opened the filing cabinet and removed a couple of leather-bound files. "This is you, Matty, old boy. Take a gander."

After the revelation of the dozens of photos he'd been studying over the past week, and the thrill of the present just received, Matthew couldn't wait to find out what delights would be revealed in these gorgeous looking annals.

As he flipped open the first page of the first file, it wasn't what he'd expected at all. Not a floating Taj Mahal, but something entirely different. "What's this?"

"This, represents nearly three years of your life, dear boy. This, is what made Marsden-Morrissey Marine the tour de force it is today, employing over a thousand grateful Bristolians to boot!"

Matthew peered down at the drawings. Some type of military craft. There were no boats like this on the marina."

Putting Matthew out of his misery, Brian filled him in. "That is your design of the amphi-tank. An amphibious armoured vehicle with stealth and ballistic capabilities."

"A tank that can go in water."

Brian nodded vigorously. "I know. But it's more than that. You won't remember, but I tried to put you off. 'It's not what we're about,' I'd said. And then with a bit of research I realised there were a lot of armoured vehicles out there that went in water too. Loads of them."

He rushed around to the front of the desk and leaned over the files. It was a performance he was enjoying thoroughly. "But your design was so much more."

Tapping an immaculately manicured index finger on the blueprint, Brian said, "See this little beauty? It can travel endlessly thanks to the hybrid solar panels. Completely covered in them, it is! There's a small generator just in case too, but it's not really needed. The solar panels power a motor that develops seven thousand horse-power!"

Matthew's eyebrows had found a new home near his hairline, raised ever-higher as Brian flipped the pages of the file to illustrate his points.

"Sounds a lot? You don't know the half of it. What's it made of? Go on, what do you reckon your floating tank is made of?"

"Well, it can't be too heavy, but it has to be armoured, so… aluminium or titanium?"

"No! Give up?"

"Uranium?"

"No. Carbon fibre!"

Matthew was stunned into silence.

"Like Kevlar, you invented this composite material inspired by the glass fibre of the hulls we were making." Brian deftly retrieved a sample of material from the cabinet. "See how light and flexible it is."

Matthew bent the fabric in his hands.

"More than twenty times stronger than steel. Lighter than aluminium. So flexible they virtually spit shrapnel back at the enemy! The MOD loved them, and now we've built thousands, and been paid millions!

Matthew whistled. "The Ministry of Defence bought thousands of *my* design?"

"That's right. Bloody love em, they do. See the shape? Undetectable by sonar or radar. They can literally travel across the sea; hundreds or even thousands at a time. Not just the sea either. Tiny draft, they've got. These babies'll go in the rivers too, and of course over all terrain! They can silently get right into the heart of a problem, unseen, and unleash their missiles whilst keeping their occupants completely safe. It's the future, I tell you!"

"Can't drones already do that? And aren't they even safer?"

"Drones aren't much bloody smaller than these, and they can't do half what these can. Once you've disposed of your enemy's despot leader, or whatever, a drone's not gonna stick around and help rebuild the devastated nation, is it? A drone is not going to take refugees to safety, is it? No. These are the future. Except they're not. Thanks to you, they're the here and bloody now!"

"Wow. I guess I'm pretty smart!"

"Bloody genius is what you are Matthew. Bloody genius. Another cognac?"

"Yeah. I think I need one!"

Chapter Forty-three

"So, what's it like… This amnesia?" Brian asked whilst taking a sip from an expensive third of a pint of local craft beer. "I mean, I know you can't remember much at the moment, but what's the prognosis?"

Matthew took a sip from his own amber oddity in its specially chosen glass (to fool the eye into not realising how small an amount you get for your fiver.) "I really don't know, Brian. I mean, I do remember you, but not as we are now. I remember you in school. It's weird."

Brian nodded along. "Weird," he repeated. "What about your family? Do you remember them?"

Matthew thumbed the rim of his glass unsure if Brian from school was the best person to talk to. He might not know him much, but he liked Brian. He didn't feel judged. "I remember them dead," he suddenly uttered.

The spluttering of Brian's beer was all the more tragic for how much of his serving the mouthful represented. Dabbing himself with some hastily grabbed serviettes, Brian's open mouth and wide eyes begged an explanation.

"I remember vividly Christmas Day when I was seven when Mandy fell over the bannister to her death." Saying the words, it felt different. The raw pain that had clawed at his heart for decades were buffeted by the new reality weaving its cotton-wool protection. "And the next year; the following Christmas, my mum took her own life, so…"

That too had changed. It needed a second for Matthew to recognise the grin on his face. Jolting in surprise, laughter followed. Perhaps fuelled by the beer on top of the smooth cognac, and maybe just sheer exuberant relief, Matthew became hysterical with mirth.

Other patrons of the Wild Beer company pub on the river were staring, keen to join in with wry smiles playing on their muddled mouths.

"Bloody hell, Matthew! It's not too bloody cheerful is it? You should be a writer, not a boat designer, blimey!"

"I know! I don't get how I came up with such a tale of woe." The more he talked, the further into un-reality his real memories sank. His mind had found a way out and he was going to cling to it and create a new truth.

"They reckon I got too stressed with Abi and the leukaemia, and that project for the MOD you showed me. Bottled it all up, apparently."

"I did tell you, you were working too hard, didn't I."

"I don't know. I don't remember!"

They cracked up again, crying with laughter. Matthew stopped, his face resetting. "A whole lifetime. That's what it feels like. It's not just that remembering is hard, my mind's created this whole other life. Like, I was in a children's home after Mum…" Matthew fought to not let himself fall back into the mire. "… and then things got really dark and I ended up in a secure institution for the mentally unwell because I tried to end it. Just like her."

Brian gasped.

"I can see it so clearly," Matthew went on. "Standing on the bridge. The water bubbling far below looked terrifying but so inviting. I knew that if I jumped it would all be over."

Brian had lost his joviality and grimly sipped what was left of his beer.

"I remember being there for years. My mind has constructed memories of a whole life there. Eventually I had enough. I wanted to take back control and I escaped. I suppose it was all a metaphor for how I was feeling." Matthew stared into the middle-distance. "But some of it must be real. I mean, I've been *somewhere* for six months, haven't I?" He shuddered.

"Where did you stay?"

Matthew gestured to everywhere. "Out there. Under bridges, in shop doorways."

"Why didn't you go back to the bridge? I'm glad you didn't, real or not, but why do you think you didn't?"

"Christmas is the trigger, I think. You can imagine. But I almost did go back."

"Almost..?" Brian left silence, his fear-filled eyes enough to finish the question.

"Yes. Very nearly. I was headed to Clifton on Christmas day with the sole purpose of ending it."

"That makes sense…" Brian joined in. "It was Christmas Day you disappeared."

Matthew nodded. "It didn't feel that way. To me I was already immersed in my nightmare - my fake life constructed by my own insanity! Everything caved in on me; the hopelessness. I remember sitting in a shop doorway, wallowing. It's hard to blame myself; I had nothing. Or rather, I *felt* I had nothing."

Matthew paused. It was so strange. He was telling this virtual stranger, supposedly a lifelong pal, an awful story that probably wasn't even true. But the memory was so vivid, it tried to infiltrate his optimism; his little rubber duck of doom ready to plop over the edge into oblivion.

With a huge sigh, he finished his story. He owed it to Brian, and he owed it to himself to know exactly what his crazy head had concocted.

"It was late. Christmas had chipped away at me until it defeated me. I heard the footsteps before I saw anyone. Well, I never *saw* anybody because I didn't look up. I refused to engage with the world. But the owner of the feet stopped in front of me." Tears dripped like a leaking tap. Matthew left them unhindered.

"He asked me if I was okay, but what could I say. 'Actually, no. I'm on my way to jump off the bridge, thanks for asking?'" Fidgeting in his seat, he carried on. "He did something that made the difference. It's the reason I'm here now. And I mean that. I don't know how much of what I'm telling you is true. I know I got things wrong. Big things. But I was missing from your lives for a long time, and that time has been dark. Very dark."

Brian's eyes were filling up as well.

"He gave me money. A fifty pound note! He didn't ask me not to spend it on drugs or booze. Didn't even ask for a thank you. It wasn't the food I bought, or anything I could have had. I mean, I don't really know what I did spend it on, but it helped. It helped so much. Because someone thought I was worth something."

"Of course you're worth something!"

"It's okay. I am beginning to realise that now. Thanks to my family, and you."

Brian gulped and padded his eye with the sleeve of his blazer.

"It's been bad since then, of course," Matthew continued. "But I knew things would change, it was just a feeling, but I knew." It felt good to get all this out and there was no stopping Matthew now.

"When the police found me, I thought they were taking me back to the mental ward I hated. When Debbie visited, I assumed she was a CPN or social worker. When they said she was my wife, I couldn't believe it. And then when she brought me back to the lovely house in Clifton and introduced me to Mum and Mandy, I nearly died of shock!"

Brian's face almost creased into a smile at Matthew's delivery, but it faded as his mind computed its inappropriateness.

"I couldn't believe them. I was angry, you can understand. But they were right, and I was wrong." Throwing himself back in his chair, he sighed. "And I don't know how I feel about that. I mean, I'm… I can't even think of a word for how pleased and relieved I am that it wasn't true. But at the same time, where does that leave me? I can't trust my own head. How will I ever make a decision of any consequence ever again?"

Brian stretched his hand across the table. Matthew eventually succumbed to the offer of closeness and grabbed it and Brian gave it a firm shake as he thumped him on the shoulder. "It's hard. But with the right help, you'll get through it. It happens all the time to loads of people. Usually the clever ones, like you!"

Matthew's eyebrows arched.

"But it does," Brian insisted. "You hear about celebrities going off the rails, don't you? And how many films have you seen where people suffer amnesia and re-invent themselves? It's a soap-opera favourite; up there with illicit affairs! They reckon one in ten suffer from some sort of mental health issue," seeing Matthew's face, he worried he was being insensitive. "But the important thing is to accept help. You'll get better, Matthew. You've come so far already."

Matthew grinned. "I know. You're right. But it's weird though."

"Weird," Brian repeated again.

Chapter Forty-four

Brian had drunk himself beyond the point of being safe to drive, so it was an Uber car that dropped Matthew in the drive of twelve Clifton Down Road before speeding Brian back to Sue's loving arms.

"Matthew! How was it?" Debbie beamed as she yanked open the door.

Matthew nodded. "Good. Really good." Smiling back at his wife, he laughed. "You didn't tell me what a complete genius I am!"

"Didn't I?" Wrapping slender arms around his neck, she cooed in his ear. "Well, I'm sorry, Mr Morrissey. How remiss of me." The lure of the bedroom was interrupted by a call to action from Mandy to come for dinner.

Walking hand in hand to the banquette hall/dining room, they pulled out their chairs and sat at the head of the table. Mandy wheeled in a trolley with bowls under cloches. "Your favourite!" she announced as she placed a steaming bowl in front of her brother and removed its dome cover. "Moules Mariniere!"

"I'll take your word for it," Matthew laughed. Sniffing the steam as it swirled from the bowl, his face lit up. "I think you're right. This smells incredible."

His exuberance fell uneasy on the guilty shoulders of Alan and Mary. It wasn't a sensation they were happy to admit to. The pressure built up with nowhere to go. Could they apologise for who they were? Mandy wasn't really their favourite, of course not. But they had to take some responsibility for how their son felt, didn't they?

"The nurse told us a bit about your struggles." He was going to say 'Matthew,' but settled on, "son."

A mussel poised on Matthew's fork dripped wine and cream onto the table cloth as it came to a sudden halt. "Really?" he answered. "That's good." But it wasn't. Just when he was beginning to accept reality.

"Yes. She seemed to think your vision of your sister falling down the stairs demonstrated you may have thought… I don't know… That we… loved Mandy, you know… Did you?"

"Did I what, Dad? Worry you loved Mandy more than me? I think I must have."

"We didn't. Of course we didn't, did we, love?"

Mary shook her head in rapid little jerks. "No."

Pushing back her chair, she rushed to her son and pulled him close. "Sorry my love. Sorry we pushed you too far. I think we were just so sure of you. We knew you'd do well," she gestured to the room's vastness. "But we should have seen the signs. I should have known." The tears fell, not just from Mary but from Matthew too.

All that time, gone. He couldn't remember a day of it. But now wasn't when he should dwell on the past; neither a past he couldn't recall nor a past that didn't exist. Now was the time to look to the future. They'd make new memories, and they'd be better than ever.

"I remember that Christmas, you know!" Mandy declared, slurping the marinade from the shell of a mussel. "It was so exciting getting that computer. I was only two or three; I didn't even know what it did until you loaded that Hunchback thing, and I wanted it!" She laughed. "But you weren't horrible to me, Matty. I knew you didn't want to, but you let me take your turn. Oh, you were so patient!"

Matthew shook his head. "It's such a clear memory. I know it can't be true but it's so vivid." Eyes glazing, he smiled a watery smile. "Is it okay if we don't talk about it? I just want to put it all behind me and move on."

"Yeah, sure," Mandy grinned. "I just wanted to reassure you, you were wrong. In case my not being dead wasn't enough!"

Chapter Forty-five

Leaning against a wall in an alley more than a mile from his childhood family home, Matthew tore at his face. The running had been therapeutic and he'd come up with an idea.

He knew the story they'd spun—the spooks, or whoever was creating his nightmare. They had told his dad that the rest of the family were dead. He had blamed Matthew, so goodness only knows what lies they'd told.

Presumably then, they were somewhere under the misinformation that Matthew was dead too. Finding them wouldn't be easy, he knew that, but he was nothing if not tenacious. He'd find them and tell them the truth. He had no choice.

Looking down at himself, he allowed his eyes to take in what he'd distanced himself from for weeks. He was a mess. He smelled, his clothes were ripped and dirty, his hair on his head and his face was long matted.

If he was going to find out what had happened to his wife and daughter and the rest of his family, he'd need to blend in. He needed to be clean.

Along the river on Spike Island, not too far from SS Great Britain and formerly-Marsden-Morrissey Marine, was a caravan site. He had to be careful, but once he was inside and in the shower, he'd mingle unnoticed with the holiday makers.

Scrunching his hair behind his head, he pulled up his coat's hood and straightened out the front, doing up what buttons remained. He didn't look smart, but a glance at the quality of the duffle jacket and the boots, he was sure he didn't look like the tramp he was.

Walking with a confident air, he strolled along the riverside. "Afternoon... Hello... Lovely weather," he greeted people walking towards him and others tending their boats. How he'd love to hop aboard and feel the freedom of the open water. Everyone smiled back, and he knew he looked okay.

The campsite was accessed by a locked wooden gate which opened onto the wide path adjacent to the towpath, so enjoyed by dog-walkers and cyclists and pedestrians whose usual destination would be the quaint public house at the end.

Without arousing suspicion, Matthew loitered near the gateway, admiring the views, loving the boats as they busied on the water. A group of kayakers were practising Eskimo rolls in the bridged off marina. River taxis with shark teeth decal hummed up and down, their skippers waiting to catch the eye of any potential fairs.

It was with an easy smile that Matthew squeezed past excited campers on their way to the pub next door. When Matthew glanced the list of facilities, he knew he'd struck gold. An easy amble allowed him to tick off all he needed—a shower block, a laundrette and even a pool. He'd have to find some coins somewhere for the washing machines, but for now, the allure of submerging in the crystal waters of the outdoor pool took his attention.

Grabbing a pair of trunks drying in the window of a caravan he passed, Matthew continued nonchalantly to the pool area. Signs invited patrons to shower before using the facilities. "Don't mind if I do," Matthew chortled under his breath. Complimentary towels along with shampoos and shower gels in little sachets were available to pick up on your way through.

Choosing a cubicle, Matthew used the shower to wash himself and his clothes. Shampoo couldn't be that different to laundry detergent, could it? Especially if he used enough of it. Saving money and time, he could swim whilst his clothes dried.

As if to facilitate his idea, the site very kindly had spin driers in the changing rooms. Designed for wet trunks, and maybe a towel or two, the little machine baulked at Matthew's clothes— particularly the duffle coat. But holding his hand on the on button did give them a good drying start.

Hanging the damp garments on the hooks lining the room, Matthew made his way through the footbath to the poolside, freshly clean, hoping he wouldn't bump into the owner of the trunks he'd stolen. "Sorry," he mouthed to the sky, but he was sure they would gladly donate if they knew his need.

It was with that belief he gained his next acquisition. Swimming up and down, occasionally pausing just to float, Matthew could feel his energy returning. The cool cleansing of the water, drying off in the heat of the sun, his body basking in Vitamin D goodness.

He spotted the Red Cross charity box before he even left the pool and he knew what he would do. Showering the chlorinated water from his skin, the trunks hung, post spin, on a hook beside his clothes ready to become his new pants.

With a whistle, he carried his coat over his arm, perfectly natural in the climate. Pausing at the counter with the charity pot on it, he drummed his finger against his clean beard. "Latte please," he said to the young girl staring boredly at her phone.

Under the cover of her turned back and the noise as the stream hissed from the machine, Mathew plucked the charity box from the counter and hid it under his folded coat. As he walked away, he said, "Never mind, I've changed my mind," to the girl. Sure she hadn't heard, he carried on walking confident her annoyed gaze would soon return to her phone screen. It could be days before anyone noticed the missing Red Cross tin.

Exiting the campsite from the front, Matthew negotiated the main road the other side of the site, quickly crossed an iron bridge that spanned the small Avon tributary that cut Spike Island off and gave it its name, and headed into the hills. He'd rest, count his spoils and come up with the best plan to find his family.

Since leaving his dad's, his thoughts had been so clear, and everything had fallen into place in his mind. He'd have to lay low; the police were everywhere and getting closer each time. He couldn't risk capture and re-admission to the hospital.

It was hard to fight the instinct to search for his girls, but they were bait. He was sure he'd be caught and it was doubtful he'd escape again. He'd be no use to them in there, so he'd wait. But not forever. He made a promise to himself, and to them, that he wouldn't rest until they were reunited. Ever.

Chapter Forty-six

"Right, young lady, time for bed."

Abi clung to her mummy's legs, unusual for a nine-year-old, but not for one who'd been through Abi's difficult life.

"Would you like Daddy to take you up and tuck you in?"

Matthew stiffened. What would she say?

Clinging tighter, she hid her face. A barely detectable shake of her head caused Debbie to smile an apologetic smile. 'Maybe next time,' it said.

As Debbie disappeared with Abi, Charlotte raised her eyes. "Am I staying here tonight, Mum?"

Mandy held tight to her mug of coffee, shaking her head. "Not on a school night, love."

Charlotte's Cupid's bow pouted sulkily. "We used to stay every night!"

"Well, that was before Uncle Matthew came home, wasn't it!"

Charlotte played with saying 'That's not Uncle Matthew,' but kept it in under a deeper scowl.

"Which means we need to leave, or you'll be late for bed." Leaning over she bade her farewells "Bye, Mum. Bye, Dad." Hugging her brother, she kissed him on the cheek. "Say bye to Debs for me."

Her Range Rover Evoque sped her to the river. Across the water she could see the business her clever brother had built with his partner as she keyed the code for the Penthouse.

"Can I watch a film to settle?" Charlotte's puppy dog eyes begged.

"Have it on quietly, and don't stay up too long. You hear me?"

Charlotte skipped off to her room overlooking the water. It was nice to be back home, really. Her own space with her own stuff, and she loved watching the boats as they scudded to and fro along the river.

"It would mean the world to Daddy if he could be close to you again. I know you were angry, sweetheart, but you must see how unwell Daddy's been."

"I didn't believe it was Daddy at first," Abi's bright eyes told as she sat up in her bed.

"I know what you mean, my love. He was very troubled, wasn't he?" Abi nodded. "But he's getting better. I mean, he doesn't remember much… of anything. But the old Matthew; the old Daddy, you can see him in there now, can't you?"

Abi's lips squashed together as she thought. Deliberation complete, she nodded hard, her head thrusting into her pillow on the final nod, ready for a peaceful sleep. As Debbie bid her goodnight, a smile crept onto Abi's cherry lips. It stayed there all night.

£170.83, Matthew gleaned from his theft of the charity tin. "I'm rich!" he declared, smiling to himself at how far he'd come down (yet how much better this was than he had been.)

He chose everything from the same shop. It made sense. Everything in The Mountain Warehouse suited his purpose of blending in with any other hiker on the Avon Gorge—the same hikers you'd find in the city centre enjoying fine dining or afternoon tea on the waterfront. And of course, he could buy a tent.

Leaving the shop; tent, new clothes and cooking equipment stowed in a tall ruck-sack, he wore more new clothes and carried his old ones in a Mountain Warehouse carrier bag.

It was with surprising reluctance that he pitched his charity-bin castoffs into the nearest bin, the duffle coat especially. Its smart warmth had certainly saved his life. But it was too distinctive. And, Matthew considered, smoothing a palm over his tangled beard, so was this.

Joining the queue in a barber's shop, Matthew had his beard shaved and his hair severely trimmed. As the old familiar face of the millionaire boat builder stared at him from beyond the mirror, Matthew stared and forced down the rage at the indignity.

Nodding along to the obligatory barber chat, Matthew looked away as the painful reminder of what he'd lost ripped him from the inside. "Soon," he muttered under his breath, then smiled and nodded as the barber assumed his verbalised thought related to the 'holiday' chat he'd been burning Matthew's ears with for half an hour. 'Soon, we'll all be back together,' the thought hovered in his head.

Chapter Forty-seven

She seemed too big for the swings, but her huge grin as Matthew pushed her as hard as he could said otherwise. She didn't say much but her giggling echoed around the playground.

"Shall I go on the climbing frame?" she asked already running towards it.

"Yeah!" Matthew ran over too, but he was definitely too big to join in. "Where do you want to go after this, sweetheart?" he asked, the words sticking in his throat. He didn't quite understand why. There was love for her, he felt sure. She even looked like him (well why wouldn't she?). There was no denying she was easy to like, but he felt completely out of his depth. He couldn't remember a time he had ever been in the company of a child.

Her unease was understandable. It was his fault, not hers.

"McDonald's? Mum never lets me!"

Seizing the opportunity, Matthew grinned. "It can be our little secret then, can't it?"

As they walked back to the car, Matthew gazed down at her pretty blonde hair, his hand jolted to stroke it but slipped back into his pocket when he couldn't be sure it was the right thing. So it was with utter delight he received her delicate hand when she took his on the way into McDonald's.

They sat on silly character chairs doing word-searches with crayons eating too many fries and burgers. Forcing in the last mouthful of chocolate thick shake, Matthew knew the onion rings had been a mistake.

"Can we do this again one day?" Abi peered into his eyes.

Squeezing her hand, he said, "We can do this whenever you like. And anything else you'd like to do as well." He was a natural. Love burst from him in her acceptance of him and he could really believe he'd been there all her life.

"What about Disney Land?"

Matthew's mouth arched in imitation of his high brows. "Well, I guess. I'll look into it."

"You got us tickets for Christmas, but we couldn't use them." Her face flushed at the hint of accusation. "Mummy phoned, and they changed them."

"Well, definitely then. Disney Land, hey. That sounds fantastic!"

"We'll need to use them soon though. They said they could be used until the end of the year and it's nearly Christmas again!"

Matthew started. "Not really, Abi! It's not even October yet. You've only just gone back to school.

"It's half-term next week, and then after that there's only half more until Christmas, and that will fly by."

"You've given this some thought, I can see. Good girl." Taking both her little hands in his, he looked deep into her eyes. "We will go to Disney Land, I promise. But you know what my memory is like. Please, please remind me; tell Mummy if I don't get things moving, okay?"

Abi nodded, but there would be no need. There was nothing wrong with Matthew's memory. Nothing at all.

"Daddy?"

"Yes, princess."

"Sorry."

"What for?"

"For being mean to you when you came home. It was Nanna and Grandpa. They were cross with you and I felt that way too. But I'm not cross anymore, and neither are they."

Matthew smiled. "That's good to know."

"I'm sorry I said you weren't my daddy." Eyes pooling with tears, her choked voice touched him. "I know you are, really." And as she threw her arms around him, her heart broke into huge sobs. "I love you, Daddy. So much. I really missed you."

As the other patrons stared at the raucous emotion disturbing their fast food feast, Matthew nuzzled her head. "I love you too, Abs," he blubbed. "I love you too."

It was a relief to be in the warm. The tent had been plenty in the milder months, but now it was inhumane. He'd paid occasional fees at local campsites and had kept on top of his personal hygiene. But as the weather turned colder, he had decided he had kept out of the way for long enough. It was time to strike.

Staring at the screen in the umpteenth cyber-café he'd visited that week, Matthew was worried he would run out of money before ever completing a successful search.

Forays into phone shops had proved difficult when his personal details didn't come up for any addresses he could name. The pattern so far, once he'd given up on having his own phone, had been to pay for an hour or two out of the charity theft he'd managed to eke out over the weeks and months, along with some food and drink in a café. Time and again he had typed in things as ideas had struck, and when they'd proved fruitless, he'd struggled for another idea.

It was a fools' approach. Too much of the time was spent thinking and not enough time searching the web. Today he would implement a different plan. He had already made a list of things to try having done his thinking in his igloo/tent.

Nothing came up for Morrissey. Nothing he could make fit to his life at any rate. So he'd tried Lewis, Debbie's maiden name. It brought a school photo from Google images where she'd been tagged by an old school friend. The account it tagged was *no longer available.* The friend's profile was closed to the public, and so far they hadn't responded to Matthew's friend request.

He now had accounts on all the major social media sites but none of them had heard of Debbie Lewis or Morrissey. Alongside the immense frustration was a grudging respect for the thoroughness of his enemy. His own social media presence had always been haphazard apart from a couple of sponsored pages for the business which Brian had been more enthusiastic about than himself, but now it was non-existent. It was like he'd never been born!

He'd thought of every possible name he could think of. Every job he'd ever known her have; where she went to college—where they *both* went; it was where they had met—nothing.

He was on the last suggestion on his list, which was to trawl through photos with the caveat of being from Cardiff, Debbie's hometown. The search result offered more than double the entire population of Wales—seven million, four hundred and thirty thousand. There couldn't be that many Debbie's in the whole of the UK; maybe the world, let alone Cardiff!

Ploughing threw them was his only choice though. Page after page he peered at photos. They had her somewhere. Her name would be different perhaps, but surely they can't have removed every image from the internet? That was impossible.

His eyes strained as hundreds upon hundreds of smiling Debbie's flashed before his eyes. Why had they gone to so much trouble? What did he know that was such a threat to national security? He considered himself patriotic. They could surely have given him a chance.

He couldn't think about that. All that mattered was keeping focussed on the pictures. If there was even a possibility he'd missed one he could never rest.

"Hi, sir. Your time's nearly up. Would you like to buy more? We do a daily rate that might work out better for you."

Matthew paused his gaze and blinked. Filling his view with the cyber-waiter's well-groomed face, he answered. "Yeah, that. Give me the daily rate."

Smiling, the waiter held out his hand. "If I could just have a swipe of your card?"

"I don't have a card on me. I'll pay cash."

Awkwardly shifting from one foot to the other and glancing at senior colleagues whilst biting his bottom lip, he stammered his response. "I don't think we can do that, sir. We don't know how much it will be."

"Thirty. Take that and give me the change when I'm done. Okay?"

The lip biting got worse. Fiddling with the end of his tie, his embarrassment was hard to watch. "I'll just pay for another hour then. How much?"

Tension lifting at once, he beamed, "£10 including a coffee."

"Great. Take this and bring me a double-shot latte, please."

"We're doing a ginger and nutmeg latte for the same price, would you like that, sir?" he offered, and then in answer to Matthew's blank stare. "It's Christmassy."

Christmas! Was it really that time of year again. Moving his focus to his surroundings, the signs were undeniable: swirling Christmas Tree decal on the windows, garlands strung on the wooden beams above his head. Even his waiter was wearing a reindeer tie.

"Just the regular," he snapped. He couldn't be dealing with Christmas. A whole year away from his loved ones. He shook his head in despair.

But quickly, his frustration at the interruption and acknowledgement of the season turned to jubilation when Matthew resumed his attention to the Debbies. "Oh my god!" he cried.

"Sorry, sir, did you say something?"

"No, sorry. Carry on. Double-shot latte, okay?"

With an affirming nod, the waiter bustled away.

"There you are, my lovely!" Matthew sighed, an air of contentment filling his lungs.

It was her, unmistakably, but it had to be an old picture because her dad was beside her. Clicking 'visit page' Matthew was able to read how Bryn Lewis and his daughter, Debbie were accepting an award for his florist's contribution to Butetown in bloom. Funny, Matthew thought. She didn't mention that. She never even said they'd worked in the florists together.

Looking again, his head pounded. It didn't say Debbie Lewis. More careful reading showed something else. It said *ne* Lewis. Before that it read Debbie *Kennedy!* Who? How could that be possible? The newspaper article was dated August 2007. That was when they got married. He'd known her for over a year before that and she never helped her dad in the florists.

A cold sweat broke out on his forehead. No, this was impossible. Bryn had died not long after he and Debbie met. He certainly wasn't winning awards for flower arranging! The government agency responsible for his torment couldn't be *that* good. And why would they insert photos into the archives of *The Western Telegraph* to demonstrate Bryn's resurrection? And why put it on page three hundred and seven of Google's search? Not for him to find. Not to add to his confusion.

There had to be an explanation. Staring at the newspaper date, he squinted his eyes, desperately willing the solution to jump off the screen.

The date of the article didn't have to indicate the date of the photo. But reading the words, he was sure Bryn was involved. They described him as 'spritely' after recovering from a cancer scare.

Bryn, alive all these years and Debbie never said? It couldn't be. With the new revelation came new searches thick and fast. More relevant results filled the early search pages now, both for Bryn, and for Debbie Kennedy.

Matthew's chest tightened as her face beamed at him from her Facebook page where she boasted nearly a thousand friends, a perusal of whom revealed no-one he recognised. No Matthew Morrissey, no Brian, Sue, Mandy, Alan nor Mary. No Marsden-Morrissey Marine, nothing in Bristol at all.

How could she have developed such a profile in such a short time? *Debbie joined in January 2004* her information page enlightened him.

"Your latte, sir. Double shot."

Matthew couldn't answer. He couldn't think. He could barely even breathe. The well groomed waiter left his coffee near him and sauntered away with a mumbled "How rude," under his breath.

The tightening in Matthew's chest grew worse. Heart attack was his first thought; and of the couple nudging each other as they stared at him. But two or three calming breaths reassured him it was just a budding panic attack. "Calm down. You haven't got time for that."

Breathing through the shock relieved the pain and he carefully refocused on the screen, pushing on with his grim research. There were hundreds of photos organised into albums: *Kennedy family holiday; Chloe's first day at big school; Christmas 2017.*

Matthew's quivering finger poised on the mouse button as his heart squeezed in his chest. Which should he torture himself with first? There was only one choice.

His eyes struggled to allow the image into his head. Forcing himself to stare at the jolly pictures through a self-preserving squint, Matthew gritted his teeth. He hadn't come this far to deny himself the truth.

A huge sigh fogged the screen as he allowed the pixels to assault him. It was a nice tree in a nice house. Not like their real home, but pleasant. A girl, a bit like Abi, but older, was grinning whilst placing decorations on the branches. There seemed to be a photo of each and every one. Who was she? Chloe, evidently, but who was that?

Searching for a distraction, his hand reached for the coffee cup. Taking an absent sip, Matthew clicked the right arrow, filling the screen with picture after picture of the smiling girl until one final shot saw the completed tree with its colourful fairy lights glowing.

One more click was a click too far. Flinching, wriggling back in his seat, the coffee pouring over the rim of his cup onto his lap spilled unnoticed. Matthew shook his head in disgust and disbelief.

Draped over a handsome rugby physique was his wife. She didn't look bothered she'd lost Matthew. In fact, he didn't think he'd ever seen her so happy. And Christmas '17? How was that possible? Had they postponed celebrations to another day? A day when they knew he would be out of the way?

She had to be in on it. Why? The money? And where was Abi? The cup shook violently in his hand. Recognising the rage bubbling within, Matthew replaced it with slow care. Their daughter had nearly died, and all along Debbie was living a double life with an ape!

He was going to find her and demand answers. No-one was going to take his daughter from him after all they'd been through. No-one!

There was no address listed on the info page, of course there wasn't, but she'd been a fool. *Moving Day* was handily labelled in one of the dozen or so albums. And there, pointing gleefully at a sign displaying the name of their new home, *Bryn Haul,* was Debbie and Mr Kennedy with face splitting grins on their conniving faces.

Knowing the florists was in Butetown, it made sense that Bryn Haul would be in Cardiff too. There were a surprising number of houses matching the description on Zoopla, but only one whose photo looked identical to the one in Debbie's bloody Facebook posts, and it was in a road called Bute Crescent!

"Gotcha!" his fist thumped the table and was too much for the ever-suffering coffee cup which gave up and threw itself to the floor. With apologetic nods, Matthew left a couple of coins from his dwindled charity heist and darted from the café.

He was going to Cardiff.

Chapter Forty-eight

It was earlier than usual, but they were all keen to get Christmas underway. For Matthew, it was to be his first Christmas. His only other recollection was the false one his mind had concocted in his darkest hours.

He was confident a proper celebration with his wonderful new (to his memory at least) family would draw a line under the whole debacle.

He'd already achieved some new ideas at the boatyard. He could remember none of the formal knowledge he'd studied at college for, but he seemed to have a natural flair. And with Brian's help, he was making great strides.

"Are we really getting the tree today, Daddy?" Matthew liked it when she called him that. He might expect her to shorten it to 'Dad' to be in with her peers, but she always acted like a cutesie little girl with him. He adored her, and this phase of their life they'd missed and were living now was the best time he could ever imagine.

"I said we would, didn't I," he confirmed with a grin.

"Can I choose it?"

"Of course you can, my little princess. We'll get whichever one you pick."

They all wore huge smiles as they drove to the garden centre they always went to (apparently).

"I love you, Matthew Morrissey," Debbie kissed his cheek as he started the car.

Staring deep into her dark eyes, loved effervesced within him, and when he declared, "I love you too," he meant every word.

"How long until Disney Land?" Abi asked from the back. She'd asked every day and they were all enjoying the countdown.

"One week and three days," Debbie confirmed.

"Yay! And are we still going on the train?"

She was so excited about a long train journey for reasons that escaped Debbie and Matthew, but her enthusiasm had made the loathsomely long trip one to rejoice.

"Yes, Abigail. The train it is!"

Seething at the duplicity was Matthew's main focus since his unpleasant discovery in the café. He'd barely slept but he knew what he had to do. He'd need money again. The coppers left in his pocket were insufficient to get a train ticket to Cardiff. He was reluctant to obtain more of the funds people had given in good faith to help the needy. It would be easy enough, but he could get caught and end up back in police custody; a risk he wasn't prepared to take.

His solution wasn't much better, but he'd keep a careful eye out for the police as he sat outside Cabot Circus and begged for change. It wasn't begging as such; he wasn't *asking* for money; just sitting in the doorway of an office building near the main thoroughfare. His view was filled with the huge glass domed shopping centre with all the designer outlets where he had frequented a year ago.

Wearing coffee-stained trousers and a dejected expression, the first pound coin scouted the way for dozens more within the hour. Matthew was grateful. He'd have enough for a train ticket sooner than he imagined, but that brought the moment of truth that bit closer. Standing on the path of his childhood home had felt pivotal, but this was the real crux. This was the real final straw. If Debbie couldn't explain her actions and give him access to Abi, what was there left to do?

He'd done very well focusing on one task at a time. If he'd given into the possibilities, he'd have been finished months ago. So, he'd keep resolute, wait until he had enough money and make his way to Haul Bryn, for which Zoopla had not only revealed its address, but its meaning—Sun Hill in Welsh.

His alertness paid off when the approaching figures of two police officers ambled his way. Headed towards him, they were still a good way off. Moving on straight away might appear suspicious, but Matthew was smart. Waiting for the inevitable distraction, he scooped the money into his large rucksack and held the handle.

When they were preoccupied with the crowd, Matthew stood and moved away, swiftly hurrying into an arcade of shops linking the newest mall to the older Galleries, and more importantly, closer to Temple Meads station.

His bag was heavy, but it helped to give his trek along the busy main roads to the railway credibility. The spires of Bristol's oldest station soon loomed into view across the river. As he strode past the traffic waiting at the lights, he realised he hadn't checked his funds. He was confident there would be enough.

Pausing at a bench, he removed his sack from his shoulders and plonked it on the seat beside him. Unclipping the front pocket, he thumbed through the coins until he got to around £30. That was more than sufficient, surely. The good people of Bristol certainly hadn't let him down this afternoon. He made the same mental note to pay them back by way of a sizeable donation when he got his life back, but this time he knew he was far from convinced he ever would.

Reaching the front of the short queue, Matthew leaned into the vent in the glass. "Cardiff Central, please." Bag poised on his knee, his mind cramped at the next question, even though it was a simple one.

"Single or return?" the lady smiled over her glasses.

What were his plans? If Debbie didn't ease his torture, where would he go? Was there any point coming back to Bristol ever again? He'd lost everything, and he didn't even understand why.

He had no clue as to the whereabouts of his own mother or his sister. Or Abi? Surely she couldn't be far from her mum. Her conspicuous absence on Facebook likely a security measure—or a device for keeping Matthew at arm's length.

Wanting to shout, to scream; 'I will be back,' Matthew knew the reality was a hazy nightmare. "Single," he barked, as though the question had been an impertinent imposition.

"Twelve pounds, ninety." That left him with plenty for a bite to eat, and another single back to Bristol if it played that way. Matthew handed over the coins and took his change. If there had been a charity collection pot, he'd have begun his repayment but there wasn't.

"Platform eleven," she said, her smile having waned in the sullen silence of her unkempt millionaire customer.

"Thank you," Matthew made a point of saying as he walked out of the door.

His modern hiking jacket was even warmer than his Stig-bin duffle coat, and a whole lot lighter. Stowing it in the rucksack as the train approached, a sickening inevitability tightened in his throat and chest.

What would he say? Would she be pleased to see him? He had been so sure their reunion would be wonderful, but now, having seen her other life, he didn't know what to expect.

Had she wanted him out of the way, or was she just doing what she was told. Questions, questions bumped up to one another, stalling at his mouth as there was no-one yet to answer.

The train pulled away, his bag successfully blocking other passengers encroaching on his dour mood. The potential joy at seeing his wife wrestled fiercely with despair he expected. Closing his eyes, the lids fluttered in his attempt to block out the world until it required his attention again.

"Tickets please," the conductor forced him from his tenuous calm. Contorting, rummaging in his trouser pocket produced the goods and he was left to re-achieve his Zen-less state.

Fingernails dug into the armrest as he shot away from his hometown at sixty miles an hour. He appeared as a death-row inmate finally proceeding to the chair. The shock he anticipated at the journey's end might be worse. Maybe he'd welcome death. No, he shook his head. He'd never give up on his daughter.

Time dragged, and closing his eyes only made it worse. Ticking off landmarks might make it pass easier, but by the time the train whizzed through the tunnel, he wasn't sure what he was even looking at.

When had she found time to live the life alluded to on social media? Was Mr Kennedy an old family friend? Was Chloe *his* daughter? And why had she kept her dad a secret? None of it made any sense and Matthew was struggling to keep his equilibrium. Chepstow and Newport flew by before the train rolled into Cardiff Central.

Matthew couldn't move. Knowing he'd risk missing his stop if he didn't, he hauled himself from his seat and shuffled with his huge rucksack from the train.

Staring at the rudimentary map he'd scrawled after consulting the computer, he squinted into the distance unsure which way to head. He had the cash, he could get a cab. They'd know where to go. It was money he'd saved for food, but he had no appetite. He may as well save his energy.

Walking to the first in the line of taxis (or tacsi's as they insisted on calling themselves) Matthew inquired if the driver knew the address he'd noted for Debbie.

"No problem, bach. Hop in."

Taking a seat in the back of the cab, Matthew closed his eyes to discourage conversation. The cabbie tried to start anyway, barking "Where you from, then?" which Matthew ignored. "On holiday, is it?" and Matthew ignored that too.

The Cardiff traffic was painfully slow, but with his eyes closed he tried to control the panic rising within him. This was the most important taxi ride he'd ever taken. The terminus of this tiny journey would make or break his life.

"There we are, bach. Eight pounds, forty, please."

"Here already," colour drained from Matthew's face.

"Ha. I don't like to hang about!"

Handing over the money, Matthew shuffled out of the car. He was forced to overcome his reluctance to move, when the taxi refused to leave until he did. "I'm not a teenage girl at four in the morning," he muttered ungratefully. As he walked a few steps, the taxi pulled away with a toot of the horn.

Standing, breathing hard, Matthew scanned the houses. They all looked very similar, but the photos he had stared at had etched a path in his brain and he was in no doubt, even before he spotted the sign hanging from its gatepost that he was stood before Bryn Haul.

Tentative steps edged him closer to the house, and as they did Matthew scanned every window for a glimpse of his wife or Abi.

Walking straight up the drive and knocking on the front door seemed too abrupt; too rapid. Skirting round the house, he glimpsed the back garden. Stopping dead, he couldn't breathe, as there with her back to him, wrapped in a thick coat, woolly hat and scarf, swinging to and fro on a garden swing, was Abi!

His heart pushed against his chest. Desperate to hurry to her, salty water flooded from his eyes clouding his sight. "Abi!" he hissed in a loud stage-whisper. "Abigail, it's me!"

His little girl. Oh the relief. Craning his neck, he leaned over the wooden fence to get closer. "Abi!" He hissed again then decided that whispering was stupid. "Abi!" he yelled, but she still didn't turn around.

"Excuse me, may I help you?" Debbie's voice but with a twinge of a Welsh accent accosted him from her place previously hidden by the house. "What are you doing?"

The rage he'd felt at her apparent crossing him dissipated the moment he saw her beautiful face. "Debbie! Thank goodness. Oh, you don't know what I've been through. But you? You've had to move out of the house, and what about Abi? She was just settled back in school after her absence and everything," he babbled, clinging to his original theory that they were both victims of some government conspiracy.

"I'm sorry," Debbie interrupted, edging towards Abi as she swung. "Who are you?"

"Are they watching? Have I put you in danger?"

"My husband will be home any second, mister. You don' wanna be here when he does!"

"Okay, I can't begin to understand what you've had to go through, but I'm sure no-one knows I'm here. I definitely wasn't followed. But, please, Debbie, don't shut me out. Help me understand."

"I don't know who the FUCK you are! But you better disappear sharpish or my husband'll knock seven sorts of shit out of you. I promise you that!"

"Debbie, for fuck sake. I *am* your husband, in case you'd forgotten. So whoever else is involved in this shitty charade won't impress me. Whatever has gone on; whatever you've been told, you won't keep me from Abi. She's my daughter for Christ's sake!"

"Chloe. Go inside. NOW!" Debbie screamed at the girl on the swing. As she turned for the first time, Matthew staggered back. That wasn't Abi.

"I… I don't understand. Where's Abi?"

"Listen, buster, I don't know who you are. You're obviously pissed out of your head, or summin, but this isn't your house. You must have the wrong address. I'm gonna call the police now, so you'd better shift before they get yere."

She took a step towards the back door. Matthew knew this might be his only chance to speak to her; his only chance to get answers; his only chance to find Abi. Placing one foot onto a fence strut, he grabbed the top and pulled himself up, vaulting the six-foot high barricade in a single leap.

Thumping down onto the patio below, Matthew lunged for Debbie. She was fast but his long reach and desperation made him faster. "Don't scream. I won't hurt you!"

Whether it was from compassion, or the implied threat that he might hurt her if she did scream, Debbie didn't know. But something told her to stay calm. Everything would be okay if she stayed calm.

Matthew frog-marched his wife through the open back door and closed it behind them. "Sit down, Debbie."

Chloe walked into the kitchen.

"Get out, Chloe. Go to your room." She forced a smile onto her face. "It's okay, sweetie. Mummy just needs to talk to the man a minute okay?"

Chloe's face paled. She could tell everything was not okay at all.

"Chloe! Go to you room. Do as you're told!"

"No!" Matthew screeched, turning the key in the lock and thrusting it into his pocket. Matthew bolted for the stairs, Debbie, grateful she had her daughter safely with her, clung to her.

Stomping two at a time, Matthew reached the landing and flung open every door: Master bedroom, little girl's room (one bed), spare room—very minimalist, and a multi-purpose office-cum-gym-cum music room. No sign of Abi or any of her things.

Leaping the stairs in three huge strides, Matthew was soon back in the kitchen. "Where is she? Where is my daughter?" he demanded.

The little girl scurried away leaving Matthew alone with his wife. "I just want answers, Debbie. You owe me that much at least."

"What sort of answers? How do you know my name?"

"Stop it!" Matthew screamed. "I've had enough of this; everyone pretending they don't know who I am! I was relying on you. My dad apparently blames me for disappearing and him and Mum splitting up, and I get it. I've obviously attracted the wrong kind of attention and it's been hard. But what do you think it's been like for me?" Slamming a flat palm on the worktop, Matthew snarled, inches from Debbie's face.

Whimpering, her trembling lips begged. "Don't hurt us… Please."

Stepping back, Matthew's eyes widened as his wife's fear was undeniable. "Oh my god. It's true. *You* did this to me, not some cold-hearted strangers. You! My own wife!"

Debbie quivered but didn't answer.

"How long did you plan all this? When did you move from Bristol back here to Wales?"

Debbie's voice, just a quiver was turned up in a pretence of haughty self-righteousness. "What are you talking about? Bristol? I've never been to Bristol."

"Don't," Matthew snarled. "I won't stand for much more of this. Why didn't you tell me your dad survived his cancer? Why pretend you'd lost him? Was it so you could come back here to lover-boy?" he screeched.

Debbie shrank in the face of his new fury.

"Oh, I've seen the pictures. All over social media, I could hardly miss them, could I?" Matthew paced feet away from Debbie as she clung to the edge of the worktop.

"I know you were with him before any of this other stuff happened! And last Christmas! Christ, I can't have been gone more than a day when you set that up. You must have planned it."

Pausing in his stride, Matthew gasped. "Why didn't I see it before? There must have been signs. I thought you loved me. I loved you!" And there it was. *Loved.* Past tense, he'd lost her. How could he ever love anyone who would do this to him?

Not the money. He didn't care about that. It was the future she'd stolen. He'd only ever worked to build a future for them, and all along she'd plotted this. "How long has this been going on? How long?" He shook, his voice high and loud.

"I don't know what you're talking about, but you're scaring me!" Debbie edged along the worktop inch by inch, snot and tears streaming from her face.

Ignoring her, Matthew was lost in his thoughts, burbling them as they tumbled unfettered from his lips. "It must have been the money. When you realised how well things were going, did you stay with me until you could cash in?" Matthew spat the words.

"Did my fucking dad tell you about when I was sixteen? My little fall from grace?" Matthew snorted. "You must have thought I'd be easy to convince I was crazy. Well it hasn't worked! I'm back and you won't get away with it. And you'll never keep me away from Abi. Never!"

Turning to face her was the first time he realised what she'd been doing.

He saw the drawer open.

Saw the knife.

Debbie lunged for him, but he was strong. The tip of the blade just caught his shoulder. Pain arced to his head and fuelled the tiger raging at the audacity of her scheming plot to overthrow him.

The quivering blade pushed further into his shoulder as Debbie used all her strength to force herself forward using leverage from the kitchen cupboard. Matthew could only give in to the crassness of what was happening to him. She would never tell him where Abi was, because she was the one hiding her from him!

Releasing his grip unexpectedly, the knife fell to the floor and Matthew stood open-mouthed. Fingering the wound on his shoulder, he recoiled from the fierce pain, but it brought him back to the present with a biting jar.

"Who the fuck are you!"

Matthew heard the yell before he felt the force. Hitting the ground hard, he cowed as he looked up at his attacker. Debbie stood behind the large bulk of Mr Kennedy, Rugby shirt flapping as he flexed his thick shoulders.

"He's crazy, Glyn. Keeps saying I've stolen his money from Bristol, or something. He was trying to get to Chloe! Nuts, he is. Really crackers!"

Lunging forward, Glyn threw a massive fist in Matthew's direction. Dodging the blow, the weight of the assailing hand propelled Glyn tumbling forward. His inebriation obvious, he crashed to the floor beside Matthew.

Wriggling free from the flailing arms, Matthew jumped up in time to see Debbie grab at the knife on the floor. Scrambling for the door, Matthew fumbled the key from his pocket and unlocked it.

Debbie stood brandishing the blade, content the threat would see him off. Matthew ran into the garden and leapt over the fence.

"I'm calling the police, you nutter!" Debbie screamed after him. Slamming the door, she bolted it top and bottom before collapsing to the floor in huge sobbing tears.

Chapter Forty-nine

Matthew ran. He didn't even know where to until he found himself back at the train station. The miles had disappeared in a fog of despair. Looking around, he realised he'd forgotten his rucksack. No tent. No coat. And bleeding from the nasty wound.

Where would he stay? Collapsing against the wall, he didn't even care. What was the point? What was the point in anything anymore?

Abi. She was his only hope; his only chance at a life worth living. How could Debbie be so callous? She must have switched off her love when they almost lost her. Matthew knew what that was like, sometimes withdrawing had been the only way to cope. Chloe and Mr Incredible must have been a coping strategy that hatched into a plan to fleece Matthew and destroy him.

He didn't understand why he'd been the butt of blame, the place where the buck stopped. But he'd been defeated—so busy with work and with Abi, he hadn't noticed his wife hating him.

Sliding down the wall, he hid his face with the hood of his sweatshirt and sobbed. His body shook as he pictured all the moments of closeness that had been a lie. The rock he'd been for her when her dad died. All the tears shed. Where had they come from? She was a bloody good actress that was for sure.

Mandy and his mum; surely they weren't in on it as well? They'd never shown they shared alliance with his wife over him, and he thought they were proud of him. They never said so, but he knew… His eyes turning to slits, he sighed; he thought he knew.

Tears turned to steely determination. The business had suffered in his absence. Debbie must have taken his shares from Brian and somehow threatened him to make him keep quiet. And his mum and dad? Their marriage had always seemed strong, but was his disappearance a test too far? Or did Debbie have a hand in that too?

What had she told them? *After what you did…* his dad's words echoed around his mind. He knew what he had to do: go back to Bristol, back to the internet cafés and back to searching. He'd find Mandy and Mum and Abi. Then he'd get the best lawyers and wreak his revenge on his conniving wife.

It was a plan without conviction. He'd lost faith in his ability to achieve anything. He was cold. He was tired, and he was unconvinced when he found them they wouldn't be just another obstacle. How many more could he take?

Ideas jumbled in his head as the new theory of his terrible circumstance clashed with the old. If Debbie is behind all this, how did she move new people into their house on Christmas Day? And why would they say they'd lived there for ten years?

If the blame was all Debbie's, and not government agencies as he'd assumed all along, how had she persuaded the mental hospital to take him and tell him such lies about never having had a wife and child?

There were more questions, rising up like terrifying faces in Night of the Living Dead. Every corner his thoughts turned for solace, another crushing question loomed. Why had old Tom King not recognised him? Why was Mandy not in their apartment? How had Brian taken down the extension they'd built at Marsden-Morrissey Marine?

One theory excluded the other. His mind screwed, desperate to find something to cling on to. But even Pollyanna would succumb to blow after brutal blow. Unfailing optimism and grit couldn't overcome everything, could it?

"Are you okay, sir?"

Matthew looked up at the smiling face of a railway guard. Grateful it wasn't a policeman, he hauled himself from the floor, wincing as his shoulder cramped. Nodding, he squeezed "Family bereavement," from his dry lips as explanation for his emotional state. And it was in a way. He'd lost everything he ever cared about.

But just like those suffering grief for loved ones they'd lost. Matthew had to carry on for those who needed him. He might not have the answers, but until he knew Abi was safe, he would never rest. "I'm heading back to Bristol," he said with a decisive glint as he felt around in his pocket, mentally totting up the coins.

"Okay, sir," the guard said with disbelieving eyes. Swallowing down guilt at his assumption that this scruffy, stained individual was homeless, he added cheerily, "Let me know if you need anything."

Matthew shuffled to the ticket office and handed over the last of his money. "Single to Bristol, please."

"Temple Meads, or Clifton Down?" the lady asked from an unsmiling mouth.

Clifton Down! How appropriate. If he were to get the answers he so desperately yearned for, where better to begin than where it had all started?

"Clifton Down, please," he said with a smirk. "I'll go back to Clifton Down."

Chapter Fifty

"Is that the last of them?" Matthew laughed as the fifth bag was loaded into the taxi. "I can see why you didn't want to walk now. These are going to be a nightmare when we change at Paddington, you know."

"Trollies. Heard of those?" Debbie snapped with a stressed smile. "And porters. I'm sure they'll help us on the train."

"I'm sure. It's just funny that you and Abi have more suitcases than me, Mum, Dad and Mandy and Charlotte put together!"

"And..?" she challenged with a grin.

There was no need to panic. They were early. Very early. Alan had been in charge of logistics and had tagged an hour on to be safe. He smiled to himself as the taxi pulled them outside Clifton Down Railway station, that they'd eaten into fifteen minutes of it already. He'd done the right thing.

They had no need to go to the ticket office. The tickets had been delivered to their door weeks ago, but Debbie still insisted the railway guard peruse them just to make sure they were in the right place.

"Yes that's right. You could have saved yourself a change if you'd gone from Temple Meads."

"We live just up there," she pointed towards Clifton Down Road and the Avon Gorge.

"Oohh. Posh!" he grinned. "Everything is in order. You'll be in Paris before seven!" Glancing down at Abi's glowing face, he bent down. "I bet I know why you're excited, young lady? Disney Land, am I right?"

Abi nodded delightedly. "We were supposed to go in the summer, but my daddy wasn't very well. But now we're going at Christmas which is even better!"

"I've heard it's great at Christmas. You give Mickey a wave from me then, won't you?"

Abi nodded.

"Have a lovely time."

"We will, thank you," Debbie and Matthew answered in unison.

"I'm starving. Can I get something?"

"You're always starving, Mandy," Matthew said. And just the familiarity that he *knew* his sister's eating habits crafted such a feeling of joy, a laugh soon followed.

"All right, Mr Skinny ribs!" Mandy said patting a burgeoning belly on her brother. He quite liked it. It was a paunch of prosperity! He'd work on it in the New Year, though, of course.

"In there, look. 'Roo Bar.' You can get some crisps or something."

"Oo, look. Scampi!"

"You've only just had a sandwich for lunch. It's three o'clock. They've probably stopped doing food now, and we don't have time for scampi anyway!" Alan stepped in. "Get some crisps or nuts, like Matthew said."

Matthew smiled. He still had no recollection of the past they shared. What he could remember was a constant nightmare, but it was fading. This was his family, and his lack of memories would soon be a moot point as the years rolled on and they made new ones.

The train rumbled out of Cardiff central and Matthew had a seat to himself, his agitated fidgeting gaining him solitude. His closest comrade was a girl who kept dropping her smartphone on the seat beside her and jolting awake to continue crushing candies.

Fingers drumming his disquiet on his thigh, he tried to focus. He'd need money again. Begging had worked well, and it felt more honest than stealing. Tomorrow he would be back online. Tomorrow he'd start the long haul to find his mum, sister and daughter. He just had to stay calm until then.

If only he'd been able to get a phone. He could search the web for anything that struck him, at once moving forward or discarding.

The bright screen caught his attention as sleepy woman dropped it for the hundredth time in ten minutes.

Edging closer, the similarity to his attempts to gain Malcolm's phone transported his mind to a place he didn't want to go. But this would be so easy. She was asleep. If she caught him, he could smile and assure her he was saving it from falling. He wouldn't keep it, but he'd use it for a while.

Shuffling in his seat, Matthew waited for the inevitable plop of the phone-on-fabric. When it happened and the woman didn't wake, he leaned across the aisle and scooped it up. He'd sat back and opened the internet browser before any other passenger registered their objection.

Staring confidently at the screen, Matthew ignored the angry stare from an elderly lady three seats away. She might say something, but he could get done as much as possible before she did.

Furious thumbs probed the internet for all it knew about Mandy and Mary Morrissey. Amongst the suggestions filling the phone's screen was ancestry.co.uk. Evidently the sleeping woman was a regular to the site. Reluctantly, Matthew tapped the screen. Heart pounding, his dad's words of disdain ringing in his ears, he entered his sister's date of birth.

Ancestry asked for date of death, but of course Matthew didn't believe she was dead, so he couldn't fill that in. He completed all the other family members, and their dates of birth, where they were born, and where they had lived, and ancestry did its thing.

His hands trembled so much he could barely hold the phone, but as he managed to complete the process for his mother, ancestry proved its mettle by directing him to information that had escaped all his other efforts.

Searching for the dead afforded subtle changes to his answers which in turn brought new questions. With the different perspective, it was with alarming promptness that ancestry.co.uk directed his attention to a news article/obituary in The Bristol Post.

Tragedy strikes again for bereft local family.

Christmas Day has not been a time to celebrate for the Morrissey family of Wexford Road, Bristol having lost their young daughter, Amanda, in a tragic accident last Christmas. Little Mandy was only two years old when she fell to her death at the family's home after an argument with her elder brother, Matthew.

Mrs Mary Morrissey suffered terribly with the loss, and it is with great sadness that I have to write she could cope no longer and took her own life by taking an overdose of sleeping tablets, also on Christmas Day.

She is survived by her son, Matthew already mentioned, and her husband, Alan...

Matthew's hand dropped and the phone crashed to the floor. The battery compartment lid flew across the carriage and the screen shattered into a million pieces.

"You broke my phone, you bloody idiot!" The woman jolted awake at the noise. "Oh, for fuck sake."

Her voice rattled on, but Matthew didn't hear a word. Falling to the floor, his head in his hands, he wailed, "No! No, no, no, no, no!"

The aching, in the depths of his being, twisted him inside out. How? Why? He had too many questions. The agony of them combined with the pain in his shoulder and they spewed from him in a wretched Technicolor torrent coating the seats and floor. Grasping at the edge of the seat, he hauled himself to his knees.

"Oh, you disgusting fucking pig!" The girl left her broken mobile, now further ruined in a puddle of puke. "You owe me a new phone, you do!"

A guard entering the carriage took in the situation at once. "Fill in a form at the desk, madam. You should be able to make a claim."

"How long will that bloody take, then? You shouldn't let people like him on trains, you shouldn't! Bloody disgrace."

"I understand, madam. If you'd rather take the phone with you…" he gestured towards the steaming mess.

"No, 'course I fucking don't, you moron!"

"Any more of that language, and I won't process your claim at all," he instructed sternly.

Mumbling, the woman edged around the mess and stepped off the train leaving the guard to deal with Matthew. "Now then, sir. You need to get off the train."

Procedure called for him to take the man's details so they could bill him for the damage, but it was obvious there would be little point. It was a wonder he'd had the money to travel in the first place. "Come on," he said leaning over Matthew.

Matthew objected to the movement towards him but had no fight in him. Staggering to the front of the train, he hobbled off, hood up to disguise his shame, and lurched down the platform.

He didn't know where to head. He didn't even know who he was. The only people who seemed to know him were back on the ward of the mental hospital. He couldn't go back there, could he?

He didn't know what happened all those years ago when his mum and sister lost their lives, but it was traumatic. Devastating. And he had made up a life for himself in his head. A wonderful life where he had a loving family, so much more than his mum and dad had offered in his own childhood.

He thought he'd got over their rejection of him in favour of his cute little sister. He thought he'd overcome the odds of a difficult childhood to build something. But it had all been in his crazy head.

Like any other nutter with a Napoleon complex, he'd convinced himself he was more than he was. They knew—the doctors and nurses on the ward—they knew what he was capable of. They knew him better than he knew himself. The place he'd detested months ago; the place he'd tried so desperately to escape was the only place familiar to him now.

His only hope? If it was, what sort of hope was that?

He'd never find Mandy. He'd never find his mum. They were long dead. And he'd never find Abi. Dear, sweet Abi. Because she'd never even existed!

Allowing the thought crushed the last breath of courage from him. A boulder of dereliction held back by a twig of hope that had finally snapped.

He couldn't think his way out of this. He could never trust his thoughts again.

Punching through the pain in his shoulder, Matthew struck himself in the head. Whack! Whack! Whack! He snarled. "You stupid, crazy fucking bastard. You made it all up. Made it all up in your stupid crazy fucking head!"

What about Debbie? The thought attacked. How had he come up with her as the focus of his fantasy when she didn't even know who he was? Shaking his head, it didn't even matter anymore. He must have seen her sometime during this whole lifetime he couldn't remember. Maybe he'd even glimpsed her with Mr Kennedy and Chloe, who didn't look unlike the fantasy of Abi he had created.

He'd never know. She didn't recognise him. He didn't recognise himself. And she certainly didn't love him.

If the delusions had manifested to protect him, where were they now? They'd make no difference. He could never go back. He could never again convince himself it was okay.

Even with the words of the newspaper flashing in his head, he still couldn't remember... He still had no recollection of killing his sister—no memory of finding his mum dead having

297

taken her own life the following year, and for that at least, he was grateful.

It wouldn't be long though. It couldn't. Not now he knew. Those terrible memories would return to torment him like a wolf worrying sheep; waiting to devour him when he was at his weakest.

He wouldn't go back to the hospital. What could they offer him? The truth? He'd had enough of that. They'd be kind and understanding and they'd explain it all to him. They'd keep him safe.

But he didn't want to be safe.

As his toes edged across the platform to the rusting iron tracks, safe was the very last thing he wanted to be.

Chapter Fifty-one

"Here it comes. Here's our train!" Mary was as excited as Abi. She'd always dreamed of going to Paris.

The train pulled in, and they heaved as one towards it. Waiting for the door to swish open and looking around for a button to press when it didn't, they shared glances of anxious anticipation like runners in the blocks.

"Come on. Paris awaits!" Alan chided the denying doors. "Is there a problem?" he asked a passing guard.

Stopping in his stride, he smiled sheepishly. "Just needs a bit of cleaning, I'm afraid. One of the passengers was taken ill and er… made a mess." Catching Matthew's eye, he did a double take before dismissing the mistake.

"Oh, okay. How long?"

The guard stared up at the station clock and squinted. "Not more than ten to fifteen minutes, I don't suppose," and he bustled away with a whistle.

"It'll be fine," Alan assured, detecting the group's concern. "I allowed some extra time for delays."

Settling on the bench beside the track, they waited for the all-clear to board. Ten minutes turned to twenty, then twenty-five then, at last, the cleaning team left the carriage.

"I think we should bagsy another one. I'm not convinced sick that took that long to clear up is ever *really* clean!" Matthew smiled, hurrying to the next coach along. Waiting in the door, he fanned other passengers away from the seats he was saving. "I'm sorry, these are taken," he said, physically using himself and his holdall as a barrier from the more persistent tut-tutting travellers.

Soon his barricade was unneeded and they sat in glorious expectation of a much needed and well-deserved family holiday.

"Are you excited, princess?" Matthew squeezed Abi's delicate hand. She nodded so hard her head looked in danger of falling off! "Me too," Matthew chuckled. The grin on his face now as permanent as a tattoo; a big smiling scar that promised never to leave. He had never felt happier, of that he was certain.

Spotting the guard from the window, Matthew fairly bounced in his seat as he saw the whistle move to his lips. The warm warble filled the air and the great bulk of the train edged forward; a hunter on its prey. The first chug of the wheels turning quickly became the rat-a-tat-tat of brisk onwards movement.

But no sooner had it started than the squeal of metal on metal screamed in the air. The carriage lurched, sending the Morrissey family tumbling forward in their seats.

"Oi! What's going on?" Alan barked, steadying his wife as she struggled to maintain her balance. Shifting back on their backsides, they tried to catch their breath as the train rested on its haunches after a false start.

People crowded out of Roo Bar and stared at something ahead of the train. Pained expressions were worn by unsteady men as they clutched wives and girlfriends to their chests.

"What's happening? What can you see?" Debbie yelled at Matthew.

"I don't know. Nothing."

"Well it's not nothing, is it? Go and find out," she bade, stroking Abi's hair. Matthew marched to the door. Pressing the button for it to open, he wasn't surprised when it refused.

The conductor entered from the intervening door. "Take your seat, please, sir. We'll be moving as soon as we can," she soothed.

"What happened?" Matthew asked, the eyes of his family falling expectantly on the woman.

"I'm afraid I am unable to divulge the details."

"You must be able to tell us something? When are we going to be on our way again?" Alan wagged a finger.

"I can't say anything more at the moment, sir."

"Well, can we get on another train?" Debbie suggested.

The conductor turned and smiled at her. Gulping down her troubled thoughts, she tried her best to reassure. "I'm sorry, that won't be possible," and before Alan's flapping lips could interrupt, she added, "There's been an 'incident.' The police have been called and they want everyone to remain on the train for the time being. The doors will remain closed until they advise otherwise."

"An incident..?" Matthew's voice was weak as he deciphered the scene outside. "Has someone jumped?"

Falling at the barrage of the truth, the conductor nodded, a tear welling in her eye. "A gentleman. We believe he was probably homeless." She gazed at the ceiling for composure. "I suppose this time of year must be especially hard to cope with." She shuffled away along the carriage to advise the other passengers of the delay.

Matthew's gaze had glassed over. The grin he believed would never leave slumped into a quivering downward curve.

"What is it, my love? What's the matter?" Debbie stroked his hand as he wrestled with words that wanted to come. He stared in turn at his mum, his dad, his sister, then his wonderful wife, and then to Abi. He drank in her very essence as they all gazed up at him.

Sniffing it up and prizing a smile back onto his lips, he whispered as his voice failed him. "It's what she said..." The others nodded. They had thought it too. "He was homeless. At Christmas. And he couldn't take it anymore, and... and... That could so easily have been me!" As his family shifted to comfort him, he mumbled over and over. "That could have been me. It could have been me..."

He would never know how right he was.

Epilogue

And so the destructive interference of Matthew Morrissey was over. The choice to share, or deny his little sister the first turn of their new computer affected more than he ever could have imagined.

Two separate realities stayed separate, merging for the first time when Matthew achieved everything he had ever wanted at the same time his alter-ego was at his suicidal lowest.

The high of one reality met the low of the other and created *destructive interference.*

His generosity killed him in the end, of course. It was the fifty pounds he donated which ensured his poor homeless compatriot set off from their chance encounter on a rare high, whilst he was brought down with a heavy dose of guilt.

They may never have met again, but the cycle of their lives kept constant—whilst one fell to new lows, the other soared to never-before-known contentment. Destructive interference became inevitable once more.

We won't ever know what would have happened if they had met again... if Matthew hadn't made the choice to end it all in front of that train.

But of course, somewhere, in a parallel reality, he didn't, did he..?

What choices have you made? You may not remember the most crucial ones; the ones which created the tangents that might one day appear and affect their devastation.

But, if you ever see your double; your *doppelgänger,* if you will, avoid them at all costs: or *you* could find yourself at the confounding conception of your own destructive interference...

We hope you have enjoyed this book

If you would be happy to leave a few words on Amazon or Goodreads by way of a review, or even just a star rating, that will be invaluable in helping other readers to find it, as well as helping the author to be more discoverable.

If you're happy to help, please follow the link.

Take me to Amazon...

http://mybook.to/Destructive

Thank you.

Remember the link to a free short story mentioned at the beginning of the book?

Join the author's reader group for updates on new releases etc. and receive *No1 hot new release in short stories*, '***Frankenstein's Hamster***' absolutely free.

https://www.michaelchristophercarter.co.uk/no-1-hot-new-release-free

Michael grew up in the leafy suburbs of Hertfordshire in the eighties. His earliest school memories from his first parent's evening were being told "You have to be a writer"; advice Michael didn't take for another thirty-five years, despite a burning desire.

Instead, he forged a career in direct sales, travelling the length and breadth of Southern England selling fitted kitchens, bedrooms, double-glazing and conservatories, before running his own water-filter business (with an army of over four hundred water filter salesmen and women) and then a conservatory sales and building company.

All that came to an end when Michael became a carer for a family member and moved to Wales, where he finally found the time and inspiration to write.

Michael now indulges his passion in the beautiful Pembrokeshire Coast National Park where he lives, walks and works with his wife, four children and dogs.

If you'd like to contact Michael for any reason, he would be delighted to hear from you and endeavours to answer all messages whenever possible.

mailto:info@michaelchristophercarter.co.uk
https://www.facebook.com/michaelchristophercarter/
https://twitter.com/MCCarterAuthor
https://www.michaelchristophercarter.co.uk

More books from Michael

Frankenstein's hamster

Monsters can be small... And furry

Harvey Collins is a seventeen year-old prodigy gifted with a scientific mind that even has Oxford University excited.

When his sister's Christmas present of an adorable hamster falls foul of their alcoholic rodent-phobic father, Harvey is the best person to give him a new lease of life.
Using what's left of the hamster and parts of a rat and even himself, Harvey soon develops a pet like no other.
Bestowed with remarkable intelligence and a thirst for revenge, Harvey's hamster is a monster in waiting.
Will anyone make it out alive?

Released just in time for Christmas, this short novella packs in Carter's renowned depth of characters and a thrill-a-minute read in a small package ideal for a car-journey to visit the relatives!

http://getbook.at/FrankensteinKindle

Or get a copy absolutely free by joining Michael's reader-group (where you'll also be first to know about upcoming releases and other cool stuff to give away)
https://www.michaelchristophercarter.co.uk/no-1-hot-new-release-free

Blood is Thicker Than Water

What is wrong with the water in Goreston's Holy Well?

When the vicar of a small Welsh community disappears after two little girls are murdered, Reverend Bertie Brimble steps into the breach.

His family are horrified at the danger he's putting his own daughter in. Especially as she looks startlingly like the other victims.

They do everything they can to keep her safe until Bertie himself begins behaving strangely, battling the worst possible desires.

And he's not the only one...

A terrible fate awaits anyone who drinks from Goreston's Holy well

Can Bertie uncover the truth about what's in the water before it's too late?

"Still reeling from the twists...

"Kept me thinking long after I'd finished reading..."

"The epitome of a great writer.."

Blood is Thicker Than Water is a remarkably thought-provoking horror tale from Wales's master of the supernatural.

Buy your copy today

http://viewbook.at/BloodWater

The Beast of Benfro

Could the truth kill them all?

When struggling dad, David Webb, survives a vicious attack from an unknown creature in the woods, his fears swiftly turn to his flirty neighbour whom he believes might not have been so fortunate.

Calling the police only serves to place him firmly at the

306

top of their list of suspects when she fails to turn up safe and well. Left to rot in jail, his only hope is his delinquent younger brother.

But as they get closer to uncovering the truth about the beast in the forest, they unleash a danger far darker: a menace which threatens everyone they hold dear.
Can anything save them from the Beast of Benfro?

Tear into this monster yarn from Wales's master of the paranormal today

http://viewbook.at/BeastBenfro

The Nightmare of Eliot Armstrong

Can you stop a nightmare coming true?

Eliot Armstrong, swarthy, handsome, head of history at Radcliff Comprehensive is jolted awake every morning; tortured by horrific, indecipherable images of a road accident.

Piecing the disturbing visions together day by day, he's horrified when he recognises one of the cars… his wife Imogen's.

Is it a precognition of his wife's fate?

Or is it a subconscious metaphor for the danger his marriage is in from his man-eating colleague, Uma Yazbeck?

He must do everything in his power to save his wife, and his marriage, But for Eliot, his nightmare is only just beginning…

Do you like thrillers with plenty of twists?
Get this paranormal noir thriller today
http://viewbook.at/nightmare

Destructive Interference
– The Devastation of Matthew Morrissey

Christmas will never be the same again...

When Matthew Morrissey takes an innocent stroll to his local convenience store to buy batteries for his daughter's Christmas present, he doesn't know it will ruin his life.

But, when he returns home, **everything has changed...** There are strangers in his home, his neighbours deny ever knowing him and he ends up attracting the attention of Bristol's finest.

Matthew has a theory about what is happening to him and who is to blame. But first, he has to escape.

Can he solve the mystery and save his family, or has he lost them forever?

Christmas will never be the same after reading this twisting thriller from
Wales's master of the supernatural
Buy yours today. You can be sure it won't be like anything you've read before.
http://mybook.to/Destructive

An Extraordinary Haunting

The Christmas holidays can't come soon enough...

Swansea student, Neil Hedges is counting the days until he can leave his terrifying student digs and go home for Christmas.

For weeks he's suffered terrifying noises in the middle of the night and things moving which shouldn't. It's all becoming clear: someone or *something* wants him out! When at Christmas, a psychic friend of the family confirms his worst fears, Neil and his fellow students can't bear to go back.

But nothing is as it seems, and when beautiful former housemate, Elin Treharne, is plagued by nightmares of her one-time home; nightmares which reveal a disturbing and life-threatening truth, even she doesn't realise the peril she's in…

Only Neil can work it out and save her before it's too late.

But Neil can't cope…

If you're looking for a paranormal thriller beyond the norm,
you've found it.
Get this twisting paranormal thriller today.

http://getbook.at/Extraordinary

You don't have to be DEAD to work here... But it helps

You hear your name, but no-one is there...

Night after night after night, growing more and more gruesome in its demands, a voice from the darkness.

What would you do?

Angharad's simple life is about to take a sinister twist...

Since retiring from working in a care home, Angharad is very much self-sufficient: growing her own vegetables, eating eggs from her hens, drinking milk from her goat and even water from her own spring flowing at the bottom of her garden in rural South-West Wales. In many ways, it seems ideal.

But who is it calling out her name in the dark when no-one is there? And what could they possibly want? Angharad doesn't know, but she must find out. Will she uncover the truth before it costs her, her life?

An intriguing and thought provoking short novel from Wales's master of the paranormal.

Open up the supernatural world of Michael Christopher Carter with this title today...

http://viewbook.at/DEAD

The HUM

If you're paranoid,
does that mean they're not coming to get you?

A strange humming noise, which seems to have no
source, is tormenting the villagers of Nuthampstead,
England, in 1989...

To the Ellis family, recently moved from the valleys of
Wales, it has a sinister significance. They don't like to
talk about it.

But Carys Ellis is only six, and she has to tell someone
about the terrifying visitors to her room in the middle of
the night when her family would not, and could not be
roused.

And that's only the beginning of Carys's plight. Her
mother is a long-term sufferer of a number of mental
health problems. Diagnosed with bipolar disorder, manic
depression, and borderline disorder, she's a drugged up
mess.

And Carys seems to be heading the same way . . .

Twelve years later, beautiful loner, Carys, is pregnant.
She's never had a boyfriend; never had a one-night
stand; she's never had any intimate contact with anyone
to explain her condition.

Not anyone human anyway.

Plagued by the dreadful humming all her life, Carys is
convinced the noise precedes close encounters of the
fourth kind; and that the baby inside her is not of this
world.

She can't tell anyone. Her mum couldn't cope, and her
dad's been relocated from Cambridge Constabulary to a
quiet Welsh village after a nervous breakdown leaving
Carys struggling with her own demons.

Can she protect her baby from its extra-terrestrial
creators, or will they whisk him away for some

unknown purpose?
Will the demons who torment her get to him first?
Or, is she just a little crazy...?

Michael Christopher Carter's stunning portrayal of one family's struggle against mental illness and other-worldly threats is a masterpiece.
Described as "Life changing," this thoroughly well-researched novel is a must read for anyone curious about what exists both out in the cosmos and within our own minds.
Get this book today and prepare to have your eyes opened...
http://viewbook.at/TheHUM

Printed in Great Britain
by Amazon